P9-BAV-606

MORE STORIES FROM THE

# TWILIGHT ZONE

MORE STORIES FROM THE

# TWILIGHT ZONE

# CURVE

Loren D. Estleman

# MORE STORIES FROM THE TWILIGHT ZONE

EDITED AND WITH
AN INTRODUCTION BY

Carol Serling

A TOM DOHERTY ASSOCIATES BOOK • New York

This is a work of fiction. All of the characters, organizations, and events portrayed in these stories are either products of the authors' imaginations or are used fictitiously.

MORE STORIES FROM THE TWILIGHT ZONE



A Tor Book
Published by Tom Doherty Associates, LLC
175 Fifth Avenue
New York, NY 10010

www.tor-forge.com

Tor® is a registered trademark of Tom Doherty Associates, LLC.

ISBN 978-0-7653-2581-5 (hardcover)
ISBN 978-0-7653-2582-2 (trade paperback)

First Edition: July 2010

Printed in the United States of America

0 9 8 7 6 5 4 3 2 1

# COPYRIGHT ACKNOWLEDGMENTS

CONTENTS

# INTRODUCTION

*There is a fifth dimension beyond that which is known to man. It is a dimension as vast as space and timeless as infinity. It is the middle ground between light and shadow, between science and superstition, and it lies between the pit of man's fears and the summit of his knowledge. This is the dimension of imagination. It is an area we call the Twilight Zone.*

—Rod Serling

Welcome to our second collection of stories celebrating the *Twilight Zone* television program, which recently celebrated the fiftieth anniversary of its first broadcast. As with our previous collection, *Twilight Zone: 19 Original Stories on the 50th Anniversary*, we've assembled a stellar assortment of writers, each of whom have given us their unique take on a story that, in another time, might have just come from that fertile realm of the imagination.

When Rod Serling created his visionary television series, he had done so with a goal in mind beyond simply supplying entertainment to the viewing public. He felt that television had the potential to be a real art form . . . to entertain, yes, but also to educate and illuminate the human condition, not to just rehash formulaic comedies and westerns. But he was repeatedly frustrated by the endless censoring from the networks and sponsors, who insisted on removing all controversial political and social commentary. Fed up with fighting this process, he knew that the only way to express himself and deal with these issues of the times would be to create and control his own show. But how to prevent the censors from watering down the themes of his new series?

It was here that Rod came up with his brilliant idea to circumvent network control; he would create a show that existed in a world of "what if" . . . a shadow land that existed just beyond the limits of imagination. Call it science fiction, imaginative fiction, fairy tales—whatever it was, it worked beautifully. Powerful episodes like "The Monsters Are Due on Maple Street," "A World of His Own," "Time Enough at Last," and "Walking Distance" were among the first of many, many celebrated episodes written by Rod, garnering critical acclaim and awards for excellence—Rod's fourth of six Emmy Awards for dramatic writing, a Producers Guild Award for his creative partner, Buck Houghton, and the first of three Hugo Awards for best dramatic presentation. Most important, it was a show that told the stories Rod wanted to tell, in the style he wanted to tell them.

Of course, *The Twilight Zone* has grown from that modest beginning to become a part of American culture for the past fifty years. Whether in syndication across the country, or in the two revivals of the television series, the title itself has entered our consciousness as a label for anything that is strange, weird, or inexplicable. And his original tales have inspired many writers to create their own stories—some of whom are showcased in this volume.

The following eighteen stories range from the unusual to the bizarre—and each would fit very nicely in that realm beyond sight and sound that is the Twilight Zone. From bestselling author John Farris comes a cautionary tale about how mankind might be its own destroyer. Kristine Kathryn Rusch gives us a moving tale of a family that still receives correspondence from a long-lost relative at the holidays. David Gerrold explores a future society where everyday men and women are given the ultimate power over the rest of humanity. From the glitter of Hollywood, M. Tara Crowl tells of a woman who wished for her heart's desire—and not only got it, but everything that came with it. We've even included a rare gem from Rod himself, about a man who is unstoppable in his own mind.

Each of these stories epitomizes everything the Twilight Zone represented—a journey into the unknowable to confront the strange and unique, which can be found everywhere, from the world around us to the deepest recesses of the human heart. I hope you'll enjoy reading these stories as much as I did assembling them.

Carol Serling

Have you ever awakened from an afternoon nap and not known where you were? In the case of Herb Tarnower, that's the rest of his life. He fell asleep in front of the television set and woke up—in the Twilight Zone.

Herb Tarnower fell asleep watching a basketball game and woke up looking at the History Channel. Penny must have changed it while he was sleeping.

They were running old footage of JFK's funeral procession.

He recognized the horse with the empty boots reversed in its stirrups and the flag-draped coffin in the back of the hearse. Something about it seemed different, though. It must have been that he was watching it in color. When he'd seen it live as a boy, it had been on a black-and-white set.

"The kids should be watching this," he said aloud. He got up and dialed the phone.

"Hello?"

"Becca, turn on the History Channel. Brian and Amber might learn something."

"There's no one here by that name. You have the wrong number."

He realized then it was a strange woman's voice. He apologized, broke the connection, and dialed again more carefully. The same woman answered.

"I'm trying to reach my daughter," he said. "Is this two-one-oh-six-four-four-three?"

"Yes, it is."

His wife came in carrying a basket of laundry as he was cradling the receiver. She asked whom he'd called.

"I just tried to call Becca. Why didn't you tell me she'd changed her number?"

"Who's Becca?"

He frowned. After twenty-eight years of marriage he didn't always understand Penny's humor. He opened his mouth to say something caustic, but she was distracted by the TV. "I thought they'd be at Arlington by now," she said. "These state funerals seem to get longer and longer."

He thought it an odd comment, but he shook his head. "After all this time it still saddens me."

"Well, he lived a long life."

"Long? He was cut down in his prime!"

"Don't be silly, Herb. You haven't made sense since I walked into the room. Are you still asleep?"

"Me? You're the one who pretended she didn't know her own daughter."

Her face became a rictus of pain. "That's—how can you be so cruel? Don't you think I'd have given you children if I could?"

He was alarmed then. She'd never taken a joke this far. "Penny, are you all right?"

She dropped the basket on the floor and ran into the bedroom, slamming the door behind her. He heard her crying.

The television commentator's deep voice broke in on his confusion. "For those of you who just joined us, you're watching continuous coverage of the funeral services of John Fitzgerald Kennedy, former president of the United States, who died Thursday at the age of ninety-two."

Herb saw then that the vehicles in the procession were all late models. Some of the people lining the pavement were using cell phones—science fiction back in 1963, when Kennedy was assas-

sinated. And the distinctive boxed H was missing from the corner of the screen. It wasn't the History Channel.

Alone in the living room, he wondered if Penny had guessed the truth, and that he was still asleep. When he tried to change the channel, the remote was different, with none of the buttons in the same place. He had to study it a moment to figure it out.

The funeral procession was on every channel, a live broadcast. He wanted to check the satellite stations, but couldn't find that feature on the remote, and then he noticed the satellite box was missing from the entertainment center. He turned off the set, feeling woozy. It was Sunday—at least it had been when he'd gone to sleep. He tried to remember if he'd been drinking Saturday night and was still under the influence, but he wasn't much of a drinker. They'd spent a quiet evening at home watching a movie. On satellite.

Other things had changed. There were no pictures of Becca, her husband Rick, or their kids anywhere in the room. The new carpet they'd had installed last spring had been replaced by the old one, stained in places and showing wear.

Practical joke? An elaborate one if so, and he couldn't picture his wife planning or cooperating in any such scheme. She considered that kind of humor mean-spirited and in poor taste.

No, he was dreaming. But in the past, he'd always awakened the moment he realized it.

Sinister thought. He was fifty-two, in relatively good shape for his age, although he knew he should eat better and exercise more. He and Penny had discussed retiring before they were too old and sick to enjoy it. The last time he'd had his cholesterol checked it had tested borderline high, and for a few weeks afterward he'd eaten a lot of oatmeal and taken walks, then had slipped back into comfortable old bad habits. Was this a stroke? Or more frightening yet, the onset of Alzheimer's? His father had lingered for

years in a nursing home, and in the end recognized no one in his own family.

If it was dementia, which things were right and which were wrong? Had JFK died in 1963 or 2009? Had Herb imagined he was a father and grandfather, or was he hallucinating that he was neither?

He shook his head. If he was losing his grip, it wasn't from age or hardened arteries. That started with misplacing things, like one's eyeglasses, and became serious when one forgot one wore them. But then, how could he be sure how long this had been going on? Maybe what had seemed like a short nap had actually been a coma.

No, he rejected that, too. If that were the case, Penny would have reacted to his confusion with pity, not hurt and anger.

That was as far as he could investigate on his own. He knocked at the door of the room that contained his most reliable counselor.

"Go away!" Her voice was hoarse with anguish.

"Please, honey. I'm sorry for anything I said. I don't know what's happening to me." His throat caught. "Penny, I'm scared."

There was a silence. Then bedsprings shifted, and after another pause the lock snapped. She opened the door just wide enough to show swollen red eyes and the stains of tears on her cheeks. Penny had good genes and took better care of herself than Herb did. The only time she looked her age was when she'd been crying.

He saw her expression change from pain to concern. His face felt cold, the blood drained from it, and he knew he was pale. She opened the door the rest of the way. He followed her and sat down on the edge of the bed while she turned away to dry her eyes and blow her nose delicately. She put the handkerchief on the night table and turned to face him. "What's going on, Herb?"

"I wish to God I knew." Staring at the floor, he told her about some of the things that were different: the carpet, the remote, the missing satellite box. He didn't mention JFK—that was too

complicated—or the pictures that had vanished, or who was in them. He sensed that would have upset her all over again.

When he finished, she sat beside him and took both his hands in hers. She spoke in a calm, measured tone, maintaining eye contact, the way he'd heard and seen her do while reasoning with their daughter when she was small, and more recently with their grandchildren when they misbehaved—or had she? He forced his mind to stay in one place and concentrate on what she was saying.

"We're saving up for a new carpet," she said. "Right now, it's not in our budget. You know we can't afford satellite TV on your salary."

"We don't have to depend on my salary. You're head of Pediatrics at Burgess General. You make more money than I do."

"Herb, I'm a housewife. I gave up nursing when we got married. Burgess doesn't have a female doctor on staff. Few hospitals do."

He took away his hands and held his head. Suddenly it was pounding. Maybe he was having a seizure after all.

Her voice remained steady. "Tell me everything you can remember, the way you think things are."

He lowered his hands and drew a deep breath. Complicated or not, he had to go into it. Somehow it seemed to be at the core of all that was wrong. "Kennedy—"

"Not Kennedy. Us. You tried to call a daughter we don't have. I was diagnosed with ovarian cancer when we were engaged. I had to have a hysterectomy. When I came out of the anesthetic, I offered to release you from your proposal, because we'd talked so much about having children. You said it didn't matter, that nothing mattered as long as you got to live the rest of your life with me. We never mentioned children again, until today. Does any of this sound familiar?"

"You had a hysterectomy, but only after we'd been married two years. The way I remember the conversation, I told you one child was plenty, that we'd give her all the love we'd have divvied up among the lot. We spoiled her. She gave us some bad times, but she turned out all right in the end. She married a good man and they have two children, a boy named Brian and a girl named Amber. Our *grand*children."

She shocked him with a bittersweet smile. "Goodness. All that, and I'm a doctor, too? When did I have time to go to medical school?"

"I was a junior executive with an advertising agency; I quit to stay home with Becca. We had to scrimp, but with a loan from the GI Bill we got along until you'd graduated and served your internship. When you joined the staff at Burgess, we could afford regular day care, and I went back to work. I'm a senior executive, you're a chief of staff. Penny, we're very well off."

"How could you qualify under the GI Bill? You never served with the military."

He held his head again. It felt as if the back of his skull would fly off. "But I did! If I hadn't, you and I would never have met. A land mine nearly took off my leg in Vietnam. You were the nurse assigned to me in the VA hospital when I came home. I proposed to you when I was in therapy."

"Vietnam? I haven't heard of that place in ages. We never were at war there. You work for Meredith and Klugman Advertising, but as a copywriter. You were passed over for promotion so many times, you stopped applying. You're not one of those cutthroat, get-ahead-by-any-means corporate sharks. That's one of the many reasons I love you."

Less than half of that sank in. "How could there have been no Vietnam War? It's the defining event of our generation!"

"Herb." She settled back into that reassuring one-note tone. "We met on a blind date. Your friend Brian Hurley fixed us up. He was dating my cousin. You and I hit it off right away. Wartime romances are for novelists."

This news was even more of a blow. He couldn't tell her that Brian Hurley, his best friend since kindergarten, had died in a rice field during the siege of Khe Sanh. They would have named their child after him if they'd had a boy. Instead, his daughter had honored his request to christen her firstborn Brian. "Brian's alive?" was all he could manage.

She pressed her lips tight, then opened them wide enough to say, "He's your supervisor at Meredith and Klugman. If I were mean enough to wish death on anyone, it would be that snake."

Penny made an appointment with Dr. Martin Sprague, who by luck happened to be in his office on Sunday and had a cancellation. "You're overworked, is all," she said, sounding unconvinced herself. "That Ipana account has been eating your lunch for weeks." She offered to drive him, but he insisted on driving there alone; to clear his head, he said. Actually that monotonous catechism had begun to wear away at the last nerve he had left. He refrained from pointing out that Ipana toothpaste had gone out with *The Dick Van Dyke Show*. If she'd said, "Who's Dick Van Dyke?" he'd have dived straight off the deep end.

Assuming he hadn't already.

His car, at least, was the late-model Chrysler he knew well; he'd never cared to flaunt his affluence with a Cadillac or some sporty foreign job. The seat belt and airbag had vanished, but today that kind of discovery seemed to be the norm. He didn't even register surprise when the billboard that had advertised a credit union on Friday was now flogging Marlboro cigarettes, complete with a stubbled cowboy puffing away with no Surgeon General's Warning in sight. After the first hour or so, insanity seemed to have come with its own rules of consistency. He was sure now he was crazy, and even if political correctness did or did not exist in this strange new landscape, he felt he was entitled to use the term "crazy," just as an African-American could be excused the N-word.

He switched on the radio. It seemed he couldn't punish himself enough on this day of all days.

". . . And they are mild! Returning to the news, President McCain is on his way to Cuba to meet with President John Gotti, Junior, regarding—"

He punched another button.

"Dr. Martin Luther King, Junior, used the occasion of his eightieth birthday celebration to call for renewed efforts to reverse the Supreme Court's decision upholding the constitutionality of the so-called 'Jim Crow' laws in the South. Negroes throughout—"

He punched another button.

"—which will mark the Detroit Lions' third straight trip to the Super Bowl. In late-breaking news, John F. Kennedy, Junior, was seen arriving at the funeral of his father, the thirty-fifth president of the United States, in the company of pop star Madonna, who wore a provocative—"

The juniors had inherited the earth. He punched another button.

"—despite rumors of a reconciliation, and possibly a new musical collaboration between John Lennon and Paul McCartney—"

He switched off the radio.

"Hahahahahahahahahahahaha!" he confided to the headliner; and was embarrassed to observe the driver of a Studebaker with the dealer's sticker still adhering to the passenger's-side window staring at him at a stoplight.

Herb Tarnower found a space next to the entrance of Dr. Sprague's office (there were no handicapped spots in the lot) and amused himself with the latest issue of *Collier's* until a nurse called his name. She, at least, wore one of those floral-print smocks that had taken the place of starched whites. That ruled out time travel.

Dr. Sprague's appearance shocked him. He'd always been overweight, but now he was positively obese, entering the examination room with a pronounced waddle, and Herb had never seen him smoking a cigar at the office before. He mentioned the cigar.

The doctor took it out of his mouth and looked at it. "Yes, if the antitobacco lobby gets its way, I won't even be able to enjoy one in a building I pay rent on."

Herb tried to remember when the state had passed a law against smoking in the workplace. Everything seemed to have been set back either a few years, or dozens.

"Marty, I think I'm losing my mind. Penny thinks I've just been working too hard, but suddenly nothing makes sense anymore."

"Penny? Oh, yes, Mrs. Tarnower." Sprague was looking at a sheet on a clipboard. "How is the little woman?"

"See, that's just the thing. You know her as *Doctor* Tarnower. You've been colleagues at Burgess General Hospital for fifteen years. You and I play golf."

"I gave up golf years ago, too fat to swing a club. Are you a drinking man, Mr. Tarnower? What you're describing sounds like symptoms of prolonged alcoholic poisoning. It warps and destroys brain cells."

"If you'd asked me that this morning, I'd have told you I drink moderately when I drink at all. Now, for all I know, I'm a hopeless wino. Everything's upside down."

"Well, undress and we'll examine you head to toe. That should help determine whether your complaint is physical or psychological."

When it was over, Herb sat up in his paper robe while Sprague folded his stethoscope. "You're a long way from a wreck. You could lose a few pounds, but look who's talking. Tell me some more about these illusions you've been having."

"It might speed things along if I ask the questions. What do you know about President Kennedy?"

"He's dead; there's no denying it if you own a television. He was okay in the White House, although I thought he showed the white feather when he withdrew his military advisors from Southeast Asia and failed to stop the spread of communism. He never faced the kind of challenge that separates the great leaders from the so-so ones. Lincoln had the Civil War, FDR the Depression and World War Two. JFK helped Jackie pick out the colors in the West Wing."

"What about the missile crisis?"

"The nuclear arms race? Well, he did what he had to do to keep up with the USSR, but he became obsessed with it to the detriment of his other responsibilities. We'd have beaten the Russkies to the moon if he hadn't let them distract him."

Herb couldn't afford to bog himself down with that revelation. "I meant the *Cuban* missile crisis. He faced down Moscow and spared the world atomic annihilation."

"Cuba's one of our closest allies, Mr. Tarnower. McCain and Gotti are discussing affairs of state right now."

"That's another thing. John Gotti, Junior, is a notorious gangster, not a foreign leader. So was his father. John McCain lost the U.S. election to Barack Obama last November. We have our first African-American president."

"African-American?"

"Black."

Sprague put out his cigar. "That's a terribly racist term. 'Colored' is the polite designation. Those people aren't making much progress in Washington, but that's no reason to mock them."

"I'm not a bigot! I contribute to—"

"I'm prescribing sleeping pills." The doctor scribbled on a pad. "If you're still feeling disoriented after a good night's sleep, call the office and I'll give you a list of names of recommended psychotherapists. Your wife is probably right. I see by your file you write copy for an advertising agency. That's a high-pressure business, and your job requires a healthy imagination. You've just been overworking it. Gotti a gangster—that's rich. A Negro president. And I suppose Jerry Lewis is the president of France."

Herb took the prescription sheet. "He's not, is he?"

"Go on with you! I have sick people to treat." Sprague lit a cigar.

He felt a little better with this professional opinion. It was just possible he *had* been putting in too many hours downtown; obsolete employment information in his medical file was nothing to panic over and he supposed a man could get his wires crossed and distort what he was hearing. It was inconceivable that Neil Armstrong had not been the first to take that giant leap for mankind, or that JFK could be discussed as a nonentity even by someone who disapproved of his performance as chief executive.

Halfway home it struck Herb that he should have asked the doctor about 9/11; but better to let sleeping dogs lie, and more particularly get some sleep himself. He filled the prescription at his neighborhood chain pharmacy, whose personnel turned over so often he seldom saw the same face twice, told Penny of Sprague's reassuring diagnosis, and they went to bed. The pills worked their magic as soon as his head touched linen.

The clock radio clicked on during a Viagra commercial. That wasn't conclusive, so he lay holding his breath until a news announcer described Barack Obama's first meeting with Raul Castro, the president of Cuba, and his brother Fidel, who for health reasons had stepped aside but remained chairman of the Communist Party. He whooped, bringing an alarmed Penny out of the bathroom, clutching an electric toothbrush.

He had to be sure. "You're a doctor, yes?"

"Herb, are you all right?"

He hated that question. "Please, just humor me."

"Of course I'm a doctor, but you're a little older than most of my patients. Should I call Marty?"

"Marty, good old Marty. Your colleague, Marty Sprague."

She started to say something, but he leapt out of bed and padded in his pajamas into the living room. He felt like Jimmy Stewart in the last reel of *It's a Wonderful Life*. Bedford Falls was still Bedford Falls, there was a satellite box on the shelf under the TV, and the carpet was new. Most wonderful of all, there were Becca, Rick, and the kids in their frames on the mantel. It had been a dream after all, a terrible nightmare that made a man grateful to be alive and awake.

The clock radio clicked on during a Fizzies commercial. That sweet treat had not been available since cyclamates were banned by the FDA. The news announcer reported that Jerry Lewis had appointed three new members to the French cabinet.

He'd been dreaming. The nightmare was the reality.

Sanity was the illusion, and the situation was deteriorating. It wasn't *It's a Wonderful Life,* and he wasn't Jimmy Stewart. He was Bill Murray in *Groundhog Day,* only much, much worse.

He went through the motions of a normal Monday morning, showering, shaving, brushing his teeth, and dressing in a suit cheaper than any he'd owned in years. Penny had breakfast ready when he entered the kitchen. She asked him if he felt better.

"Considerably." He'd always heard that deranged people were skilled at feigning rational behavior. Sprague's shrinks would commit him if they heard his story. He drank coffee and ate a slice of toast. Against his better judgment (assuming he had any) he glanced at the morning paper. The Soviet–based company that provided satellite service to the world was raising its rates; no wonder he couldn't afford it on a copywriter's pay. It stood to reason that the country that won the Space Race would run the industry. Reason was a relative thing, he was learning.

Penny expressed concern when he told her he wasn't hungry,

but he kissed her good-bye and said he was late for work. He hoped Meredith and Klugman was where he'd left it Friday.

Waiting for a light change, he saw a big white policeman snatch an elderly black man by the collar and haul him onto the curb when he failed to finish crossing before the pedestrian signal stopped flashing. He bellowed in the old man's face, shrinking him inside his clothes.

Herb rolled down the window. "Leave him alone, Officer. Can't you see he can't walk any faster?"

"What's it to you how fast them people shuffle along?" snarled the cop. "Mind your own business, or I'll run you in for obstructing justice."

The light turned green. He resumed driving. Much, much, *much* worse than *Groundhog Day*.

The radio offered no diversion. A number of women had been charged with creating a public nuisance by burning their bras in Central Park. Even the feminists were running slow.

His corner office belonged to a man named Shatner, the lettering on the door informed him. He found his own name on a plate in a cubicle the size of the front seat of his car. He hung up his coat and turned to find himself face-to-face with Brian Hurley.

Heavier and grayer, yes, but it was a face he'd once known as well as his own, and had had no chance to say good-bye to because Brian was sent home in a body bag and buried in a closed casket. Incredible joy surged through him—and withered in the glare of his childhood friend's anger.

"Tarnower, I'm sick of you thinking you can sneak in here late without my knowing it. From now on every minute you show up past the hour is a day off your vacation time."

"Why the attitude, Brian? We used to be close."

"That was before your wife tipped off her cousin I was running around on her. That was the money end of your crummy family: I had to bust my hump twice as hard as anyone else in the office for every promotion when I could've been slacking off, like some losers I could mention."

"Brian—"

"That's Mr. Hurley. Another slip like that and I'll write you up for insubordination. I want that Ipana copy on my desk by noon sharp, or you can clean out your desk at twelve-oh-one."

Alone in the cubicle, Herb's face felt hot. He had to re-educate himself on how to operate a model of computer he hadn't seen in three years, but that wasn't so bad because he'd been afraid that Silicon Valley was just a Herban Legend. When he accessed the writing program, however, he couldn't motivate himself to find a new way to say "whiter teeth." If he was going to survive in the Bizarro World, it was time he found out something about it. Google was still Google, thank God, even if the high-speed connection he was accustomed to had been scrapped in favor of an antiquated service that required patience. He got no hits on Lee Harvey Oswald, so he clicked on "Kennedy, John F.," and spent the morning boning up on what he had come to regard as The Last Half-Century: The Director's Cut.

Kennedy, it developed, had served one lackluster term as president trying to make good on the anti-Communist platform he'd campaigned on. With no Cuban Missile Crisis to avert (and give the U.S. leverage over the Soviet Union), he had drained the budget struggling to match Moscow weapon-for-weapon. This caused him to underfund the space exploration program and fail to fulfill his inauguration promise to put a man on the moon by the end of the decade. When Russia landed there first, the ineffectual JFK made an unlikely assassination target; hence obscurity for Oswald. The desperate decision to push the arms race forced Kennedy to ignore Southeast Asia, and when Saigon fell to the Communists in 1964, he was defeated for re-election by Richard Nixon, who had lost to him in 1960.

With no war to distract him, Nixon made an early diplomatic

trip to China, leading to a free trade agreement that boosted the domestic economy. No war meant no student riots. Prosperity at home gave Nixon another term, unclouded by a Watergate, and a return to the postwar euphoria of the 1950s after four years of malaise under the previous adminstration. The only cloud on the horizon was the continuing Cold War, which kept the population busy digging fallout shelters and not thinking about civil rights or women's liberation. Those seeds would be planted under President Goldwater.

Lyndon Baines Johnson returned to the Senate. There would be no national office for Kennedy's vice president, nor a chance at one for Kennedy's brother Robert, who resigned as Attorney General on the day of Nixon's inauguration as custom required. RFK served Massachusetts as governor for three terms and died aged sixty, a victim of lung cancer. Herb got no hits on Sirhan Sirhan.

Gerald Ford: Former Michigan congressman, deceased. Jimmy Carter: Former Georgia governor, retired.

Habitat for Humanity: No hits.

Ronald Reagan: Former motion picture actor, deceased.

George McGovern denied Barry Goldwater a second term in a close race attributed to liberal backlash after twelve years of conservative government. McGovern survived a challenge by Spiro Agnew, but right-wing pundits insisted that his timorous attempts at diplomacy missed a golden opportunity to bring down the Soviet Union with a hard-line stance. Actor Warren Beatty looked good in the Oval Office, struggled with the economy, but was relatively successful in foreign affairs; one affair in particular led to an international scandal, and he was pressured into resigning.

In the most recent contest, Democratic hopeful John Edwards had lost by a landslide to John McCain. In a world at peace, both candidates' lack of combat experience (no Vietnam, no POW

McCain) was less important than the victor's long tenure in the political arena: Change was dangerous. Typing in Barack Obama produced no results.

Herb sat back, his brain reeling. It fit together somehow, or most of it, like a jigsaw puzzle assembled from separate boxes, but with some pieces left over.

No President Reagan meant the Iron Curtain was left intact—and incidentally no Presidents Bush, which meant no Gulf wars.

A powerful Russia crushed Afghanistan, handily preventing the Taliban from gaining traction there, therefore:

No al-Qaeda.

No 9/11. The date scored no significant hits.

Which was good. No war in Vietnam was good, too, sparing fifty thousand American lives, although it had dealt a devastating blow to the Tarnowers, delaying Herb's marriage to Penny until it was too late to raise a family. For him it was as if his daughter and grandchildren had been swept away by a tornado, leaving no trace, and Herb alone in his grief. Penny couldn't share the burden, having no memory of them.

Maybe God, or whatever force drove the universe, had decided it was Herb's turn to make the sacrifice for a world without terrorists or meaningless conflicts. But he had not paid the price alone. A dominant world power based in Moscow was no good thing, no matter what situation one compared it to, and he had *no* idea why Ipana and Fizzies survived, or why it was suddenly okay to smoke in a doctor's office, or for that matter why his best friend had been rescued from dying young only to become a jerk. Some things just seemed to have turned sideways and fallen through cracks in the cosmic renovation.

Everything seemed to have come unglued under Kennedy. But it had not been JFK's fault. Apart from its tragic conclusion, his administration was remembered chiefly for his masterful resolution of the Cuban Missile Crisis. Faced with his determination not to back down, Russia had relented, withdrawing its weapons of mass destruction from Castro's country and showing the first tiny crack that would eventually lead to the Soviet Union's collapse less than thirty years later.

Castro.

That was the name that was missing. The ogre—or saint, depending on one's point of view or experience of life in that island nation lying only ninety miles off the coast of the United States—that iron-fisted dictator whose presidency had outlasted nine U.S. commanders in chief (in the world Herb knew), had been conspicuously absent from the long roll of western history just examined. The answer to the puzzle lay not in the little pieces left over, but the big one that was missing.

He had to work fast. It was two minutes to noon, which was when he would lose his computer privileges—along with his job. Herb typed in CASTRO, FIDEL.

The number of results bewildered him. If world history had passed the man by . . .

But, no. They were all sports-related.

He scrolled to the most recent date, clicked, and waited for the download. "Come on, come on." Another minute passed as the horizontal activity bar crept across the computer screen at a snail's pace.

At last a video clip staggered onscreen. At a special ceremony preceding the New York Yankees' last game in the venerable stadium, Hall of Famer Fidel Castro was being honored for his long, spectacular career as a starter with the pitching staff. A frail but distinguished-looking old man came out on the field with the aid of a cane and a youthful supporter on either side to accept a plaque and deliver a short, moving speech. He was clean-shaven but for a closely clipped white mustache.

"My English is not sufficient to express my gratitude to this great land of opportunity," he began, in his heavy accent. "That it should embrace so humble a stranger to its shores—"

"Baseball?!"

Herb jumped at this cry of rage. He hadn't heard Brian Hurley approaching his cubicle.

"I give you a clear assignment with a deadline, and you waste three hours of company time watching *baseball*? If you're not out of this building in fifteen minutes, I'll have security—Tarnower, are you listening?"

Herb had risen and walked to the elevator, leaving his boss standing there. Whatever personal items he left behind he would never miss—not compared to what he'd lost already.

Driving home, he vaguely remembered hearing somewhere that Fidel Castro had once tried out for the Yankees. The coach was unimpressed, and the dejected athlete returned home to study law and then lead a revolution that would topple the Batista government in 1959. First to go were the casinos owned by the American Mafia, whose bribes to corrupt officials had paid off in huge profits from high rollers who flocked there to drink and gamble. The mobsters fled to avoid firing squads and the casinos were destroyed or converted to uses more in keeping with a Communist state.

But in this alternate reality, none of that had happened. Castro had signed with the Yankees and was too busy throwing strikes to involve himself in politics back home—who wouldn't, given the choice between governing and having his picture on a bubblegum card? Meanwhile, men named Albert the Butcher and Vinnie Bigs had continued to gain wealth and power and established a sovereign nation devoted to vice. When Batista died, possibly even before, the need to pull strings from behind the scenes existed no longer. Cuban presidents Lansky and Luciano had led the way, and now John "Junior" Gotti, offered his hospitality to a U.S.

president eager to forge an alliance between capitalist countries against the threat from the Soviet Union.

There was an eerie familiarity to it all. No matter how good the first draft, it could always use improvement. Lord knew Herb had burned through reams of paper working his way toward an angle that sold better than all those that had come before. In some ways, things were worse—as few would predict—with one less dictator in the world. In others, they were better. It all seemed to even out, except for Herb's personal anguish. But the pain was his alone; Penny seemed to have made her peace with being childless, so long as he didn't belabor the point. And since Becca and Brian and little Amber had never been born, they had suffered nothing by their passing. In time, Herb himself might learn to come to terms with his loss, and perhaps even forget it. Already he found it difficult to picture their faces, remember the sound of their voices.

Whatever the reason for this . . . this revision (for he found himself thinking more and more like an advertising copywriter), it seemed the race might survive, even benefit. This belated start toward equal rights might mean a smoother transition than had been the case in the rough draft—no riots, no assassinations, no Bobby Riggs vs. Billie Jean King. Maybe he could find a job writing speeches for the leaders. It beat hawking toothpaste.

As Herb Tarnower was planning out this bold new future, a pneumatic hatch opened soundlessly in the hull of the Soviet space station *Potemkin,* located approximately one-third of the distance between the earth and the moon, and released an interplanetary ballistic missile armed with a nuclear warhead capable of destroying an area roughly the size of New England. Its purpose was to punish the United States for its friendly overtures to Cuba against Russian interests in the Western Hemisphere, and its primary target was the World Trade Center, identified in coded radio transmissions as Ground Zero.

Of course, Fidel Castro was rejected by the Yankees and went on to become one of the most powerful, beloved, and despised dictators in history. Who among his enemies would have thought that in the Twilight Zone that would be good news?

# REVERSAL OF FORTUNE

Robert J. Serling

The locale is a college campus in Arizona. The featured players are two college professors on their way to hear a lecture on the battle of Midway. Not much of a backdrop for a tale of time travel, is it? Except that this particular university is really parked in the middle of a place where time travel is more a reality than a fantasy. And our two professors are walking toward a lecture hall located somewhere . . . in the Twilight Zone.

The two professors walking toward the lecture hall in the Social Sciences building personified an academic odd couple.

Dr. Alan Petibone, B.S., M.S., Ph.D., headed the department of Astrophysics at the University of Southern Arizona. Dr. Gerald Redmond, B.A., Ph.D., labored in the department of Music, where he valiantly but futiley tried to convince students that the works of such giants as Wagner, Chopin, and Cole Porter were vastly superior to the discordant, tuneless, deafening din regarded as legitimate music by the younger generation.

Petibone was a tiny man whose large head would have been more in sync if attached to the body of an NFL defensive tackle. Redmond, who was tall but reed-thin, had to shorten his stride when he noticed Petibone was beginning to pant while trying to keep up with him. The little man shook his head impatiently.

"We have to walk briskly, Gerry. He'll be starting the lecture in a few minutes."

"Are you sure it'll be on the battle of Midway?"

"Confirmed it when I talked to Joshua earlier this morning. He was delighted, if surprised, that we're hearing him tell the Midway story again."

"I don't wonder," Redmond muttered. "This'll be the fourth time."

They reached the lecture hall entrance and stopped momentarily so Petibone could catch his breath. Redmond rubbed his chin thoughtfully. "Alan, are we *ever* going to tell him?"

"Only when we're absolutely sure he'll keep it to himself."

Redmond said soberly, "Remember, Joshua Endicott is a distinguished historian. Frankly, I think he'd keep our secret."

"Maybe. Perhaps if I show him absolute proof."

"Is our item of proof in that envelope you're carrying?"

"It is."

"How come you're bringing it today? You didn't at any of the previous lectures."

"Just a hunch. He came close to triggering a rebuttal *last* year, but not quite close enough. Time to go in, Gerry."

They found two isolated seats just as Joshua Endicott, chairman of the department of History, waddled to the podium. He was a beer barrel with legs, yet although portly he gave the impression he was made of iron, not fatty tissue.

He spotted Petibone and Redmond, nodding in their direction with a friendly smile. Somehow, that smile increased Gerald Redmond's uneasiness.

"Alan," he whispered, "how long do we keep this up? It's a wonder he hasn't gotten at least curious."

"I told him last year he was so mesmerizing, we never tired of hearing about Midway. His ego replaced his curiosity."

They settled back in their seats to listen, for the fourth consecutive year, to a story they both knew was untrue.

". . . and in summary, I must again emphasize the vital role played by the Doolittle raid in what became the miracle of Midway.

While the raid inflicted very little physical damage on its targets, the psychological impact was enormous. The emperor himself might have been injured or killed, and that alone called for massive retaliation.

"Yet the Japanese military could not believe that twin-engine B-25 bombers could have taken off from an aircraft carrier and must have come from Midway Island. This erroneous assumption marked the turning point of the Pacific war. Thanks to the efforts of band musicians from the sunken battleship *California*, we broke the Japanese naval code, and ambushed the task force that tried to invade Midway. The Nips lost four of their best carriers and many of their top pilots, shifting the balance of power in the Pacific to the U.S. Navy. Any questions?"

A husky black student rose.

"Dr. Endicott, what might have happened if we *hadn't* won at Midway? Do you think a defeat might have cost us not just Midway, but the war?"

"Absolutely not. Remember what Admiral Isoruku Yamamoto is reported to have said after one of his officers congratulated him on the success of the Pearl Harbor attack: 'I fear we have awakened a sleeping giant.'

"So, even with a defeat at Midway, the sleeping giant already was fully awake. Yamamoto himself warned that America's arms production superiority would inevitably doom Japan. It's almost lunchtime, so if there are no more questions . . ."

He stopped as he saw Alan Petibone waving his arm like a stranded motorist frantically trying to attract someone's attention.

Endicott chuckled. "I see my distinguished colleague, Dr. Petibone of our Astrophysics department, has a question. He has been attending more than one of my lectures on Midway and I appreciate his obvious interest. Alan, what's your question?"

The students stared curiously at the gnomelike Petibone as he rose. His voice was deep and gravelly, as if the words were rolling over pebbles.

"I have no question," he began. "I'd just like to respond to the one that young man asked. In a more accurate fashion than the grossly inadequate hypothesis you provided, Joshua, which was pure bullshi—bull manure. No offense, I hope."

"None taken," Endicott laughed. "Continue, Alan."

"With due respect," Petibone continued, "I think you have greatly underestimated the consequences if Midway somehow hadn't resulted in a decisive victory. As you correctly pointed out, that crucial moment in history hinged almost entirely on two supposedly unrelated events that suddenly became very much related. First, the effects of the Doolittle raid on the Japanese psyche. Second, the application of musical notes to deciphering Japan's naval code."

"I've already acknowledged the importance of those two events," Endicott said defensively. "I don't see why—"

"Let me finish. The raid's psychological effects could easily have worked *against* us. Of far greater importance was the decision to use musicians as code-breakers. Eliminate that one factor, and you have created a disaster of catastrophic proportions.

"The Japanese, still assuming such large bombers had to have come from the nearest U.S. land base, the island of Midway, would have invaded it without our even knowing they were coming. Midway then would have become the launching pad for further intrusions on American soil—namely, the seizure of Hawaii, and in all likelihood a full-scale occupation of Alaska.

"All we had to stop them with were a few carriers that lacked effective cruiser and destroyer screens. Many of our destroyers dated back to World War One. Our heavy cruisers were notoriously thin-skinned. Our carriers were damned good, but would have been destroyed one by one, before we could finish building new and better warships of every category.

"No, Midway was far more than just a turning point. It was the difference between winning or losing the whole damned war—not just the Pacific conflict, but the war against Nazi Germany. I apologize for cutting into everyone's lunchtime, so maybe I'd better let you all go."

Much to his surprise, he heard audible murmurs of "Keep going" and Endicott, too, was nodding agreement.

The gravelly voice resumed its path over invisible pebbles. "I shall be as brief as possible, knowing that young stomachs may demand a higher priority than young minds. But I feel it essential that you hear a more realistic 'what if?' hypothesis than Dr. Endicott has postulated.

"I fear he is terribly wrong in assuming that defeating Japan merely would have taken somewhat longer if Midway had been lost. On the contrary, it eventually would have led to a humiliating peace based in considerable part on Japanese-dictated terms. You must remember that a *world* war began in 1939. A war the free world easily might have lost. I am convinced that our triumph at Midway prevented that from happening.

"Why? Because if we had lost that battle, we would not have been sending lend-lease aid to Britain and the Soviet Union. All of our production efforts, not only by necessity but by the force of public opinion, would have been utilized against a Japanese juggernaut running wild. In such a climate, Congress never would have passed a lend-lease bill.

"Let me remind you of the America First Committee, a prewar organization opposed to any involvement in a European conflict. It had considerable public support at the time, and would have been even more influential in the aftermath of a Midway defeat. So the American people very likely would have swallowed the bitter pill of leaving Russia and even Britain to shift for themselves.

"It is even very possible there would have been no Manhattan

Project, no war-ending atomic bomb attacks on the Japanese homeland, because our strategy would have been almost entirely defensive, with little or no emphasis on something as theoretical as nuclear weaponry. The United Nations wouldn't have existed. Ditto a free, independent Jewish state.

"I submit that these possibilities really should be categorized as probabilities. Because we would have been a discouraged, disillusioned nation fed up with FDR; a people with no stomach for getting involved in another European war. Yes, Germany already had declared war on us right after Pearl Harbor. To use a boxing term, however, we very likely would have been willing to settle for a draw in the Pacific while quite logically figuring that Germany wasn't a real threat to invade the United States. Even crossing the English Channel to invade England posed a formidable task.

"So a face-saving peace treaty with Japan would have been acceptable while taking a chance that the Soviet Union would either defeat Germany, or weaken it to the point where even the victors were tired of war.

"Roosevelt almost certainly would have never won a third term and Republican isolationists would have dominated Congress and the White House. How does 'President Robert A. Taft' sound to you?

"Without our help, Britain would have surrendered, despite Churchill's eloquence, and might have been occupied by an invading Nazi army after an exhausted Royal Air Force finally lost control of the air over the British Isles. So England never could have served as a kind of unsinkable aircraft carrier.

"There would have been no Normandy invasion, no strategic air war against Germany, and Dwight Eisenhower would have been just another army officer who never would have become president.

"These are more than hypothetical suppositions. They are based on logic and what we already know about World War Two. A war in which our becoming the arsenal of democracy was pivotal. There would have been no such arsenal, because we would have been totally committed just to saving ourselves.

"I greatly admire Dr. Endicott as a historian, but I felt you should at least consider Midway's *true* significance."

He sat down, not really hearing the applause, conscious that he probably had lost Joshua's friendship. Endicott, however, graciously thanked him for his "stimulating words" and conceded that "Dr. Petibone's ideas deserve serious thought." As the lecture hall emptied, Endicott approached his two colleagues, shaking his head mockingly at Petibone.

"You rascal, why did you wait until today to undress me in front of my own students? You've heard the same lecture three times before."

Petibone smiled wryly. "Josh, the cockamamie answer you gave that kid just pissed me off. I've never before heard you dismiss Midway's long-range importance to that extent."

"I didn't dismiss it. I've always stressed its significance. But my comments are based on what *actually* happened, not on what *might* have happened."

Petibone stared at him, so long that Redmond put a hand on his shoulder, with a squeeze that urged caution. He was too late.

"So were mine," Petibone said quietly.

"What in the hell is *that* supposed to mean?" Endicott demanded.

"Exactly what I intended it to mean. I know what *really* happened at Midway. There was no miraculous victory."

He paused, knowing he was about to drop an extremely heavy anvil on Joshua Endicott's complacency.

"Josh, do I have your solemn promise that what I'm about to tell you will never be repeated to another human being—not even to your wife?"

"Of course."

"Good, although I doubt very much if you'll believe me anyway."

He took a deep breath, as though he were taking on the fuel he needed to propel the next words out of his mouth.

"I swear to God, I've gone back to 1942 in a time machine I designed and built myself. And if you don't believe me, ask Gerry because he went with me. Back to Pearl Harbor as it was less than four months after the attack, and about a month before the Doolittle raid. Gerry, tell him this is no joke."

Redmond nodded. "He's telling the truth, Josh. That contraption of his really works . . . although I'd never recommend time travel as a pleasure trip. It does something to a few basic senses like smell and appetite, plus sense of balance. It seems to raise hell with metabolism in general. When we returned to the present, we were terribly dizzy for almost a week, and we couldn't even look at food."

Endicott gave them a look that ran the gamut from amusement to utter disbelief.

"Okay," he said, "I know you're both pulling my leg right out of its socket. But for the sake of argument, Gerry, what was a professor of music doing on this H. G. Wells expedition?"

Petibone answered him. "It was Gerry's idea to enlist help from the *California*'s band. He had written his doctorate dissertation on the theory that musical notes seemed to resemble the cipher codes used by the military."

Endicott shook his head scornfully. "Baloney. That theory surfaced as early as 1939."

"Correct, but Gerry was the first to think of applying the theory to the naval code the Nips were using in the early forties, stuff we were picking up on shortwave radio with no idea of what it meant.

"So when we went back to forty-two, I passed Gerry off to naval authorities at Pearl Harbor as a cipher code expert, while I already had my current FBI security clearance as a consultant on rocket weaponry. I put a 1939 date on Gerry's much later dissertation and showed it to the Navy brass. They were impressed and desperate enough to let him use that collection of stranded ship's musicians to prove the theory would work on Japan's naval code.

"With help from some Japanese-speaking linguists and Gerry's expertise, they broke the code, the Midway invasion force was ambushed, and we shortened the war by at least two years while saving Britain in the process, not to mention Mr. Stalin's ass, with lend-lease aid. By that look on your face, I gather you don't believe us."

"No, I don't!" Endicott snapped. "You're telling me the two of you changed history. And I'm telling you such a thing is impossible. Answer one more question, Alan. Why did you decide it was necessary to tamper with real history?"

"Because that supposedly theoretical scenario I gave your class wasn't theory. When we left the present in my machine, the world was not what it is today. If you think things are bad now, they were a hell of a lot worse when we decided to do something about it.

"Listen well, Josh. This is how things *really* were in 1987, the year after I finished building and testing the time machine, and when Gerry and I decided to use Midway as the pivotal event that *had* to be altered.

"Britain, which the Nazis occupied for more than a decade, had become three separate nations—England, Ireland and Scotland—and was just beginning to consider re-unification. A defeated Russia had split into five different countries, all neo-fascist. So the Axis was victorious, but war drained Germany—which incidentally, still revered Hitler, who died a natural death in 1949, instead of committing suicide in forty-five—which still stayed very carefully out of Japan's way.

"As well it might. Japan ruled half of China and most of the

Far East, including all of Korea. Incidentally, the Korean War never happened. Japan also was dictating much of our own economic policies. Every automobile plant in the U.S. was Japanese-owned. GM, Ford, and Chrysler no longer existed. Japan also owned our TV networks, movie studios, and forty percent of America's banks. It had become the world's richest nation, a status made possible by the true story of Midway, the one we had to rewrite.

"These are just the highlights of what the world was like because there was no miracle at Midway. A world of which you and everyone else have absolutely no memory whatsoever, because we went back and made sure the real aftermath of Midway never happened. Any comment?"

Endicott's jaw had dropped like the hinged prow of a ferry boat. It took several seconds before he could reply, and when he did, his voice had descended to the lower decibels of uncertainty.

"I'll be damned if you're not serious. But you didn't have to swear me to secrecy because nobody would believe me anyway. And frankly, I still don't. Words, however convincing they sound, are not proof."

"Agreed. So here's visible proof."

Petibone opened the envelope he had been carrying and took out an eight-by-eleven, black-and-white glossy photograph that he handed to Endicott.

"This was taken at Pearl Harbor, on March 28, 1942, almost one month before Doolittle's B-25s took off from the carrier *Hornet.* The musical group you're looking at happens to be the band from the *California.* See that capsized hull in the background? That's what's left of the old target ship *Utah,* which the Jap pilots mistook for a carrier. Visible proof of the photo's vintage.

"Now, very closely, look at those two men in the front row of the band, the ones wearing civilian clothes. Care to identify them?"

Endicott stared hard at the photo, then looked up at Petibone with an expression of absolute shock.

"It's you and Gerry," he breathed. "Will you give me your word that photo hasn't been doctored?"

"I'll do better than that. Turn it over and read what's on the back." Endicott complied. "It's stamped 'Official U.S. Navy photograph. Classified and not for publication.' Then a date . . ."

He paused, took a deep breath, then muttered, "March 28, 1942." Petibone put the photo back in its envelope. "Satisfied?"

"Up to a point. How about showing me this alleged time machine of yours?"

Petibone shook his head. "No can do."

"I'm not surprised. Why not?"

"Josh, I just don't want *anyone* to see it, to find out it exists. In effect, we've been playing God by tampering with time itself, and there are people who'd stop the U.S from ever using it again, on moral grounds."

"You're going back in time again?"

"Gerry and I are going to make one more trip, despite our concerns about the long-range effects of the metabolic disruptions. When we return, I'll dismantle the machine and destroy all the technical data I used to build it."

"I'd be willing to risk those effects. So how about taking me with you?"

"The machine can handle only two people safely. Believe me, with three passengers one of us wouldn't survive."

"Then let me go instead of Gerr. You said yourself that he went because he had to teach those band members."

Petibone shook his head. "Too dangerous. Look, neither Gerry nor I have any kids. You have three. Besides, you weigh well over two hundred pounds, and our early experiments with relatively large animals, like obese hogs, showed that the more weight, the more drastic the metabolic problems. Death is possible, and shorter life expectancy almost a certainty. Gerry and I accepted those risks because we felt changing Midway was all-important to the world's future."

Endicott sighed. "All right, but can you tell me how far back you're going this time? It must be tremendously important or you would have already destroyed your machine."

"Yes, it's for damned important reasons. We're returning to September 11, 2001. Trying to prevent three airline flights from taking off."

Professors Petibone and Redmond have not yet returned from their second and final voyage. Are they still trying to complete their mission?

Did Petibone's time machine prove to be their coffin? Or have these two intrepid time travelers ended up at the wrong destination? Such as being trapped forever in what we know as the mysterious and unpredictable world of . . . the Twilight Zone.

# BY THE BOOK

Nancy Holder

Respectfully submitted for your approval . . . The place is here, the time is now, and Deb, the harried housewife of our story, is just another victim of our times: an unsung heroine battling the unreasonable, unending demands of modern life. Someone who is too busy, underappreciated, and more than just a little bit desperate to find her way through the chaos that has become her world. Deb needs some help, and she gets some . . . but not in the manner in which it was intended, and not with the results you might imagine.

What you need," Ellen told Deb, "is a little something for yourself. And I've got just the thing."

Picture-perfect, Ellen reached into her embroidered tote bag, which was decorated with Halloween pumpkins and candy corn. Deb, slouchy and unprepared for visitors, had her arms filled with a tower of black construction paper topped with a black cat invitation template, and she desperately kept Ellen blockaded in the entryway of the house. The place was a disaster; Kevin had stayed home from work with the flu and there were wads of tissues everywhere. Andy's pajamas were wadded up in the middle of the floor, and the kitchen was covered with ants because Sarah hadn't put away her Sugar Pops before informing her mother that Deb just didn't understand, that Sarah hated her, and she might as well be dead.

Ellen had just given Deb the paper and the pattern to transform the paper into invitations for the Boy Scouts' Halloween party. Both their sons were Cubs. It was going to be a big 'do, and suddenly Deb had sixty-three black cats to cut out. Today. And speaking of cats, the cat box reeked. Deb hadn't noticed it before, but now as she stalled Ellen, who clearly thought coffee and something fragrant and homemade should come forth during the handoff, her eyes were almost watering. Cleaning the cat box was Sarah's job. So were last night's dishes, but Deb just wouldn't understand why they'd gone undone.

"Okay, well, thank you," Deb said, as Ellen topped the tower with a thick paperback book. Deb stared down cross-eyed at it. It was a romance novel. Silver-embossed letters read *No Time for Love.* Below the title, a woman with waist-length curly blond hair, dressed in a silver gown with a plunging neckline, clung to a sharp-profiled man wearing a pirate shirt that exposed his bulging pecs. He had miles of curly dark brown hair. Their lips were open, their eyes were closed . . .

. . . and Deb couldn't even remember the last time she'd thought about romance, much less had any. Her ponytail was held back with a rubber band; she wasn't wearing any makeup; and she had on a ratty old sweater, a pair of too-tight jeans, and one blue sock and one green sock.

"It saved my life," Ellen said, tapping the book with one of her perfectly manicured fingernails, and there was something in her voice, an odd sort of catch, that made Deb blink. "You really should read it."

"Okay, thanks," Deb replied. "I'll get the invitations done by tomorrow."

Ellen sneezed. Maybe it was the cat box. Mortified, Deb closed her eyes and willed her to leave.

"Be good to yourself." Ellen's charm bracelet—witches, pumpkins, and black cats—jingled as she patted the book. Then she reached back into her tote and pulled out a key ring. The enameled heart shape said WORLD'S #1 MOM. She had five kids. Deb had two.

At last she was gone, and Deb shut the door—and her cell went off. Balancing the tower of paper and the book, she fished in her jeans for the phone. Everything tumbled to the floor, the paper flapping like bats. And it was then—and only then—that she discovered the cat had left a gift on the floor, perhaps in retaliation for the filthy litter box: a round little—

She closed her eyes in shame as the purring motor of Ellen's car hummed down the street. The phone trilled again and she managed to connect.

"Mom, I don't have my gym shoes!" Sarah shrieked. "I thought I put them in my locker but they're not here! I'll get a nonsuit! No field trip!"

"Oh, no," Deb said. Sarah's PE class was going to a performing arts center tomorrow. Sarah was a dancer and an actress; she hardly ever wore her gym uniform, hence no need for shoes.

*"Mom!"* Sarah wailed.

"I'll find them. I'll bring them," Deb promised.

They were underneath Kevin's briefcase in the hall. And on the way to Sarah's school, she ran out of gas.

"You should have made sure you had your shoes," Kevin said to Sarah that evening, as he blew his nose again and dropped the tissue onto another stack beside the couch. Sixty pounds overweight, in need of a shave, wearing his favorite sweats and a ragged bathrobe, he was draped with a fuzzy dark-blue throw covered with cat hair, and he had been there all day, watching TV. Deb had told Andy to pick up his LEGOs, but the TV had him hypnotized.

"I *did* make sure," Sarah huffed. She rolled her heavily made-up eyes. She was thin and wiry, a dancer. Her black hair was long and dramatic, a drama student. "Andy must have hidden them."

"Why—?" Kevin began, but something on the TV caught his eye. He picked up the remote.

"God!" Sarah bellowed. Then she stormed out of the room. Deb heard her door slam. Andy didn't move. He hadn't heard a word.

Kevin blew his nose and put the tissue on coffee table. "Sorry again about the gas," he said. "I thought *you* had gassed up."

"I want a baby brother," Andy announced.

"I think something's burning in the oven." Kevin picked up the remote and continued to surf.

It was after one in the morning. Kevin was asleep on the couch, so Deb would have the bedroom to herself. Which was nice, because Kevin snored. The doctor said if Kevin lost a few pounds, the snoring might go away.

From the chuckles and clacking emanating from Sarah's room, Deb guessed she was on her laptop, chatting with her friends. Sarah's punishment for not doing the dishes last night was to do tonight's as well, but she hadn't emerged from her room all evening, not even to eat. Sarah also still hadn't cleaned the cat box. Better to leave her alone and let her get over her sulk, Deb decided. So Deb did all of them, loading the dishwasher with great care so as not to wake Kevin.

Then she picked up the construction paper and the black cat pattern from the breakfast bar, where she'd left them, and absently grabbed Ellen's romance novel as well. Wearily, she shuffled into the master bedroom, flicked on the lights, and shut the door.

*Scissors,* she thought, as she laid everything on the bed. Sighing, she turned to go back into the kitchen. The silver letters of the book cover gleamed, catching her eye. *No Time for Love.* That guy was so handsome, in an outrageous sort of way. Huge chest, arm muscles bulging all over the place . . .

*It saved my life.*

As she rummaged through the kitchen drawers for the scissors, Kevin snuffled from the couch and she tried to look more quietly. They weren't anywhere; she was about to knock on Sarah's door when she noticed that the sliver of light beneath it was gone. Sarah had gone to bed. She tiptoed into Andy's room, her stockinged foot coming down hard on a LEGO block. She winced and bit her lip as she spied the prize on top of a pile of paper, markers, and glue sticks: some bright blue kiddie scissors about three inches long.

She plucked them up and limped back out of the room, down the hall, and into the master bedroom again. She picked up the black cat template and three pieces of black paper, and looked down at her scissors. This was ridiculous; she *had* good scissors. If whoever had taken them would have just put them back . . .

*No Time for Love.*

She sat down on the bed and moved the scissors around the tail of the cat pattern, then along the arched back toward the head. It was hard to cut through three layers with the funky scissors. Her thumb was already hurting. Then she accidentally ripped the tail.

Frustrated, she unthreaded her fingers and flexed them, cricking her neck left and right. This was crazy. She could do it tomorrow. After the carpool and paying the bills and seeing what she could do about the ants.

She put the whole mess on the nightstand. The book was left behind on her mattress. Feeling a little sheepish—she'd never read a romance novel in her life—she opened it to page one.

*He stood on the beach, his rough muslin shirt dangling open, the cold air washing his broad chest, his muscular thighs girded with chain mail.*

She blinked. Did the man on the cover have on chain mail? She checked. No, no chain mail. Leather trousers. Snug, too. Wow. Very snug.

*Aidan's long, brown, curly hair waved in the wind as he thought of his woman in the arms of the sheikh . . .*

"His woman gets a pirate *and* a sheikh?" she murmured.

*He balled his fists and swore that nothing would come between them, not even his honor . . . or hers . . .*

"Wow." Flushing, she felt a little thrill at the base of her spine. This was pretty hot stuff. She kept reading.

*She was his, and his world would end if he could not have her. . . .*

Then she thought she heard something, some kind of rushing noise. Was it the TV in the living room? They kept the heater down low for a reason, and that reason was called *money.*

She looked up from the book, dropped it, and would have screamed if the man looming over her hadn't covered her mouth with his large hand and gazed into her eyes with fiery passion. It was Aidan, from the cover, with his pirate shirt and his broad, masculine chest and his legs girded in chain mail.

"Mmmwh," she managed behind his hand. She had to be asleep. She was having a dream.

Gently he pushed her back against the pillows, moving one clanking leg onto the bed. Her eyes widened. The sound she was hearing was the ocean, and she smelled salt and . . . whoa . . . *him* . . .

*"Nothing shall come between us. Nothing,"* he whispered in a deep, masculine voice. With his other hand, he caressed her cheek. His fingertips were calloused. His eyes burned with lust.

*I am definitely asleep,* she thought, as her heart pounded and she tingled all over. *But I sure don't feel like it.*

*"I, Aidan, am here,"* he declared, with a smoldering look as he trailed his fingertips over her mouth. *"And all I want . . . is you."*

In the morning, Deb jerked awake to the blaring alarm as the black construction paper cascaded, once again, to the floor. She rolled over the other way, and found Ellen's book under her hip. She smiled. Nice dream. Then she laughed. Who was she kidding? It had been a great dream. The best dream of her life, in fact.

But the morning was here way too early and she had carpool. She slung her legs over the bed.

"Mom, there are ants *everywhere!*" Andy shouted.

"You little freak!" Sarah screamed. "You freak, you freak! *Mom!*"

"Thank you so much for doing this," Ellen said, taking the invitations as Deb blocked her view of the house once more. Ellen was wearing *another* Halloween-themed ensemble—a black sweater with silver moons over matching black trousers, and silver moons dangling from her ears. She even had a crescent-moon watch with a black leather band. "I hope you didn't go to a lot of trouble."

"Oh, no, it was fine," Deb lied. Her fingers were killing her. She had never found the good scissors. Andy had dribbled ketchup all over Sarah's costume for her dance performance and Deb had spent the majority of the day first trying to clean it, then figuring out how to replace the ruined sections. Andy swore it was an accident. He'd been trying to kill the ants that had also invaded the bathroom. With ketchup. Kevin had done nothing but snuffle and cough on the couch.

"Did you start the book?" Ellen asked. Her smile was sly.

"Um, yes, it's great," Deb replied vaguely, trying to translate that smile, blazing with embarrassment over her hot, hot dream. As she looked down, she discovered a spot of ketchup on her black sweatshirt. Then she nearly choked as she noticed the time on Ellen's half-moon watch. "Our cat has a vet appointment," she announced.

"Oh. My husband takes care of our dog." Ellen smiled very sweetly. "If I could trouble you to make some cupcakes for the party?"

Inwardly, Deb groaned. But she smiled and said, "Of course."

"Thank you *so* much. Well, I'll get out of your hair." She glanced at Deb's hair, and Deb blanched. She'd been meaning to get a cut. . . .

*"You are perfect just the way you are,"* Aidan murmured into her frizzy shag six hours later. Kevin was still on the couch, thank goodness. *"I adore you."*

"You're really here," Deb whispered, touching his broad chest with her fingertips. She'd been on page seventeen, third paragraph down, when suddenly he'd appeared, as he had the night before. Except tonight . . .

. . . no chain mail.

"Mom!" Sarah bellowed. "Mom, I need a towel!"

She sighed. He caught her hand and brought it to his lips. *"I am really here. And all I want is . . . you. Kiss me, my beauty."*

"Mom!" Sarah cried. "There is cat hair all over the floor and my wet feet will get all gross! *Mom!*"

"Shut up!" Andy shouted. Pounding rattled the hallway wall. "Me and Dad are watching the game!"

*"Stay here, with me,"* Aidan begged her, grabbing her hand. *"Stay here."*

"Sarah needs a towel," she told him.

*"But I need you."* He eased her back against her pillow. *"I need you as no other needs you."*

"Here!" Andy yelled. "Catch!"

"Ouch! *Mom!*"

"Stay." He kissed her.

And she stayed.

"Thanks," Deb said absently to Kevin, whom she had convinced to stay on the couch by claiming that she had caught his cold. He'd been there for four nights now. He seemed perfectly content, eating potato chips, drinking beer, channel surfing. As thunder rumbled overhead and rain poured down the sliding-glass door, she glided away, the hem of her light blue chenille bathrobe catching on one of the heaps of tissues, sending a cascade to the floor. In the hall, she stepped on a LEGO, and then on a wet washcloth.

"We're out of Sugar Pops," Sarah informed her from the doorway of her room. "We're out of *everything.* And I don't have any more clean jeans."

"I'm so sorry, sweetie," she said, gliding on.

"What is *wrong* with you?" Sarah demanded, then huffed and slammed her door as Deb glided past. "I don't know," Sarah muttered behind the closed door. "I swear my mom has gone psycho."

Deb went into her bedroom . . . or rather, where her bedroom used to be. Now it was their secret tropical cove of passion. Aidan's pirate ship, *The Treasure,* bobbed in the distance, and Aidan himself lay bare-chested in the fine filigree bed he had carried from his quarters aboard ship and settled firmly in the fine, warm sand. A canopy of shimmering Indian silk was strung from one gently curving palm tree to the other, and he was lying on his side, his broad chest glistening with a sheen of manly perspiration, his long brown hair hanging low. A parchment map was spread on the bed; he was drinking finely spiced rum from a sterling silver goblet. At his tanned elbow, an empty silver platter studded with jewels gleamed in the sun.

*"My love,"* he said, eyes drinking in the sight of her. *"I've been waiting an eternity for you."*

"Sorry, sorry," she murmured. "My family . . ." She shrugged and held out her hands.

*"I am your family now,"* he said, reaching for her wrists and drawing her toward him. *"Come to me, my beauty."*

Her stomach growled. She had made tomato soup and grilled cheese sandwiches for dinner, and burned the last of the bread—her own sandwich—while reading chapter twenty. Thirty-six pages of love scene.

She could hardly wait.

She sat down beside him on the bed. His eyes blazed with pleasure. Her stomach growled again and she said, "What were you eating? Is there more?"

*"Iced shrimp and papaya,"* he told her. *"Of course there's more."*

He leaned over the side of the bed and brought up another platter laden with delicate pink shrimp and golden slivers of papaya. And chocolates.

"You're a lifesaver," she murmured, as he began to feed her.

"Yes, I really do still have a cold," she told Kevin, blowing her nose as if to make a point. It had been a week. She looked down at the pile of tissues beside the couch, and wondered why on earth he hadn't thrown them away himself. He was back at work, which got the daytime TV off, thank God.

The hallway was littered with dirty clothes and there was a paper towel roll outside the bathroom. The kids had been making do since the toilet paper ran out. Kevin kept apologizing for forgetting to get some at the store on his way home from the strip of fast-food restaurants he had begun to frequent. Sarah wasn't talking to Deb; she had forgotten to do the carpool and everyone had been late for school. *Twice.* She felt a twinge. Slight, but present.

She heard someone crying in Sarah's room.

"I don't know what's wrong with her, Andy," Sarah said. "Maybe she's got a fever and she's delirious."

"But I *have* to bring the cupcakes to the Scout party. It's my responsibility!" Andy ground out.

"Maybe Dad can buy you some," Sarah ventured.

Deb stepped around the hallway clutter and went into the bedroom. And there he was, lying in bed, sipping rum and eating a banana. Sun-streaked highlights gleamed in his hair. When he saw her, he beamed with joy and held out the cup to her.

*"Where have you been, my beauty?"* he demanded hotly. *"The hours have dragged like years."*

She climbed onto the bed. "I don't suppose you know how to make cupcakes."

He slid his arms around her. *"No, but I know how to make you happy."*

Sighing, she picked up the goblet and swallowed down the rum. He kissed her. Again. And again. He ran his fingers through her hair and marveled aloud at how exquisitely, achingly beautiful she was. He wept with joy that they had found each other at last.

"What about the cupcakes? I have to make cupcakes. I'm supposed to take them to Ellen's after drop-off tomorrow."

He eased her onto her back and gazed with limpid desire into her eyes.

*"Forget them,"* he urged her in his deep, barrel-chested voice. *"There's nothing but you . . . and me. Nothing in the world but our passion."*

He was almost right about that. But Andy's tears echoed in her mind as she slumbered beside Aidan. She tossed and turned. Then at four A.M., she got up and started making the batter. She'd bought all the makings the first day she'd read Aidan into her life. While digging for the extra package of butter in the freezer, she discovered a treasure trove of microwave meals and frozen vegetables. Kevin and the kids didn't have to eat so much fast food. They'd had food in the house all along. But no one had looked for it. No one else seemed to be able to cook. And why was that?

In the next room on the couch, Kevin snored on.

Yawning, exhausted, Deb made chocolate cupcakes with orange frosting, each one topped with a gumdrop spider and legs of black licorice. Four dozen. Her eyes were bloodshot and lined with sandpaper by the time she finished, just as the sun came up. And as she awakened her son with the wonderful news, he just stared at her in horror.

"Four dozen? You were supposed to make *six* dozen," he said.

She realized with dawning horror that he was right. She'd miscounted. She'd been too distracted—too tired, and too eager to get back in bed with Aidan.

"Ellen, hi, I'm sorry," she said, calling Ellen on her cell phone. "I hit a snag," she said. "I'll bring the cupcakes over a little later today."

"Oh," Ellen said, sounding surprised. "All right."

Andy didn't talk to her the entire way to school. He sat in the back, sulking beside Sarah, who was also sulking, because she was gaining weight and her face was breaking out from all the fast food.

"Sarah, if you don't like all the stuff Daddy's been buying, why haven't you zapped any of the meals in the freezer?" Deb asked her daughter.

*"Me?"* Sarah asked, stunned. "*You're* the mom."

Deb jerked as if she'd been pelted with a water balloon. She blinked, stunned, at what a curt, spoiled, thoughtless child her daughter was. And her son, glowering at her because she was two dozen cupcakes short of a Halloween party.

*I'm the mom,* Deb thought, as she dropped her kids off at their schools. It became a litany with the swish-swoosh of the windshield wipers as the sleet crackled down on her windshield. *The mom, the mom, the mom.*

She did feel guilty, but more than that, she was angry. She went home to her filthy house, half-covered with ants, and the cupboards and trash cans overflowing with fast-food containers and tissues; and the nest Kevin had made on the couch, and the remote on the floor. She looked at it all and she blasted into the bedroom, where she found Aidan lying in bed, the light in his eyes leaping to life as she stomped toward him.

*"At last,"* he said. *"How I have been pining for you, my beauty."*

She stared at him. "Do you love me?"

His chest swelled. His eyes welled with tears. *"Oh, yes. I love you, with all my heart, and my soul. You are my life. Without you, I'm . . . I'm nothing."*

"Then why didn't you help me with the cupcakes last night?" she demanded. "Because I'm the *mom*?"

*"You are my one true love."* He looked puzzled. *"Come to me, be with me . . ."*

"I can't," she said miserably. "It's all getting worse. It's going to be overwhelming if I don't get back to work." She broke down sobbing. "Because I'm *the mom*."

*"No, you are my beloved. My darling. My life."* He enveloped her in a loving embrace and kissed her tears away. *"Don't cry, my heart, my wonder, my sweetling."*

"Can't you help me?" she asked him. "If you love me?"

*"Help you . . . yes, I will help you, yes, my darling,"* he said. *"We'll weigh anchor in an hour and be gone from here forever."* He pulled the rubber band from her hair and clutched her face, kissing her long and hard.

*"My beauty."*

"Make it two hours," she pleaded.

*"For you . . . an eternity,"* he whispered moistly into her ear. *"Soon, we will leave all this behind."*

She left the bedroom, but she didn't make the extra two dozen cupcakes. Trembling, she loaded what she had into the car and drove straight to Ellen's house. She'd never been there before, but as her arms shook around the Tupperware containers loaded in her arms, she noted the impeccable lawn, the little Japanese footbridge, and the stone lanterns on either side of the entrance. WELCOME FROM THE DEWITT FAMILY, said a little sign on the door with two big cherry blossoms and five little ones.

Balancing the containers, she rang the doorbell and tried to catch her breath. She thought she was going to faint. As dots of yellow swam before Deb's eyes, Ellen opened the door. Every hair in place, she was dressed in her black moon sweater, jeans, and black Uggs. She was taking off a pair of rubber gloves.

"Oh, good," she said. "Come on in. I was just cleaning up."

Deb stumbled across the foyer into a homey living room filled with antiques. Pushed against the wall beneath a painting of an old forest, there were five large plastic bins, each one labeled with a name: SEAN, MARCIE, HAILEY, DOUG, STEPHANIE. The names of her children.

Deb and Ellen went down a hall where various certificates were framed—soccer, softball, good citizenship, honor roll—and a large white board labeled "CHORES." The children's names were written there, too, with a series of checkmarks beside each one. To the right of that were at least half a dozen calendars, hung up side by side, each with a different theme—puppies, baseball, France, sunsets, motorcycles. The squares for October were all filled in, with different handwriting for each calendar.

Ellen caught her looking. "Each of my children has their own calendar," she said. She laughed. "Of course I have one for my husband, and one for me. And I keep it all on a spreadsheet."

Deb stared at Ellen as if she were speaking a foreign language. She swayed behind Ellen as she led her into her kitchen. It was blue and white, and it was immaculate, from the white grout between the white tile squares on the counter, to the white tile floor and the white appliances. Tidy refrigerator art. A pumpkin candle sat in the kitchen bay window, overlooking a perfectly manicured yard. There was one orange coffee cup decorated with a black cat in the dish drainer. Ellen laid the rubber gloves on a stand that hung over the sink, wiped her hands on a brown dish towel with a smiling jack-o'-lantern on it, and reached for the containers.

"I'm sorry, I'm so sorry, there are only four dozen," Deb said in a rush, "but I had to talk to you. What did you do? Did you come back, or . . . or . . . ?" She trailed off as Ellen cocked her head quizzically and set the containers beside each other, burping open the nearest one.

"What *adorable* cupcakes. Did you run out of supplies? I always keep some mixes on hand. I get them when they're on sale."

Deb stared at her. "Ellen, what did you do about *Aidan*?"

"Aidan?" Ellen said, opening her cupboard. She pulled out a box of chocolate cake mix. "Who—"

"*You* know," Deb said. "The man . . . in the book."

"Oh." She laughed. "You see, I have it all blocked out." She smiled at Ellen. "On my calendar." As Deb blinked, she walked back to the row of calendars and pointed to the one closest to them, themed with sunsets. She tapped her finger on Wednesday's square. "See? Nine to ten P.M. tonight. Mom's Reading Time. I'm halfway through a great new one about a highlander." She leaned toward Deb. "Scorching. I'll give it to you after I'm finished."

"Reading time," Deb said, trying to make sense. "Scorching."

"My husband teases me about my romance novels, but I'd go crazy if I didn't have some 'me' time, you know?"

"Me," Deb said.

"No one better interrupt my reading time," Ellen declared. "It's my lifesaver."

Deb flopped backward against the wall. Ellen peered at her. "Are you all right?"

"Dinner," she blurted desperately, scanning the chore list. "Do they make dinner? Do you have . . . what about the store? If you run out of toilet paper . . ."

"Let me get you a glass of water." She left Deb, who had slid halfway down the wall, and went back into the kitchen. She got Deb some water and brought it back to her. "It's Doug's turn to make dinner. Of course all of them have chores. And if they don't do them, well, they might say I'm too hard on them but it's all about consistency, you know?" She wrinkled her nose. "And boundaries."

"Oh, my God, I'm going crazy," Deb said, gulping down the water. "Completely crazy."

"Is there someone I can call?" Ellen ventured, taking the empty glass. "Do you need something, some medication or—"

"I need to go," Deb announced. She pushed herself away from the wall.

"You can keep the book," Ellen assured her. "I just recycle them when I'm finished."

Deb lurched to the door. "Okay. Okay, thank you."

"Are you sure you can drive? Is there anything I can do? I'll make the last two dozen cupcakes. Don't worry about that."

Ellen hovered at the door of her perfect home as Deb staggered out to her car. Her messy, stinky car that was almost out of gas again.

*I'm the mom I'm the mom I'm the mom.*

*I* am *the mom,* she thought. *Me.*

She did a lot of thinking on the way home. Once there, she threw open the door to the master bedroom. Aidan had on his shirt, and the bed was gone.

*"At last. I have been waiting,"* he said.

She crooked her finger. "We're not going anywhere."

Six months later, and the dark days were over. It was spring.

The calendars were up. The bins were in the hall. Andy was

putting away the groceries, including the items Sarah had requested for her dinner preparation. As indicated on her calendar—ballerinas—it was her turn.

"Hey, are you ready?" Kevin asked Sarah, as he strode into the room in his new track shorts and a freshly laundered T-shirt. It had been Andy's turn to fold and put away. Kevin was clean-shaven, and he had lost forty pounds. Deb had promised Ellen she would have the bright green Camporee invitations finished by this evening at seven.

"Yes. Hold on," she told him.

While Kevin jogged in place, she went to the master bedroom and rapped lightly on the door. It was their code, giving Aidan permission to exist.

She opened the door and there he was, lying beneath the canopy of Indian silk, naked from the waist up. His eyes beamed with joy at the sight of her.

*"My beauty, my joy,"* he whispered. *"How I need—"*

She glanced down at the paltry pile of invitations beside his elbow. The scissors in his hand caught the light. "You should get the sheikh to help you," she told him.

He sighed unhappily. *"But my beloved, I need—"*

"*I* need those invitations. Pronto." She blew him a kiss as he huffed and picked up the scissors.

Smiling, she shut the door, and retraced her steps back down the hall. Stopping at Sarah's door, she gave it a soft rap.

"How's it going?" she asked.

"Mom," Sarah said, "do I *have* to make dinner *and* the dishes?"

"Yes," Deb replied. "You forgot to clean the cat box. That's the punishment."

"It's not fair!"

"I know." Deb smiled to herself.

"But then why do I have to do it?"

Deb couldn't wait to say it. She loved saying it.

"Because I'm the mom."
And Deb set sail for her walk.

"Books fall open, you fall in," or so the saying goes. But sometimes books fall *out* into our world, and take us to a place we've never been before . . . a dimension where imagination trumps reality every time . . . the Twilight Zone.

# EARTHFALL

John Farris

For millennia men have looked to the sky for signs and portents of Earth's destruction—will the end come in a fiery collision with a comet or asteroid that will leave only barren debris in what once was Earth's path around the sun? Or is it possible that, all along, men have looked in the wrong direction for their doomsday, which quietly, almost undetectably, already has begun?

Lenny (for Lenora) Vespasian, just twenty-two and with enough money to buy Portugal, had been a gilded filly flawless in form but with the heavy-lidded sated eyes and languor in her limbs of a burnt-out post-deb, stale cake for brains and the vocabulary of a stevedore. Right now, at eleven twenty on the bright cloudless morning of August 13, she was just a stiff, having expired in the night while her current lover, the crackhead rocker Bobby Benedict, lay deep in noddy land beside her on Lenny's Dux bed.

The Suffolk County police weren't calling it murder yet, but one of the crime scene investigators had opened a week's worth of neglected e-mail on Lenny's laptop and come across the ominous message YOU'RE NEXT.

That detective was waiting on the lawn of the 24,000-square-foot brick house that faced the glistening sea near Amagansett, shading his eyes (even though he wore tinted glasses) as a helicopter circled to land near the tennis courts. The passengers were a top-rank FBI agent and one Pierre Saint-Philèmon, a heavyweight from Interpol in Brussels. They comprised the two-man spearhead of an international task force. Two more helicopters were on the western horizon, approaching the estate.

The special agent in charge of the FBI's team introduced himself. Nobis. No first name. A tall graying man, fit as a triathlete, with bronze skin and triangular sapphire eyes that made the sky look dingy.

"Bud Podokarski," the detective said. He was sweating and nervous, awed that one phone call of his had rung loud bells in D.C.

"Big damn house," Nobis commented as they approached from the west lawn the bedroom wing where Lenny Vespasian lay forlornly nude and stone dead.

"And wide open," the Interpol investigator said as he looked around. "Although the family must employ security."

"Twenty-four hours, two-man patrols, Dobermans," Podokarski replied.

"They saw and heard nothing unusual, of course."

Podokarski shook his head. They paused at the edge of the wide tri-level terrace outside the late Lenny's suite, which was easily accessible through French doors. The terraces were paved with flagstones. There was a hedge-bordered path to Lenny's private swimming pool.

At the pool a boy and a girl, prepubescent, were lounging in swimsuits beneath an umbrella, looking at them. The boy was playing with what looked like a Matchbox car.

"Who are the kids?" Nobis asked.

"They belong to the caretaker and his wife. Apparently Miss Vespasian let them use her pool whenever they want."

Podokarski mopped the back of his neck with a handkerchief. Hot, hot, hot. Nobis wore a dark suit with his white shirt and tie, but even with the sun full on his face, he wasn't sweating. Nor did he blink as he looked at the kids. Podokarski wondered what it would be like to be interrogated by this guy.

"Want to have a look at the body before we have it removed for autopsy?"

"What I'm looking for," Nobis said, "won't be visible to the naked eye. And you won't be taking Miss Vespasian anywhere. She's going back to Washington with us."

The other helicopter descended on the lawn a hundred yards away and blew in their direction the fine sand from the beach that had collected at the roots of the close-cut Bermuda grass. Nobis looked at the sand sifting lightly over the terraces and abruptly left the others, walking down the path to the pool.

The kids studied him warily. The boy picked up the car he'd been rolling across the glass tabletop where they sat and spun the toy wheels idly with a finger. The car the boy had in his hands wasn't much larger than a good-sized cockroach. Dark and sleek-looking, tapered cowling, a racing model with NASCAR wheels. Four sets of exquisitely crafted tires.

"Good morning," Nobis said pleasantly. "Could I talk to you?"

The girl said, "What happened to Lenny? Did she OD?"

"We don't know yet. Did you ever see her using drugs?"

The girl had a thin face and a thinner mouth. She kept it closed. The boy snorted.

"I seen her do lots of things," he said wisely.

"Shut up, Rog," the girl said, taking an openhanded swipe at his head and missing as he grinned. She looked down and sniffed sorrowfully. "Lenny was always nice to us. Show some respect."

Rog wouldn't shut up. "Maybe she killed herself," he said helpfully. " 'Cause I heard her say she couldn't stand the idea of going to jail."

"You are *so* naive," the girl said. "What she did was an *ac*cident, dummy. And Lenny was really truly sorry anybody got hurt."

"What happened?" Nobis said to Rog, although he already knew what they were talking about.

Rog shrugged and spun several wheels of the car.

"DUI. Her *second* DUI. This time she drove up on a sidewalk in the village and nailed some people waiting to get into Sea Fare. Nobody got killed, but I think one's still in a coma." He shrugged again. "Yeah, her lawyers probably had it fixed already. Not that it matters now, *does* it, Chrissy?"

"Shut up—and this time I mean it," his sister said, making small fists.

"Mind telling me where you got that flam car?" Nobis asked the boy.

"Lenny gave it to me 'bout a week ago. I thought I lost it, but I found it again this morning."

"Where?"

Rog pointed to the terrace. "It was just sitting there outside the doors to her bedroom. So I went up and got it." He folded his lower lip between his teeth. "Doors were open, like always. I didn't know she was dead then. I mean, I didn't look inside."

Chrissy said, "Lenny always likes to sleep with the doors open. She says air-conditioning dries out her skin. She has . . . beautiful skin." A look of pain crossed the girl's face. "I mean . . . I can't think of her being, like, dead." She trickled tears.

Nobis took out his ID folder.

"Rog, I have to ask you for that car. It could be part of an ongoing investigation."

Rog made a face, but he seemed impressed by Nobis's tone of quiet urgency. And anyway you didn't say *no* to the FBI. He put the shiny black speedster on the table and heaved a sigh.

"Can I get it back, d'you think?"

"Do my best," Nobis said. "And thanks for your cooperation."

In Lenny Vespasian's *luxe* bedroom, Nobis showed the little car to his team. Saint-Philèmon's only comment was a raised eyebrow. Nobis put the toy into an evidence bag and handed it to one of the Bureau's evidence response techies who had taken over the crime scene investigation.

"Turn a chopper around and get this to Ludecke and Hopkins at DARPA right now."

The Interpol inspector said, "You will want to see what has been found in the recreation room."

Nobis glanced at the bed where Lenny, a pale sack of blood, was being zipped into a body bag for transporting. The techies handling her wore surgical masks, and it was a special kind of body bag. Nobis heard Lenny's superstar boyfriend blubbering and moaning in another part of the four-room suite. He followed Saint-Philèmon.

Two other members of the FBI's ER team were measuring and photographing a spill of what Nobis assumed was cocaine on the marble floor. He kneeled for a closer look and saw little tire tracks from four sets of wheels through the white powder.

"Playing with their little toy while they were getting high?" the inspector mused.

"Miss Vespasian gave the car to the caretaker's kid. I don't think she knew it was here last night. And not conscious while it was on the move." Nobis looked at the bedroom, turned to a techie. "Microscopic particles of coke would have rubbed off the tires as it rolled along. I want to know if the car went straight to her bed."

"The bedroom's carpeted," the techie said. "Cashmere, but still tough going for a toy car with wheels less than a millimeter in diameter. Unless something was pushing it along."

"Something, or someone, was," Nobis said. "As for the obstacle of a carpet—I've seen one of these roach chariots roll up a vertical wall and across a ceiling upside down. The big question is, when they get where they're going, how do they kill? And why?"

"*Two* questions," Saint-Philèmon said with a slightly haunted smile. "Two deeply perplexing questions, *mon ami.*"

"And to answer them I think we had better be both lucky and quick. So far eight people with no apparent connection to one another have died after being informed *You're next.*"

"No apparent connection," the inspector said. "Yet all of the victims seemed to have had a notable deficiency in moral values, and all enjoyed a certain level of notoriety that unfortunately has been enhanced by the mystery surrounding their deaths. Is there a plan? Who or what are we looking for?"

Nobis rarely smiled. He did so now.

"Another god gone mad."

Dinner at the Wrixtons' showplace home, a mid-nineteenth-century Victorian in Washington's Georgetown neighborhood, ends, as do all of their intimate and socially-significant gatherings, at a few minutes past eleven. Wry Wrixton and his coltish third wife Julia, half his age, are fitness fanatics who arise early and play hard at their health club. Tough daily schedules demand of them at least six hours of sound sleep nightly in their third-floor bedroom, overlooking a walled garden and an additional wall of backyard oaks and red maples to further ensure their privacy.

August in Washington is usually hot enough to boil sap out of the African tribal wood carvings Julia collects, but even with the central-air thermostats set at sixty-eight degrees, Julia still likes to sleep with one window partly open near her bed, to enjoy the sweet midnight breath from the garden below.

Private security on the perimeter of their property and inside the house has been doubled following the latest, cryptic (death?) threat that appeared three days ago in Wry's personal e-mail. Just a precaution, Wry tells his wife, while he must be in Washington at the wrong season and for the most part under the radar, conducting secret confabs at the Pentagon.

He's in his pj's and using his ultrasonic toothbrush, eyeing himself for flaws in the old barbershop mirror mounted behind his-and-hers sinks. *Shave and a haircut, four bits.* Wry moves armaments and ammunition around the world for hefty fees to legitimate governments—and also to less visible tribal and religious trouble-makers. He has, at sixty, the shrewd mien, the pitchman's polished baritone, the eerie essence and urbane lech of a wholesaler of death.

Julia comes into the bathroom looking perplexed, something in her hand.

"Wry, where did this come from?"

He puts down his toothbrush with another overly wide grin of self-approval (he's always had marvelous teeth), and turns for a better look at the object.

"Toy car."

"I know, but—"

"You mean the four sets of wheels? Don't think I've ever seen one like—where did you find it, sweetheart?"

Now Julia is looking at herself in the kitschy old mirror. Even at the end of a long day, aswirl in frothy, clingy night clothes, she illumines Cecil Beaton's famous dictum: The Truly Fashionable Are Beyond Fashion.

"Oh . . ." Julia reties her hair with a velvet ribbon so it is well off her shoulders and the back of her neck for sleeping. "It was there on the sill when I went to raise the windows by my side of the bed. Probably belongs to Myra's little boy. He follows her around the house while she does the vacuuming."

"Great workmanship," Wry observes, picking up the little car Julia has left on the marble sink. He gives the four sets of wheels a spin, sets the car down again, and instantly it's in motion, rolling straight and true to the edge of the sink, where it stops as if sensing an abyss before it.

"You know, I used to collect those when I was a kid," Wry says fondly. "Matchbox cars, they're called. Can't remember now what I did with all of them."

Special Agent Nobis and Pierre Saint-Philèmon were on hand for Wry Wrixton's autopsy, as they had been for all of the autopsies, some postburial, of the nine victims. The findings of the pathologist remained consistent and as puzzling as ever.

"In each case," Nobis explained to a packed house in the largest conference room available at FBI headquarters the afternoon following Wrixton's funeral, "certain proteins concentrated in the heart valves of the victims were ingested by agents widespread in nature, found in—among other taxonomic species—the Venus flytrap and the venom of the Japanese hornet. In each case the delivery system was contained in one of these hobby cars."

He picked up one of the eight identical black racers from a table beside him. The components of the ninth car (some so small a strong magnifying glass was required to see them) were arranged in orderly fashion a little distance away. While Nobis spoke, another of the components, somewhat like a near-microscopic Swiss Army knife with dozens of tools, was robotically rebuilding the ninth car.

"The metal is a nickel-titanium alloy called nitinol," Nobis continued. "Motive power is contained in nickel hydride batteries, each the size of a grain of sand." He gave the wheels of the car he was holding a spin and put it upside down on a leg of the table. The car descended and, with a version of eight-wheel drive, smoothly made the transition from table leg to floor. It then made a right turn and stopped half an inch from the FBI agent's right foot. Nobis returned the little car to the table.

"The wheels are coated with a substance similar to the adhesive found on the hairs that sprout at the ends of a gecko's toes. It provides sticking power that nevertheless doesn't impede smooth forward or reverse motion."

There was dead silence in the room until the director of Carnegie-Mellon University's Autonomous Mobile Robotics Lab spoke up.

"Where in God's name did the technology come from? *We* can't do this!"

The Pentagon's rep, bristling with gold stars, said darkly, "And who's funding it? Not us."

Other representatives of world governments or R and D divisions of biobusinesses who were present via satellite looked puzzled; or they shook their heads emphatically.

"*Tant pis,*" Pierre Saint-Philèmon said softly. "It gets worse. Or better, perhaps, depending on one's scientific viewpoint."

From Prague a Nobel laureate in integrative biology asked, "Do you have an explanation of how the bacteria confine their destruction to the heart valves? Can the bacteria distinguish one protein from another? As we all know, there are millions of different proteins in the human body, thus far uncatalogued."

The chief pathologist for the FBI took over.

"No, we can't answer that. But examination of each victim's tissues by electron microscope reveals an infinitesimally small borehole through the sternum and into the heart wall." A computer graphic on another large LCD screen illustrated his remarks. "The secondary delivery vehicle, which we believe is off-loaded from one of the toy cars—a nanobiomimetic 'creature,' for want of a better word—completes the drilling process into the heart wall, then disperses bacteria that immediately set to work, um, replicating themselves."

"Have you isolated the bacteria?" asked the director of Singapore's Institute of Molecular and Cell Biology.

"No. The chief characteristic of the bacteria is that it seems to be amazingly fast-acting, and somehow genetically engineered to, um, cease to exist once the heart valves are destroyed."

"How contagious is it?" the head of the CDC in Atlanta wanted to know.

"Not contagious in the sense of disease pathogens. I've tried to make it clear that what we are dealing with are, um, robotic bacteria."

He winced at the ensuing uproar, with the kindest word distinguishable in several languages being "Preposterous!"

"That remains our, um, most viable theory to date."

"Let us have some order, please!" the deputy director of the FBI demanded after another twenty seconds of outrage, denial and, possibly, fear.

His counterpart from the Hong Kong police, a small ravishing Eurasian woman, said calmly, "Assuming for the moment we accept the hypothesis that extremely advanced work in robotics has been conducted somewhere in total secrecy—rather like the plot of a James Bond movie—what then is the logic behind the selection of victims, which required too much diligence to be considered random? A Mexican drug lord, a Hong Kong hedge-fund swindler, a rogue nuclear scientist, a wife-killer that an incompetent American prosecutor failed to convict, and our most recent victims. From the intelligence available to date, these people—of no particular significance in a moral context—were unknown to one another."

Nobis took the floor again.

"The dominant, or Alpha Perpetrator—let's deal with only one for now, although we believe there are several brilliant individuals working together—deliberately courted our attention. Which he certainly has at this point. He's been . . . toying with us, so to speak. There probably is no personal revenge motive behind the murders. Nor are we dealing with a serial killer. The choice of victims is largely irrelevant, although there is a definite aspect of self-righteousness. Our profile suggests the Alpha Perp considers himself to be ethically and morally superior to just about everyone else on the planet, thus justifying his killing spree. A towering intellect, a scientific genius. Give him that. But emotionally he is a despot, a failed human being, a common voyeur, probably impotent and totally insane."

"Then you know who he is?" asked the Hong Kong police commissioner.

"No. I only know he's here today. Like I said, he's a voyeur, and childishly infatuated with the investigation in which he has played an invisible part. So far."

Everyone assembled in the conference room was suddenly preoccupied with trying not to look around. Another uproar began, like the alarm of vulnerable animals at a water hole smelling carnivores in their midst.

Nobis smiled thinly, and gestured for quiet.

"Although not physically present," he amended. "But we should hear from him soon. I believe the first phase of the scheme that has been set in motion is complete."

Nobis picked up the demo car again, this time dropping it into an evidence bag.

"I doubt that it will be long before we hear directly from our Alpha Perp. Thank you for your time, ladies and gentlemen. The bureau will keep you fully informed."

Outside the conference room in the Hoover building, Nobis and Saint-Philèmon were approached by a cadre accompanying the president's National Security adviser, Neal Hullinger.

"I think it's time, from all I've heard today, to bring the president up to speed," Hullinger said.

Nobis nodded.

"I think, by way of illustration, he should see what you have in that evidence bag."

"Doesn't the president have grandchildren visiting the White House this week?"

"Yes, he—" Hullinger took another look at the nanobiomimetic toy car. "Good God, you aren't suggesting—"

"There's vehicular homicide and, in this case, a homicidal vehicle. But if you want the responsibility—"

"No, no!" Hullinger said, backing away. "You've got to find this monster, Agent Nobis!"

"He's more likely to find me," Nobis said.

Promptly at six o'clock that evening, Pierre Saint-Philèmon knocked on the door of a sixth-floor apartment at the Four Seasons Hotel. Special Agent Nobis let him in.

The small apartment was immaculate. Bedroom, sitting room, kitchenette. The furnishings not unlike what Saint-Philèmon would have expected of a first-class travelers' lounge at the Charles de Gaulle airport in Paris. No personal touches, unless one counted an unopened bottle of an important-looking wine and two crystal glasses on a silver room-service tray.

The nanobiomimetic toy that Nobis had brought with him was motionless beside the tray, yet sinister in its lack of activity.

"Only two glasses?" Saint-Philèmon commented, picking up the bottle of wine, which he held reverently: a near-priceless Château Mouton Rothschild. "You assured me we would be having company."

"He'll be along," Nobis said, almost indifferently. "Is that the vintage you told me you enjoyed?"

Saint-Philèmon whistled softly.

"And can never afford."

"Please," Nobis said, gesturing.

Saint-Philèmon poured a glassful of the Château Mouton Rothschild and offered it to Nobis.

Nobis smiled enigmatically, declining.

The nanobiomimetic car moved on the seventeenth-century, richly lacquered end table. It seemed to Saint-Philèmon, as he raised the glass in a silent toast, then sipped with an expression of ecstasy, that the car was spinning all of its wheels. He heard a very faint sound of acceleration that prickled hairs on the back of his neck. Although he knew that none of the toy cars had workable engines.

*But if it should want a powerful engine, probably it could build one for itself,* he thought.

A black-and-white movie was playing on a wall-mounted TV screen. Nobis had turned his full attention to the movie. Saint-Philèmon dimly recalled having seen it as a child. He savored another sip of wine. Obviously the golden oldie had been filmed on location in Washington. The sequence playing out now was set in a park or playground, with the Washington monument visible in the background. Foreground, a flying saucer was confronted by armed and nervous troops and spectators. They stared at a large silvery robot walking down a ramp that had appeared from the base of the saucer. And there was a tall, stern-looking space traveler with a British accent. The soundtrack hummed eerily.

"Isn't that movie called *The Day the Earth Stood Still*? But—?"

"I like a little joke now and then," the normally humorless Nobis said. "Say, about every twenty thousand years or so."

Saint-Philèmon shot him a look and nearly choked on his third sip of the precious wine. He coughed and reached for his handkerchief and looked back at the wide screen on the wall.

Where a man on horseback had appeared in the movie's background. But unlike the somber tone of the film, he was three-dimensional in glorious living color, riding slowly toward the camera. His horse was a black Arabian.

Nobis said, as they watched the newcomer on the screen, "The most dangerous of human beings are those who are born congenitally evil. Fortunately there are only a few of them. The next most dangerous category of humans are those who devoutly believe they are always right."

"Evil as a wretched excess of good," Saint-Philèmon commented, having gotten his cough under control without spilling a drop of the expensive wine.

The man on the black Arabian horse, who wore faded jeans and a calico shirt and a kerchief knotted at one side of his throat, was now in the midst of the ongoing motion picture. He gazed around at the flying saucer, the robot, the awestruck crowd of people. Then he draped the reins over the pommel of his saddle and leaned forward in a relaxed attitude, patting the horse's neck, smiling. Waiting.

"Good afternoon, Dr. Walpole," Nobis said.

The man on horseback nodded agreeably.

"Agent Nobis. Can that be you?"

"Yes, Dr. Walpole. Inspector Saint-Philèmon is with me."

"But none of my former colleagues at SAIL or Berkeley? Those who I assume—how would you say it in your profession?—*fingered* me?"

"No. None of them have had knowledge of your whereabouts during the past ten years. Or knowledge of those who were most likely to be your associates. Nate Kronenwald. Sven Ullberg. Francois Beguelin. Mian Zhang Choi. Zane Red Star. Other than yourself, the most brilliant minds on robotics and bioengineering of the past two decades."

"You're very good, Agent Nobis."

"I have many resources."

"And you knew where to find me. Quite a good job of mind-reading."

"I don't read minds. I study them. Thanks for making yours available."

Edward Walpole smiled indulgently, then straightened in the

saddle and looked around again. "I appreciate your sense of irony, but it *is* distracting to find oneself in the middle of an old flick."

The scene from *The Day the Earth Stood Still* vanished from the LCD screen, and was replaced by a vista of red and ochre canyon lands.

"Thank you," Walpole said. "Now, I suppose, squadrons of helicopters are about to swoop down on me, and I shall conclude my retirement years alone and forgotten in some state dungeon. A 'failed human being,' isn't that how you described me?"

"Doesn't work that way, Dr. Walpole. We both know you're untouchable."

The man in the saddle nodded, thinking, savoring his advantage.

"So what is it we can do for you now, Dr. Walpole?" Nobis said.

"Why don't we talk further, Agent Nobis? But not under these circumstances. Please accept my hospitality. And perhaps you would be interested in meeting my associates?"

"I would, Doctor."

"Well, then . . . shall we say, this same time tomorrow afternoon? In my location of the moment? Let me tell you how to find—"

"I know where and how to find you. Until tomorrow, Dr. Walpole."

"*Hasta luego*," said the man in the saddle, turning his handsome stallion around with a flourish and cantering away. The sun flashed on the silver-dollar headband of his black Stetson.

The LCD screen went blank.

Saint-Philèmon poured himself another generous slug of the Mouton Rothschild. He saluted Nobis with his glass.

"Someday you must tell me how you do that," he said cheerily. "Meanwhile, do you propose to confront our renegade madman alone?"

"Sorry, Pierre. I appreciate your contribution to the investigation, but I can't put you in harm's way. The risk factor is now at a level where the primary Law applies."

Saint-Philèmon nodded. "In your case as well. You are not invulnerable, Nobis. And I believe Dr. Walpole's scientific curiosity has him on full alert."

"Which works to our advantage." Nobis smiled. "I'm well past the boundary of what even his brilliant mind can conceive. Excuse me. I think it's time to dispose of this."

Nobis raised the sleek little car, number ten of a lethal series, to his mouth. He bit it in half and began to chew nickel, rubber, and titanium as if they were a chocolate chip cookie.

"Be careful you don't catch something," Saint-Philèmon advised, grimacing. He drained his glass and immediately poured more wine. Having reached the limits of his usefulness, he had decided he might as well get drunk.

At three forty Mountain Time the next afternoon, Nobis left the car he had driven from the Tucson office of the FBI to a remote Indian nation close to the Mexican border. He walked another two-thirds of a mile through a gradually deepening arroyo to the place where Dr. Edward Walpole was waiting.

Walpole had brought an extra saddle horse, a usually placid paint gelding that nonetheless began acting up at Nobis's approach. As did Walpole's own mount, Hooligan. Walpole was forced to let go of the paint's reins in order to keep Hooligan under control. The paint lit out for home through lengthening shadows.

Edward Walpole smiled crookedly at his guest. "He's never acted like that before."

"I don't get on well with animals," Nobis said with a shrug. "And I don't mind walking."

"It appears you will have to, Agent Nobis," Walpole said. "I must ask you if you're armed."

"Only with my wits."

"Very good, sir," Walpole said, as if an excellent chess match had been proposed.

He took Nobis through a canyon that featured spectacular swooping walls sculpted by wind and flood, and into a narrow valley where sheep grazed. There was a sprawling adobe house blending with the land and several warehouse-like outbuildings, all covered with camouflage netting. Also parked beneath the nets were a number of dusty but expensive four-wheel-drive vehicles.

"How many employees do you have, Dr. Walpole?"

"About thirty men and women. Yaquis from both sides of the border. They are largely uneducated but highly skilled with their hands. They have been provided with a standard of living they could never have achieved elsewhere. Needless to say they are clannish by nature and intensely loyal."

"How many of them have an inkling that they're accessories to murder?"

"I hope we're not about to get off on the wrong foot with each other, Agent Nobis."

Walpole surrendered his horse to a ranch hand wearing a broad-brimmed sombrero, mopped his face with a large yellow bandana, and peered at his guest, who wasn't sweating.

"You seem remarkably adaptable to our ungodly heat."

"So far."

Walpole looked more closely into Nobis's unblinking sapphire eyes.

"Shall we go inside? The others are waiting."

The technical geniuses Edward Walpole had rallied to his cause also wore casual Western-style clothing. Walpole's wife, the nanomimeticist Mian Zhang Choi, who had been the key innovator in downloading her husband's mind into the bacterial computers aboard the robot cars, was confined to a wheelchair that was also a technological marvel, controlled by her mind.

They all welcomed Nobis with good cheer and intense curiosity. It was, apparently, their cocktail hour.

"I don't suppose you would care for a drink?" Mian said, smiling at Nobis.

"Now, Mian," Walpole chided her.

"Agent Nobis knows I'm just having a little fun."

"I never drink . . . wine," Nobis said, doing his part to be convivial, but there was a glint in his sapphire eyes.

Sitting lifelessly in her chair, Mian motored closer to their guest and looked into his eyes. She spoke to him in Mandarin. "So you have a sense of humor."

"About some things," Nobis said, also in Mandarin.

Zane Red Star, who wore a beaded tribal vest and whose specialty was cognitive science, shifted them back to English. "That's fascinating. And were you programmed with other emotions?"

"Sure. Logical thought, hard-coded algorithms, is only part of a complete system of information processing. Without emotion I can't make decisions or form reasonable judgments. Or protect myself, if it comes to that."

"Where are you from, Agent Nobis?" Sven Ullberg asked. "Not from around here, I assume."

That had them laughing, but it was nervous laughter.

"Just a little dot on the map."

"Star map?" someone else asked.

Nobis shrugged. There was silence, except for the rattle of ice in a couple of glasses.

"Don't be foolish," Mian said to the last questioner. And to Nobis: "Whoever you are, and knowing what you must know of our purposes, do you think you have the power to stop us?"

"I'm not interested in power," Nobis said. "Because I have no capacity for delusion, I can't be a politician, judge, or diplomat. I'm just an investigator."

"We're prepared to die for what we believe," Walpole said. "But of course you know that, having . . . studied my mind."

"And I detected high explosives when I entered your compound. As for your convictions that you can change society for the better by intimidating world leaders with your nannies—that's primitive thinking. Fear only breeds more hostility and irrationality. You're simply proposing a different sort of warfare: in one historical context, you're replacing the longbow with cannon. But war will find a way: It's a disease pathology of human nature. Your technology is brilliant; your motives are flawed and naive."

"You don't understand us at all!" Francois Beguelin protested. He was the team's nano-designer. "Your own technology is astounding. So lifelike. But still you're a machine."

"And have been, for half the modern era of this planet. A long time ago I was a scientist like the five of you, except for certain variations of form. That was in my old neighborhood, another little dot on the map. The rise of technology followed a similar course there—slowly, impeded by the rise and fall of hostile cultures and pathological religious convictions. But I grew up during a century of accelerated scientific progress, one product of which were self-replicating nanobots. I built them, loved them too much, didn't recognize the danger. Because my carbon-based nannies, like yours, had no programmed intelligence. No conscience. They were infinitesimal eating machines."

Walpole said, "But we do know the dangers of—"

Nobis stopped him with a look.

"And you only intended to kill a few key leaders, persuading their political heirs to fashion lasting peace treaties with one another. The wrong means justifying righteous ends. That's what I had in mind as well."

The silence that followed became as oppressive as a thick cloud in the room. Nobis didn't look at anyone. The brightness of his eyes had dimmed. A couple of the men freshened their drinks. Walpole stood behind the wheelchair of his wife. They both stared at Nobis.

"Did you build yourself, Nobis?"

"Yes."

"Only one of you?"

"One is enough."

"So that your mind, everything you've gained intellectually for a millennium, will never be lost?"

Nobis shook his head slightly. He seemed tired.

"I left most of that stuff out. Like I said, I do investigations."

"What happened on your world, Nobis?"

"It got smaller. It's just a piece of rock now, the size of one of your lesser asteroids. My self-replicating, robotic bacteria were carbon-based. In a matter of decades they destroyed every living thing on the surface of the planet. Then they ate the planet. Only then did they stop replicating, although I don't have any doubt a few of them are in interstellar space right now, looking for a galaxy to gobble up."

"My God," Zane Red Star said. He lost his grip on his whiskey glass and it shattered on the tile floor.

Walpole said sharply, "We have nothing to fear! *Our* nannies were designed to live on proteins unique to the human heart valve! When their food supply is exhausted, they—"

"Mutate," Nobis said.

A Mexican houseman appeared in a doorway to announce, "Dinner is served." Nobody moved or looked at him. He shook his head and retreated.

"Impossible," Walpole said.

"Very little remains of the corpses of your first nine victims. What's left has been placed in sealed titanium containers; they're on the way to the deepest hole in the oceans—the Mariana Trench.

That will slow the nannies down, but not stop them. They'll continue to multiply from the minerals in seawater once they're exposed to it. As for the tenth victim—"

"There is no tenth victim!" Mian cried. "We only wanted to make it clear to five of the world's most powerful men that they must cooperate or they would be next."

"There are men who are pure in their faith, others who are pure in their evil. I'm sorry. At your level of social development conflict never stops. As for the tenth victim—I ate one of your little cars yesterday; what it contained is now eating me. Doesn't matter. I've had a dozen different bodies since I was removed from my planet and given a second chance."

"Removed? By whom?" Mian asked. There were tears on her cheeks.

"Other galactic investigation teams. There are four hundred billion stars in this galaxy alone, and it's not one of the biggest. My dot on the map contains a hundred million star systems with cognitive life on at least that many planets. Some as pretty as this one. But there are always kids who like to play with matches, and supposedly grown-up scientists who come up with foolproof schemes to ensure a more perfect world. You ought to have considered unintended consequences. Too bad."

Sven Ullberg said, "Are you telling us Earth is—"

"On the endangered list? I wish the news was that good, Sven. No, we're writing the planet off."

"We?"

"The Intergalactic Union."

Walpole said, "B—but . . . there must be something—"

"No. I am sorry about that. Our only concern is that the nannies you've infected yourselves with don't spread to other planets in the system. Anyway, I'm being removed. The work goes on, sniffing out other misguided tinkerers before they succeed in destroying entire planets."

"Is that all we are?" Walpole said in a fit of ego. "Misguided tinkerers?"

"What are you going to do to us?" Mian asked Nobis.

"There's something worse than what you five already have set in motion?"

"I . . . I guess not."

"But we're always on the lookout for talent. I think if you hadn't been turned into a quadriplegic ten years ago by a drunk driver, you would've been thinking a little more clearly, Mian. Your mind is the best of the lot. I've been downloading it for the past ten minutes."

"But I'm—"

"We'll fix you up, when we get to my little dot on the map."

"What about me?" Walpole said. "You can't just take my wife away from me!"

"How do we get there, Nobis?" Mian asked.

"We close our eyes."

"It's that fast?"

Smiling, she closed her eyes. No farewell glance at her husband.

Pierre Saint-Philèmon and various government and local law enforcement officers were watching from a mesa four miles from the hidden valley when the dwelling and outbuildings of Edward Walpole's compound blew sky-high. Behind them the sun was going down. After a minute or two of silent watching, they all walked down to where the SUVs were parked with motors running.

A senior bureau official said to Saint-Philèmon, "So that appears to be that. What do you think, Pierre? Could Nobis have been right? We've only got ten years, maybe twenty?"

"*Je ne sais quoi.*"

"So what's next for you? Back to Brussels?"

"To pick up my early retirement check. Then I shall catch a

flight to Guadeloupe, buy a small boat, and spend as much of my days and nights as possible enjoying the sun, the sea, the women, the cognac. And the stars. Ah, the stars."

"Sounds like a plan," the FBI guy said wistfully.

Infinitely small, self-replicating eating machines going about their singular business until nothing remains of our planet but another lonely rock tumbling in space. Just call it an anomaly in the progression of scientific ingenuity. Or, to put it another way—there are no limits to the perversity of human beings, and even the most brilliant among us are merely carbon-based fodder for the appetites of our own creations.

# DEAD POST BUMPER

Dean Wesley Smith

For your consideration, the desert-preserved remains of one Elliot Leiferman, successful businessman, world traveler, and husband. He had earned everything he felt he needed: a beautiful home in Malibu and all the money he could spend. Talk of the world ending annoyed him, nothing more. His world was orderly, well-planned, and in his control. And he planned on keeping it that way, no matter what his wife believed. What he didn't plan on was an afternoon drive to the end of the world, and the edge of . . . the Twilight Zone.

*Elliot Leiferman: Summer 2016 near Death Valley*

The dust and light sand swirled along the edge of the ancient road like a runner fleeing a threat, twisting in streamers on the dry desert wind, vanishing, then appearing a step or two later. The sagebrush whipped back and forth, its faint rustling quickly snapped away by the force of the hot wind and the empty nothingness of the desert. A fence of rusted wire and old wood ran ragged beside the road, sometimes upright, other times nothing more than a remnant of splinters mostly covered in sand.

The road, gray with age, vanished under sand drifts and piles of dry sagebrush as it stretched into the distance. Nothing but dust and sand and waves of heat had traveled down it in a very long time.

The rusting hulk of an old automobile rested on four flat tires, tipped slightly in a shallow ditch. One of its two doors hung open and the hood of the car was tucked against a still-upright fence post. The metal figure of a leaping wildcat adorned the hood, and the word JAGUAR in metal script rusted on faded blue paint.

A man's body sat behind the steering wheel, the skin mummified in the heat and dry air and constant wind, the old seat belt still holding the body in position. Dead eyes stared at the fence post against the hood of the car as if it were an insult to even the living.

Dust swirled inside the car for a moment and then settled over the thick layer already covering the seats and floor. Sand was building a dune against one side of the car, already up to the bottom of the windows. In ten more years the car and man inside would be nothing more than a large pile of sand, and the highway would be completely covered.

*Elliot Leiferman: December 20, 2012, Malibu, California*

Elliot watched in disgust as his wife, Casandra Lieferman—Candy, to her few remaining friends—grunted as she lowered her large bulk into a chair beside the bed. She had a chocolate-covered maple bar in one hand and a large vodka-tonic in the other, three limes of course, more vodka in the tumbler than tonic by a factor of two.

Nothing he could say, no amount of pleading, begging, threatening, had helped Candy to either stop her drinking problem or go on a diet. His thin bride of eighteen years had ballooned in the last three years to over 350 pounds and she now regularly downed ten vodka-tonics in tumblers before dinner. He gave up counting how many she had every night after her huge dinner. She just passed out in her bedroom, eating and drinking while watching television.

He had moved into his own bedroom almost two years ago.

Something had gone horribly wrong in both of their lives and their marriage, and he had no real idea what. He had remained thin, actually five pounds under their marriage weight, and he seldom drank anymore. His work took him around the world on business trips and for years Candy had gone with him on many of the trips.

But then, three years ago, it all changed and changed suddenly. She started drinking and eating and quickly grew tired of the traveling as well, deciding instead to simply stay at home and indulge herself.

At one point, a year ago, he had begged her to go to counseling with him and she had shrugged and gone along. But in the sessions it quickly became clear she was never going to stop either overeating or drinking. She just didn't seem to see why she should.

When the counselor finally got her to tell him why, clearly, so that he, the counselor, could understand her, she had simply said, "Why not?"

"I *still* don't understand," the counselor had said.

Candy had looked at him with disgust, then said simply, "You haven't heard? The world is ending December 21, 2012. So why shouldn't I enjoy this last year?"

Since that point, Elliot and Candy had argued many, many times over her belief. He had kept asking her what if she was wrong, what then? She had flatly said time and time again that she wasn't wrong.

He had demanded over and over for her to explain how she could be so certain.

"The Mayan calendar is ending on that date," she always said, as if that explained everything. "I just know my life, your life, will end that day. I can feel it."

Now, as he unpacked from his last trip, she sat in his bedroom on his dressing chair.

"Tomorrow's the big day," Candy said between bites of the maple bar and sips of the vodka-tonic. A large smear of chocolate streaked her cheek, but she didn't seem to care. She hadn't been out of her bathrobe in weeks, and he doubted from her sour smell that she had even taken a shower in that amount of time either. He had been in Europe the last two weeks and had only gotten home a few hours ago.

"So," Elliot asked, repeating a question he had asked every time she said something about her insanity, "what happens if the world doesn't end tomorrow?"

"Oh, it will," she said before taking a huge bite of the maple bar, chewing twice, then washing it down with a large gulp of vodka.

Elliot just shook his head. How could a woman he had loved so deeply, still loved, actually, gone so far off track? He had read a dozen books about insanity and nothing about Candy's seemed to even fit a pattern. He could even remember the night it had started. Back in 2009 she had come to bed late after watching a History Channel special on how the world was supposed to end on December 21, 2012, the last day of the Mayan calendar. She was both excited and agitated at the idea, and he had listened only halfheartedly to what she said that night.

Over the next few weeks after that, she never stopped talking about the topic, even on a trip together to London, one of her favorite cities. At one point she had stood looking up at Big Ben and asked, "Isn't it a shame that all of this will be gone in three years?"

He had changed the subject, hating even talking about predictions of any future. That was for those crazies who believed in that mumbo-jumbo. He was a believer in right now. The present. Today. The future would be what the future would be. And Candy, up until that point, had been as down-to-earth as he was.

Not anymore. She was as crazy as they came.

He turned from his unpacking and looked at the mess of a human being his wife had become. "I guess tomorrow we shall see, won't we?"

"That we will," she said, smiling. "I plan on spending the day on the deck, watching the world end over the ocean. Would you like to join me?"

"Thank you, dear," he said, turning back to his now almost empty suitcase on the bed so that she wouldn't notice how disgusted at her he felt. "I'll do my best to make it back from the office in time."

"With the world ending, why bother to go into the office at all?"

He shrugged, keeping his back to her. "I just like the routine is all. It's comforting."

"Well, do hurry home," she said. Then grunting, she hefted herself out of the chair and waddled down the hall toward the kitchen.

He had no intention of being home tomorrow, end of the world or not. He'd deal with her the following day, after her fixation had been proven wrong.

Then maybe he could help her, get her the help she needed.

*Elliot Leiferman: December 21, 2012, near Death Valley*

The car hit ninety easily as he took the Jaguar down the straightaway out onto the desert road headed toward Death Valley. The old highway was almost never used anymore, and to even get on it he had had to move a road-closed sign, but he loved the freedom of the straight pavement and the speed at which he could safely drive without worrying about any patrols stopping him.

Thunderclouds threatened in the low hills in the distance, but the cab of the Jaguar kept him comfortable from the intense heat and safe from the blowing sand. This morning Candy had been like a schoolgirl in her excitement. How anyone could be excited about the end of the world was beyond him, but for weeks the news reports had gone on and on about the Mayan calendar coming to an end today, and this morning's headlines were END OF THE WORLD?

The entire thing just annoyed him.

It was not only stupid, but it had cost him the woman he loved. He wanted this over and done with, he wanted to help Candy get healthy again, stop drinking, lose weight, become the woman he had married.

But that wasn't going to happen until he got home tonight and the world hadn't ended. Then he could start helping her recover for real and maybe even get to the root cause of why she had believed the end was coming anyway.

The Jaguar's smooth ride ate up mile after mile of the old road, taking him deeper and deeper into the desert. Even at this time of the year, the temperature outside was a baking ninety degrees and he had the air-conditioning holding him in comfort. He had come to learn that there were real advantages to having large amounts of money—the beautiful home in Malibu was one, this car was another.

He loved this car, and lately had taken more and more long drives in it when home, just to get away from Candy.

He looked out over the expanse of desert around him, letting himself relax into the drive. Wouldn't it be funny if the world actually did end today while he was in the desert? He snorted to himself and snapped on the radio, letting it search for a radio station.

Normal music playing, no alarms, nothing different.

Nothing was ending today.

He let the miles drift by as he thought about all the wonderful times he and Candy used to have and the hope that starting tomorrow, they could rebuild that old life once again.

The sun was starting to touch the horizon; the day was nearing an end. Candy was going to need him later tonight. He had no doubt she would pass out from all the drinking, but at least he could be there to take care of her. For the first time in a year, he felt he wanted to. Something that she had believed in deeply was about to not happen and she would need help getting through that.

He let the car slow down to under sixty and glanced around at the vast expanse of nothingness. Amazing that in such a crowded place as California, there could be so many thousands of square miles of nothingness.

At that moment he noticed a faint light on the dashboard. He slammed on the brakes and came to a stop in the middle of the old road.

The gas warning light was on.

*Oh, God, no.* He had no idea how long it had been on, but it was unlikely he had enough gas to make it back to the roadblock. That had to be seventy or more miles back, at least.

It had never occurred to him to get gas before he left. His thoughts had been on Candy and the end of the world, not his wonderful car.

He swung the Jaguar into a quick three-point turn on the narrow old road, and started back west into the glowing orange of the sun as it sat over the Pacific in the far distance.

He had to stay calm, think this through.

At that moment the finely tuned car that had run so smoothly for so long sputtered, caught again, then sputtered and shut down.

He was out of gas.

On a closed old highway near Death Valley.

*Oh, God, oh God, oh God, what have I done?*

The steering was heavy in his hands as he took the car out of drive and coasted to a stop.

At the last moment he eased the car off to the side of the road, letting the Jaguar come to rest in a very shallow ditch, its front bumper resting lightly against an old wooden post of a long-gone fence. No point in taking a chance that someone else out speeding on this old road would plow into his car in the middle of the night. He just hoped that bumping the old fence post hadn't scratched the bumper.

He snapped out his cell phone and looked at the signal.

Nothing.

And he'd never bothered to have a tracking satellite system installed, even though the dealer had suggested it. He had never figured it would be needed in his drives around Malibu.

He glanced around.

Death Valley.

A closed road with no traffic.

Nothing within seventy or more miles of him.

*God, oh God. What can I do?* His stomach twisted as if he were about to be sick.

He couldn't let himself panic. He had to think this through. If he panicked, he was as good as dead.

He pushed open the door and let the hot wind of the early evening blow dust into his just-cleaned car. In front of him, the sun had set.

He glanced at the clock on the dashboard. Five thirty.

Six and a half more hours for the world to survive, to prove he was right and Candy and all the other doomsday shouters were wrong.

He unbuckled his seat belt and climbed out of the car, standing in the middle of the road in the fading light and looking in both directions, fighting down the panic that threatened to choke him at any moment. His only hope of getting out of this stupid mess was to stay calm.

No point in trying anything until daylight. Even with the sun just barely set, he could feel a bite to the air. It was going to be a long, cold night.

He went back to the Jaguar and checked for anything that might help him pass the time more comfortably. Nothing. He kept the Jaguar's trunk clean enough to eat out of, and he had not thought to bring either food or drink with him.

He had on light slacks, a light shirt, and not much else.

He went back to the car, buckled himself back into the driver's seat, reclined the seat just slightly, and shut the door.

He had no idea just how cold it got later that evening. But it was already colder than he had ever experienced or imagined possible.

*Elliot Leiferman: December 22, 2012, near Death Valley*

The cold had drained Elliot more than he had ever imagined it could. His stomach was threatening to claw its way out of his body from hunger, and his lips were chapped from no water and the extreme dry air.

At sunrise, he'd managed to stagger out of the car and back onto the road. Then he had started walking back toward the roadblock at the same pace he used on the gym's treadmill, a steady four miles per hour.

After an hour his speed had slowed and he knew, without a doubt, that he had no chance of making that walk clear back to the roadblock. The intense cold of the night was already being replaced by the hot, dry heat of the day, and the constant wind and blowing sand seemed to suck every ounce of moisture from his body.

His only hope was to return to the car and pray that someone either spotted him from the air or happened to drive by. Even if Candy noticed he was missing and reported that to the police, no one would know where to look. He'd never told anyone he used this old highway to take drives on.

He barely made it back to the car, again snapping himself into his seat with his seat belt and leaving the door open for ventilation.

Yesterday clearly hadn't been the end of the world, at least not for Candy. But it might have been for him unless he got very, very lucky.

That night, after a long, very hot day, the night again got bitingly cold and thunderstorms echoed through the desert, sending flashes of bright white light to show him the vast wasteland and how hopeless his situation really was.

A flash flood also washed out the bridge near the roadblock that night, making it impossible for any car to travel the old county road again.

The next morning he again started the walk out, but this time turned around after just a mile, almost too weak to make it back to the car.

He slept off and on through the rest of the heat of the day and into the biting cold of the night, his seat belt holding him in place. The hood of his car and that fence post leaning against the bumper of his Jaguar became his entire world as he drifted in and out of consciousness.

By the third day, Elliot's strength was gone. He could barely keep his eyes open as the intense heat of the day drained what will to live he had away.

His mind escaped the constant of the old fence post, drifting back to the good days with Candy, the fun they had had, the trips they had taken.

Candy had been right.

If he had just listened to her, drunk with her, eaten with her, gotten fat with her, enjoyed the last three years as she had done, he wouldn't be sitting where he was, dying from the heat and thirst and hunger, staring at an old fence post.

He had caused the world, as he and Candy knew it, to end on the last day of the Mayan calendar.

He had caused it by not believing it could happen.

Yet it had. The world had ended.

"I'm so sorry, Candy," he managed to whisper through cracked, dry lips.

As he slipped off into his last sleep, the sun beating down on the top of his Jaguar, he asked one last question, hoping somehow that Candy could hear him all the way out in Malibu.

*How did the Mayans know?*

An old, rotting, time-worn fence post resting against the perfect metal bumper of an expensive car. A man facing his final moments, staring at the post, wondering why he had doubted the seers, the prophets, the prophecies about the end of the world. They had all been right. So very right. *His* world had ended on December 21, 2012 . . . in the Twilight Zone.

# THOUGHTFUL BREATHS

Peter Crowther

Come meet Boswell and Irma Mendholsson, both of them—in the nomenclature of the day—"good people" . . . everyday folks with everyday dreams and, particularly in Boswell's case, a yearning for away-from-it-all locations. But, when life's power pitcher throws an unexpected curveball at them, Boz and Irma get to sample the rare and exotic delights on offer in that most fascinating of all off-the-beaten-track retreats—the Twilight Zone.

*And now I see with eye serene*
*The very pulse of the machine;*
*A being breathing thoughtful breath;*
*A traveller between life and death.*

—William Wordsworth,
*She Was a Phantom of Delight* (1807)

In Forest Plains, just the way it is in many thousands of communities the length and breadth of these United States (and, for that matter, all around the world), the quality of life centers on the relationships formed by people with other people. Small towns, campuses, apartment buildings, and office blocks all thrive with the buzz of connecting.

There is an indefinable magic in the way we react with others, whether those relationships are business-orientated contacts, simple platonic friendships, schoolyard liaisons, tempestuous love affairs, or the gentle settling together of two people committed to the long haul. But it's just one of these—the last one—that we're concerned with here.

Boswell Raymond Mendholsson met Irma Jayne Petschek ("—and that's Jayne with a 'Y,'" Irma would always say, her voice Katharine Hepburn-ballsy, hand on hip and chin thrust out) when Boz worked the summer at the water purification plant over on the interstate about sixteen miles out of the Plains. It was 1947, the war over two years and Boz looking to find some stability with a regular job, toying with the idea of the GI Bill and trying to forget Iwo Jima. He was twenty-three years old, a look of a young Robert Taylor—complete with widow's peak and steely-eyed stare—his face gradually smoothing over the telltale craters of acne, and his feet once more finding their spring.

Irma was the third-stringer from a six-sister family of semi-strict Presbyterian stock come down from Providence in the 1930s when jobs were hard everywhere, not just in the Dust Bowl that that Guthrie feller sang about. She had a wide mouth, full lips, a front tooth—the left one as you faced her—that curled over its partner slightly, legs fit to make Betty Grable throw in her hose, and a laugh that sounded like water running across wind chimes.

Boz thought Irma was the cat's pj's, and when Irma caught sight of Boz—no matter how far away he was—her knees buckled fit to snap right in two, like they were made of modeling clay that old Miss Timberlake gave out to her first- and second-graders over at the schoolhouse.

When a job came up at the real estate office down in Forest Plains, Boz applied. He didn't know diddly about selling houses, but he had an air to him that seemed to calm people right down. Folks trusted him and that counts for a lot in real estate selling, just as it counts for a lot in life.

Those were the days when fellows took candy and flowers around to their dates' houses, promised to have them home by a reasonable hour, and took them maybe to the soda shoppe on

Main Street or out to the "WI-I-I-IDE SCREEN" drive-in over on the canal road. There was no fooling around permitted by the Screen's head honcho, the matriarchal Josepha Hjortsburg who, ever since the death of her beloved Gabby out in the Pacific, wouldn't show war movies and so made things difficult for herself and her clientele with a string of romances and comedies that tended to make the kids more amorous than when they'd been waiting in line to buy tickets. But, through making constant rounds, the flashlight-laden Josepha made sure all the canoodling stayed right up there on the screen and not out in the parked cars.

On those dates when Boz and Irma made it out to the Screen, Boz liked the newsreels the most. He might have had it with war—which, like most folks in those magical far-off days of the late 1940s, he surely had—but the lure of far-off places burned inside him like a furnace. Boz maintained that joining the fighting forces was the best way to see the world and he figured there was no way he was ever likely to make it over to ride a trolley car in 'Frisco, never mind climbing the age-worn steps of the pyramids or sailing the canals of waterlogged Venice. But Irma would squeeze his hand tight when he sounded kind of down-in-the-mouth and she'd tell him that it was good to have a dream. "A person should always have something to aim for in life," the twenty-year-old Irma would proclaim sagely, nodding at the words as though she were underlining them a mite. "One day," she'd finish off, letting the words trail away all by themselves. And Boz would squeeze her right back and consider leaning over to give her a kiss on the cheek, risking the flashlight treatment from Josepha.

The "one day" that Irma had long dreamed of—even before she knew Boswell Raymond Mendholsson existed—came on a drizzly fall day in 1949, with the bottle-green leaves of summer turning russet-red and muddy brown. That was the day that Irma, resplendent in a wedding gown (specially made by Boz's Auntie Mildred), walked slowly down the aisle of the Forest Plains

Presbyterian Church on Canal Street, her arm in her father Ted's and him looking like the cat that got the cream while his wife, Annie, sitting in the front pew on the left, looked at the two of them with tears rolling down her cheeks onto an angel's smile. Boz himself glanced over his shoulder, at first a little nervously, and then all the nerves faded away like ice in a glass of summertime lemonade.

Married life passed without a hitch—so long as you don't count the little problems we all get from time to time—but money was never something the Mendholssons had in abundance. Truth to tell, things started off tight and just got tighter. But they doted on each other right from when the two of them said, breathlessly, "I do," their hearts skipping more beats than Joe Morello. They meant it then and they never had cause to go back on it in all the days and weeks and months and years that were to follow . . . happy times indeed.

Life for the Mendholssons seemed like a summer meadow—beautiful, fragrant, and set to go on forever. They were rich in ways that had nothing at all to do with money . . . mainly just through their own company. Irma kind of drifted away from her family and even her friends—excepting Jeannie Gustavson and her husband, Ray—and Boz pretty much followed suit. He did, however, stay in close contact with Phil Defantino. A childhood friend and Boz's best man, Phil had landed a job with ICI Industries down in Philadelphia and he rose quickly through the ranks at a time of great expansion for the company. Within less than two years, Phil was spending a lot of time away from home . . . initially traveling the U.S. and then moving on to worldwide travel to cities that Boz had only ever read about, advising small businesses on how to maximize their profits.

Whenever Phil was home for any length of time, he and his wife Jackie would come out to Forest Plains, the old hometown, to spend time with Boz and Irma. At first, they stayed at the house, giving Boz more time to quiz Phil about his latest trips, but when the house got a little more "crowded" with the so-called patter of tiny feet, they stayed at the Holiday Inn over on the interstate. "I reckon I know more about Holiday Inns than the folks who work in them!" Phil said on more than one occasion.

Truth to tell, Irma was a little embarrassed about having house-guests who stayed in the local hotel, but Phil always let her know the plain and simple truth: that bringing up a family needs all your attention—and that, according to Phil, meant *you need folks getting under your feet like Custer needed more injuns!* Phil and Jackie never had children and neither Boz nor Irma ever felt comfortable in asking them why. They had their suspicions, of course, but they believed that if Phil and Jackie had ever wanted to discuss it, then they would have.

The first product of the Mendholssons' union came into the world kicking and squawking just a couple of days before Thanks-giving 1950, and Irma and Boz had a lot to be thankful for when the Thursday arrived. Sitting alongside Irma's hospital bed, with little James cradled in his wife's arms, Boz told her that he loved her more than anything else in the world, the tears in his eye-corners underlining that a few times.

While the arrival of Baby James served to erode still further the already shaky Mendholsson fortunes, the tough financial situation served only to deepen Boz's determination to provide for his new family. Thus he took an additional job in the kitchens of the For-est Plains Bar 'n' Grill, Irma having nixed other ideas of additional income by virtue of the fact that it wouldn't do for folks to see the guy who was trying to interest them in property also serving drinks at Max's Bar over on the Canal Road, or mowing lawns on Satur-days and Sundays. But at night, after chores were done, Boz would disappear into his den—a lavishly mysterious title for a small room that he'd decked out with shelving—where he sat and perused travel books and city guides and the occasional foreign language tome.

It was in here that, after a visit from Phil and Jackie to see the new baby, Boz discovered that Phil had left his billfold—he remembered Phil taking it out of his pants pocket because it was giving him a numb backside. But when he'd called his friend to give him the good news, Phil had said blankly, "Not my billfold, Boz. Must be yours." Boz had laughed at that. He'd flipped it open while he was talking on the phone and there were five twenty-dollar bills in there. "Well," Phil had said—and was that just a touch of a smile Boz heard in his friend's voice?—"whyn't you check if there's a name in there?" Boz did just that and discovered a handwritten card—handwritten in the unmistakable scrawl of Phil Defantino—proclaiming THIS BILLFOLD AND ALL THAT IT CONTAINS IS THE SOLE PROPERTY OF BOSWELL MENDHOLSSON. "Oh, Phil . . ." was all that Boz could think of to say.

Then, in 1952, the day before Independence, along came Nicola, a gloriously raven-haired companion for young James and whose cherubic face and open, trusting smile filled Boz and Irma with levels of love that even they had not dreamed possible. As the summer was already showing signs of turning to fall, Boz discovered another "lost" billfold.

Evenings and weekends, the Mendholssons walked their charges along the park paths and the sidewalks, passing the time of day with anyone they happened to meet along the way. These were the magical days of America, a time of peace and plenty, when everything was possible. A time when the picket fences of Rockwell's *Post* covers could still be found in pretty much any small town up and down and left and right across the country. A time when guys still presented their dates with candies and flowers. A time when the human spirit still retained some dignity.

Dignity, the Mendholssons had in abundance. Money—with the exception of the miraculous billfolds that continued to show up in Boz's inner sanctum of travel tomes—they had not. But Irma and Boz never allowed their restricted finances to affect their home life, and their house over on Cedar Avenue rang constantly with the sound of happiness . . . a sound that was a tinkle of baby chuckles for a while, then preschool mirth, then youthful laughter until at last, in the closing days of the sixties—a troubled decade, in Boz's eyes, when the magical and exotic landscapes on the other side of the world took on a sinister cloak of danger and threat—just a couple of weeks after man set foot on the moon, the quartet was reduced to a trio with the departure of James Mendholsson to Boston U.

They were all happy for him, of course—after all, what had they strived for so hard all of their lives except to improve their children's lot?—but on the day he drove their son out of Forest Plains, the air in Boz's old Pontiac was so thick you'd have needed a knife to cut it.

Now forty-six years old, with the big five-oh straddling the horizon like a gunfighter who had called him out onto Main Street for a showdown that Boz knew he couldn't win, Boswell Mendholsson retreated into the den still more, leafing through books on Paris and Provence, the waterways of Venice, the jungles of Peru, and wistful train journeys through China and mainland Europe. In the pages of these books—repeatedly- and often-read pages that Boz would occasionally hold up to his face as he breathed in the imagined aroma of the far-off lands the words described—Boz's life was different. It wasn't that he didn't love or want Irma—the truth of the matter was that he loved and wanted her more than he had ever done—but rather that he felt, if only a tad, unfulfilled. Even the occasional visits from Phil and his tales of airport lounges and cab rides in alien cities (plus the inevitable Grand Den Discovery, which, in line with inflation, had increased in value over the years) did little to assuage Boz's feeling of despondency. To put it plain and simple, he was getting older. Old, even.

The specter of the mortality gunslinger darkened a little more when, one sunny morning in April 1973, Nicola announced that she and Bobby Eads were planning to marry. Irma shrieked with happiness like a drunken banshee, her arms lifting and lowering as though she were about to take off and soar right up into the sky. Boz meanwhile adopted a fixed smile that made him look like he'd suddenly discovered a worm in that last bite of apple. He had known, of course, that Nicola and Bobby were getting kind of serious but "kind of serious" in Boz's book was a mighty long way from actual marriage. But as he watched his wife and suddenly-not-so-baby-anymore baby daughter dancing around the worn work surfaces in Irma's kitchen, Boz couldn't hold back the out-and-out Cheshire cat grin and he leapt into his women's midst, took their proffered hands as they all danced around like witches around a cauldron on All Hallows'.

But later that night, in the den, Boz's stomach was knotted like a pretzel and it was all he could do to hold back the tears. The door opened slowly alongside him, Boz sitting in the old rocker he'd inherited from his mother while he read John Hillaby's *Journey Around Britain,* and Irma's face peered in at him.

"You okay, honey?"

Boz looked up and gave her a half-smile, intending to tell her *sure I'm okay* and *why shouldn't I be?* but just that question and Irma's face and the fact that their little girl was going to be leaving home . . . all those things just gathered together like street-corner hoodlums and ganged up on him. And the tears came.

"Oh, Boz," Irma said, her voice soft and loving, as she came fully into the room and, hunkering down beside him, threw her arms around her husband. "You big silly," she said.

"I know," Boz said, agreeing in a self-deprecating wish-I-was-different kind of way.

"What am I going to do with you?"

"I dunno," Boz sniveled.

"She's not going far away, you know."

"I know." And he did. Nicola and Bobby's plan was to buy an apartment across town, so Bobby could carry on working at the bookstore on Main Street. But it wasn't so much Nicola's actually moving that so tore at Boz's heart as what it represented—and what it represented was an end to the feast. What once had been a sumptuous spread that looked set to last forever now, in Boz's eyes, more resembled picked-over carcasses and emptied bowls and plates.

"We'll be okay," Irma whispered into Boz's ear, and then she kissed him on the cheek.

He nodded. "I guess we will," he said, looking down at a photo of John Hillaby standing on England's south-west coastline, staring out to sea. *It's almost as though he's looking right at you, Boz,* a small voice seemed to whisper in Boz's ear. "We'll be fine," Boz reiterated.

And so they were. For a good long time.

James graduated with a good degree from Boston and took up a job with a small design and communications firm, running their business from North Square, just a few yards from Paul Revere's house. He married Angie, the girl he'd met while at university, and the couple bought a nice apartment overlooking the Common. Three children arrived in rapid succession: Anthony Boswell Mendholsson in the spring of '74, Jennifer Jayne (with a "Y") Mendholsson in the fall of '75, and Maria Spring Mendholsson in November '77. Viewing Maria Spring on a freezing cold December day just six weeks after her initial appearance, Boswell agreed she was a beauty . . . and then said to his very obviously delighted son (and a mock-disgusted wife), "So, number three is here fit and well. You figured out what's causing it yet or is this likely to be an annual event?"

But while things were going well for one Mendholsson offspring, they weren't so good with the other. Nicola and Bobby split up when Nicola found out that her husband had been looking into more than old books with the store's new and shapely assistant. That was in 1976, Bicentennial year, and, just like the country itself, the Mendholssons' daughter had regained her independence. But nothing lasts forever and by 1980 she had met and married an insurance services manager from the bank where she worked—Jim was his name—and both Boz and Irma agreed they liked him a whole lot more than the philandering Bobby.

Nicola's first child was miscarried and, for a while, the unspoken feeling was that, of all the Mendholssons, she was leading a tainted life. "I know just how you feel, honey," Jackie Defantino told the gaunt-faced Nicola. "Believe me when I tell you just how much." She and Phil had headed over as soon as they'd received the news from Irma, and when Boz and Irma heard what Jackie had to say to Nicola, they both looked at each other with a mixture of revelation and understanding. Turning around from where he was sitting, at Nicola's hospital bedside, Phil caught the exchange and gave a weak smile. Boz reached out and ruffled his friend's hair the way he'd always done when they were both first-graders at Forest Plains Elementary, and when Phil got up, his eyes were brimming with tears. "I know," Boz told him, wrapping his huge bear arms around the more diminutive Phil. It would seem to outsiders a strange thing to say to a friend under the circumstances, but it felt just right to everyone present.

Jim was hugely supportive and, in 1985, when Nicola was thirty-three, Margaret-Jayne (again with a "Y"—seemed nobody much cared for the name "Irma" anymore) Boswell Henfrey let the world know she had arrived in no uncertain terms. "I reckon she's going to be an opera singer," the increasingly tired-looking Boz announced, and everyone laughed.

Phil and Jackie came right out once again, Phil having retired from ICI and seeming to be enjoying spending time at home. The word was that they were planning to move back to the Plains but it would be in a different area to the one where Boz and Irma resided. It was the summertime. Boz was sixty-one years old and having trouble peeing.

"You need to go see D. Fredricks," Irma told her husband. "I will, I will," he told her. And the sad fact was that it was going to have to be true. By now, with the leaves turning red on the trees, Boz was reduced to sitting on the toilet bowl while he peed to avoid getting dead legs from standing there waiting for the drip-drip trickle to empty his bladder. Even Phil was leaning heavily on him. And so Boz bit the bullet, made the call, and went into the M.D.'s office out on Jefferson Place.

Jack Fredricks couldn't make much of a diagnosis without getting inside for, as he put it, "a look-see" and so he arranged for Boz to come back the next day for an endoscopy. This entailed a tiny seeing-eye tube being inserted into Boz's penis and shoved up inside so the doctor could take a look around. Boz wasn't sure which hurt the most, the tube going in or the so-called lubricant (which felt like having toxic jelly squirted into your dick) that preceded it. But the simple physical pain was soon overshadowed by what the seeing-eye saw.

"Prostate," Jack Fredricks announced with a sigh when the investigation was finished. He sat down on the gurney next to Boz while Boz nursed his crotch and fastened his pants.

"Is that bad, Jack?" Boz asked, hardly hearing the words over the thumping of his heart.

"Not going to know until we do a biopsy."

"Biopsy?"

"Got to take a slice off and send it for analysis," he explained, complementing the words with a sawing motion with his hands. "Won't hurt," he said, patting Boz on the shoulder. "But it will mean an overnight stay in hospital."

Boz nodded, zipping up his fly. "So," he said as he slid off the gurney into his waiting shoes, "what's your gut feeling?"

Jack looked at Boz for a few seconds and then looked down at his knees. "I'd say it looks bad," he said. "But let's wait for the—"

"How long?"

"Boz, I said—"

"Jack, you've been up enough guys' dicks to know what you're seeing in there. Let's go for the worst-case scenario—I take it we're talking prostate cancer here, yes?"

"Looks that way to me . . . God, but I wish it didn't."

"Okay, so, worst-case scenario, it's prostate cancer. From what you've seen, how long?"

Jack sighed and looked up at Boz. "I think you'll see Christmas but not Easter."

When Boz spoke again, his voice was shaking. "You *think* I'll see Christmas? Christ, Jack, it's already September and I feel as fit as a horse . . . just having a little difficulty peeing is all."

"I know," was all Jack Fredricks could think of to say. "That's the way it goes, though. You'll feel fit right until—" He let his voice trail off.

"Until I don't, huh?"

Fredricks nodded.

Boz felt a great pressure behind his eyes, like there was something inside his head that wanted out, like rats on a sinking ship; and it—this thing, whatever it was—had decided that the easiest and fastest way out was through his eye sockets. His breath felt short and his chest hurt. And his legs felt like jelly. "Jesus, Jack," Boz said.

Fredricks nodded again. "I'll give you some pills that may slow the growth down a little—they're actually designed for high blood pressure but they have this side effect, you know?—but the tumor looks pretty big."

Watching Fredricks, Boz was reminded of when he and Irma had bought a rabbit for James. James named the rabbit Shadow and kept him out in the yard, where he even built a special run for it out of wood-ends that Boz had left over after extending some shelving in the den. One day, when Phil and Jackie Defantino had come out to the house, James had excitedly shown off his pet and, still excited and maybe just a little careless, he'd dropped the heavy run onto Shadow's neck. A hysterical James had appeared in the house while Boz and Irma were handing out coffees and slices of cake, the deceased and almost decapitated Shadow lying limply in his outstretched hands. *Daddy, Daddy . . . make him better,* five- or six-year-old James had pleaded. But one look at the rabbit and the single eyeball hanging out of one socket showed there was absolutely no hope. Boz reckoned that Fredricks now felt a lot like the way he himself had felt all those years ago: helpless. Like a parent, he was looked up to by his patients as some kind of god, able to dispense life and healing whenever he fancied. Boz didn't feel anyone should feel so wretched.

"Okay," he said, "so give me the pills already. We'll get this thing started right away and maybe we can make medical history."

"Right," Jack Fredricks said, emphasizing their determination with a clap of his hands, but Boz knew just from watching the M.D.'s back that this was going to be one trip that nothing could prevent him from taking.

The results of the biopsy confirmed it. It was an aggressive tumor, big as a baseball (though, when he looked in a mirror, Boz couldn't figure out where the damn thing was hiding itself), and there were signs of secondaries. And while he couldn't figure out whether it was his actual condition or a psychological thing, he was starting to feel sick.

On the day they flipped over the calendar to October, Boz and Irma went in to see Jack Fredricks for the lowdown. It wasn't good. There was no point in trying to operate because there was a 75–80 percent chance he'd die under the anesthetic. And even if he didn't, it would only extend his time maybe over Christmas, and all of the extra gain would be spent in a hospital bed. Boz decided that, if he was going to go, then it was best not to drag it out unnecessarily, and he preferred the idea of being around somewhere he knew with people he cared about, and who cared about him without being paid for doing it. No, he would soldier on until he got too tired, at which point he would take to his bed and wait to start The Great Adventure. Jack Fredricks said it wouldn't take long at that point. Maybe three, four days.

To say there were tears would be an understatement.

Neither Boz nor Irma could imagine life without their partner and this whole thing had happened so quickly that it took a couple of days for the realization to set in. After that, they decided to tell the children. More tears followed.

The atmosphere in the Mendholssons' home grew dark and somber. Even Boz's den failed to provide the relief and respite from the everyday world that he'd grown used to over the years. When he was sitting in there, it seemed as though the books were whispering behind his back . . . asking what was to become of them when he'd— He didn't like even to think about it. But the thing that worried him the most was how Irma would survive without him.

Then, with Halloween approaching, Boz hit on an idea.

"Honey, Phil's coming around."

"Oh, fine. Did he call? I didn't hear the—"

"No, I called him a few days ago—last week, if I recall. I just remembered about a half hour ago." Boz stretched to his full height in the kitchen doorway and breathed in the smell of baking. "Smells good."

"Jackie coming, too?"

"No, just Phil."

"Any particular reason?"

Boz shook his head. "Just fancied shooting the breeze. Now that they're back in town I figured I'd spend as much—" He paused and re-phrased. "Spend a little more time with him. You know."

"I know, honey. I'll set out the table in the front room and—"

"That's okay, sweetie, we'll have coffee in the den."

"But it's so cramped in there, honey."

He walked over and gave her a kiss on the cheek. Then he licked a finger and rubbed at a patch of flour on her forehead. His heart ached when she allowed her eyes to close and moved her head against his hand like a cat wanting to be stroked. "Don't worry about me, okay? I'm fine."

The truth, however, was that Boz was actually far from fine. He was now starting to feel weak and the pills designed to keep his prostate growth down to a minimum seemed to be less successful than they'd been at first. But he kept this information to himself.

"Nicola said she'd maybe call you."

"Well, if she does, just tell her I'll call her back. I don't really want to be interrupted when Phil's here."

Irma looked at him, a slight frown on her face, but it passed quickly, like a cloud across the moon, when Boz smiled at her. "I'm sure looking forward to cake," he said. "And the coffee'll help me pee."

She shook her head and waved him away. "Oh, you," she said.

The doorbell rang and Boz said, "That'll be Phil," as he disappeared out into the hall. Irma heard their voices and she stepped out to say hey.

"Hey, Irma," Phil said, his voice wreathed in smiles and consolations. "How're things?"

Irma did a little jig with her head, side to side, and then nodded. "We're doing okay, I think. Aren't we, honey?"

"We're doing fine," Boz agreed. Then, to Phil, "Well, come on into the den. Irma's been cooking all morning so I think fresh cake is heading our way."

Irma smiled bravely at Phil and saw him give her the slightest of nods that would have been all but imperceptible to a casual onlooker. When she dropped her gaze from his eyes, Irma noticed that Phil Defantino was holding a briefcase in his hand. When she looked up at Phil again, about to ask why he'd brought a briefcase, Phil shuffled the case into his other hand and said to Boz, "Okay, show me to a chair—I'm pooped." And the two of them turned around and moved down the hallway to Boz's den.

"You go on in and make yourself comfortable," Boz said as he ushered Phil over the threshold to his book collection. "I'll get the coffee."

"I can bring it in for you, honey," Irma said.

But Boz was already making his way back to the kitchen. "I don't want you waiting on me, sweetie," he said. "And anyway," he added, "I want to have a nice long talk with Phil without any interruptions. It's not you, baby," Boz said when Irma frowned at being labeled as an interrupter, "but you know how Phil can gabble on."

Irma watched Boz open cupboard doors and place mugs on the breakfast conuter. She watched the whole process of her husband preparing a tray—milk from the refrigerator, sugar bowl, two plates, two pieces of cake—and all the while she tried to think back to a time when Phil Defantino had gabbled on. For the life of her, she couldn't come up with a single one.

Phil stayed with Boz in the den for over two hours, the pair of them speaking in hushed tones in there. It wasn't that Irma was eavesdropping, but just that whenever she went past the den door, all she could hear was a dim and distant drone of voices. When Phil emerged, Boz hurried him out of the door while he explained loudly that Irma would be preparing lunch. She took that as a hint and went straight back into the kitchen to make them a couple of omelettes. As she switched on the Mister Coffee, she heard Boz shout, "Okay, same time tomorrow," and then close the door.

"He's coming back tomorrow?" Irma asked when Boz appeared at the kitchen door.

"Yeah," he said. "He sure is a sucker for punishment."

"What was in the case?"

"Huh?"

"The briefcase. Phil had a briefcase with him?"

"Oh, yeah," Boz said as he leaned over the frying pan and sniffed in the smell of eggs cooking. "He wanted to show me some stuff he'd picked up on his travels. Books and stuff."

"More books!" Irma said, smiling, and she shook her head. She wondered how she was going to get rid of all those books when the day came, but just as quickly as the thought presented itself to her, she dispelled it. And so the moment passed, and as it passed she never gave a thought to the fact that Phil's briefcase looked just as full as it had been when he had arrived.

"More books?" Irma said when she answered the door the following day and saw Phil standing there in the rain, his arms wrapped around his briefcase.

"Excuse me?" Phil said, stepping past Irma into the house.

"It's okay, Phil. I told her."

Irma turned around to see her husband walking along the hallway, a big *aw shucks* smile etched on his face.

"You told her?" Phil said, smiling, glancing from one to the other.

"Yeah," said Boz, taking Phil's coat from him. Phil moved the case from one hand to the other during the process. "She knows you're smuggling books into the house." He shrugged. "I think maybe she's worried I'm going to spread to the other rooms."

Irma smiled, cocking her head on one side as she watched Boz. Was it her imagination or did he seem to be losing a little weight? Maybe she needed to fatten him up a little. "Coffee and cake?" she asked Phil.

"Irma, you are a beacon of sustenance in a wasteland of famine."

"I'll take that as a yes. Honey? Would you like cake or maybe a sandwich to set you on until lunch?"

"Cake will be fine, sweetie," he said, and kissed her on the cheek. Irma threw her arms around him and, just for a second, wanted desperately to absorb him into her, the way those vampire-type creatures did on that *Outer Limits* episode, but the moment passed and she relaxed her hold.

"Hey, careful there," Boz said with a grin. "Don't you know I'm a sick man?"

"You've always been a sick man," Phil chided, "and it hasn't done you any harm far as I can make out."

They all laughed, though perhaps a little dutifully—just three normal people making polite banter—and then Boz said, "Come on into the den." Turning to Irma, he said, "I'll come get the coffee and cake, sweetie. I'll just get Phil settled in."

*Jiminy,* Irma thought to herself in the kitchen, *it sounds like he's about to send him into orbit.*

The following day, Boz came into the kitchen and turned on the Mister Coffee. "You got any more of that cake left?" he asked as he rummaged in different cupboards. "Phil just can't get enough of it."

"He coming around *again*?"

Boz shrugged. "I guess," he said. "I think he's bored. Since he retired, I mean."

"Well, he could at least bring Jackie along. Be nice to have someone to talk to while you two are in the den."

She opened the one cupboard that Phil seemed to have missed and produced the plate containing the cake, wrapped in tinfoil.

"What is it that you talk about in there anyways?"

"Oh, this and that," Boz said. "This and that."

When Phil came around, the entire process was repeated: the slightly awkward look on his face as he shuffled the briefcase around, the somewhat contrived pleasantries, the ushering of the guest by her husband into the den, and the profuse declaration that Boz would save her the trouble of bringing in cake and coffee by taking it himself.

On this occasion, however, Irma noticed that Boz's hands were shaking a little. She watched the hands intently as he loaded cake onto the top plate and straightened the mugs so that the handles were accessible. She thought about how those hands had travelled her body and her face over the years, pleasuring her and making her feel safe, and she wondered, just for a few seconds, where those years had gone and how they had gone away so quickly.

When the hands stopped shaking and stayed exactly where they were, Irma looked up and saw Boz watching her. There was a profound sadness in his eyes, a sadness borne of love and a long relationship that could now be measured in weeks . . . possibly even days, though neither Boz nor Irma would acknowledge that possibility. But that very morning, it had taken Irma some time to get Boz out of bed and into the shower. In fact, she had been considering asking Chris Hendricks, the family odd-job man these past twenty years or more, to come around and investigate putting up a handrail—she just didn't trust Boz's balance anymore.

"I'm okay," Boz said, "before you ask."

"I know, honey," she said, lifting a hand and tracing a line with a fingernail along the back of Boz's left wrist. "I do so love you," she said.

Boz nodded. And as pale and exhausted as he looked—even a little jaundiced around the eyes—there was a twinkle of mischief in those eyes that made Irma frown and narrow her own eyes.

"You up to something, Boswell Mendholsson?"

"Just taking some cake and coffee through is all, sweetie," he said. And with that, he backed out of the kitchen and into the den, closing the door firmly behind him.

And so it went on for several weeks, almost daily visits from Phil Defantino with each stay restricted to the den, usually for between one and two hours. The visits were in the mornings mostly, which was also when the children called around whenever they could—children! what a ridiculous thing to call them, Irma thought to herself on more than one occasion: they were both in their thirties now but, of course, they would always be a little boy and a little girl. And they did so love their father. When they left—they rarely brought their other halves or the grandchildren—they would hug Irma tightly, asking if she was okay and managing to keep things under control. Each time she would tell them emphatically that she was fine. And she was.

Irma believed you got an almost spiritual strength from someplace in these situations. She had heard of that before. And while she did not dare to consider what life would be without her husband, she managed to cope with his steadily deteriorating condition with determination, patience, and even good humor.

Boz himself seemed to wind down around lunchtime or early afternoon, retiring to the couch where he would watch game shows or, occasionally, the Cartoon Network. Sometimes he would simply call it a day and go straight to bed. Irma would take him a sandwich and a bag of potato chips around five or six o'clock and then Boz would drift in and out of sleep until Irma came to bed herself at around ten thirty.

As the November winds buffeted the house and Thanksgiving approached, there were increasingly clear signs that Boz's downhill slide was gaining acceleration. It was just the little things that they both noticed—the swollen ankles from the steroids, the drowsiness from the painkillers, the sickness from the tumor itself—any of which by itself could maybe have slipped beneath the radar. But taken all together, things were starting to look a little bleak. And now Boz was starting to wheeze like an old steam train. "It's got into his lungs," Jack Fredricks told Irma one late afternoon as he was leaving the house, the setting sun framing him there on the porch as he buttoned up his overcoat.

Then, one day, Boz cried out in pain as Irma was trying to get him out of his bed. "It's no good, sweetie," he said, his words coming out like knife stabs, in breathless staccato. "Let me be . . . just let me be." And with that, he slumped down onto the pillow and fell immediately back to sleep, his mouth wide open, stealing as much air from the room as it could manage.

"Hey, Irma," Phil Defantino said when Irma opened the door. They looked at each other in silence, neither one of them making a move, and then Phil said, "Boz not so good?"

She shook her head and wiped at her eyes. She knew that Phil could see she had been crying.

Phil nodded. "Well," he said, drawing the word out and hunching his shoulders against the wind, "maybe it would be better if I called around another time."

"Yes," Irma said, trying to keep from glancing down at Phil's briefcase, "maybe it would at that. I'll get him to give you a call when he's feeling a little better."

When Phil said, "Sure," his voice sounded hoarse and broken. He nodded once and turned around, head hanging down, and made for the street along the path through the Mendholssons' front yard. He never looked back. And he never saw Boz alive again.

Irma spoke in whispers to Nicola on the telephone.

"Hey, honey," she said.

"Hey, Mom. Everything okay? Is it Dad?"

She glanced around to make sure the bedroom door was still closed. "He's not too good, honey."

"Not too good?"

"No, not too good at all. Dr. Fredricks says . . . he says . . ."

"Mom?"

"He says your daddy will be leaving us soon."

"Oh, Mom."

"I know, honey, I know." A single tear dropped from Irma's cheek onto the telephone cradle and she wiped it away with one finger, rubbing the spot back and forth until there was no trace of it at all. "I called your brother. He's coming home tomorrow. Catching the red-eye out of Boston—should be here by midmorning."

"Will that . . . will that be—"

"Oh, I hope so, honey. I surely do hope so, but he's not so good."

"I'll be there."

Irma replaced the telephone and listened to the resulting silence, absolute at first and then, slowly, giving way to house sounds—boards settling, the wind outside, the occasional clank of the heating system. It was all familiar and yet, with the absence of her husband's movements around the place, it was completely alien.

She went back down the hallway and gently eased open the door to the bedroom she had shared with Boz these past thirty-six years or so. He was still there—*where would he have gone for goodness' sakes?*—but only just, a mere shape beneath the bedclothes, made eerie by the dim nightlight on the bedside table, his chest rising and falling very slowly and with apparent difficulty. She moved silently across the room and sat down on the bed beside him, took one of Boz's thin hands between hers, and watched his face.

"Irma?" he croaked without opening his eyes.

"I'm here, honey. I'm right here."

"Irma . . . I feel pretty rough."

"I know, honey. You must rest, save your energy."

Boz opened his eyes and looked straight ahead, past Irma, at the covered shelving and rails that contained all their sweaters and coats, pants and shirts, a lifetime of clothing and shoes. *Half of that will have to go,* Irma thought, following Boz's line of vision. *Oh, dear Lord, give me the stren—*

He turned toward her and, when she saw his milky, watery eyes, Irma let out a small gasp.

"Irma . . ."

"I'm here, dear," she said.

"Irma, you have . . . you have to be strong."

"I know, honey. I will be. You be strong, too."

Was that a laugh he gave or just a cough? Irma couldn't tell anymore.

"Irma, I'm going to be going soon and—"

"Hush, please hush, saying those—"

Boz shook his head. "Shhh. Let me finish. I always wanted to go traveling," he said, his voice soft like unfurling parchment, "and now I'm going to get the chance. After all these years . . ." He coughed again and Irma wiped his mouth with a paper tissue.

"After all these years I'm going to visit all those places we wanted to visit together. Think of me there," he said.

"I will," Irma promised. "I'll think of you."

"Just pret—" He closed his eyes and gave another little shake of his head. "Just *think,*" he continued, "that I'm away from home, seeing wonderful sights and . . . and missing you." He turned to her. "I *will* miss you, sweetie," he said.

"And I'll miss you, too," she said.

He nodded and closed his eyes. After one long, wheezy breath, Boz's chest was still.

"Honey?" Irma said, even though she knew, deep down, that her husband was now too far away to hear her. Even so, she said it again. And then once more. After a while, she just sat with him, holding his hand, reminding him of all their times together and telling him how much she loved him.

The funeral was held on a rainy Wednesday in November.

James held tightly onto his mother's arm all through the service, with Nicola standing on her other side, watching Irma carefully throughout the hymns and the sermon. At the end, to the strains of a Glenn Miller tune, they trooped out into the graveyard for the internment.

Irma hadn't realized how well-thought-of her husband truly was. They had kept themselves pretty much to themselves all through their married life and yet here were lots of people—people Irma wasn't entirely sure she had ever met—standing out in the driving drizzle to celebrate her husband's life and to mourn, with her, his passing.

"Who *are* all these folks, Mom?" Nicola whispered.

Irma shook her head, her eyes locked onto just one figure standing almost directly across from her, above the open grave beneath Boz's coffin: Phil Defantino. She had not mentioned Phil's stream of visits to either of the children and now, seeing him acknowledge her with the faintest nod of his head, she wondered why.

James's hand grasped her arm and she turned her head just as the coffin began lowering.

On the way back to the car, Irma stopped and talked to many of the mourners. Everyone said pretty much the same thing, which wasn't much at all. But what could you say? He was gone and that was it. Phil Defantino was different, though. Phil took Irma in his arms and hugged her close to him. "Anything you ever want, Irma, no matter what it is, you only have to call me. Okay?"

She nodded. "Thanks, Phil." They stood looking at each other for a few seconds before James helped his mother into the waiting car. She kept her eyes closed all the way home, praying to her heart to stop beating. But it didn't. Nothing was that easy.

Having made arrangements for Angie and Jim to look after their respective children, James and Nicola had decided to stay on at the house, though the first day after the funeral, Thanksgiving, was a baptism of fire. "If I can make it through today," Irma said when Nicola brought her a cup of Earl Gray tea in bed, her voice tired and her eyes bagged from crying all night, "then I can make it through any day."

Nicola made a wonderful turkey dinner with all the trimmings and the three of them spent the day looking through old photo albums, listening to music, and crying like babies. When Irma finally made it into bed, she was so completely exhausted that she even refused one of the sleeping tablets prescribed by Jack Fredricks.

As soon as she closed her eyes, she dreamed of Boz, and when she woke up the following morning, with shafts of watery sunlight angling through the gap between the curtains, it was like losing him all over again.

"Okay," James announced as he plopped onto the side of his mother's bed, "we need to have a plan."

"James *always* had to plan things, Mom," Nicola observed from where she was standing, leaning against the door frame. "He won't be happy unless he has a list so you might just as well let him get on with it."

Irma forced a brave smile and nodded.

"So, first, Dad's clothes," James said, writing *clothes* in his notebook.

"I don't think I can—" Irma began before being startled by a thud out in the hallway. She looked up and, just for a moment, there was a girlish excitement in her eyes. But the excitement evaporated just as quickly as it had appeared when she realized it was the mailman.

"I'll get it," Nicola said, and she backed out of the room.

"Okay, Mom, I know how you must feel, but—"

"James, you truly have absolutely no idea at all how I feel. Those are your father's clothes . . . his shirts, his pants, his favorite shoes, his—"

She stopped when Nicola reappeared at the door clutching a bundle of envelopes. Her eyes were wide and her mouth seemed to have been chiselled into an O shape.

"Nick? What is it?"

Irma frowned at her daughter. "Nicola?"

Nicola walked across the room and lifted one of the letters from the small bundle, handed it across. Irma accepted it and saw that it was not a letter at all: It was a postcard. From Venice. The picture showed the Bridge of Sighs and a gondolier guiding his craft between high stone buildings, backdropped by a sun that appeared to be sinking into the canal behind him.

Her heart beating, Irma turned the card over and gasped: The message was written by Boz—she knew his handwriting anywhere.

*Dearest Irma,*

it began.

"Mom?" James said, hardly daring to move.

*Well, here I am in Venice. The trip was less traumatic than I expected. I wish you could see this place—I'll have to bring you when we meet up again. The sound of the gondoliers calling to each other—and singing! My, but they have wonderful voices. The smell is a little strong—kind of fishy—in places but the canals and the buildings—such wonderful buildings—more than make up for it. Anyway, must go. We're on a tight schedule. I'll write again soon.*

*All my love as always,*
*Boz*

"Mom, you okay? What is it?"

"It's a postcard," Irma said, her voice reverently hushed.

"A postcard?" Nicola moved over alongside Irma, but only managed, "Who's it—" before she saw the handwriting. "That's from Dad!"

"A postcard from Dad?" James was half tempted to add something along the lines of it must have needed one hell of a stamp, but decided against it.

"From Venice," Irma added, checking the front of the card again before turning it over and re-reading the words.

"I don't understand," Nicola said.

"It's some kind of sick joke," James said as he reached for the card.

Irma shook her head. "No, it's not a joke. It's a very clever ruse on your dad's part to make me feel better."

And she went on to tell Nicola and James about the daily visits from Phil Defantino, mentioning the mystical briefcase, the secluded sessions in Boz's den, the fact that Phil had spent his entire life traveling to distant countries so he must have built up quite a database of contacts . . . people who, as a favor to Phil—and for such a good reason—would probably not be averse to sending a pre-written card from their home city to Irma here in the United States.

After studying it for a while, Irma said, "I'll bet this is the way it works:

"Phil organizes the card from Venice, gets it across here and brings it around for your dad to write. Then Phil takes it away and sends it back to Venice, and that same person then sticks a stamp on it and pops it into a box."

"But the timing is so perfect," Nicola said.

"Well, maybe Phil held onto the card until—" She paused and shrugged. "Then he sends the card and tells whoever that it's fine to send it right back."

" 'I'll write again soon'? What's that mean?"

"Exactly what it says, I guess, James," Irma said.

"You mean . . . you mean there'll be other cards?"

Irma smiled at Nicola and nodded. "I guess so. I don't know just how many, but . . . they were in there a long time every time Phil came around. And Phil came around pretty much every day until your dad got too weak."

James watched his mother turn back to the card and read it again. "How do you feel about it, Mom?"

"I think it's pretty weird," said Nicola, and she gave a little shudder. "It's like Dad speaking from beyond the grave."

"That's exactly what it is," ventured Irma, "but it certainly doesn't bother me. After all, that's what a will is, isn't it? The deceased speaking to his loved ones from beyond the grave . . . with all the statements and clauses in that will written when the deceased was still alive. This is really no different than that and, of course, it's a delightful idea."

"Still pretty weird, if you ask me," Nicola concluded.

But Irma was smiling. "I think it's sweet. And I think I'm ready for a cup of coffee." She went into the TV room and placed the card on top of the television, standing it up against a bowl containing nuts and dates.

"Pride of place, huh?" James said.

Irma nodded without taking her eyes from the card. "Pride of place."

When Phil Defantino called around, James answered the door.

"Hey, James," he said, nodding awkwardly. It had started to snow outside—just a fine powder now but everyone knew that as soon as it warmed up a degree or so, they'd get it knee deep—and Phil was wearing a peaked cap like hunters wore, complete with earmuffs, a thick scarf, and mittens that made him look like he was hiding freak hands of enormous size. He was a shopping mall dummy on which some overzealous window dresser had decided to drop every piece of winter clothing in the store. James had to smile. Phil frowned at the smile and then said, "I thought I'd call around to see how your mom's doing."

"Oh, she's fine. Thanks to that—"

"Hello, Phil," Irma said. She moved quickly along the hallway and reached around her son to pull Phil into the house.

"I was just going to say to Mr. Defant—"

"Hey, James . . . it's Phil. You're not a kid anymore."

James laughed. "Okay, yeah, Phil." He turned to Irma. "I was just going to say how well—"

Irma flashed a wide-eyed stare at him and gave a single slight shake of her head. "Why don't you go make us some coffee, honey?" Then, to Phil, "You going to stay for a few minutes, yes?"

Phil nodded enthusiastically and started to pull clothing off, depositing it in a heap on the floor just inside the door.

Phil and Irma sat in the TV room for almost an hour, drinking coffee and eating cookies and generally just shooting the breeze. Phil checked to see if Irma was okay and made sure that she didn't need any money or anything and Irma said she was fine on both counts, with Irma telling him that one of his magical lost billfolds was not required. She had forgotten all about the postcard and she saw Phil notice it there on the television, but he didn't say anything so she didn't say anything either. When the snow started to fall heavily outside the window, Phil decided it was time for him to hit the homeward trail. He gave Irma a kiss on the cheek and a big bear hug—God, how she missed her man's strong arms around her!—and then, once more suitably attired, he ventured out into the elements. Irma watched him trudging along the path to his 4 × 4, watched the lights come on as Phil got in, and then watched the car move off. She waved energetically at the little toot on Phil's horn and closed the door. When she turned around, James was leaning against the stair banister, watching her.

"Why didn't you want me to say anything? About the card, I mean."

"Wasn't anything to do with him."

Irma walked past James, heading for the kitchen.

"Wasn't anything to do with Phil? Didn't you tell us that—"

"James," Irma snapped, spinning around at the kitchen door. "However or whyever this thing happened and no matter whose help was used, that card is to me from my husband. My *dead* husband. Writing to me from one of the most wonderful cities on

Earth." She shrugged and her stern expression mellowed. "Sure, I could maybe track down the whys and wherefores of it—talk to Phil, ask him to come clean and so on—and where would that leave me? What benefit would I gain from that?"

James could feel the color draining out of his cheeks.

"You think of religion, right? All those folks traipsing to chapels and churches, synagogues and mosques . . . and all of them doing it, week in and week out, on the back of a fairy story? Oh, it's a pretty widely held and widely believed fairy story, but it's still a fairy story. There's no proof. It's like the old saying goes: If you had proof, then you wouldn't need faith. And right now, when I thought my life was pretty well over, I get a postcard from the one person on this planet who means more to me than anything else in the world . . . a postcard from Venice, for crissakes—excuse my French—and yes, sure, there's a part of me, maybe just a tiny itsy bitsy part, that thinks, well, maybe he is *in* Venice! And maybe I will get to go there with him one of these days. And until that happens, he's just going to stay in touch with me, writing little messages to me. It doesn't hurt, does it? To believe that, I mean? But you want me to seek out the proof that he just sat in his den day after day, concocting silly meaningless little notes using his travel books so's he could send me postcards from exotic locations for me to read while his body—the body I loved and cherished more than anything else, and that I miss so very very much—just decayed to mulch in the—" Irma slid down the wall, sobbing.

James went across to her and crouched down beside her, his own tears rolling down his face. "Oh, Mom . . . I'm so sorry. So very very sorr—"

Irma patted his arm and rubbed her eyes with her sleeve. "No, you haven't done anything, honey. It's me who should be sorry."

"No, you—"

"Shh. Let me finish. You just wanted me to rationalize everything so's I wouldn't fool myself . . . so's I would face the fact that your dad is dead and gone and I'm alone now. You didn't want me to allow myself to become dependent on . . . on a fantasy. Is that about right?"

James nodded. "That's about right, yes."

"Well, honey, let me reassure you that I'm absolutely fine. I do know the score. Maybe your dad and me . . . maybe we'll meet up again"—Irma waved her hand and shrugged, eyebrows raised as though challenging her son to disagree with her—"someplace else . . . be it Heaven or wherever. And then again," she said with a shrug of resignation, "maybe we won't. But the possibility—no, the *faith* that I have—that I *will* see him again is all that's going to keep me going. And that postcard and maybe others just like it, is a part of that faith.

"Even though, deep down, I know—and I *do* know—that your dad wrote those cards when he was still alive, there's just this wonderful *what if?* element about it . . . like when you see a squirrel gathering nuts and you imagine it going home to a tree-hole where its partner is cooking dinner for it, or on Halloween when you look out of the window and you wonder whether, just maybe, the ghouls and the ghosts are gathering down at the cemetery gates just waiting for some shmuck to wander by . . . or Christmas Eve, looking out of that same window into the snow and trying real hard, no matter how old you've become, to hear sleigh bells.

"The whole thing about the *very idea* of the cards and that he even thought of doing it and that Phil got so involved—God only knows how much effort *he* had to put into this . . . and maybe is *still* putting into it—well, how could anyone not *want* to believe? It comes right down to this: my man is dead and I have to go on without him. I can make that portion of my time on Earth *very* hard or I can make it just hard—it could never be easy. The postcard helped. God forgive me that I needed such help, but I guess I did. And I still do. And if I speak with Phil about it, then I break the spell. So all those people he's had lined up and all those visits to the house when your dad was so sick . . . all of that would have been in vain."

The sudden sound of water draining from the bath upstairs broke the silence and Irma smiled, running a hand through her gray hair and sweeping it back from her forehead.

"You're right, Mom," James said, and he threw his arms around her once again. Breathing in the smell of her—her soap or perfume or whatever it was—suddenly made him realize that he wouldn't be smelling his father's unique smell ever again. "I miss him, too," he whispered into his mother's ear.

"I know, honey," she said. And then, because such a revelation and the enormity of its implications needed to be acknowledged more than once, "I know."

They made a pact that night, Irma and James and Nicola, to keep the postcard—they hardly dared speak of it in plural, not yet at least—a secret amongst themselves. They had a small celebration to mark their decision, a late-night feast of port and cheese and crackers, raising their glasses to the continued success of Boz Mendholsson's travels and adventures. When James went to stand outside in the wind and snow for a cigarette, he looked at the surrounding houses and listened to the snow-muted sounds of the neighborhood and the susurrant hum of the traffic on the interstate, and he steeled himself to face a world that was now minus one of the half-dozen people who mattered most to him. It was easier than he had imagined.

The second card—the one from Paris—arrived the following week, wedged between a credit card statement and a letter from Suzanne, Irma's eldest sister. The statement and the letter were ignored until much later in the day, but the other item was devoured voraciously by Irma right there on the doorstep, the wind blowing her hair around her face. Casual passersby who knew of Irma's loss might have been surprised and possibly even dismayed by the huge grin on her face. "And *au revoir* to you, too, honey," Irma whispered when she reached the end.

From then on, the cards arrived with dependable regularity—always one per week and very often two. It seemed that Boz was on a whirlwind tour of the entire world, jetting across continents and time zones with casual disregard for jet lag or budgetary constraints. Berlin, Amsterdam, Vienna, Austin, Reykjavik, Milan, Rome . . . and every card cross-referenced and referring to ones that came before it. It was a veritable *where's where* of cities, countries, and cultures, each card bringing her up to date on how Boz was and providing snapshots of local cuisine and landmarks, the smells, sights, and sounds of the world delivered every few days into the Mendholssons' mailbox.

James and Nicola fell into a routine of telephoning Irma purely to get the lowdown on their dad's latest adventures, and whenever they visited the house, they relished holding the postcards and reading them for themselves, marveling still, way down inside of them, at the ingenuity and sheer meticulous dedication being employed in this scam of scams. But as the days and weeks rolled into months and seasons, that attitude was eroded and, even in spite of themselves, the cards became the reality of their situation . . . their father off on a prolonged world trip with a brief communication coming from every stop along the way.

By the time Irma flipped the calendar over into 1987, Boz had sent her seventy-one cards. The one she received on January 7 was from Moscow—or St. Petersburg, as Boz informed her in his note—where he had spent New Year's Eve celebrating in Red Square. In a nice touch at the end he said it was a good thing he didn't feel the cold because it was ten degrees below.

Irma kept the cards in a special rosewood box by the side of her bed, the cards all filed in date order. There had been a couple of screwups in the summer when cards arrived in the wrong order, but now she had marked each one with a number and there was a complementary sheet with all the numbers and the dates the cards arrived. At night, before she went to sleep, Irma would sit in bed, with the wind whistling around the streets of Forest Plains, picturing Boz in all these exotic locations. He hit his one hundredth card in late June—the card even emblazoned with a hand-drawn rosette in red ink proclaiming Boz's literary century.

Irma was glad of the warmer weather. The winter—her second as a widow—had been cold and long, and it had taken its toll on her stamina and her constitution. Nicola insisted that she go to see Dr. Fredricks and, though she refused at first, James was quick to remind her of what she would have said to his dad in a similar situation.

Jack Fredricks said that Irma's blood pressure was up a little, but it wasn't anything to worry about. He gave her some pills and congratulated her on dealing with her loss so magnanimously. "You're an inspiration to us all," he told her as he showed her out of the surgery.

"Well," Irma said, "I've had a lot of help." And then she was on her way.

Phil and Jackie Defantino had stayed in close contact over the twenty months since Boz's death, and though Phil was often tempted to mention something to Irma about his special project with Boz, he refrained. He had quickly recognized the danger of stealing the magic from what Boz had conceived and so he never said a thing . . . not even a knowing smile. And Irma, in what Phil considered to be remarkable forbearance, never let her own face slip when he would ask her how things were.

But when James and Nicola were shown the one hundredth postcard, they saw something that must have been happening for a while but which they had missed. They didn't say anything as such, but James had to ask his mother to clarify some of the message as the words appeared to have been smudged. "Probably dropped in a puddle someplace," was all Irma could say as she took the card and read aloud the whole message. While she read, James looked across at his sister and saw the same concerns in her eyes as he felt sure were present in his own: Boz's handwriting was deteriorating.

The following day, James called around to take his mom to the mall, but she wasn't ready. He shouted into the bathroom and asked if it was okay for him to flip through Boz's postcards. "Go ahead," Irma shouted over the noise of the shower. "They're in the box beside my bed."

Sitting on the bed, flicking through the cards, James saw that it was worse than he had first thought. Boz's penmanship had become uncontrolled, the words slanting into each other and littered with misspellings and grammatical errors, inconsistencies and duplications. He wondered just when, in his father's illness, these cards had been written.

But, as it was to turn out, James's concerns were overtaken by events.

The following Monday, James took the day off from work and drove up to Forest Plains to see Nicola. They met up at the coffee shop on Main Street, the plan being to discuss what they were going to do when the cards dried up. It was something they had never really considered, having been swept away on Irma Mendholsson's flood tide of optimism and wonder. Maybe, for just a while there, they too had signed onto the belief that their father truly was enjoying a long vacation, writing home every few days to keep them aware of where he was.

"She's going to crash," James said, shaking his head in desperation. "Crash and burn."

"Oh, I don't know that—"

"Nick, she has never mentioned the whole thing ever since that first couple of cards came. Not once. And neither have we. She actually believes now that he's simply out of the country."

Nicola nodded thoughtfully.

"And when the cards finally stop, it's all going to come back to her. It'll be like he's died all over again."

"So what'll we do?"

"I think the time has come to have a long talk with Mom."

With great reluctance, Nicola agreed.

They realized that something was wrong as soon as they saw the folded-up Sunday newspaper lying on the porch.

"Oh, God, Nick," James said as he fumbled for his key.

"Stay cool, it might not mean anything," Nicola said. "Let me try the doorbell." She reached past her brother and pressed the bell. The distant sound of *bing bong* from inside the house only seemed to exacerbate their feeling of impending doom.

Inserting the key in the lock, James turned the handle and opened the door. "Mom?"

They both stood on the porch for a couple of seconds, each of them convincing themselves that they simply didn't want to frighten their mother. But it was more than that. It was something both profound and sublime. So long as they remained outside the house, then anything that might have happened in there stayed in the future as a mere possibility. Once they went in and confronted what they now believed to be inevitable, there was no turning back . . . no alternative but to accept.

"Maybe she's sick," Nicola said, taking the first step.

"Slept late?" James offered.

"James, it's two o'clock in the afteroon."

"We should have called," he said, moving along the hallway.

"Mom?" Nicola shouted. "It's Nicola and James."

Irma was in the TV room sitting in Boz's chair. She could just have been asleep, but they knew immediately that she wasn't.

"Oh, Mom," was all James could think of to say.

Nicola remembered what Frank Garnett had said about when he found his own father dead in bed. *You know,* Frank had said, a look of something approaching wonderment on his face, *he just wasn't there any longer. It was his body, but it was completely empty. Like a drawing of my dad rather than the actual article.*

And that was exactly how Irma Mendholsson looked, one foot tucked up beneath her leg and her head slumped over to one side.

James knelt down by the chair and felt her forehead. It was ice cold.

"James!" Nicola snapped, her voice barely above a whisper. "Look."

James followed his sister's pointing finger and saw, clamped in his mother's clasped hands resting in her lap, the edge of what appeared to be a piece of paper.

James pried her hands apart and there was another of his father's postcards, this one featuring a picture of the Sydney Opera House. He tugged at the card—

"She doesn't want to let go of it," Nicola said softly.

—and, through the tears, he read out the message on the back:

*Hey swetie*
*Im in Astraylia. It's veryy hot. God, im so tired. i'm*
*missing you like mad. i don't think i can carry on*
*much lonegr. It is very hot here. i love you more than*
*I can say.all my love*
*Boz*

"Doesn't sound too good, does he?"

"It's worse than that," James said. "The spelling and punctuation are adrift as well." He handed the card over to his sister and thrust his hands into his pockets. "Oh, Mom," he whispered.

This time the funeral was a quieter affair. Neither James nor his sister wanted a lot of people, so the only others in attendance were Jim and Angie, with Anthony, Jennifer, and Maria, and baby Margaret-Jayne, plus, of course, Jackie and Phil Defantino.

At the end of the service and the internment, while Jim and Angie took the children back to their respective cars, James and Nicola stayed back to speak with Phil and Jackie. When they had exchanged the customary commiserations, Phil asked Jackie to wait for him in the car. She looked a little puzzled but did as she was asked.

The three of them watched her walk away and then Phil turned to James and Nicola and, with a deep sigh, reached into his inside coat pocket and produced a brown paper bag that was about the shape and size of paperback novel. He handed it to James.

"What is it?" Nicola asked.

"I think I know," James said as he opened the bag. Without removing the contents, he peered into the bag. For a few seconds it did indeed look like a paperback book, viewed from the page edges rather than from the spine. He folded the bag over again and handed it back to Phil. "There's nothing there that we want, Phil," he said. "Just some cards."

"James—"

"Nicola, remember what I told you Mom had said about destroying the magic?"

Nicola nodded.

James turned back to Phil. What were they like, those last dozen or so postcards? How much did he deteriorate by the time the end came? Suddenly, James felt thankful that his mother had died when she had. He couldn't imagine the heartbreak she would have gone through having to read them right up to the end, and then for the cards to stop completely. He said, "Just get rid of them."

"You sure?"

"We're sure."

Nicola nodded and turned away.

"Will you be needing any help? With the house, I mean. Boz's books and magazines . . . all that stuff."

James shook his head and breathed in deeply. The intake of breath made him appear bigger and stronger than he felt. "We're going to get a dealer in, sell the lot. We could do it ourselves, advertising them, but it'd take too long. And we'd sooner see it happen in one hit."

"I understand," Phil said. "Well, if you need any help with anything at all, just give me a call."

"Will do. Nick and I are staying at the house for a few days to sort out all the furniture and, as you say, all of the books. Dad's old firm is doing the realty."

"He'd like that."

"That's what we figured. Anyway, by the end of next week, it'll just be a shell with a *FOR SALE* sign in the yard."

Phil sighed and looked around. Jackie was standing by Phil's 4 x 4—she waved when she saw him looking and he nodded before turning back to James and Nicola. "Well, I guess that's it." He shook James's hand and gave Nicola a kiss on the cheek. "Keep in touch, huh?"

"You bet," James said.

Watching him walk away from them, they saw him remove a handkerchief from his pocket. In the stillness of the cemetery, the nose-blow—when it came—sounded like a clarion call or *Last Post*. Neither James nor Nicola could decide which.

The weekend wasn't as traumatic as they had feared it would be. And though they had both expected to be wracked with nostalgia, going through their mother's clothing and furniture proved to be relatively easy, with most of the stuff being either thrown away in a collection of garden refuse bags or stacked in neat piles for the thrift and charity stores off Main Street. In addition, they had a guy calling around early the following Tuesday to take all the furniture they didn't want or need—as it turned out, they didn't need anything and kept back only a couple of items that had earned a place in their memory.

The man from the Realtor's office—a guy called Dane—came around on Sunday and prepared a notice on the property. When he left, after less than an hour, James and Nicola stood watching the FOR SALE sign long after his car had disappeared.

Monday morning dawned and with it came a sense of closure. The sun was shining, the house was pretty well cleared, and they were both looking forward to getting back to their own homes. The grieving process had started but, as James said—and had said repeatedly over the weekend—things could have panned out a lot worse than they had done.

By midmorning, Nicola had wiped down all the paintwork and vacuumed the house from top to bottom. Now it was just a house: All the evidence of its life as the Mendholssons' home was stored as memories in the cerebral databanks of James's and Nicola's heads, to be accessed whenever they were required.

The one thing they hadn't thought of doing occurred to James as he watched the mailman walking along the sidewalk.

"Hey, we need to get in touch with the post office to have Mom's mail forwarded to one of us." He got up from his seat on the floor against the side wall when he saw the mailman turn into Irma's yard. "You want to do it, or me?"

"I guess me," she shouted after him, "because I'm here in town and I'm home with Margaret-Jayne most days."

James opened the door. "Makes sense to me," he shouted. Then, to the mailman, "Hey, how are you today?"

"I'm fine, but tired. Seems like I work harder at home on weekends than I do during the week." They both laughed. The mailman handed a small bundle of envelopes to James and expressed his sympathy for his loss. "How you doing anyways? It's a sad time for you."

James nodded as he flicked through the letters. "Yes, it is, but I think—"

He stopped when he saw the postcard. He recognized the picture immediately—Venice . . . the Bridge of Sighs, the gondolier, the stone buildings: Everything was there, just as it had been on the very first card that Irma had received from Boz.

James turned over the card. The first thing that he noticed was that this card was not addressed to his mother: It was addressed, in his father's hand—a strong hand once again—to him and Nicola, care of his mother's address:

*Dearest James and Nicola,*

the message began.

*Well, this is going to be the last card, I'm afraid.*

"Is everything okay?" the mailman asked.

*Your mom arrived here yesterday morning—I can't tell you how good it was to see her again. Adventuring all by yourself is such a lonely business.*

"James?" Nicola called from the room, her voice echoing in the empty house.

*She wants me to show her everything else and while we've got a mighty long time together now, there's* such *a lot to see!!! Look after each other and your wonderful families.*

*Love as always. Dad*

And there was a P.S. at the bottom.

Nicola appeared alongside him just as James was finishing reading. The mailman was walking back down the path, shrugging repeatedly to himself.

Somewhere off on the interstate a truck horn sounded, dopplering from soft to loud and then back to soft again, like some kind of animal.

"I don't believe it," James said, shaking his head.

He handed the postcard to Nicola and put his hands up to his face.

Nicola read.

"My God," she said. "His handwriting is back to normal and he sounds lucid again. But all this stuff about Mom—how could he have—" She stopped, looked up at her brother, then back down at the card.

*P.S. I'm sure the past few days have been difficult for you both but I'm absolutely fine. Couldn't be happier. Have a wonderful life, both of you. We'll be following your progress—whenever our busy schedule permits it!*

*Much love,*
*Mom*

"How—"

James interrupted her. "I'll tell you one thing," he said, "about that card, and the one that came before—the first one."

Nicola, wide-eyed, simply nodded her head for him to continue.

"I think we were wrong . . . about the sun setting, I mean."

Nicola turned it over and looked at the photograph closely.

"I'm betting that's a sun*rise!*" He turned and smiled at her. "The start of a brand-new day."

> *The undiscovered country from whose bourn*
> *No traveller returns.*
>
> —William Shakespeare,
> *Hamlet* (1601)

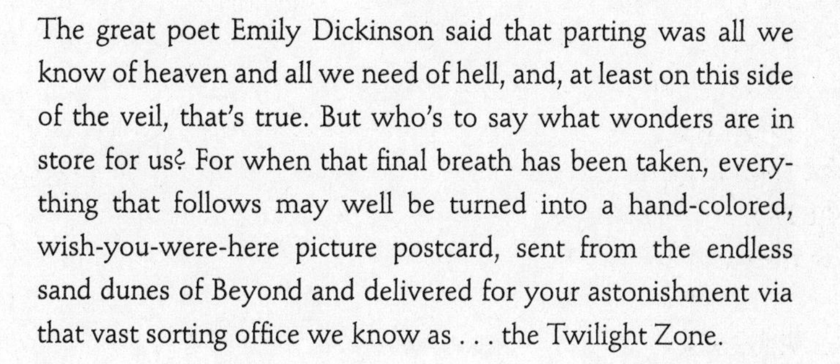

The great poet Emily Dickinson said that parting was all we know of heaven and all we need of hell, and, at least on this side of the veil, that's true. But who's to say what wonders are in store for us? For when that final breath has been taken, everything that follows may well be turned into a hand-colored, wish-you-were-here picture postcard, sent from the endless sand dunes of Beyond and delivered for your astonishment via that vast sorting office we know as . . . the Twilight Zone.

# OBSESSION

David Black

For your consideration: Paul Keller, citizen, husband, father—who went to a party looking for laughs, and instead met his future, in which laughter would be rare. Because your future is never what you expect in . . . the Twilight Zone.

## 1

Paul Keller had the perfect marriage, perfect kids, the perfect job—the perfect life. Perfect but, one might also say, perfectly dull. No edges or surprises. As Mark Twain said, "Heaven is great for the climate but terrible for society."

One Saturday night at a party, Paul (who was a senior trader at a successful brokerage house) and his wife, Claire, were chatting with friends when, across the room, Paul saw Lily Sass and realized for the first time he had been missing something in his life—her.

He always thought Claire was his soul mate. That's what he told her at their wedding seventeen years ago.

That Saturday night, he realized he was wrong.

"Are you okay?" Claire asked. "You look like you've seen a ghost."

"Just a chill," Paul lied.

"In this room?" Claire said. "It's overheated! I'm dying."

"Maybe," Paul said, "I'm coming down with something."

On Monday morning, at work, Paul's father-in-law and boss, Ben Kipfer, stuck his head into Paul's office.

"If you're coming down with something," Ben said, "take the day off."

"I wish Claire wouldn't tattle to you," Paul said.

"She said ever since Saturday night, you've been under the weather," Ben said, studying Paul for signs of flu. "Said you woke up sweating last night. The sheets were soaked."

"Ben," Paul said, "you know how much I love and respect you. But what goes on in my bedroom, soaked sheets and all, is none of your business."

That day, Paul had lunch with his best friend and coworker, Laurie Traynor, at a Japanese restaurant on Fifty-seventh Street.

"You do look a little pale around the gills," Laurie said.

"Has Ben been spreading stories?" Paul said.

Laurie shrugged.

"No one wants to catch the flu," Laurie said. "Not with the market the way it is."

"What I tell you stays at this table?" Paul said.

"Have I ever betrayed a confidence?" Laurie asked. "Even something as innocuous as taking Viagra."

"I just needed something to perk things up," Paul said.

"There are lots of other guys who'd perk things up outside the marriage bed," Laurie said. "Married as long as you've been, using Viagra is like renewing your vows."

"Saturday night," Paul said, "I met someone. Well, not exactly met her, but saw her."

"What's her name?" Laurie asked.

"I don't know," Paul said.

Laurie fiddled with her sake cup.

"What are you going to do about it?" she asked.

Surprised by the question, Paul said, "Nothing. I love Claire."

"Your life is too good." Laurie laughed. "You can't help flirting with disaster."

That evening, at home, Paul was helping his thirteen-year-old son, Jason, with his math homework. His sixteen-year-old daughter, Kelly, left to go "study" with friends. Claire was pasting pictures from the family's last vacation into one of their many photo albums.

Paul couldn't stop thinking about Lily—although he didn't yet know her name. He didn't imagine her figure or her face, but the heat he felt when he saw her, a tingling that slithered up his spine like a snake.

The next afternoon, at his usual coffee shop, Paul sat at his usual stool at his usual spot at the counter. He ordered his usual lunch—a BLT, bacon extra crisp—when he glanced into the long narrow room and saw Lily, opening her mouth to eat a forkful of chicken salad.

Her mouth closed. She chewed and looked over her still-raised fork into Paul's eyes.

Paul felt the snake in his spine again.

Lily's tongue darted out and licked her lips. And she smiled. At Paul.

Paul smiled back. Folded his newspaper to the editorial page and had to read a paragraph in Gail Collins's op-ed piece three times before he realized he was too distracted to focus.

When Paul again glanced at Lily, the booth she'd occupied was empty.

She had left.

At work, for the rest of the afternoon, Paul was in a foul mood. He uncharacteristically snapped at his secretary when a sheet of paper she put on his desk sailed onto the floor.

At home, he was unusually silent.

He went into the bedroom early and was sitting on the bed, his laptop in front of him, when he overheard Jason ask Claire, "What up with Daddy?"

"Yeah," Kelly said, "what's his damage?"

"Probably a bad day at work," Claire said.

"Well," Kelly said, "that's not my fault."

When Claire came into the bedroom later and curled up in bed next to him, Paul stiffened and said, "Can't you see I'm trying to work?"

Claire studied Paul's face—she couldn't recall the last time he had spoken so coldly to her—and then slipped out of the bed and went into the living room to read.

Two days later, Paul spotted Lily's reflection in the window of a cigar store as he was going in to buy some Gloria Cubana Churchills. He whipped around, but was too late. She was gone.

The day after that, on the way to work, Paul saw her at the far end of his jammed subway car. By the time he had elbowed his way through the car, she again was gone.

*Must have gotten off at the last stop,* Paul thought.

But had they stopped?

He had gotten on the subway at Eighty-sixth Street. They were just now pulling in to the Seventy-ninth Street station.

Had he somehow made a mistake and gotten on at Ninety-sixth Street? Then, she might have gotten off at Eighty-sixth Street.

His cobbler was on Ninety-fourth. But he couldn't remember dropping off shoes before heading to work.

Paul determined not to let Lily distract him anymore.

But at lunch, at the diner, she was in the same booth she had been in a few days earlier.

Paul slipped off his stool and walked over to her, offering his hand.

"Paul Keller," he introduced himself. "I saw you at the party the other day."

"And all over town," Lily said, taking Paul's hand. "Lily Sass."

Feeling her touch made Paul weak. Looking into her eyes made Paul dizzy.

"Can I buy you lunch?" Paul asked.

But he had already sunk into the booth across from her. He couldn't help it. He felt his legs were about to give out.

Her tongue darted out and licked a spot of coffee off her lips.

"I would like that," Lily said. Fixing his eyes with hers, she said, "And after lunch, why don't we play hooky?"

They ended up in Lily's apartment—on Riverside Drive and West Eighty-eighth Street.

"I don't do this with just anybody," Lily said.

"No, no," Paul said, sitting beside her on the couch. "Of course not."

They had been necking. No petting, just kissing. Something Paul hadn't done since college. No, Paul thought, not since high school. By college, the distinction between necking and petting—between petting and fucking, for that matter—had become quaint.

But every time Lily seemed to invite Paul to go further than just kissing, Paul thought of Claire, of Kelly, of Jason, and stopped himself.

"I'm not crazy," Lily said. "You feel it, too."

"Yes," Paul said. "It's like I've found—"

"Yourself," Lily finished for him.

"I was going to say that," Paul said, shocked to realize that the connection he felt with Lily was real.

"Like you've found yourself," Lily said. "At last."

That night, Paul suggested he take Claire and the kids out to dinner.

"What's the occasion?" Claire asked.

"I just feel like doing something all together," Paul said.

In the restaurant, Paul worked too hard to make conversation, asking Kelly and Jason the kinds of questions about school and their friends he rarely asked. Trying to get Claire into a discussion about a recent movie he'd read about in the *Times*, but in a stilted, cocktail-party chatter way. By the time the check came, all four of them had lapsed into silence.

"Well," Claire said, standing, "that was fun . . ."

Over the next month and a half, Paul met and necked with Lily three more times. At their last meeting, Paul explained he had to cut it off.

"I don't know where I am anymore," Paul said.

"You don't have to explain," Lily said. "I figured it was too good to last." She gave a rueful smile. "Timing is everything, huh?"

For a month, Paul buried himself in his work. But the more he tried to forget Lily, the more he thought of her.

On every street, he thought he glimpsed her. In movie theaters, he was sure she was sitting a few rows ahead of him. In restaurants, he heard her laugh.

"Who is she?" Claire asked one night.

Paul didn't answer. They were lying in bed, side by side, staring at the ceiling.

"Do you want to sleep with her?" Claire asked.

"I haven't," Paul said.

"But do you want to?" Claire demanded.

Paul's silence was her answer.

"I could have handled anything," Claire said. "If you lost your job. Cancer. But not this. I have no way to fight this."

"I ended it," Paul said. "Weeks ago."

"Whoever she is," Claire said, "you might as well go to her. You're not here anymore." Claire whipped back the sheets and swung her legs over the side of the bed. "This isn't any kind of life," she said.

Shrugging on her bathrobe, she said, "Go to her, get her out of your system, and come back. Or, if she's what you want, I'll give you a divorce."

## 2

"It's perfect," Paul told Laurie, after his first month with Lily.

"Just like you imagined?" Laurie asked, not sure whether she was being sarcastic.

"What we're like together," Paul said, "it's something I never could have imagined."

Laurie wanted to believe a relationship could be that good, but experience told her Paul must be living in a hopeful fantasy.

"In the morning," Paul said, "when I open my eyes, she's there, standing by the bed with my coffee. Yesterday, on the way to lunch, we saw someone so intent on his BlackBerry, he went around a revolving door twice before getting out of a building. We share—"

"The pleasure of seeing other people act foolishly?" Laurie said.

"—a sense of the absurd," Paul said. "Laurie, you're too cynical."

"How's the sex?" Laurie asked.

"Telepathic," Paul said. "Otherworldly."

Paul had moved into Lily's apartment. Intimate, cluttered, fragrant. Lily had collected artifacts from her travels around the world. A jade figurine Lily had found in China was worth, according to one of Paul's friends who came to dinner, at least $100,000.

Paul found everything about Lily intriguing, exciting, surprising, new. She was the woman who would—in Goethe's phrase—"kiss him and make him eternal."

But every gift has its price. And every paradise has its serpent.

At work, the price was a "wonderful opportunity" offered by

Paul's father-in-law, Ben. The head of the firm's Hong Kong office was being rotated back to New York. Paul could move the family to Hong Kong, do his two years there, and come back to the home office a full partner.

In Ben's mind, this was a win-win. Either Paul took the gig and broke it off with Lily. Or he turned it down—leaving Ben no choice but to fire him.

Paul turned down the offer—and cleared out his desk.

He saw the kids every Tuesday and every other weekend.

Kelly was sarcastic to Lily.

Jason was silent, sitting on one of the beds in Lily's guest room, cross-legged, plugged into his iPod.

Meals were a strain. If Lily cooked, Jason picked at the food, and Kelly claimed it made her sick.

If they went out to eat, the kids could never agree on a restaurant.

"You're not being fair to Lily," Paul told his kids one evening, sitting on the edge of Jason's bed.

Kelly lay on her bed, facing the wall. Jason sat next to Paul, cross-legged as usual, listening to his iPod.

Kelly sat up. Violently.

"I don't want you to *tell* me everything's going to be all right," she said. "I want you to *make* everything all right."

"Why can't you just come home?" Jason asked, still plugged into his iPod.

"They'll get used to me," Lily told Paul later that night.

By the end of the second month together, Paul began to notice . . . odd responses to his questions about Lily's past. She wasn't evasive, but the answers didn't add up.

She grew up outside of Boston in Newton, she told Paul once. But another time, she mentioned how much she loved the St. Patrick's Day parades she used to go to in Savannah, Georgia.

When Paul asked her about the apparent contradiction, she waved it away with a not unreasonable explanation. Part of her childhood was spent in Newton, part in Savannah.

One time, she said her father was in the aerospace industry. Another time, she said he was in the military.

"He worked in aerospace *for* the military," Lily reasonably explained.

But the after-the-fact explanations seemed improvised to Paul. When he tried to dig deeper, Lily would kiss him and distract him with sex.

"What do you think she's hiding?" Laurie asked.

"I don't know," Paul said. "But I don't really know that much about her."

"Except what she tells you," Laurie said. "It sounds like you don't trust her."

"I trust her," Paul said. "Enough."

But he began waking up in the middle of the night, panicking. Who was she? What did he really know about her? What if she were a crook—or a con artist?

"Why would you think that?" Laurie asked when Paul admitted his night fears.

"Everyone she knows in New York is a new friend," Paul said. "She appeared in town just a few months before we met."

"You love her?" Laurie asked.

"Of course," Paul said.

"You're feeling guilty about leaving Claire and the kids," Laurie said, "and projecting your guilt onto Lily."

For another month, Paul tried to ignore his suspicions.

But by spring, he began contacting the high school Lily claimed to have attended, looking up her homes in old telephone directories, checking the businesses where she claimed her father had worked.

The high school explained they had no record of Lily; the files for the years Lily said she attended had been destroyed in a fire. Other people seemed to have lived in the houses in which she'd told Paul she'd grown up. Her father's work record was unconfirmed—Lily explained it was because he was working on top-secret projects.

The fire in the high school—well, that had nothing to do with her. The houses in which she said she'd grown up—what could she say? She grew up in those houses—which she described in detail.

When Paul visited one of the houses and, using a phony excuse—saying he had grown up there—got inside, the interior checked out with Lily's description.

"What about the auction gallery you said you worked at in Boston?" Paul asked. "It has no record of your employment."

"Of course not," Lily said. "I was a temp, paid under the table—at the employer's request, so he could avoid paying FICA and benefits."

The address in Boston, where she claimed to have lived, was an empty lot. She'd lost her lease and decided to move to New York when the apartment building she lived in was torn down.

The hospital where she said she was born had no record of her birth.

"Why should it?" Lily said. When the hospital where she was born merged with another hospital, the records were lost—something that made it hard for her to get her passport years later.

She was vague about the extent of her travel—six years of circling the world: Hong Kong, Calcutta, Rome, Oslo . . .

When she grew up in Newton, she said, it was so provincial she had determined to see the world when she grew up.

"What's so suspicious about that?" she asked Paul. But Paul couldn't figure out where she got the money for so many trips, and trips of such long duration.

Although Lily always had a reasonable explanation for the

discrepancy between what she told him and what he found out, Paul got more and more uncomfortable.

When Paul met with his lawyer to discuss the divorce settlement, Lily was oddly combative, insisting that he not allow Claire to take advantage of the situation. Even after the divorce, Paul still would have plenty of money. But Lily seemed a little too concerned about protecting that money.

Lily explained, if no one was looking out for Paul, his guilt might cause him to give it all away.

"What do you think?" Lily demanded. "I broke up your marriage so I could get your money—you think that's what we're about? This is what I think about money!"

She grabbed the valuable jade figurine and threw it against the wall, shattering it.

Paul put his arms around her to comfort her. Comfort ignited passion, and they made love wildly into the night.

But the next morning, Lily was still upset.

"I can't believe you've been checking me out," Lily said. "I'll bet if I started checking out your past I'd find as many discrepancies."

"You're going to blow it," Laurie told Paul.

"During the day, I don't have any problems," Paul said, "but when I wake up in the middle of the night, and look at her, sleeping next to me, as still as a corpse, I get this weird feeling . . . For all I know, Lily could be a psychopath. A serial killer."

If only Paul could have regained his trust—made a leap of faith, believed in the love he and Lily had shared when they first met—he could have saved himself from his growing obsession. An obsession that was beginning to affect both his physical and mental health.

Laurie was becoming concerned. Paul was slowly going to pieces.

He started to shadow Lily, listen in on phone calls, spy on her.

One night, when she found Paul following her, Lily lashed out at him.

"Without trust," she said, "there can be no love. You're destroying something that could be, should be only good, something you sacrificed your marriage, your work, everything to win."

But Paul couldn't help himself. He was, by now, in the grip of what seemed to be madness.

"Get your mind off it," Laurie said. "Take her away for a weekend."

## 3

Lily rented a house on Cape Cod for a week.

"It's on this bluff overlooking the ocean," Lily said, excitedly showing Paul photographs the rental agent had e-mailed her.

The drive up to the Cape was pleasant. The weather was overcast and the forecast was storms, but they didn't let that bother them. They sang along with an oldies rock station. Stopped for a leisurely lunch and dinner. Played word games like *Ghost*.

After dark, they arrived at the house, which was stark, silhouetted against the gathering clouds in the sky.

Lily called Paul to dinner. He came into the room as she was lighting a thick, squat candle.

A chill crept up Paul's spine—not the erotic charge he used to get in Lily's presence, but something clammy. Uncanny.

"What's that?" Paul asked.

"A candle," Lily said.

"A Santeria candle," Paul said. "A voodoo candle."

Lily shrugged.

"I was in a hurry shopping," she explained. "I stopped into the bodega on the corner . . ."

The air was heavy. Thunder rumbled in the distance.

All through dinner, Paul studied Lily. Before this trip, he'd been afraid Lily might be after his money. Or his life.

Now, maybe because of the isolation, maybe because of the thunder and occasional flash of lightning, he began to have a creepy feeling she was after something more valuable.

His soul.

When he saw her in the bathroom plucking hairs from his brush, he confronted her.

"I want them for a locket," Lily said.

Paul grabbed for the strands of his hair.

Lily dodged him and ran out of the bathroom.

"What do you think I'm going to do with your hair?" Lily asked. "Use it to cast some hex?"

Clutching the hair in her hand, Lily ran out of the bedroom, out of the house.

Thunder cracked right above them.

"You're being crazy," Lily said.

Paul backed her up to the edge of the bluff.

"You're the spider," Paul shouted over the storm. "I'm the fly. You trapped me at the party to eat my soul at your leisure."

Behind Lily, lightning split the sky.

Paul reached for the strands of his hair—as Lily, pulling back her arm, lost her footing and fell sixty feet to the rocks below.

Despite his lawyer's attempt to get Paul off with a defense that Paul was temporarily insane, Paul was convicted of manslaughter-1, a class B felony.

"You might not have to serve the full twenty-five-year sentence," Paul's lawyer told him.

When Laurie visited Paul in prison, she looked at Paul with pity and contempt.

"You schmuck," she said. "You had twice what most people never get once. Real love. You had heaven and turned it into hell."

A month later, at a Seattle cocktail party, Robert Duhamil—a man like Paul, with a perfect marriage, perfect kids, a perfect job, a perfect life—went to get his wife a drink.

When he looked across the room and saw Lily, he knew he had found his soul mate from the tingling that slithered up his spine like a snake.

A man alone in a cell, pondering on the heaven he has lost and the hell that remains. He believed too much in love, and love is not what it seems . . . in the Twilight Zone.

# SALES OF A DEATHMAN

David Gerrold

Meet Justin Moody, a young man in search of a career—not just a job but a way to contribute to the people of his community. Not surprisingly, he's going to accept a much greater responsibility than he has ever imagined, because the employment office is in the Twilight Zone.

"Whatever else people say about this job, it's a necessary part of society. It's work that needs to be done."

Justin scratched his head, rubbed his nose, and shifted uncomfortably in his chair. "Yes, I know all that. I mean, the job counselor explained it. More than once. She said I had an aptitude. That's why she sent me here. She said I was good with people. People trust me. People like me. At least, that's what she said."

"Yes, that's all here in your file." The woman behind the desk had an oddly dispassionate way of speaking. Soft-looking, quiet and managerial, she glanced through the file, turning pages slowly. "Actually, she said that you present yourself as unintrusive and nonthreatening. That's what makes you perfect for this job."

Justin nodded politely. "I suppose that's supposed to be a compliment."

"It is. You have no idea how many people come to us with the wrong idea about what we do here. Or simply the wrong attitude. People motivated by fear, anger, jealousy, revenge, or even the vain hope that this is a way to cheat the system. It isn't. It's about service. We provide a service necessary to the maintenance of our technological society."

"Yes, that's what the orientation video said."

She closed the file. "What we're looking for are people who can submerge themselves so completely in the job that they disappear. All that's left is the service. Maybe you're up to it, maybe you aren't. There's only one way to find out. What do you think?"

"I don't know. Are you trying to talk me out of it?"

"Let me be candid," she said. "The job does take an emotional toll. It requires a level of inner stamina that most of our applicants are incapable of maintaining for very long. That's why we have a probation period. That's true of any job, of course, but here your probation period is indefinite."

Justin took a deep breath. "I live with my dad. He's not the easiest person in the world to live with, but he needs me. So I take care of him. I've done it for eleven years now. I had to quit school, but he's my dad. I think that proves something. I mean, about my ability to be strong inside."

She nodded without expression. "Yes, we'll see. Do you have any other questions?"

Justin started to shake his head, then stopped. "Um. How are the health benefits?"

The old man sat alone in his wheelchair, staring out the window, staring down at the street below, the torn awning of the secondhand shop, the sign-plastered window of the liquor store, the groaning bus that farted black smoke as it rumbled past. The same view every day, the same people, hurrying, hunched over, caught in the desperate struggle to keep up with their own lives. The old man grunted and pushed his wheelchair backward away from the window.

In the corner, a television set babbled soundlessly. Eleven minutes of shallow people pretending to be concerned, then four minutes of even shallower people explaining all the different ways a person could smell bad. Lather, rinse, repeat four times an hour. "Pfeh." He turned away from it, facing the front door instead.

At last, he heard the sound of a key in the upper deadbolt, the second deadbolt, and finally the bottom one. Justin pushed his way in, carrying two grocery bags. "I bought a chicken for dinner, Dad. Roast chicken, just the way you like it. To celebrate."

"You're late. I need to pee. You want me to piss my pants again?"

"It's only five." Justin put the bags on the kitchen table and came back to his father. He bent and kissed the old man's forehead, then went around to the back of the chair to push him to the bathroom. "Come on, let's get you taken care of, and then I'll start dinner. I bought a roast chicken at the market. Your favorite. To celebrate."

"I'm not in the mood for chicken. Chicken is Sunday. Why were you late? Why didn't you call? Help me onto the toilet."

"I went for a job interview. And that's why we're having chicken."

"You got a job? You can't get a job. Who's going to take care of me?"

"I'll still be here. It's a service job. I can set my own hours. And I haven't accepted yet."

"What kind of a job is it?"

"It's a very good one. It's for the Department of Enabled Actuarial Transitional Health. I could make enough money I could even hire a part-time nurse for you, if you want."

"I don't want a nurse. And what's the Department of whatever you said anyway? What are you going to do for them? Stare at a screen all day? You already do that here. I'm done. You can help me off the toilet now. I can pull up my own pants. I'm not a baby."

"Yes, Dad. Let me wash my hands now and I'll start dinner."

Justin wheeled his father into the apartment's tiny kitchen. It would make the preparation of dinner a little more difficult, but it was easier than listening to complaints from the other room, always punctuated with calls of, "What? What'd you say? I can't hear you!"

Justin cut slices of chicken, cut them into chewable pieces, placed them carefully on his father's plate. Rice and peas and salad. A glass of iced tea for each.

They ate in silence, the old man chewing each piece of chicken slowly and carefully because his teeth hurt. Finally, he said, " 'Course, on the other hand, if you had a job, you wouldn't be underfoot all day, annoying the hell out of me with your constant complaining."

"Yes, you'd have some quiet time for yourself."

"Hmpf. Like I need that. Nobody ever comes to visit anyway."

"You could go down to the park."

"It's not safe. I'd rather stay here." He peered across the table. "What kind of a job is it?"

"The Department of Enabled Actuarial Transitional Health. I'd be a—a field worker. A service provider."

"Service provider? What's that mean?"

"If I take the job. I'd be a—a deathman. But I'm not sure I'm going to take the job."

"A deathman. Hah. Everybody thinks about it, but nobody ever wants to actually do it. Serve death? Uh-uh. Scares the screaming hell out of them. But it's still gotta be done. Like collecting garbage or cleaning sewers. Society breaks down if nobody does it." The old man grumbled. "At least it's clean work. You wouldn't come home stinking of garbage or shit."

"No, I guess I wouldn't."

"They pay good?"

"Twelve hundred and fifty dollars per service, to start—plus expenses, if any, like transportation. I can set my own hours. If I get assigned to a major facility, I can make several thousand dollars a day."

"That's a lot of money."

"Death isn't cheap, Dad."

"'Course money isn't worth anything if you don't have your health."

"You're right about that."

"You gonna take the job?"

"I don't know. I have to go back on Monday."

"This thing about death. They say it's a public service. Cleaning up the sick and old and useless. Because they're a drain on the public body. Parasites. You're helping society. Making the world a better place. Make more room for the real people."

The old man paused to pick apart a stringy piece of chicken with his fingers. "When I was your age . . . except your mom didn't want me to. Might have done it anyway, except you came along. But I looked into it, I did. Lots of us did. Easy work, easy money." He popped the meat into his mouth and chewed for a bit. "Takes a special somethin', though. You gotta feel for people, like you're doin' them a service, helpin' them along. Otherwise, y'know, y'start to feel bad about yourself. Whatever. If you have the backbone for it, it's good work. Nobody ever gives you shit. That's for sure."

Justin stopped. He laid his fork down next to his plate. And considered carefully what his father had just said.

"Do you want me to take the job?"

"Ahh, you'll do what you want to do. You always do. You never listened to me in the past, why would you listen to me now?"

"I want your opinion. Your advice."

"My advice? Hah. Make up your own mind. I wish I had. If I had, you wouldn't be here nagging the hell out of me."

"It's really very simple," the training supervisor said. "You get a gray suit, a gray car, gray gloves. You go in, you lay your hands on them, they transition peacefully and without pain. That's really all that's required. And if that's all you ever did, you'd be earning your salary.

"But the good caseworkers, they make the service personal. They respect their clients, they sit with them and chat for a bit. They take the time to know them, learn something about who they are and how they lived and what makes their lives special and worth remembering. If you can see them as real people, then you can give them their transition as a gift of release. Some agents just go in and out, wham-bam-thank-you-ma'am. But the great agents take the time to make sure the client is ready to go. Every case is different. Your job, your real job, is to be a generous listener. In a sense, you have to fall in love with each client, look for the love in their hearts and the dignity in their eyes. Give them peace in their soul and you can feel good about giving them an easy and painless release."

Justin nodded slowly, hearing the words but not yet understanding the depth of meaning. All of the words, they were starting to blur together like so much jargon. In butt-simple language, the deathman kills people. He takes lives. He does it legally. As a service of a benevolent society. He does it with a transition warrant, signed by a panel of three judges who have reviewed the life-quality of the client and determined that it has depreciated beyond recovery. More jargon.

It's still death.

"Yes," agreed the training supervisor, even before Justin could finish speaking it aloud. "Everybody has that conversation. *That* one. The one about morality and conscience and isn't this a mortal sin? No, it isn't. We'd be merciful to a horse with a broken leg or a dog with distemper, wouldn't we? Why would we want to deny such a generous mercy to our loved ones? When you can achieve that level of understanding, then you can see your job as what it truly is—a service."

"I understand what you're saying," Justin replied. "It's going to take me a while to actually experience it that way."

"Don't worry. You will. Eventually. If you stick with it."

The hospital smelled of disinfectant and flowers and air freshener. The lights were too bright. His footsteps sounded heavy on the floor, as if his shoes were soled with granite. Maybe it was the way that people turned to look at him, then turned hastily away.

A crisp gray suit, shiny gray shoes, a pair of silent gray gloves. Except he wasn't wearing the gloves yet. Not yet. Not until the client was ready. But they still recognized him, still knew why he was here.

Justin felt uneasy; he hoped it didn't show. Could they tell that this was his first case, his first time? His face flushed with embarrassment. He bit his lips tightly together and hoped it looked like determination.

Room 223. Mrs. Bellini.

He had to ask at the nurse's station. The male nurse barely glanced up. "You should have been here a week ago. We need the bed."

"Paperwork," mumbled Justin.

The nurse jerked a thumb over his shoulder. "Back there." He punched a button on his phone. "Yeah, I've got a code gray. I'll need a DC and a gurney in five. No, make it ten. The gray's a noob."

Justin followed the general direction, found the room, and gently pushed the door open. "Mrs. Bellini?"

She didn't answer. She was a small still form beneath a pale blanket. Her skin was sallow. She had an IV in her left arm. What was left of her hair hung down in yellow strings. She was intubated and her breath rasped painfully. Her yellow eyes were open, staring blankly at the ceiling.

"Mrs. Bellini?" Justin moved into her field of view. Her eyes flicked sideways, then drifted away. "Mrs. Bellini, do you know who I am? Do you know why I'm here?"

No answer.

"My name is Justin. I'm here to ease your transition."

She lifted her right hand as if to wave him away. He stepped back. The hand fluttered helplessly in the air, like an injured bird. It had a life of its own.

Justin glanced around, grabbed a chair, and pulled it close. He sat down and leaned forward. Because he didn't know what else to do, he reached out and took her hand. Her bony fingers wrapped tightly around his.

"Do you know why I'm here?"

She blinked. Once, twice. She moved her head, almost a nod.

"That's good, yes."

He started to say, "Is there anything I can do for you—" then stopped himself. She couldn't speak. She didn't have the physical strength to write a note. He couldn't even offer her a sip of water. She was helpless beneath the tubes and wires.

"All right," he said. "This won't take long." He reached into the inside pocket of his coat and pulled out his gray gloves.

Her eyes widened as she watched. Justin hesitated. He stopped fumbling with the gloves and just met her gaze. He watched as her eyes filled with tears. Finally, he said, "It's time to go, sweetheart." He finished pulling on the gloves. They felt cold and smooth, they tingled. He closed his eyes and issued a wordless prayer to himself for strength, then reached over and took her hand again, pressing it between both of his. He held it for a long time, waiting and listening to the sound of her breath leaving her body for the last time.

The first few weeks, most of his clients were like Mrs. Bellini. A few could talk. Some of them said, "Bless you," or "Thank you."

One old man called him something in Italian. Justin wasn't sure if it was a good thing or not.

A nine-year-old girl, only a few wispy strands of hair left on her head—her sunken eyes never left him. In a voice like the rustle of parchment she asked if it would hurt. "No," Justin promised. "It will be just like going to sleep."

"Will I go to heaven?"

The question startled him. "What do you think?"

"I took my sister's doll and broke it. Isn't that a sin?"

"Did you apologize to her?"

"Yes. But I didn't mean it. Daddy made me."

"Are you sorry now?"

"Yes, please. I don't want to go to hell."

"Well, I'm pretty sure that God doesn't send little girls to hell. Especially not someone as sweet and honest as you."

That seemed to satisfy her. "Okay," she said quietly, and a moment later, "I'm ready."

Justin stepped out of the way, so Mom and Dad could hug their little girl one more time. He used the moment to pull on his gray gloves, still so cold and smooth. When the parents finally moved away from the bed, he sat down. "Okay, close your eyes," he whispered. "And now you count to three with me, and on three, you let go. Okay?"

On three, he took her hand in his.

On Thursday, Justin was sent to a small house in the suburbs, where a teenager had overdosed on drugs. The paramedics were just sliding the gurney into the back of the ambulance when he arrived. They looked at him, annoyed. Justin held up the transition warrant.

"He's just a kid."

"He's had his three strikes. He's out." Justin regretted the words even before he finished saying them.

"You don't believe in rehab?"

"I do, yes. But apparently this boy doesn't." He offered the warrant for their inspection.

Neither of the paramedics reached for it. One of them said, "We've seen that paperwork before. We know."

The other added, "We also know that in cases like this, you have the right to make an on-site adjudication."

The first one said, "But you don't get paid if you don't serve, do you?"

The second one nodded over Justin's shoulder. "That's his mom, over there. She's the one who called it in."

Justin looked. A worried-looking woman, clutching her sweater close to her. He turned back to the paramedics. "I can let him go. But you know we'll all be back here again in a week. Or a month."

"Or maybe not. Maybe when he finds out that a deathman let him live, just this one more time, maybe he'll straighten out. It's your call, of course. It's your conscience."

Justin put the gloves away, back into his inside coat pocket. He couldn't think of anything else to say, so he just turned and walked back to his car. The gray car.

Friday morning, Justin went to see his supervisor. He knocked politely on her door, waited for her to say, "Enter," then stepped quietly into the room.

Without looking up from the screen she was studying, she waved him to a chair. After a moment, she finished and turned to him. "Problem?"

"No. Yes. Maybe. I don't know."

She glanced at her watch. "Mm-hm. You're right on schedule. Three weeks. Which conversation are we going to have? The one where you tell me you can't do this anymore? Or the one where you ask for reassurance that you're doing the right thing?"

Justin flushed with embarrassment. "I guess I'm not the first person to have . . . I guess you could say, misgivings."

She laughed gently. "No. You're not the first. Which one was it? The little girl?"

"No. She was sweet. It was easy because she understood we were ending her pain. And she knew she was loved. No, it was the boy last night."

"The drug overdose?"

"Uh-huh."

"You gave him a pass."

"Yes."

"The paramedics talked you out of it?"

"And his mother was watching."

"Yes, I heard. In fact, that's why I expected you this morning. Everybody gets one of those warrants, sooner or later." She added, "You did the right thing. You erred on the side of caution. Maybe the boy will learn, maybe he won't. Probably he won't. But if there's even the slightest chance that he will, you were right to do what you did. It doesn't hurt you to be merciful. It doesn't hurt us."

She took a deep breath. "But sometimes, it does hurt the client. Sometimes in our eagerness to be the nice guy, sometimes all we do is extend the pain, stretch it out a little longer than it needs to be. It's a judgment call, and I promise you, I'll always stand behind you, no matter what you decide in such a case. As far as I'm concerned, you're a deathman, you don't make mistakes. But just be aware—sometimes, in some cases, it happens that being merciful isn't the most merciful thing you can do. Do you understand what I'm saying?"

Justin nodded. "I was thinking about his mother. I didn't sleep very well last night. If I had . . . exercised the transition warrant, the boy would be out of his pain. And so would the mom. I mean, yes, she'd have to deal with her grief for a while, but the warrant would have released her from the trap she was in. This way, he goes to the hospital, the clinic, the rehab center, he begins the cycle all over again, one more time—and the mom, she has to go through the whole cycle again, too. Until the next time she finds him on the floor choking on his vomit. I could have spared her that pain. How many weeks or months or even years?"

Justin's supervisor nodded. "What you just said—that's true compassion."

"It's in the training. I paid attention."

"Yes, you did."

"I get it now. It's not just about the client. It's about the client's family—releasing them from their burdens, too. That's what I'm upset about. I'm not sure I did that woman any favor."

"No, you probably didn't. Oh, if you were to ask her, she'd say you did, and she'd be enormously grateful. But in actuality, no. Her quality of life will not improve as long as she is carrying the burden of that boy and his addiction. No, Justin, you didn't do anything wrong last night. It's a lesson we all have to learn. Mercy isn't always nice. Sometimes mercy is ruthless."

She sighed, not in exhaustion but in sympathy. "Do you need to take some personal time?"

Justin shook his head. "I'm fine. I think."

"If you want to take the rest of the day, or even a couple of days, go ahead."

"Thank you," Justin said, rising. "I, uh—I think maybe I should. Thank you."

On the way out, Justin ran into the dispatch officer. He was holding a fresh warrant.

"Um, no, I probably shouldn't. I'm supposed to take a personal day."

"Sure, okay. No problem. I was just thinking convenience."

Justin rubbed his nose. "Okay." He took the transition warrant and shoved it into his coat pocket without looking at it. "I can take care of it tonight."

"Or tomorrow," said the officer. "Whenever it's convenient. The client isn't going anywhere."

In the morning, Justin helped his father out of bed and into the bathroom. He sat him down on the plastic chair in the shower and helped him bathe, using a showerhead on a flexible hose so the old man wouldn't have to twist or turn more than necessary.

After he dressed his father, he lifted him into the wheelchair and rolled him into the kitchen. "Would you like some bacon and eggs this morning, Dad?"

"Too expensive. Why are you spending all this money? Oatmeal."

"We can afford it now. Remember, I have a job."

"Eggs and bacon. Cholesterol and fat. Trying to kill me, are you?"

"No, Dad. I'm trying to make you happy. Sunny-side up? Or scrambled?"

"Scrambled. Hmpf."

"And what channel would you like today? History or Animals or National Geographic?"

"Doesn't matter, they're all the same. And don't get so uppity. I know how to use the remote."

"Yes, you do know. It's right there for you."

"Don't you have to go to work already?"

"Not today. I'm taking a personal day."

"They fired you already?"

"No, Dad. They said I did good. They just want me to have some time to—to think about some things. It's part of the job."

"Hmpf. I know what happens when you start thinking. You tie yourself in a knot. You get all stuck. Well, don't you do that now. You have a good job. It keeps us in bacon and eggs. Don't you give up now. What? No toast?"

"It's in the toaster, just a minute more. And no, I'm not giving up my job. I'm just—sorting some things out."

"Sorting? Hah. Nothing to sort. Just do it. Don't be a damn wussy."

While his father sorted through his breakfast, complaining his way through the meal, Justin busied himself with little things. Washing the pan, putting away the bread, pouring himself a cup of coffee. His gray coat was on the back of his chair. He picked it up and started for the closet, then remembered the unfulfilled warrant in the pocket.

The warrant had a blue stripe across the top. He'd never gotten one of those before. It meant "Optional." To be exercised at the discretion of the server. Another judgment call.

Actually, it was an acknowledgment. This is how much we trust you now.

He didn't open it, he just tapped it against his fist for a moment, thinking. Remembering his orientation, remembering his training. Remembering what his supervisor had said. "You're not just releasing the client, you're releasing the family as well."

Maybe she'd said it to make this kind of decision easier, but in Justin's mind, no—it only complicated the matter. Who was he really serving?

But he already knew the answer to that one, too. Again, from his training. Step back from the immediate circumstances. You're serving everyone. Figure out where the real service is and you'll know what to do.

He shook away the thought. In theory, it was an easy conversation. In practice, it wasn't about conversation. He unfolded the warrant without looking at it. Okay. If nothing else, it would get him out of the apartment for a bit. Maybe some fresh air, a walk through the park, a chance to sit and not think.

The old man wheeled himself into the living room. "You're doing it, boy, aren't you? Thinking yourself into a corner."

"No, Dad. I'm not thinking at all."

"Well then, why don't you do something useful? Go to work. Make some more money."

"Yes, that's probably a good idea." He glanced down at the paper in his hand. He wasn't surprised. He'd been expecting it. All the myriad little conversations fluttered around him for a moment, then evaporated. He understood.

He understood everything.

He reached into his inside coat pocket.

He began pulling on his gloves.

"Dad? Have I told you today how much I love you?"

"To everything, there is a season and a time for every purpose under Heaven. A time to be born, and a time to die." To which we might add, "Especially in the Twilight Zone."

# THE WRITING ON THE WASHROOM WALL

Jane Lindskold

Words written in purple ink. Words speaking of destiny, warning of death. Marj tries hard to deny that these words are written to her, but eventually she must accept that someone is speaking to her from . . . the Twilight Zone.

The words were pursuing her.

Aghast, Marj stared at what was written on the right side of the bathroom stall. Amid the names of rock bands, recitations of undying love, mild obscenities, and even a fairly good limerick was the Palmer-method perfect handwriting she'd already seen twice that day. The words, written in what looked like dark purple marker, were simple.

*Why do you wait? Neither destiny nor death can be denied.*

Shivering, Marj tore off a length of toilet paper but, as she finished her business, she couldn't rip her attention from the words.

"Neither destiny nor death can be denied," she murmured.

Then the chiming of the clock on the campus green reminded her that other, more immediate (at least she hoped more immediate) responsibilities also could not be denied.

Tucking herself back into order, Marj quickly washed her hands. She studied her reflection in the mirror as she touched up her makeup and hair. Neat brown locks professionally cut in a professional style. Green eyes that contact lenses made just a little brighter. A trim figure set off well by a stylish suit. Expression, just a little worried . . .

Marj schooled her features to project order and confidence, then, half-running, hurried to the second floor lecture hall.

As Marj moved to take her place behind the podium on the raised dais that dominated the hall, the other words in purple ink she had read that day echoed counterpoint to the tap of her low-heeled pumps against the floor.

*Why do you wait? Surrender to fate.*

That one had been written across a birthday card stacked on top of her mail in the Psych Department main office when she'd come in that morning. She'd thought the inscription was a department prank—in rather bad taste—but when she'd gone to show the envelope to the secretary, she couldn't find it.

*Why do you wait? Open your heart.*

That had been written on the reverse of a lawn service flyer stuffed into the mailbox for her small house. She'd found the note when she'd stopped home on her way to a birthday lunch with her mom.

Although these two ominous warnings had shaken her, Marj had eventually concluded that they must be student pranks. Although she did not precisely advertise where she lived, the information could be found easily enough. The note defacing her birthday card would have been easier still to pull off, but this last one?

Who would have known she was going to stop in that particular ladies' room? She certainly hadn't intended to do so. She'd been on her way back to her office from lunch when one of her students had stopped her with a question. By the time they had finished their impromptu conference, Marj had realized she didn't have time to go all the way back to the Psych Department and had raced for the faculty lounge.

That was another puzzling element. Normally, students—except for a few privileged graduate assistants—did not have access to the faculty lounge. How did the graffiti artist get into the private bathroom?

Of course, if it was a faculty member . . .

A slight rise in the hum of student chatter alerted Marj that her failure to hook up her laptop and begin her lecture on schedule had been noticed.

She resumed her focus with some effort, unpacked the laptop, and set the first of her slides running.

"Good afternoon," she said, deciding that apologizing would be an error, would make her vulnerable. "Today we're going to begin a detailed examination of Freud's early theories."

"Dr. McKinley!" The interruption came from Ivy Perkins, a young woman Marj already knew to be a disruptive element. "I really don't understand why we're bothering with Freud at all. I've been doing some independent reading . . ."

Pausing to shape her pretty mouth into a slight, self-deprecating moue, Ivy Perkins turned her profile to her assembled classmates. The expression said more clearly than words, *I know you know that I'm smart and ambitious. I'm also terribly pleased with myself.*

Marj thought Ivy knew she was sending the first message, but was she aware of the second?

"Yes, Miss Perkins?" Marj prompted dryly.

"Not only have Freud's theories been largely discredited, but there is ample evidence that he falsified some of his case studies when the data did not support his conclusions."

Clearly, Young Miss Perfect thought she was dropping a bombshell. Equally clearly, most of her classmates didn't care. A few looked vaguely interested, but since this discussion wouldn't be on any test, most were staring down at their crotches, believing for some reason that this would conceal their covert texting or video-game play.

*I suppose,* Marj thought with resigned viciousness, *it's better that they're playing with electronics rather than with themselves—which is what it looks like they're doing, or would if they didn't look so bored.*

At least Young Miss Perfect wasn't bored, so Marj decided to address her question.

"Miss . . ." Marj swallowed the impulse to say "Perfect," and corrected it to "Perkins," "what you are saying is absolutely incontestable. However, whatever the flaws—and they are many—Freud's theories remain the bedrock of modern psychology. All the approaches that have come after have been in reaction to those early proposals. Without understanding Freud, you cannot understand anything that has come since."

Miss Perkins looked offended. "I don't see why we need to memorize failed theories. It seems to me that we're wasting a lot of time learning what we will need to unlearn."

"Perhaps," Marj said, "but understanding reaction is very basic to psychology—both the science and the practice. If you cannot resign yourself to attending to the material for any other reason, then consider it practice in understanding what is, in many ways, a classic parent/child reaction pattern."

"With Freud as the parent," Miss Perkins said brightly.

"And as a child of sorts," Marj agreed, "for he was reacting to what he saw as the superstitions and religious restrictions that he felt were crippling human intellectual development."

"Interesting," Miss Perkins said.

Marj could tell the young woman would have liked to continue the discussion, but although the forty-seven other students might have appreciated the distraction, they would only have done so until they realized an exam was coming. Then they would have whined and panicked about how "not fair" Dr. McKinley was being, expecting them to learn without bullet points.

So Marj lectured on ids, egos, and superegos for the next forty minutes. Then she managed to slip out before Ivy Perkins could corral her for a heart-to-heart.

Most days, Marj probably wouldn't have minded. At least Ivy Perkins cared about the material. She'd already declared her major. Most of the department had admitted that they felt as if they were auditioning for the dubious distinction of being her adviser.

*Ivy Perkins cares,* Marj thought as she slid behind the wheel of her car. *So many of the students don't even attend physically. Those who bother to show up are often mentally absent. Was I like Ivy, bright, eager, challenging?*

Marj considered, exchanged a rueful smile with her reflection in the rearview mirror.

*Probably. I was so grimly serious, so determined to break the chains that bound me—poverty, superstition, the lack of education that held my family back. Reaction, again. Here I am with both my Ph.D. in Psychology and my M.D., teaching "Introduction to Psych," despite the fact that I could have a much more lucrative private practice. Why? Because I want to get the word out. There is no mystery we cannot solve. The intellect rules. Nothing will hold you back if you don't let it.*

Marj glanced around to check a four-way stop. Written neatly at the top of the stop sign were four too-familiar words: *Destiny cannot be denied.*

Even though another car was starting to roll forward, Marj floored the gas and rocketed through the intersection.

"Oh, yeah?" she said. Only after the words had echoed around her car did she wonder just to whom she was speaking.

The next morning, Marj woke feeling that her panic had been utterly and completely stupid.

Since she lived alone, she settled for lecturing her two cats while they crunched through their breakfast kibble.

"A fraternity stunt. A viral marketing gimmick. I bet if I cruised the 'Net I'd find the messages already being discussed."

But she didn't check the 'Net. The explanation fit too perfectly, relieved her anxiety almost completely.

*Reaction,* she thought as she read a new note in which purple ink warned her not to wait, to "Awaken. Open. Permit yourself to see." *That's why I responded as if those notes were to me in person. Probably didn't help that the first one I saw was on a birthday card. Reaction, cultivated by a childhood steeped in superstition. Next thing I know I'll be making signs against the evil eye and crossing myself before I enter a dark room.*

She sniffed, crumpled the note (this time written on the envelope holding her bank statement), and tossed it into the trash. Her sense of superiority lasted all the way to dinner that night.

The Psych Department was entertaining Dr. Juan Schimdt, a visiting lecturer from Argentina. That evening there was a private banquet followed by an informal discussion of the role psychology played in all aspects of Argentinian society.

"In my country, psychoanalysis is part of daily life," Dr. Schimdt explained as they sat over their coffee. "There is no shame associated with seeing a 'shrink.' Nor is such a derogatory term—it is derived, as you know, from 'headshrinker,' which is associated with witchcraft—employed for those who practice the profession. Our people are curious as to how the subconscious mind affects conscious decisions, even how it affects personal preferences."

"Preferences?" asked Paul Adams, the department chair. "Isn't that going a bit far?"

"Not at all," Dr. Schimdt replied. "Take Dr. McKinley as an example. I have noticed that although the food here is excellent, she has avoided both the soup and the bread."

Marj hated being singled out, but decided to be polite.

She grinned in a self-deprecatory fashion. "I don't much care for oregano, and both were rather heavily seasoned with it."

"I thought that might be the reason," Dr. Schimdt said, obviously pleased with himself. "I noticed you ate heartily from both your main course and dessert."

"Maybe I was saving space for what I liked," Marj challenged.

The guest lecturer waggled a finger at her. "But you have already admitted to not liking the taste of oregano. I find that very interesting, because your full name is not 'Margery,' as one might assume from hearing you called 'Marj,' but 'Marjoram.' I noticed this on your department's roster. And the scientific name for 'marjoram' is 'origanum.' Now, I am not saying this is so in your case but, if I had a client who disliked very much something for which he was named, I would ask him whether the reaction was to the taste or to the name."

Dr. Schimdt leaned back and folded his hands on his little paunch, obviously pleased with this demonstration of both his erudition and his psychological acumen.

Dr. Adams broke the uncomfortable silence that followed with a somewhat forced chuckle. "Well, I dislike chocolate, a distaste my wife assures me makes me subhuman. What would you make of that?"

Dr. Schimdt laughed and went into an involved diagnosis of the chair's presumed psychology that set most of the table laughing. Marj realized that her own tension had made her react so strongly to being singled out.

*If I wasn't so strung out already,* she thought, *I would have also realized that I am one of the few unattached women here. What I was being subjected to was South American gallantry, not psychoanalysis.*

She rejoined the conversation, but the little voice in her head wouldn't let the matter rest.

*But he was right, wasn't he? You have hated your name, ever since that teacher in second grade looked at you and said, "Like the cooking herb?" and everybody laughed. Then in fourth grade there was that girl who insisted on calling you "Margarine." There was the boy who called you "Toe-Jam." Was that the same year? No. Fifth grade.*

When dinner and discussion had ended, Marj made sure she wasn't the first to leave. She didn't want anyone to think she was in a snit. In her eagerness to make a good impression, she found herself walking out with the guest lecturer after everyone else had left.

"I am sorry," Dr. Schimdt said, "if I embarrassed you at dinner. I did not intend to do so."

"That's all right," Marj said, then added impulsively, "You were completely right. I've always hated that name. I was teased over it when I was a kid. Besides, I always thought it sounded ugly. My grandmother named me: Marjoram Sweet McKinley."

"You could change it," Dr. Schimdt said, "couldn't you?"

"My name?"

"Why live with something you dislike? There is no need, is there? Isn't getting beyond our pasts and moving into a healthy future what our profession is all about?"

They'd reached the parking lot. Marj felt huge relief as Dr. Schimdt turned in the direction of the nice hotel where college guests were always put up.

"May I give you a ride?" she said, gesturing toward her car. She didn't really want to do so, but felt she must offer.

"The hotel is only a few blocks away," the lecturer said. "And after that dinner, I need the exercise." He gave a sly, playful grin. "After all, I ate not only the main course and the dessert, but the soup and bread as well. Good night, Dr. McKinley."

"Good night."

Marj drove home, thinking about holding onto the past, rejecting the past. She kept her gaze on the street, trying not to be distracted by messages in purple ink. She couldn't avoid the one written across the top piece of mail in the stack waiting for her.

*Closing your eyes only causes you to run into things.*

"Confucius say . . ." Marj snarled, ripping the envelope in half.

Over the next few days, Marj did a pretty good job of ignoring the purple writing, although it popped up everywhere, including, with peculiar persistence, when she was in the washroom.

*Catching me with my pants down?* Marj thought wryly. *Isn't that an expression for "off guard"?*

She was mildly puzzled no one else had mentioned the writing. She guessed that everyone was already in on the gimmick, that it was old news. She thought about mentioning what she'd seen, but didn't want to seem behind the times.

Then her chicken noodle soup started talking to her.

"I hadn't realized the cafeteria was serving alphabet soup," she said, stirring the broth so the white letters swirled and danced.

Paul Adams, the Psych Department chair with whom she was dining so they could go over a committee report, blinked. "Are they? I didn't get soup."

Marj watched the letters settle, a few, as always, floating for a moment longer than the rest. These settled into orderly lines: *Accept your gift. Death awaits. Why wait?*

Her mouth went dry. She blinked, thought about showing Paul the words, felt terrified he wouldn't see them.

"Maybe it's just barley," Marj managed as she spooned up the offending letters and swallowed them. "Now, about the library committee . . ."

Later that day, keeping office hours for the students who never came, Marj forced herself to concentrate on her notes for a new seminar she was teaching.

She tilted the contents of the little teapot she kept by her desk into her mug. Only a thin stream of pale liquid came out. Lifting the lid, Marj peeked inside. The few stray tea leaves that always escaped her strainer arranged themselves into curving letters.

*Death cannot be denied.*

Swallowing a scream, Marj dropped the pot onto to the carpet. The driblets of tea spilled out, writing in cursive on the tightly woven industrial carpet: *Destiny cannot be denied.*

Shutting down her computer, Marj called to the office secretary, "I'm leaving early. If anyone wants me, I'll be back on Monday."

"Have a good weekend!" came the cheerful reply.

*As if . . .* Marj thought.

At home, no neatly scripted messages in purple ink defaced her mail. Marj wanted to hope that the viral campaign was over, but she no longer believed that threadbare excuse.

If a viral marketing campaign of that magnitude had been going on, someone would have mentioned it, even if only to question who would bear the cost of cleanup.

Ivy Perkins would have wanted to discuss the psychological implications of vaguely threatening messages. Why were they written in a shades of purple? The other students would have actually gotten into that discussion.

No. This had been meant for her from the start, and when she had found an excuse to ignore the written messages, a new, less explicable avenue had been found.

"I'm going crazy . . ." Marj wailed, and took little comfort when both cats rubbed themselves against her ankles, rumbling comforting purrs. "What am I going to do? Go to a shrink?"

Her laughter echoed harsh and shrill off the walls. "Physician, heal thyself! If the word got around that I was having a breakdown, my reputation would be shot. Tenure or not, the news could cost me my job. Extenuating circumstances. I might lose my license. Find myself on the streets."

Marj wished Dr. Schimdt was still in the area. She could consult him. Then he'd go safely back to Argentina, out of her world. He wouldn't tell anyone anything.

"No. Couldn't talk to him," Marj babbled, picking up Poppet and squishing her face into the cat's long fur. "There's e-mail. If he thought I was becoming dangerously deluded, he might report to the department. Later, he might mention the case in one of his lectures. 'The Spice Girl Who Lost Her Mind.' God! That would be horrible."

Holding the vaguely protesting Poppet, Marj paced back and

forth. Normally, she didn't drink more than the occasional glass of wine with a meal, preferring tea or coffee, but now she feared what she'd see in the tea leaves. She'd never heard of coffee grounds having significance, but she'd never heard of any of this . . .

A glass of whiskey. She had a bottle she'd bought when her brother was visiting. On the rocks. She'd be careful not to spill anything. No words uncoiling, written in whiskey on her polished hardwood floors.

An hour later, Marj was soundly drunk. Rather than the alcohol numbing her fears, it intensified her sensation of dread. She avoided gazing in anything that reflected, even tossing a towel over the polished front of her infrequently used oven.

She didn't so much fall asleep as pass out on the sofa. When she woke in the middle of the night, she was disoriented. Her mouth was furry and dry. A hangover threatened behind her eyes, making remembering just why she'd fallen asleep on the sofa, rather than in her bed, hard to recall.

Stumbling to the bathroom, Marj flipped on the light. Her reflection looked back at her from the mirror. Her own reflection and something else, a wavering image of a second face, a much older face, but one that resembled her own.

Marj leaned forward. Her reflection superimposed itself over the phantom image, sharpening it, adding details. Marj felt a horrified sensation that the image was swallowing her.

"Grandma Gloria?"

The lips moved, deep creases around them writing grotesque prophecies of age over Marj's much younger features.

"Why haven't you accepted my gift?" the lips shaped, the words perfectly clear, although there was no sound.

"Your gift?"

"My gift. I gave you a gift."

Marj shook her head, the violent action causing her hangover to germinate and her vision to swim.

"No, Grandma, you couldn't have sent me a gift. You're dead."

Marj woke late the next morning, sprawled on her bed, still fully dressed. Poppet was pressed against her side, Tuffet in the curl behind her knees. The hangover played drums in her head. Her muscles ached.

A hot shower helped amend both sets of aches. Not until Marj was on her second cup of coffee, and daring a nibble on a slightly stale croissant, did she consider what she had seen the night before.

"Grandma Gloria," she said to Tuffet. "Something about a gift. But she died when I was a child. Why would I have such a dream now?"

Tuffet chattered at a bird or squirrel outside the window.

Glancing over to see what had the cat's attention, Marj saw Grandma Gloria staring back at her.

Dropping her coffee mug, Marj screamed.

Grandma Gloria—or rather, her reflection, for now Marj realized she could see through the image—made a gesture as if writing with the index finger of her right hand.

The puddle of spilled coffee on the table elongated into words: *Why do you wait? Neither death nor destiny can be denied.*

"Are you threatening me?" Marj said, her voice shaking. "Are you some omen of death?"

*No,* Grandma Gloria wrote. *You are threatening you. Accept my gift.*

"Gift?" Marj said. "If you mean the savings bond you left me, I was waiting to cash it until I needed . . ."

*NO!* Grandma Gloria shook her head disapprovingly. *How long will you deny me? Deny your destiny? Deny what I knew you to be?*

"I don't know what you're talking about," Marj said, although she was beginning to remember.

*Come then . . .*

A gnarled hand, too solid to be a mere reflection, emerged from the windowpane. Tuffet hissed, but the cat's warning came too late. The hand grasped Marj firmly by her right earlobe and dragged her in the direction of the window.

"I will show you," came a commanding voice Marj would have sworn she had forgotten, but was unmistakably that of her grandmother. "I will show you what you have never forgotten."

Marj felt herself enter the reflection, moving through light that shifted like molten quicksilver, coating her body, covering her, compacting her, packing her into herself as she had been at age six.

Child Marj knelt next to a low table. Its polished teak surface was all but swathed beneath a fringed shawl of red damask. Set on the shawl were several items: a crystal globe, a small pitcher and matching bowl, an overly thick deck of cards.

The room was lit by candles set in high sconces, these positioned so that their glow illuminated the table but left the rest of the room in shadow. Incense saturated the air of the enclosed room with the smoky scent of sandalwood.

The ringing sound of brass against brass and the aroma of freshly brewed tea announced the arrival of Grandma Gloria.

Grandma's attire was quite different from how she normally dressed. Instead of a tidy floral print housedress, nylons, and comfortable shoes, she wore a long skirt that came nearly to the floor and a full-sleeved blouse trimmed with lace and thick with embroidery. Both were so dark a purple that they were almost black. She had a fancy velvet shawl over her shoulders, and another tied over her skirt. Her hair was wrapped under a scarf. The brass chimes Marj had heard came from rows of bracelets that hung heavy on her wrists.

As the old woman set down the tea tray she had been carrying, she gave Marj a hearty smile that—despite its cheer, or maybe because of it, since Marj didn't think of her grandmother as particularly cheerful—managed to scare Marj right down to her neat, white bobby socks.

"Well, Marjoram, are you ready for our little game?"

"Marj . . ."

"Excuse me?"

Marj looked down at her knotted fingers. "Marj. My name is Marj. I don't like being called Marjoram."

"But Marjoram is a wonderful name, full of significance. Do you know what marjoram is?"

"A plant."

"Yes, but it is a wonderful type of plant. A type called an 'herb.'"

"My friend Amy's dad is named Herb."

"Not at all the same. Can we get back to the point?"

"You won't call me 'Marjoram'?"

From somewhere under the child, Adult Marj applauded this reply. Grandma Gloria obviously didn't agree. A quick flash of anger erased the carefully genial expression she had been maintaining.

"I want you to understand what a wonderful name you have been given. Marjoram is a cure-all."

"What's that?"

"It's a special medicine that can make many sicknesses go away."

Little Marj didn't say anything, but her out-thrust lower lip made quite clear that learning this had done nothing to improve her opinion of her namesake plant.

*Poor psychology,* thought Adult Marj. *What child thinks anything good about medicine? It's only when you get older that pills and ointments are appreciated.*

Grandma Gloria sighed. "Well, 'Marjoram' is a very special name, and a very pretty plant. I'll show you it in my garden this summer when it is all covered with the flowers."

"What color?"

"White, just kissed with pink."

"I like pink."

Grandma Gloria seemed to decide that this constituted a truce. "Now, Granddaughter . . ."

*Not 'Marjoram,'* Adult Marj thought gleefully. *Round one to the kid.*

"I've brought you here to show you something wonderful about yourself. Our family has long had a gift for the Second Sight."

"What's that?"

"The ability to see what most people can't—things people don't believe are there."

"Like ghosts?"

"Maybe . . ." Grandma Gloria was cautious with her reply, obviously prepared to backpedal, but Little Marj didn't seem too worried.

"Is that why you're dressed like a witch, Grandma?"

"Like a witch?"

"I saw a movie where some kids went to a witch at a fair and she was dressed like you are, all fussy. The movie witch had big earrings, though. You don't have those."

"Did you like the witch?"

"She was okay, I guess."

"Well, I'm not a witch. I'm a seer."

"Because you have two eyes?"

"Two eyes?" Grandma Gloria looked seriously confused.

"I mean that Second Sight," Marj corrected herself. "It's not the same as having two eyes? Sometimes pirates have just one eye. They wear eye patches, then."

*Man, I was an annoying kid,* Marj thought, but she felt a little delight, too. She was remembering more and more now about her early childhood.

Lucky days, unlucky days, holy days. Going to Mass in a

church that was fully modernized in the best post–Vatican II style, but seeing another side of religion in the homes of older relatives where statuettes of saints leaking gore were proudly displayed and where the same Jesus the priest told them was gentle and mild hung tortured in elegant detail from the Cross.

The evil eye. Not stepping on a crack unless you broke your mother's back. Black cats. Not going under ladders. Don't open an umbrella inside the house. Don't speak ill of the dead.

Robins have red breasts because a robin pulled a thorn out of Jesus' forehead. Dead rooster proclaiming the resurrection. Animals kneel on Christmas Eve.

Religion and superstition, all blurred together in a storm of contradictions, a storm held together by a fearful logic that almost made sense.

Grandma Gloria had been at the heart of that storm. Other old ladies and sometimes old men came to see her. These people called Grandma a wise woman and praised her skills for healing with herbs and prayer. Sometimes Marj heard another word whispered: witch.

Grandma Gloria had seemed very much a witch on that day in her parlor when she had persuaded little Marj to look into the crystal ball on the table.

"Look and tell me what you see," Grandma had coaxed.

"Can I have a cup of tea?"

"After you look."

"With sugar?"

"And cookies. Now, look and tell me what you see."

And Marj had looked. At first she'd seen nothing but the candlelight giving back distorted images of the room, then . . .

"I see the church! Our church. There's a service. A coffin. Grandma! Grandma! You're in the coffin! You're dead!"

"So you remember now," Grandma Gloria said, her tone almost wistful.

Adult Marj found herself sitting across from her grandmother. They were in the same candlelit room, but now Marj was dressed not in Little Marj's party dress, white socks, and penny loafers, but her fluffy robe and slippers. There was even a small, damp spot on the sleeve of the robe where coffee had splashed when she'd dropped her mug.

"I remember. You tried to convince me that I had the Second Sight, that I should train to be your apprentice. I didn't want to have anything to do with it."

"I didn't try to convince you," Grandma reprimanded. "I proved it to you. You panicked. You ran away. You've been running ever since, what with your silly study of psychology—a fancy name for study of the spirit, the very thing I offered you when you were six."

"You offered me nothing of the sort! You tried to capture me in a well of superstition and fear, tried to make me part of this dark world." Marj gestured wildly with one hand and the candle flames flickered. "I wanted light, not shadows."

Grandma Gloria ignored her. "I am here to offer you another chance at the destiny you refused."

"What? Why now?"

"You were six. You are now thirty-six. The numbers are aligned."

"What if I don't want what you're offering?"

"You didn't want your name, but I notice it remains a part of you."

Marj blinked. "What does my name have to do with anything? I thought about changing it to 'Margery' when I went to college, but it would have been a hassle. Anyhow, changing a word wouldn't change me."

"Denying you have the Sight doesn't change the reality. You are gifted. Why must you deny your destiny?"

Grandma Gloria's words were silky, persuasive. Marj felt a desire to reach out for the crystal ball, to pour water in the basin, add a drop of oil, gaze into the liquid. Images would appear for her, as surely as writing had appeared on walls.

*Messages from the dead or from my own subconscious? Has my recent birthday given me a yearning to go back to the imagined security of childhood?*

Grandma Gloria's expression softened.

"I frightened you, child, all those years ago. I should have waited until you were older, but I had been blessed with a warning of my own near death. I knew you had the Sight, and I wished you to be my heir. Instead of winning you over, I chased you away. And because I wronged you, my soul cannot rest."

Unwilling pity touched Marj. Perhaps Grandma Gloria saw some sign of this and took heart. She leaned forward and picked up the deck of cards that rested on the table between them. From the thickness, Marj knew it must be a tarot deck.

"Can't you draw just one card?" Grandma pleaded. "See what it tells you?"

"I shuffle," Marj insisted, accepting the cards. "And cut."

"That is how it is always done."

The cards were worn, polished with long use, but crisp enough that they shuffled with appropriate clatter and snap. Marj riffled the pack together enough times that she was certain any attempt to stack the deck would have been defeated.

("But this is a dream," a small part of her mind screamed in protest. "This entire vision is a stacked deck.")

Marj cut the deck a half inch from the bottom, rather than near the middle as was usual. Then, peeking up through her lashes so she could see Grandma Gloria's reaction without the other realizing she was being observed, Marj held up the card for the older woman to see.

Instead of the satisfaction or smugness Marj had expected, she saw puzzlement flicker across the lined features.

"That isn't a card from my deck," Grandma whispered, and for the first time Marj looked to see what she'd drawn.

The card showed an androgynous figure in a chariot drawn by two horses, one black, one white. Although the horses were not pulling against each other, there was a sense that what kept them in cooperation was the firm confidence of the driver holding the reins.

"The Charioteer," Marj read the legend on the card. "You say this isn't what it looks like in your deck?"

"No. I always used the Rider-Waite deck. The Charioteer in that deck wears armor and his chariot is shown behind paired sphinxes, black and white." Grandma Gloria looked at Marj almost shyly. "Does this card say anything to you, child?"

"Balance," Marj said, speaking the first word that had come to mind when she looked at the card, "like in Plato's tale of the charioteer. Plato says that the soul is like a chariot pulled by two winged horses: the rough, passionate black horse and the powerful, spiritual white horse. Plato's message was that we need both horses but, unless the charioteer carefully manages his team, the chariot will go in circles and no progress will be made."

Marj felt her heart racing, words tumbling from her mouth almost before her mind could shape them.

"It's like Freud: the id, the ego, and the superego. The Id contains our base, animal passions. It is the fountain from which our spirit springs.

"The Ego embodies the rational self, the sense of 'I' as distinct from the rest of the universe. Various philosophers—Descartes, Kant, Hume, and others—sought to explain the Ego, feeling that if we understood the Ego, we would come closer to understanding the individual in relation to society at large.

"The Superego contains what we learn from our teachers, our advisors. The Superego is what harmonizes the Id and Ego. It provides an awareness that the universe is larger than ourselves, that we must function with an awareness of this greater scheme or become deluded that we are somehow central to all."

Grandma Gloria looked overwhelmed at this flood of words. Marj felt herself grinning.

"It's okay, Grandma. Really, it's okay. You want me to choose to accept what you call the Second Sight, but the way you present the choice it's as if I need to wrap myself up like a gypsy fortune-teller, get a deck of cards, and deny everything else I know. What this card is telling me is that I can have both. I can have it all. Black horse. White horse. Me at the reins."

She laughed. After an moment, Grandma Gloria laughed with her.

"Then I can rest?" the old woman asked, hesitant still.

"That's your choice," Marj said. "You've kept telling me that neither death nor destiny can be denied. You've been fighting death, trying to force me into a destiny you chose for me. Listen to your own words. You never were speaking to me. You were speaking to yourself."

And with that, Marj rose, bent, and kissed the old woman on one age-wrinkled cheek. There was a door visible now between two of the brightly burning candles, and Marj walked through it.

Marj was sitting at her kitchen table. She might have been tempted to believe that, after her rough night, she had drifted off to sleep again and spilled her coffee.

But words written with the coffee said: "Good-bye and God Bless."

And in her hand Marj grasped a tarot card emblazoned with the Charioteer.

Heart and head. Intellect and soul. Like Marj, we believe we must choose one over the other. The truth is so much more complex, so much more difficult. We all live between these two extremes. We all live in our own personal Twilight Zone.

# STANLEY'S
# *STATISTICS*

Jean Rabe

Meet, if you will, Stanley Rossini, a pleasant enough octogenarian who made his fortune writing best-selling police procedurals and whose thoughts are filled with the criminals and detectives who traipse through the big, bad city in his mind. Stanley worries about becoming a victim, like some of his fictional characters did, becoming one more statistic on a police blotter. One more number crunched. And so he lives in a small town, keeps all of his doors locked, and one day tries to feed his loneliness by inviting inside the wrong soul.

Josh didn't mind the smell of geezers. Good thing, since he spent a few hours every day—save Sundays and holidays—delivering food to their tidy little run-down homes.

The women usually smelled of bargain-brand perfumes they'd lathered on to war with the disinfectants sloshed all over their kitchens.

The men smelled musty, of old clothes slick-shiny-thin at the knees and elbows and a bit too baggy—shirts and pants that had an assortment of stinks and stains on the front from being dribbled on, and that Goodwill would flip a rejecting finger at if given the opportunity—but the geezers just couldn't part with because they lacked the disposable income and desire to go out shopping for something better. Sometimes the men also smelled of cheap cigars because on their pensions they couldn't afford the good kind, and of Vicks VapoRub or Bengay or some other pungent ointment Josh had learned to tolerate quite well.

He found Stanley Rossini to be a pleasant exception to the rest of his clients, and so he often took his proverbial sweet time when delivering Stanley's Meals on Wheels.

Stanley always smelled of a hint of expensive aftershave, a touch of fine whiskey, and wore over the top of his pressed linen shirts designer-brand sweaters so new there hadn't been time for even the smallest nub to appear. His pants had a pressed crease down the front—never a wrinkle, the cuffs brushing the tops of his polished black leather loafers . . . Italian, Josh wagered, because they looked like ones George Clooney wore in a romantic vineyard-set comedy he saw at the budget cineplex.

Stanley's house wasn't little or run-down, but it was tidy, and everywhere in his kitchen, dining room, and den—Josh had not yet seen the rest of the place—were antiques of various sizes that didn't have a mote of dust on them. Stanley had a housekeeper come by on Mondays and Thursdays to keep the place spotless; Josh had met her once in passing. Also on display were an assortment of trophies and poster-sized framed book covers featuring guys with guns and wide-eyed women in fishnet stockings. Josh had learned during his second delivery that Stanley had been quite the writer in his younger years and was not shy about displaying his accomplishments.

As usual, Josh rang the bell and waited ten toe-taps. And equally as usual, Stanley opened the door, motioned Josh into the living room, and then with a flick of his age-spotted hand, gestured him toward the kitchen beyond. Stanley was careful to double-latch the door behind him, put on the chain, and re-key the security system.

"Just set my lunch up on the table, Joshua, if you don't mind. The good china today, the Royal Copenhagen. I'll get to it in a few minutes. Oh, and a pitcher of ice water. Have to deal with my company first. A reporter from the local paper's come to interview me about my new book."

Josh had registered the woman seated on the leather couch, notebook in hand, tiny tape recorder whirring away on the coffee table next to a Japanese teapot and cups. This was the first time Josh had seen Stanley entertain anyone. He sat the food sack on the mahogany table and went to the cabinet for a plate, being especially quiet so he could hear the conversation in the other room.

"I'm almost finished with the final draft," Stanley told the woman. "Another week, two at the most, then it'll be back to the publisher and ready to go to print."

The old man had a soft voice, and so Josh slipped closer to the doorway so he wouldn't miss anything. He was pissed about the woman's presence, as he'd intended to pocket another Hummel figurine from the knickknack shelf on the wall behind the couch—no way that would happen with both of them sitting there. Josh was an expert on Hummel. The previous pieces he swiped from Stanley—one from that shelf and another from the desk in the den—"Umbrella Girl" and "Umbrella Boy" respectively—he'd sold for $1,200 each on eBay. Stanley also had an assortment of Royal Doulton figurines in a curio cabinet that Josh intended to pick from. And that would be just the tip of the pilfering iceberg.

Also in the curio cabinet were museum-quality Capodimonte gnomes, a set of seven of them, all playing musical instruments, in near-mint condition and made sometime between 1760 and 1800. Josh had researched the pieces and placed their value at $14,000 for the lot. Beneath them on the bottom shelf was a Meissen nineteenth-century figural grouping of Diana the Huntress in a chariot drawn by a pair of white elks, the color intense. It was worth at least as much as the gnomes. Stanley had made an off-handed comment two Meals on Wheels deliveries past that his deceased wife—God bless her beautiful soul—had inherited all sorts of figurines from a great-great uncle. Stanley kept them around to honor her memory.

Josh intended to honor her memory by selling Diana and her elks to the highest bidder sometime next week . . . along with the two terribly rare Russian Imperial porcelain fairy-tale figurines that had to have been crafted by Sabanin. The latter would go for a solid ten thousand, and the arctic white fox by Cybis on the curio's top shelf would go for more than that, as it was number forty of one hundred (Josh had taken a peek at it when Stanley was in the bathroom) and signed, no chips or cracks, and at ten inches across too big to slip in his pocket.

Three weeks ago on eBay Josh had sold an old Vincent Jerome Dubois cockatoo for a mere $3,000. He'd nabbed that from a geezer's house on Washington Street, another unsuspecting Meals on Wheels client. And a week before that, from a geezer in a rental unit, he'd managed to lift a figurine of St. George mounted on a white horse and slaying a dragon. The detail was exquisite, from the Italian studio of Pattarino, who was known for giving his pieces to dignitaries visiting the Vatican. Josh suspected he'd underpriced it at $4,000.

"Four thousand, that's how many copies of my first book sold. This one, they're going to start the print run at four hundred thousand, I understand. Never thought I'd finish the book. Never thought I'd tell my editor I was done with the first draft. Been working on it two long years. They used to take me only a few months to write, a book. But 'back in the day' a book only had to be about fifty thousand words, give or take. The publishers want double that now. More complex characters, too. More violence."

"Wow, a hundred thousand words."

"That's why it's taken so long. That and the arthritis in my fingers slowing me down some. Thought I was done writing, I say, retired so to speak. But I'd gotten the bug again, damn the arthritis. See the knobs? It's rheumatoid—RA. Have some more tea. It's Earl Grey, imported."

"How many words do you write a day?"

Stanley shrugged, the gesture setting a wrinkle in his sweater. "Don't track it that way. Been writing on one of those newfangled laptops because my editor said he wouldn't deal with typewritten manuscripts anymore."

"Your fans will snap this new book up, I'm sure," the reporter gushed as she noisily sipped from the cup. "There hasn't been a new Stanley Rossini in a bookstore in . . . what . . ."

"Nine years," he finished. "Like I said, I'd thought I was done writing."

"And the name of this new book?"

"*Statistics,*" he answered. "Comes out in hardcover next May. Hope I live long enough to see it."

That would be eight months away, and Josh felt certain Stanley would more than make it—if nothing untoward happened to him. Though Stanley had to be eighty-five if he was a day, he was in great shape. Stanley didn't need Meals on Wheels. He didn't need a housekeeper. He was spry and could well take care of himself; in fact, he drove himself to doctor appointments and town meetings in his old BMW. Josh suspected Stanley ordered the Meals on Wheels—and had to pay full price since he wasn't financially limited—because he was lonely and liked the contact with the delivery man. All of the geezers Josh delivered to were lonely. And none of them, Stanley included, seemed to miss the figurines Josh helped himself to.

Geezers had so many dust-catchers sitting around anyway that they probably couldn't remember precisely what they had. Bits of jewelry, Meerschaum pipes, ivory letter openers, 14K thimbles, and all manner of things strewn here and there that the geezers probably didn't know were valuable. Josh was careful never to take too many pieces from any one place . . . unless a geezer was sick and on his or her way out. Then Josh got a little greedier. Only on a few occasions had Josh helped a geezer to the hereafter so he could take some bigger pieces.

Well, a few more than a few occasions.

But he'd never been caught.

Never would, he figured.

Working for Meals on Wheels paid very well.

"*Statistics*?" the reporter pressed. "Did I get that right? The name of your book is *Statistics*?"

"I always favored one-word titles. Lets them set the print on the cover bigger."

"And it's about—"

"—a number cruncher in the police department who finds trends in crime statistics and uses them to break a burglary ring and later track a serial killer."

Josh poked his head out farther and watched the woman scribble furiously in her notebook.

"So, Mr. Rossini—"

"Stanley. I like to be called Stanley."

"So, Stanley, I heard this book doesn't feature your usual hero, Sergeant Alfonso . . ."

"Detective," he corrected. "Alfonso got a promotion and his gold shield in the seventeenth book. No, *Statistics* is not about Detective Alfonso, but he puts in a cameo just for old-time's sake. The number cruncher is a new character—based him on my father, actually."

"Interesting," she said.

"My father used to work for the FBI's UCR division—helped form it, in fact. And I got a lot of the statistics I use in my book from the UCR—well, double-checked them, actually. There's magic in statistics, but only a few people know that. The numbers have a life of their own, you see. Statistics have been following me my whole life, just like they followed my father—and eventually got him the day after his sixtieth birthday, hit-and-run in downtown Manhattan. Every nine days someone in

New York City is killed by a hit-and-run driver. And of those drivers, twenty percent leave the scene. I know statistics, I know that this is a cruel world, and I protect myself as much as I can. That's why I have so many locks on my doors and the most expensive security system I could buy—keeps me from being one of the statistics. I drive an older car, dark blue, statistically safer on the road. I have to be so very careful. The statistics want me badly."

The woman politely bobbed her head, but stopped writing. Josh could tell that she'd figured Stanley had ventured into that twilight zone of addle-brained geezerhood. Alzheimer City.

"The statistics can be quite malicious, you know," he continued. "So I decided to finally, after all these years, write a book about them. Should have done it earlier, just didn't occur to me. My editor thinks it's going to be a sure-fire best-seller and will open on the *New York Times* list in the top ten."

"Uhm . . . UCR." She bobbed her head quicker. She had a long neck and a long nose, and so the gesture reminded Josh of a pigeon. When Stanley didn't get back on track, she tapped her pen on the notebook. "What's the UCR?" Even her voice sounded all twittery and birdlike.

"The Uniform Crime Reporting Program. Like I said, my father helped establish it back in . . . oh, 1929 I think it was. I was just a little tyke. By the way, Stanley was the forty-third most popular baby boy name in 1925, the year that I was born. A pretty harmless statistic, that one."

"UCR . . ." she pressed.

"Right. There was this organization called the IACP—the International Association of Chiefs of Police. My father was heavily involved in it for years before joining the FBI, and the Association had pushed for an archive of crime statistics. The FBI . . ." He paused, probably waiting for her to ask what those initials stood for, Josh guessed. "The FBI collected all the statistics from police and sheriff departments across the country, gathered them all into the Uniform Crime Reporting Program, the UCR. Back then it was all on paper. Now it's computerized."

"Statistics," she stated.

"They have lots and lots of statistics, the UCR." Stanley puffed out his chest, the first time Josh had seen him do that. "I usually can rattle off statistics for this and that without much thought . . . the statistics follow me around, you know, whittle their way into my brain and beg me to become one of them . . . one more statistic. But I called the UCR before I started my novel just to verify everything, all the statistics I wrote about and had my number-cruncher character analyze. I hadn't needed to bother though, as I instinctively had all of them correct."

"The statistics?"

"Yes. The UCR's statistics—and the statistics that pop into my head—come from almost seventeen thousand police agencies, and they're bundled under all sorts of categories—general crime, hate crimes, law officers killed and assaulted, thefts, drunken driving, what-have-you. More tea?"

Josh bit his lip when the reporter reached for the teacup and nearly knocked it over. The tea service, he'd researched after yesterday's delivery, was circa 1890, and all totaled had eighteen pieces, each stamped on the bottom and signed with Japanese letters. The pot had a blue picture painted on it of a delicate-looking house that was perched over a stream and wooden bridge. When Josh stared at it, he imagined he was in Japan. The cups displayed a thick gold border lining, which given the immaculate condition of everything put it easily at $5,000. If the reporter broke the cup, the value of the set likely would be halved.

Stanley would have to die soon, Josh realized in that moment. Very soon. There were too many large pieces in this house that had to be filched and sold before anything happened to them.

The set of "good" dishes, for example. Josh tiptoed back to the kitchen table and touched the edge of the plate he'd put out.

Stanley had said his wife received the set from a relative during their twenty-fifth anniversary party. Stanley had no clue what they were worth—at least $87,000 according to a collector Josh had contacted. The china set was exceedingly rare, Flora Danica in near-perfect condition. The plates had hand-painted flowers and bore maker's marks on the undersides.

Yes, Stanley would have to be helped to the hereafter very soon, before a single piece of Royal Copenhagen got a chip in it. Before the Japanese tea set was ruined.

Josh had only been in three rooms . . . he tried to imagine the valuables on display in the rest of the house. He would have to bring several duffel bags on the day that Stanley would die. A couple of cardboard boxes. Maybe borrow a friend's van so he could also make off with the early French Art Deco Macassar chair that sat in the entry. Josh put it circa 1915, faux ivory border, caned seat, veneer only slightly weathered and easily worth more than a grand. The signed Norman Rockwell print that hung above it was probably worth something, too.

He returned to the cupboard and took down a pitcher, filled it with water and ice, and set it on the table. It was an Anthony Shaw Burslem Peruvian horse hunt pattern, hard to find in this condition and color—lavender, made in 1850, Josh had learned, likely something else Stanley's wife had inherited. Josh had stolen and sold a few other Shaw pieces through the years and was familiar with the artisan, who was born in Cheddleton, Staffordshire, in 1827, married in 1833, and established himself as a potter in 1851.

Josh couldn't help but smile. Stanley thought he knew all about statistics. Josh knew about statistics, too. He knew that the top-selling antiques on the Internet this week were an American cherry secretary desk that went for $16,000, an Armenian Kazak rug from the nineteenth century that went for $11,000, an art nouveau inlaid dining set that sold for $8,600—that one had been his, stashed for two years so it wouldn't be traced back by nosy relatives of a geezer who died after lunch—and a bronze Putti clock garniture from the early 1800s that went for a whopping $11,000.

Stanley made a harrumphing sound and Josh returned his attention to the conversation in the other room. "No one knows more about statistics than me. For example, your little daily dates back to 1886 and currently has a subscription base of forty-six thousand, down twelve percent in the past eighteen months, a little greater than the national trend given this current sad economy. But I don't need to tell you about your own statistics. You want to know about my book."

"That would be nice," the reporter said. "Can you give me an example of some of the statistics in your book?"

"My fictional city is New York City in disguise," he admitted. "But most of my readers know that. So I used crime statistics from New York for an authentic feel. Last year there were eight hundred and thirty-six murders, two thousand eight hundred and one rapes, sixty-five thousand home and apartment burglaries, and—"

"—and your number cruncher finds patterns."

"Oh, yes. There are even patterns to the crime statistics in this small town . . . though thankfully there's not as much violence as in the cities. Statistics say it's safer to live in smaller places, like this. Using double-locks and a security system helps, too."

"And driving older model cars," she added a little sarcastically.

Stanley seemed not to notice her tone. "Yes, it's important to protect yourself from the statistics. For example, women in your age range—"

"Your lunch is getting cold, Stanley," Josh called from the

kitchen. "And I have to get going over to George Brenner's. He'll be hungry." Josh felt only mildly bad that he'd tarried here so long. The rest of the meals in his car—despite their thermal wrapping—would be delivered lukewarm at best. "I need to be on my way."

Stanley made a tsk-tsking sound. "Can you heat it up in the microwave?"

"Sure."

"Are we done?" Stanley asked the reporter as he stood.

"I have enough material," she answered politely. "Thank you for taking the time, Mr. Rossini—"

"Stanley. I like to be called Stanley."

"Thank you, Stanley. I look forward to reading your book."

*"Statistics."*

Josh waited a while longer, so Stanley could finish the broccoli fettuccini. He carefully washed the Royal Copenhagen plate and put it back in the cabinet, wanting to make sure that it would still be intact when he came tomorrow to retrieve it.

Yes, Stanley would die tomorrow, Josh pronounced. He'd poison the Meals on Wheels, with something from his basement chemical box that would be fast-acting and practically nondetectable. At eighty-five, there wouldn't be an autopsy on Stanley . . . there hadn't been on any of Josh's other deceased clients. Natural causes, the coroner always ruled. Geezers.

Josh felt sad, in a way, because all he would have left would be clients that smelled of cheap cigars and bargain-brand colognes, who wore old clothes slick-shiny-thin at the knees and elbows and a bit too baggy—shirts and pants that had an assortment of stinks and stains.

"See you tomorrow, Stanley," Josh said, heading to the front door. While he waited patiently for the geezer to undo the chain and the double-locks, Josh glanced at the French Art Deco

Macassar chair and the Norman Rockwell print. "See you tomorrow."

As usual, Josh rang the bell and waited ten toe-taps. This time Stanley didn't open the door. Josh rang the bell again and again, and considered going around back to see if maybe Stanley was in another room and making some noise so he couldn't hear the doorbell. But Josh worried that he might trip some security alarm, and so he tried the bell one more time, and then he cautiously tried the door . . . it wasn't locked.

Josh tentatively pushed it open and edged into the living room, half expecting to see Stanley flick his age-spotted hand to gesture toward the kitchen and to say, "Just set my lunch up on the table, Joshua, if you don't mind."

Josh had the tainted Meals on Wheels package in hand. He'd left the duffel bags and packing material in the van he'd parked out front; he intended to retrieve them after Stanley was dead.

"Stanley? Oh, Stanley?"

No answer.

"I've got your lunch! Hot ham and scalloped potatoes. Green beans, too. Applesauce."

Josh padded through the living room and into the kitchen, sucking in a great breath when he saw Stanley slumped at the table, facedown next to an empty Royal Copenhagen plate.

"Put the food out for him, on the plate, nicely arranged." It was the female reporter. She'd come up behind Josh, so quiet he hadn't heard, leaned in the doorway, and leveled a pearl-handled antique pistol at his chest. He'd seen the pistol in a display case on Stanley's desk in the den. "Do it now."

Josh did as he was told, his fingers brushing Stanley's face; the geezer was still a little warm, hadn't been dead all that long.

"I don't understand," Josh said. "What is—"

"Going on?" she asked. Her head bobbed, reminding Josh of a

vulture this time. "Isn't it obvious? I helped Stanley become one of his statistics . . . victim of a burglar. Crimes against the elderly are soaring, you know. His book even hinted at that. He told me yesterday that in *Statistics* a number cruncher discovers a burglary ring and later tracks a serial killer. I figure he didn't realize it, but he was writing about you and his own demise. You *do* have your own little burglary ring running, Joshua, and you *are* something of a serial killer."

Josh stepped back from the table and looked around for a weapon. She waved the gun. He wondered if it worked.

"So you're a thief, like me, not a reporter," he said. "A con artist. You conned Stanley into thinking you were interviewing him."

She smiled evilly. "I *am* a reporter, and I *did* interview Stanley. The article is running in tomorrow's edition. It'll go above the fold, right over his obit, which I'll volunteer to write, too. I am a very good reporter, an investigative one. Been following the statistics myself, the deaths of elderly people in this town . . . the ones dying after eating a Meals on Wheels–delivered lunch. And then I ran across the deliveryman who sells antiques on eBay under the handle GeezerGod."

Josh paled, his gaze darting between Stanley and the gun. Were there bullets in it? "But . . . but . . ."

"So here's how it will play out. The housekeeper will arrive later this afternoon to find Stanley poisoned at this table, having finally joined those precious statistics he thought were chasing him. And you'll be dead on the floor . . . Stanley apparently had just enough energy to shoot you before he succumbed. Easy to believe, given the statistics on home invasions and crimes against old people."

"But . . . but . . . why?" Josh's mind whirled. Should he rush her? Should he offer her a percentage? Was she really going to shoot? Would the gun fire? Should he—

"I don't care about the knickknacks, I care about the manuscripts Stanley Rossini collected. I learned about his collection by accident from researching him in the newspaper morgue. He collected signed, antique manuscripts worth thousands upon thousands upon thousands. And now they're mine. All of those precious, priceless manuscripts . . . along with a half-finished novel about Alfonso before he made detective. All of them out in my car, waiting for me to sell them and start a new life far from here."

Josh took a step toward her, trembling fingers reaching for the gun.

She fired and watched him fall.

"You're just one more of Stanley's statistics," she said, firing again.

She'd hit him twice in the chest, below his heart. He felt the blood spill down his shirt, and he tried to hold it in with his fingers. Josh fought for air and stared up at her, seeing her wipe the prints off the gun and press it into Stanley's age-spotted hand.

"And I'm just filthy rich."

Say good-bye, if you will, to Stanley Rossini and Joshua, men who embraced numbers and percentages, two disparate souls who were poisoned by the statistics they fed on . . . in the Twilight Zone.

# THE MYSTERY OF HISTORY

Lee Lawless

Consider the mysteries of the human heart . . . a place where time knows no bounds, where more knowledge only leads to more questions, and where the spiraling strands of existence intertwine in a fine web that captures both fate and chance. A place quite commonplace in . . . the Twilight Zone.

The bar did not seem to fit in anywhere. It had the usual local-dive trappings—a half-dozen smoke-stained televisions high on the wall, two pool tables lit by funnel-shaded lights, and a beer-stained, pockmarked dartboard in the corner. Mounted on dark walls, a sun-bleached longhorn skull and a massively antlered moose head glared portentously at one and all. A pair of 1960s blue-striped downhill racing skis hung crossed on the front of the upstairs balcony alongside a set of crisscrossed poles. Both were strewn with lacy bras suspended in a silky swoop a few feet above the stage. Against the far wall, the Internet jukebox was decked out with the chrome and glowing tubes of some ancient machine harrowed out of jukebox hell.

The polished maple bar itself spanned the room. Behind it stood a dazzling array of bottles, their backlights illuminating the liquor with an ethereal glow. Large mirrors to the rear of the bottles magnified the bar's luminosity. Various lighting devices—ranging from candles to ancient oil lamps to futuristic cylinders roiling with brilliantly lit lava—completed the mood. Two separate rows of ten beer taps were at each end of the behemoth bar.

Photographs of the neighborhood and a collection of New York City–themed visual art adorned the walls. Local patrons had contributed these artworks, and they were the only indication that this was a New York City pub.

Otherwise the bar would not have looked out of the ordinary anyplace else.

"Can we bring it back to the here and now for a second?" the smirking young female bartender yelled down the bar at a prim college girl who was reading a thick book. "Beatrice, there are live men from this century here. You and Al Hamilton need to split up."

Beatrice Baxter, the studious history major who spent most Monday nights sitting silently immersed in a book at the end of the bar, gave the bartender the finger without looking up.

The girl did have other entertainment options besides her tome. Old-style mind games—made of twisted steel rings to untwine and wooden Peg-Boards to negotiate—festooned the forty-foot bar, while nearby a beautiful imported foosball table featured two teams of painted foosball-kicking Irishmen, who were mounted and manipulated on swivel rods and looked like soccer players. *Big Buck Hunter* and *NYPD Shootout!* arcade consoles flanked each restroom. Then there was the artwork on the walls to look at, including the old rock 'n' roll posters and photos framed by thousands of shellacked pennies . . . the photos taken at long-ago shows in other long-forgotten New York bars. If anyone had the skill, they could have hammered out tunes on the black upright piano stage-left.

Tonight, however, the joint was unsettlingly empty.

When no one was on stage, the place always felt empty. It was a Monday, and the bar could only presently afford bands on the weekends, and only when the bands drew enough fans. In short, business was slow. None of this was lost on the bartender, a fetching twentysomething with an intricate sleeve of tattoos on her left arm, dark skinny jeans, and a tight black T-shirt that read TROOLEY'S TOURIST TAVERN.

As she poured a beer for Beatrice Baxter, the librarian major, she noted fleetingly that her love life was as empty as the bar. God, she was bored, and Library Girl was sure as hell not about to liven things up. Beatrice spent most Monday nights—including football season Monday nights—silently immersed in a book at the end of the bar, hair wound into a loose pencil-stabbed bun, reading glasses locked on the page, her long, slender legs crossed under a modest plaid tweed skirt. Her pale cashmere button-up sweater was probably the most demure garment any woman had worn in the bar since it had opened.

"You gonna do a few straight shots and stop sulking?" the bartender asked amiably.

Beatrice looked up. "I'm not sulking, I'm studying. You're sulking, Reli." She pronounced the bartender's name as "Really." They both took a good long gaze around the nearly empty bar. A few construction guys were shooting pool in the back over a pitcher of cheap beer. "Not that you don't have anything to sulk about here."

"Yeah, well . . ." Reli trailed off. Trooley's Tourist Tavern had been a downtown watering-hole staple for over a century, slinging martini-and-beer breakfasts, lunches, dinners, and power meetings to local Wall Street hotshots who wanted to pretend they were slumming. With the economy nose-diving, many were slumming for real and no longer drank there. Some of the Freedom Tower construction workers—along with a few locals and music fans—would hang out but only if a band was playing. The Pussycat Pleasure Palace strip joint around the corner had recently sucked up most of them.

"Let's do a shot," Reli decided, "before this library turns into a morgue." She poured two four-ounce rock-glass shots of Jack Daniels and belted hers back. Beatrice sipped hers politely.

"Would you rather have the place full of creeps," Beatrice asked, "who sit around with one drink and try and act cool? Or who dress like bohemians and try to talk like poli-sci professors?"

"At least they'd spend some creepy money," the bartender replied.

"I still say you should have a poetry slam," the college kid said, putting down her book and looking Reli in the eye.

"I'm *not* going to put on some hippy-poetry-folk-coffeehouse-acoustic-contest thing. I'm not *that* desperate. This isn't the Village. This is Tribeca—this district has more money than goddamn *countries.* I just gotta get it in here."

As she said this, a tall man entered the bar, removing an archaic homburg from his head. He hung a long, black leather Gestapo-looking trench coat on a bar chair near the entrance, unbuttoned a dark olive suit jacket and sat down. He had long sideburns, an imperial goatee, and a pointed mustache.

"What's your very best whiskey?" the man asked.

"A hipster," Beatrice whispered.

Reli nodded her agreement, but nonetheless treated the customer to her best booze-slinging smile. After topping off the two rock glasses, she brought him a very vintage Jameson's. Absorbed in her book, Beatrice didn't even notice. She still had a lot of work left on her master's thesis on American history.

Returning to Beatrice, Reli tossed her tip on the bar. "Think Al Hamilton would have liked this in his central bank?" she asked Beatrice, who stared incredulously at the shiny gold coin in front of her. "That guy just tipped me with this. It's like he just walked out of another century."

Beatrice examined the coin. It was a fairly heavy chunk of gold emblazoned with a picture of a mountain, the words PIKE'S PEAK on one side, and $2.50 DENVER 1860 on the other.

Beatrice shrugged and returned to her book.

"Hey, you are sulking," the bartender said.

"Greg broke up with me," Beatrice finally said, "so he could have more time to write his opera, and then my fighting fish, Kurosawa, died."

The bartender scoffed. "Eh, forget Greg. I never liked him. What kind of guy writes operas?" She paused and, raising her whiskey glass briefly en route to a sip, added, "I'm sorry about Kurosawa, though."

"Thanks."

"You should move on to some more modern musicians. Or how about a jazz guy? That's classic, I could introduce you to some really cool jazz guys."

"No, I shouldn't be dragging anyone else into my boring life right now. I should buckle down and finish my boring thesis."

"You've got to know when to be boring and when not to. Be boring at home all you want. But don't be boring at my bar. It makes us look bad. A book about Alexander Hamilton? Read something interesting, or *talk* to someone. Go blast off a few rounds on *Big Buck Hunter* or something. You're wasting a whole social experience here."

"I'm talking to you."

"*Everybody* talks to me. I'm better than a shrink, a scientist, a newscaster, and three priests—from three different religions, all rolled into one."

"Why only three priests?"

The ladies stared at Dapper Doubloon Dude at the end of the bar.

He repeated the question in the same deep, commanding voice. "Why only three religions' priests? There's hundreds of religions out there. I daresay you're worth at least ten organized religions' priests, a cadre of shamans, even a deity or two."

Reli smiled broadly, first at Dapper Doubloon Dude, then Beatrice. "What's your name?" she asked the stranger.

He strode the length of the bar to where they were sitting before offering his hand to the ladies and replying, "My name is Devin MacCleary. Pleased to meet you."

"Madame Aurelia Trooley," the bartender said with overabundant flourish. "People call me 'Reli.'"

"I'm Beatrice Baxter," Beatrice said, trying really hard not to sound meek. Up close, MacCleary was not a creep. His dark olive jacket and matching well-tailored pants did not look tacky, like some secondhand-shop bargain find. The color even matched his curious eyes. His black boots gleamed and his accoutrements—a pocket watch, two unobtrusively elegant rings, and a big bright belt buckle—all appeared to be silver. His dark brown hair was stylishly pomaded. He smelled faintly of fine leather.

Up close, Beatrice concluded that his sideburns, imperial goatee, and mustache looked surprisingly handsome on his striking face.

"Charmed," MacCleary said, returning and emboldening Beatrice's smile as he politely shook her hand, then turned to the bartender. "A pleasure, Madam."

"Call me Reli."

He smiled, bemused, as many did at her nickname. "Really Trooley. Wonderful. Are you the proprietor?"

"Family heirloom, but my pop's still alive in Florida. He hates New York in winter."

"Your sign says you've been here since 1866," MacCleary noted.

"Yeah, and it feels like it on slow nights," Reli replied.

"It used to be a brothel," Beatrice said pleasantly.

"Well, thank God it stopped, or I'd never meet you two lovely ladies. And smart, too. What are you reading, Miss Baxter?"

"A biography on Alexander Hamilton. It's for school."

"Hamilton was an intriguing American . . . even though he lost that duel?"

Beatrice laughed shyly. "I've read about it. In fact, my thesis concerns whether Burr murdered Hamilton in cold blood."

"He wrote the night before that he intended to waste his first shot, perhaps even the second, and that afterward he warned the doctor that the gun was still loaded. We also know now that their Wogdon and Barton guns had secret hair triggers. In other words, Burr could have aimed, changed his mind, then shot Hamilton by accident. Did you know that Hamilton's brother-in-law had shot a button off Burr's coat with the exact same weapons in an earlier duel?"

. This time Beatrice was serious. "Yes, I'm familiar with the facts surrounding the duel, but your observations are pretty deep for the casual reader. Are you a practicing historian."

MacCleary grinned. "I'm in finance—I get good tips from the best sources."

Reli already had a bottle in hand—more top-shelf Irish whiskey—with which to refill MacCleary's glass.

He took a languorous sip. "Ah, superlative spirits. Where did you ever find a bottle of this?"

Reli sipped gracefully while she answered. "My great-grandfather Arthur Trooley started it and ran the place from when he came here from Ireland. He beat out all the other New York bars because he had the best whiskey, which he distilled himself in the subbasement. But there was a massive raid on the place during Prohibition thanks to the Pussycat Pleasure Palace ratting them out, and the feds smashed the stills . . . obviously we've never been able to hook those stills back up. Anyway, we stocked a lot of the good stuff to make up for it."

"So what was the secret ingredient that made it sell?"

Reli shrugged. "The fact that it was fifty cents a bottle? Maybe they put cocaine in it? Who knows?"

"Hmmm . . . fascinating. Two lovely ladies with a thirst for knowledge, and a knowledge of thirst."

The jukebox began to play the Rolling Stones' "You Can't Always Get What You Want."

"Nice," said Beatrice. "I love this song."

"Who's singing it?" MacCleary inquired.

"This is a joke?" Reli asked.

He shook his head.

"The Rolling Stones," Reli near-snarled.

"Do you like them?" MacCleary asked Beatrice.

"I'm more the Bob Dylan fan—especially his early folk music," Beatrice said. "You know his stuff?"

"I do, and I now like this Rolling Stones song as well," said MacCleary, pausing to listen to the song's lyrics. "Speaking of getting what I want, however, may I smoke in here, Reli?"

Reli shook her head. "Nah, dude, it's not the same bar as the 1860s. You gotta go outside."

"Indeed," said MacCleary. "Miss Baxter, would you care to join me?" He removed two scrupulously hand-rolled cigarettes from a silver case in his shirt pocket.

Beatrice seldom smoked. She decided not to tell Devin MacCleary that. She donned her plaid scarf, black peacoat, took a deck of the bar's "TTT" logo matches from a jar on the bar, and followed MacCleary out the door.

Reli plucked a condom from a cookie jar on the bar and threw it at Beatrice, snickering.

Outside the street was tranquil and dark. MacCleary lit both cigarettes with an antique-looking silver lighter and handed Beatrice one. They smoked in silence.

"May I ask you a silly question?" MacCleary asked after a minute. "What's a seen-esther? The newspaper said the bar may be full of them if there was a music show."

Beatrice giggled. "It's pronounced 'scene-ster.' It's a person . . . usually a younger person . . . who will hang out at a bar just because they heard the bar was cool, not knowing anybody there, not knowing the band's music, not dressing up at all, not ordering anything interesting or expensive, and . . . well, basically just lurking. Putting in face time."

"I see. But what about just coming to the bar to be there because you like it?"

"That makes you a regular. Scenesters are the type of people who will call friends just to say, 'Oh, I'm at *this* bar,' just to sound important or cool, then not come back, even if they had fun, because 'the scene' is somewhere else."

"And this is one of those bars?"

"Well, it sometimes is, when there's a band or something."

"I see. See and be seen at the scene. Scenester." MacCleary pondered. "On a more solemn note, there is a scene down the street that I feel I must visit, but I'm unsure if I want to go there alone. Would you walk with me for a few blocks?"

"Yeah, sure." They began to walk. "You're not from around here, are you?"

"No, no, I am not. I'm from Montreal originally," MacCleary said.

*Canadian. That explains a lot,* Beatrice thought.

She knew instantly to where they were walking.

"So . . . your degree is in American history?"

"It is," Beatrice said.

"Why?"

"History to me is like this endless riddle—I'm fascinated by why and how great events actually happened and who were the players who made them happen . . . what they were really like."

"You then plan on writing great books?"

"If I could just teach history, that would be enough."

"Noble idea, that. Not enough good ones around anymore." MacCleary dragged deeply and contemplated. "I got this tobacco from George Washington's farm, you know, speaking of history."

"Oh, did you?" Beatrice giggled, playing along. "Well, that's very nice. I don't like supporting slave labor, though, so maybe I should stop smoking."

"Ah, it's all right, I picked it myself . . . though, I suppose, they planted and tended to it. Enjoy."

They walked by steel gates shuttering pizzerias, sneaker stores, a few chic delis. They strolled past the ornate art deco front of the post office.

"So which historical figures do you admire—other than Mr. Hamilton?" MacCleary inquired. "Adventurers? Warriors? Artists?"

"Well, I just saw a brilliant movie about one artist . . . well, I guess he's an adventure artist . . . this guy Philippe Petit. Have you heard of him?"

MacCleary shook his head.

"He was a French guy—just a kid, really—who sneaked into the World Trade Center in the 1970s and strung up a tightrope between the two building tops with his buddies. When dawn broke, he walked from one building to the other on the wire."

"Perhaps he thought it safer than dodging the traffic below."

"That seemed to be his attitude. He was an adventure-artist."

"What happened to him?"

"He went back and forth between the buildings for a long time, and then the police arrested him. A lot of people, however—myself included—thought it was cool."

"Doubtless."

They reached their destination. Before them was a chain-link fence surrounding the gaping pit that had been the World Trade Center.

MacCleary removed a slim, shiny personal data organizer from his pocket and tapped the screen a few times, presumably to an Internet search engine.

"Yes, here it is," he said. "Frenchman Philippe Petit wirewalks over New York City, August 7, 1974."

He looked up into the abyss before him, his eyes suddenly hard. Beatrice had seen this look on many other tourists who were faced with the tragic reality of the barren Trade Center site. He lowered his head and tapped at the screen again, sternly.

"Beatrice, would you like to go to a date with me?" MacCleary finally said.

Beatrice raised an eyebrow. Maybe the Canadian's English wasn't as perfect as he tried for. "Don't you mean *on* a date, Devin?"

He didn't miss a beat. "Is that a yes?"

"I guess," she said, somewhat nervous.

MacCleary returned her smile. "Wonderful." He offered her his hand. She took it and began to turn, to walk back to the bar, but MacCleary remained rooted to the spot. With a mysterious smile, he said, "Close your eyes."

She did so. MacCleary pulled her close, touching their lips together in a gentle, chaste kiss.

Beatrice could have sworn she had been hit by lightning, so great was the flash and the jolt through her body.

She was staring into his forest-green eyes when she opened hers. Nor did she break her gaze—not even to notice that the bright morning sun glinted in all its splendor off the Twin Towers.

Three guys and a girl entered Reli's bar. Two of the guys and the girl held guitar cases. The guys with the guitars looked like college professors in glasses, black dress shirts, and clean, pressed jeans. In contrast, the girl and the other guy looked like rock 'n' roll ruffians.

"Hey, guys," Reli said brightly. "Get ya some drinks?"

"Four Jameson shots," the girl said.

The rocker-looking asshole gave a low whistle. "Damn," he said, "this place is Death Valley."

"Where are the tumbleweeds?" the girl asked.

"That's us," the guy said.

"Goddamn ghost town," the girl said.

Reli hated cooler-than-thou musicians who sneered at her place, implying it wasn't chill enough for their genius talents and superstar extravaganzas. She especially hated condescending rockers who didn't enter with fans in tow. When Beatrice came back in a few minutes, she'd probably give last call.

"Too bad ghosts don't pay cover charges," the taller of the guitar-toting prof-types noted.

"Don't suppose you have a few fans who could change all that?" Reli asked.

"Maybe," the rocker girl said with a supercilious smirk, "but right now we're on recon."

"It's all cool," the other prof said, looking around.

Reli placed the shots in front of the band, including one for herself. "Okay, Recon Patrol, here's the deal. You wanna play here, cover is ten bucks a head. We keep the first ten fans' cash for the sound guy. You can keep anything after that, but don't expect to get a second date if you ain't making me at least three bills in the bar till. No pyro, no security issues, and we got no stage lights, green room, or backline amps to speak of."

"Drinks?" the lanky long-haired guy asked.

"Half off," Reli said. "Still cool?"

The band looked at Reli, each other, the shots, and the ornately empty room.

"Let's start with some drinks," the rocker guy said.

Reli wondered absently if they had enough cash for the tab or whether she should charge them per round.

A cop car passed on the street behind Beatrice and Devin, finally distracting her gaze. The car was dark green and cream-colored, with a single red domed light on top.

"Is someone shooting a seventies movie?" Beatrice asked. "Wait—what time is it?"

All around them, Tribeca's pedestrians ebbed and flowed. A

woman with a huge, halolike Afro brushed past in tight brown leather bell-bottoms on platform heels. Two shaggy-haired businessmen in bright blue plaid suits and large dark sunglasses checked her out as they strode by from the opposite direction. The street was full of cars—Cadillac Coupe de Villes, Buick Rivieras, a Triumph TR6. A girl in a flowery hippy dress with flat long hair rode by on a chromed chopped hog behind a biker guy with a very serious pair of muttonchop whiskers and a Pancho Villa mustache. An open car radio was jamming Led Zeppelin's "Communication Breakdown."

"It's not a movie," MacCleary whispered. "Turn around."

Beatrice turned. Her entire field of vision was overwhelmed by the Twin Towers.

"But . . . but . . ."

"I told you I was taking you *to* a date," MacCleary whispered.

"What kind of joke is this?"

"Most assuredly not, my dear. Come now, you're well-versed in history. Does anything here look like a joke?"

Beatrice took a long look around. A checkered cab grumbled by. *They disappeared decades ago.*

"Does *that* look like a joke?" Devin asked, pointing straight up.

A small, barely visible figure was stepping out onto a thin, taut line, strung between the two towers, supported by two cavalettis—guy lines—that kept the cable taut. He'd planned the feat well.

He held a long thin pole for balance. And, wide-eyed far below, Beatrice and Devin watched him in silence.

Three or four minutes passed before another pedestrian spotted the man and pointed him out. Soon a crowd of onlookers stared up at the man on the line.

"Oh, my God!" gasped a black businessman in a dark, three-piece, pin-striped business suit. A cigarette fell unnoticed from his hand. Instantly, all heads tilted upward.

"Who is that man?" a woman shrieked. "He'll kill himself!"

Beatrice shook her head, entranced. "No . . . no, he won't . . . he'll be okay." She broke her upward gaze momentarily to stare incredulously at MacCleary. "It happens the same way? The exact same way?"

Devin MacCleary nodded, smiling. "Unless you think you can change his mind from down here."

MacCleary's gorgeous green eyes smiled right along with him. This was for real. Strangely assured, Beatrice craned her neck up again. Eyes on the sky, the pair's hands met without even needing to glance back down.

With her free hand, Beatrice waved at the sky. "Go, Philippe! Yeah! You can make it!"

A few cheers went up in the crowd.

"If that ain't the damnedest . . ." the businessman in the three-piece pinstripe chuckled. "Hell, yeah! *Break* the law of gravity, man!"

More cheers went up. Petit was almost across.

So he turned, and returned back the other way across the wire.

"I like the idea of those buildings," the businessman mentioned, to no one in particular. "The reality is a lot uglier." A few people around gave a still-dumbstruck laugh in agreement.

"I still don't see them as the tristate center of commerce," another Wall Street exec in a six-hundred-dollar suit said.

The street was almost completely stopped. Horns honked either in anger at the human gridlock or in support of the man on the wire, as cabbies leaned out windows for a better look upwards. A policeman with an almost impossibly bushy mustache was speaking into his radio with slow, deliberate words, his eyes also fixed upward.

"I got an unidentified guy walkin' on a tightrope at One World Trade Center," the cop stated, sounding like he barely believed his own words even as he spoke them. "On *top* of One World Trade Center. Goddamn."

"Come on, Philippe!" Beatrice enthused, clutching Devin's hand. Even though she knew what happened, it detracted nothing from the situation.

"Don't mention him by name," Devin whispered. "The cops might think you're an accomplice and take you in. The fun part is being incognito."

"This is incredible," Beatrice whispered. "All of this."

"I thought you'd like it." MacCleary gave her a quick sideways grin. "Even though I'm not a *practicing* historian."

A quarter of a mile in the air above them, Philippe Petit paused on his wire in the middle of the void and slowly, reverentially, knelt down.

After the squad cars, paddy wagon, and NYPD helicopter had all descended on the scene, a full forty minutes later, Petit was arrested. Beatrice and Devin watched as the sweet-faced, mischievously grinning young Frenchman was thrown, handcuffed, into a police cruiser and carted away, amid cheers from the vicariously invigorated crowd. Devin turned amiably to Beatrice.

"All this action makes me hungry. May I buy you dinner?"

"But it's morning!" Beatrice pointed out.

"It's whenever we want it to be," Devin responded. "Besides, when we left the bar, it was night, and your body probably still thinks it is. You can only reset so many clocks."

He had a point. Beatrice hadn't eaten since lunch that day, which was now over thirty years in the future. She wasn't thirty years' worth of hungry, but she was hungry.

"I know a great place in the Village," continued MacCleary. "Shall we?"

*This sort of thing could get addictive,* thought Beatrice, who replied, "Definitely." She put out her hand for a cab.

"No need for that," smiled Devin. "Follow me."

Devin took her arm in his, led her around a vacant street

corner, and pulled out the shiny device. A few taps of his finger later, and they were standing beneath the gnarled limbs of an ancient oak tree in Washington Square Park.

Beatrice looked around furtively. No one had noticed them. It was dark out, but the street traffic was still active. Not removing her arm from his, they began to walk.

Almost instantly, Beatrice realized they were farther from more than the Twin Towers site. The cars on the street had fins and lots of chrome. Almost every woman passing by wore a skirt or dress; nearly every man wore a hat. Devin noticed her noticing as they walked.

"Guess," he cajoled.

Beatrice was amusedly awestruck. "I . . . I can't say!" she stammered. "The fifties?"

"Close! It's 1960. Forgive me, I just find it much more charming."

Beatrice could not even *begin* to tell him how charming she found all of it.

They strode smiling toward the neon and noise of Bleecker Street. "So you can travel though time *and* space," Beatrice asked, more confidently than she had thought it would sound.

"That's the deal," Devin replied, casual to an almost absurd degree. "Einstein called that one, not me. They go hand in hand. The real trick is not getting noticed. Ending up in the wrong space at the right time, or vice versa, gets kind of messy. That's why I like jumping around in New York, because people appear at random here all the time . . . it doesn't seem out of the ordinary . . . most don't even need a time-travel machine."

"That's what it's called? 'Jumping'?"

"Jumping, jaunting, hopping, skipping, skedaddling, whatever you like. I've never met anyone else who's been doing it at the same time as me . . . *any* of the same times as me . . . so I guess I get to coin the term."

"You're the only one? You're all alone in this?"

"I don't know about that, honestly. But thankfully, I'm not at the moment." MacCleary smiled his magnetic smile at her, disconcertingly handsome again. They were outside a bar with a staircase leading into an unseen subterranean spot. "Here we are. Do you like folk music? You said something about liking . . . Bob Dylan."

Beatrice almost gasped. "I thought I was the only one left."

Devin laughed. "Not anymore, my dear. Not by a long shot."

They walked, still arm in arm, down the stairs.

The subterranean spot opened up into a long, large room filled with tables, benches, a stage, a bar. Dim lamps and candles illuminated faces, smoke, reflections from cocktail and beer glasses. A smoky-voiced young guy in skinny jeans and a black corduroy fishing cap jammed on acoustic guitar from the small stage. A waitress dressed in beatnik black led them to a small table off to the side of the stage and lay down a menu.

"Wine or beer?" the waitress said, bopping casually to the raucous harmonica line in the tune being played.

"I'll have a glass of red wine," said Beatrice, trying not to sound too dreamy.

"Well, I'd like to have an old-fashioned . . . but I guess I'll have a beer," MacCleary said.

The table was small and circular and their legs entwined beneath it. She was loving this more than any date she could ever remember being on. No, wait, the future. No, wait, *her* past. No, wait . . . oh, whatever. This was awesome, so flipping cool.

"So you said you're in finance," Beatrice said, trying act nonchalant, as if time travel was no big deal.

"Yes, but it's boring," MacCleary said. "My work life is very boring. I just buy stocks. I have stocks from here to next Tuesday. And the Tuesday after that, and the Tuesday after that. Oh, and from a thousand Tuesdays *before* that."

"That's nice," Beatrice said.

Devin nodded knowingly. "It's nice that I enjoy the simpler pleasures—music, the arts, hanging around, good conversation. What about you?"

Beatrice took a deep breath. "Well, my work life is pretty boring, too. As I said, I'm into history, struggling to understand how people lived and what they really did with their lives. It's like I'm trying to solve this great big puzzle. But I love music and art, and I'm pretty sure that with all of your adventures, I could ask you questions until you begged me to shut up."

"Don't worry, I won't do that. What adventures do you want to hear about?"

She was reluctant for a moment. "Um . . . well . . . I mean . . ."

Devin knew the word she was looking for. "How?"

Beatrice giggled, a little embarrassed. "Yeah."

"A fair enough question. You already know the who, and the why, and the where, and certainly the when, but it is the what and the how that you require. And I shall tell you." He pulled the personal data organizer from his pocket. It was a rectangle about the size of his palm, with only a smooth glass screen on the front and a shiny silver back. He tapped the screen and instantly a photo of the Egyptian pyramids appeared. He touched the middle pyramid and a menu appeared. With a flick of his finger he scrolled down to an icon that said simply SETTINGS, then, DATE AND TIME.

"Very straightforward really, an exceptional piece of technology. All one must do is scroll here"—he dashed his finger over a slot-machine-like wheel of numbers and dates on the screen—"and there you have it. That's the time, any time, down to the second. As for place"—he went back to SETTINGS, then to WORLD MAP—"you just zoom in and fly out." He was careful not to alter the settings. "Of course, there's the homepage, which tonight would return us back to Trooley's in the same time we left—that's my default setting for now . . . otherwise, we're anywhere." He touched the bottom of the screen and it went black. "It's also got a camera and music storage, but you know, everyone's got that stuff onboard their phone these days."

"Those days," Beatrice giggled.

"Yes," Devin smiled. "Those days. Of course, the phone and Internet only work if I'm jumping into an era with satellites capable of such transmissions . . . I can break the rules of time and space, but I can't break the constraints of technology. It's only as perfect as the times."

The waitress brought their drinks. As she left, Devin raised his glass in toast.

"May our futures' least be more than our pasts' most," he stated.

The youthful, undiscovered Bob Dylan was really into his set now, groaning and yowling through his Woody Guthrie phase, whanging on his guitar and wailing on his harmonica. Beatrice had never had an experience—not even a dream—as good as this. She and Devin clinked glasses and sipped.

Devin stared deep into Beatrice's eyes.

"In the year 2027, you break my heart, Beatrice."

Beatrice blinked.

"That's when I'm from, my dear. I meet you . . . I *met* you . . . at Trooley's in 2031, when you're forty-nine, and I'm twenty-one. That was a few months ago for me, so I traveled back to you here from then. In 2031 you've become what people used to call a 'cougar,' an older woman who chases young men, and in my case, you broke my heart. I'm here tonight to make sure that it doesn't happen, that we will be together. I know we're technically in another dimension, and that the laws of space and time get iffy when run through gadgetry, but I love you. I don't care when or where."

*What . . . the hell . . .* Beatrice thought.

"I know you love bike riding, and good mystery books and Bob Dylan," MacCleary stated. "You're brilliant and successful in every time frame I could probably think of landing in. When I met you, in 2031, your chateau in Quebec was on a ski mountain and had a wall-sized shark aquarium. But I can't take you to where you already exist, so I'll take you to where you haven't existed yet, and we'll take in the sights and try out some new drinks. Okay?"

"That's Bob Dylan playing up there, isn't it?"

"Indeed it is."

*"I had a shark tank?"*

Beatrice was in a daze, as if she were watching herself think. "You can't do this all the time. There's no way."

MacCleary nodded solemnly. "I was born in Montreal in 2010, and Montreal, 2031, was my primary residence when I obtained the device. I have a self-designed home on the beach that I've visited for my last three summers, respectively during the years 0001, 0003, and 0007. I made most of my money in stocks and a little trading of vintage champagne in the Russian imperial court, but that's a whole other story. Ditto Hamilton and Washington. Oh, and wherever I am, Friday is Ride Day, and I go out prospecting for gold with an old friend of mine in the Wild West of the 1860s."

"And it doesn't change . . . I mean, we can't . . ." Beatrice had no idea how to put it into words, present or past tense.

"It doesn't seem to. Perhaps because there are many other dimensions, worlds, and universes out there in which our lives go in all kinds of directions—so many that this device does not impact on ours. Whatever the case, I don't believe I've altered anything in *our* world."

"Where did the device come from?"

"That's too long a story for our first night. Also, I'm not sure how much I should tell you about the future. The less you know about the future, the less you'll surreptitiously surrender to it."

He studied her intently. "My God, and I thought you were gorgeous at forty-nine."

Back at Trooley's, the band became intoxicated and now talked quite loudly about doing a music video for something called "a Partnership for a Free-Drugs America." Reli looked at the six different cuckoo clocks over the bar. Beatrice and MacCleary had been gone almost ten minutes.

She thought that if her shy friend didn't get MacCleary into the sack, she, Reli Trooley, might take a run at him. Wall Street sharks, punk-ass musicians, and slimy construction workers were starting to bore her. Reli could seriously use a change of pace.

They were sitting beneath the Statue of Liberty, all alone by the water reflecting the city's lights brighter than stars. Beatrice had asked to go somewhere quieter so they could get their thoughts together.

"I abide by camping rules—take only photos, leave only footprints. And I prefer peace. It's amazing how much of history will run its course with or without one person's input. So I choose not to get in the way."

Beatrice nodded gently, head nestled on MacCleary's shoulder as they gazed at the skyline from the grass.

"I'm sorry I broke your heart in 2031, Devin."

"Try not to do it this time."

He pulled her close. Beatrice Baxter, now a scholar of space and time, then experienced the best kiss *ever.*

He left her on the cloudlike feather bed in the modest stone-and-palm hut he had spent most of the summer of 0001 constructing, near a beach in what would later be known as Costa Rica. She slept soundly, naked in the warm ocean air.

MacCleary wasn't tired at the moment. He put his dark green suit back on again, switching the homburg hat for a black Stetson.

"LAST CALL!" shouted Reli.

The bar had been empty most of the night—not enough patrons to justify even an open-night mike—and the band, the only bar patrons left, all looked at each other.

"Bottle of champagne, please," the lead guitarist, Doc, stated.

"Veuve Clicquot only. Hundred bucks."

The band responded by cheering wildly and slapping the bar. "And we wanna play, too," the bassist, T.J., pronounced.

Reli waved a hand at the stage. "Go ahead, audition. Even if you suck, you get some good bubbly."

Arthur Trooley was pissed.

Not only was the bar getting too rowdy, but the goddamn cowboys were back in town for more whiskey. Or, as they put it, "put their winnings into the whiskey business"—to which end they were buying up his extra whiskey kegs and wholesaling them out west.

Trooley shuffled down the long stretch of his stupendous bar, his greatest creation, his American Dream. Hailing from Dublin, he had landed at Ellis Island in the Year of Our Lord 1865 and the bar had been slinging hooch and hoochie-coochie in lower Manhattan since early 1866. Maintaining decorum was crucial to his establishment, he felt, a fact that was reflected in his immaculate white tuxedo shirt, black suspenders, bow tie, and slacks. The other patrons ranged from the distinguished gentlemen-about-town to the decent-to-better class of skilled worker, a fact the latter tried to hide by dressing in the cleanest clothes they could procure and perhaps even deigning to bathe.

Then of course there were the two goddamn cowboys who

had invaded his place like banshees from hell. He'd have thrown them out except that they made so much money for him. Pooling their funds, they bought his famous basement-distilled Irish whiskey by the barrel and peddled it to the hundreds of batwing-door saloons back west as top-shelf liquor. Everyone was getting rich off their enterprise, so Trooley humored them.

The bar had been about evenly divided that evening among the newspapermen, who were jovial and drank a lot; the bankers, who were more reserved but also drank a lot; and a boisterous battalion of barbers, bakers, butchers, and horse-carriage jockeys, who were often mad as a mud pit full of fighting pigs, but paid well to drink a lot and didn't rough up the girls any more than the other customers.

The girls. The goddamn cowboys had bought his four most beautiful ladies with their damn Wild West gold. At this very moment those Wild West Horsemen of the Apocalypse were ravaging them in the upstairs bedrooms, stealing that gorgeous tail right out from under his other patrons, particularly the bankers, who were furious at having to wait for a little of their own hoochie-coochie.

April and Autumn, the seventeen-year-old Norse blonde and the olive-skinned Italian brunette, had gone with that loudmouth rancher named Brough, whom Trooley only tolerated because Brough claimed his father came from the same part of County Louth as his own father had. The second cowboy, MacCleary, had commissioned the other two—Summer, the tanned, sun-blond-haired half-Dutch girl from the faraway Caribbean (and Arthur Trooley's personal favorite), along with Snowy (who, via a plantation in Virginia, came from the even-farther-away Congo).

The bankers had never previously faced any competition for Trooley's high-priced honky-tonk courtesans. The bankers were at the very moment discussing how to attack the mine owners when they returned from the whores' quarters upstairs. Their arsenal included concealed handguns, daggers, and a shocking array of brass knuckles. The bankers occasionally needed to let off some serious steam.

Then the cowboys appeared at the top of the stairs, smirking.

Rudy MacCleary, the shaggy-haired frontiersman, had slid almost completely down the gleaming wooden banister when the bankers charged him and his partner. Rudy took on two tweedy-suited, bowler-hatted, knife-wielding financiers with his fists. Rudy's partner, the one in the inexplicable suit with his cowboy hat, kicked an attacking banker back down the stairs, but took a thrown whiskey bottle in his right temple and tumbled down the steps himself, crashing into the prostrate banker. The liquor in the opaque bottle—marked only "XXX TTT," Trooley's legendary Irish whiskey—was fortified with authentic American Wild West fulminates. When the bottle shattered against the westerner's skull, the elixir's secret ingredients—the severed heads and tails of various venomous rattlers—were marooned atop the man's head.

His New York crowd always enjoyed the adventure of drinking genuine Wild West whiskey, so Trooley accommodated them.

Trooley watched MacCleary rise unsteadily, while the same banker who had hurled the bottle kicked MacCleary unceremoniously down a second descending corridor of stairs to the sub-basement. He booted a stray snakehead—still steeping in the lower half of the broken bottle—down the stairs after him.

Arthur Trooley couldn't bloody well stand for this mayhem. His precious whiskey was not to be used as a weapon. He pulled out his shotgun from behind the bar, blasted a load of rock salt into the ceiling, and hollered, "MIND YAR DAMN MANNERS!"

With that, the fighting stopped, and four bankers shrugged with studied insouciance and ambled up the stairs to the ladies.

He was just so damn handsome, it was a serious shame to see his gorgeous face all bloody and messed up. The blood dripping . . .

almost *coursing*... down from a gash over his right eye looked awful.

He tried to make a joke of it, leaving his cowboy hat on as he stagger-strolled back into Trooley's, a grin/grimace on his face. His face and olive suit were bloody, and he was drunk.

Filling a bar towel with ice, Reli tended to his wounds.

"Dare I even ask?" Reli snarled.

"You wouldn't believe me if I told you." MacCleary winced as the ice chilled the bruises. Reli cleaned and sterilized the wounds with napkins soaked in bar vodka.

Reli wondered in passing where the Stetson had come from, but decided she didn't want to know.

"Did Beatrice . . . ?" Reli asked instead.

"Beatrice is safe. She had nothing to do with this. She'll be back in a moment." He shifted the ice on his head. "Ow. Can you do me a favor and make sure there's no glass in there?"

Reli grimaced, but her eyes were still warm. *What the hell is this guy's story?* she wondered. *And why do I always get interested by guys like this?*

She poured two rock-glass shots of whiskey and scowled at the intricacies of the messiest wound, the one on his temple. Dark shards of glass gleamed in it. She pushed one of the shots to Devin.

"Hold still. This is probably going to hurt."

From the stage, the band struck up an upbeat song they called "Black and Blues."

In August of 0001, in the Costa Rican palm beach hut, Beatrice awoke. She felt glorious.

Until she spotted the large jungle cat . . . a cheetah? A leopard? A jaguar? . . . prowling along the beach in the morning sunshine.

She hoped Devin had some sort of firearm here to deter

ferocious felines. She was about to ask him as much when she realized he was gone—the device with him.

She hoped he was just getting some breakfast from the future.

"That's the Universal Truth Machine, isn't it?" MacCleary queried, as Reli patched up his head.

"Sorry?"

"The band onstage . . . it's got to be the Truth. Right?"

"I guess that's what they said. I dunno, never seen 'em before."

"They're huge in 2031."

"I'm sure they hope so."

"No, I mean, they're the stuff of legend by then."

Reli sighed. "You know, if you were going to leave the bar to get stoned, you could have invited me."

"I'm not stoned. I travel through time. That's all."

"Okay, now you're hallucinating, and I'm worried. How hard did you get hit on the head, dude?"

Devin stood up abruptly, as Reli was finishing wrapping gauze around his skull.

"Fine. I'll prove it. Mostly because I like hanging out here. I've been in and out of the scene here for almost two hundred years."

"Riiiight," Reli said.

"I'll be right back," said MacCleary. He eased his cowboy hat down over the bandages and sauntered to the bathroom, removing something shiny from his pocket as he did so.

The band onstage was singing a new song. It went:

*If you think we're losing our minds*
*If you think we're fallin' behind*
*If you think we're none of a kind*
*Well, you're right—it's time to fight!*

*If you think we're losing our hearts*
*If you think we're falling apart*
*If you think it's time we got smart*
*Well, you're right—it's time to fight!*

*If you've got a way with it, you've got to get away with it*
*If you've got a hand at it, you've got to take a stand*
*If you've got a way with it, you've got to get away with it*
*If you've got the swing of it, you've got to come out swinging*

*That's the State of the Art, now*
*That's the State of the Art, now*
*That's the State of the Art, now*
*All right!!*

They weren't half bad, Reli figured. Maybe Crazy Devin was onto something.

She hoped he wasn't doing coke in the bathroom. She preferred men who drank.

MacCleary reappeared in Costa Rica and took Beatrice by the hand.

"Awake, my dear? Care for a morning mimosa?"

"Where did you go?" Beatrice asked anxiously. "There was a cougar on the beach . . . I mean a jaguar . . . I mean . . . Devin, you're bleeding . . ."

"No, no, I *was* bleeding, I'll be fine. Let's go have brunch in Russia."

Later on, Beatrice couldn't really recall what happened next—something to do with Catherine the Great's court, and a lot of champagne. No one except the lower-class Russians spoke Russian, so everyone spoke French. MacCleary could communicate with them all just fine, anyway. Beatrice's college French helped her follow half of the conversation . . . barely.

There was champagne everywhere, in bottles that appeared almost comically oversized and everywhere else. It was all Veuve Clicquot champagne. For some reason she remembered that Russia had purchased 70 percent of the Veuve Clicquot supply by the turn of the twentieth century.

A man was playing a piano that overflowed full of champagne. Dancing along the strings inside were a hundred live sardines.

They were in an opulent home's library along with several other merchants from France and Russia, all of whom had something to do with champagne. They sang cheerfully at the gurgling, champagne-drenched piano.

And drank.

And drank.

And drank.

At one point, the men all focused on Beatrice. She smiled politely until the men began tossing her from one to another, after which she began shrieking. *Maybe they invented crowd surfing?*

Finally Devin caught her. Toasting the merchants with his free hand, he walked off, Beatrice slung over his shoulder.

He grabbed one sealed bottle of champagne from a silver stand before heading up the stairs—an 1811 Halley's Comet–vintage bottle.

"Let's play a trick on Reli," MacCleary declared. "Hang on."

Halfway up the stairs, MacCleary and his device sent them back to the present day and the dark, cool subbasement of Trooley's, where he placed the priceless bottle on the back of a shelf in the darker of two walk-in beer coolers. Without even bothering to walk out of the cooler, Beatrice still slung over his shoulder, he returned them to the stairway in Russia, which he continued climbing.

Upstairs, in a room with a large claw-foot bathtub as well as a fireplace, Devin opened a window and pulled the biggest bottle of champagne Beatrice had ever seen from inside a drift of snow on the roof.

"This is what we in the trade call a Balthazar," said MacCleary. "Twelve liters apiece. And I have six bottles." He grinned wickedly. "Shall we have a champagne bubble bath?"

The band at Trooley's was playing another song. It went:

*Word to your crew:*
*I came to stage a coup*
*This revolution's evolution's*
*Never usin' fools*
*Word to your agents:*
*Excess in moderation*
*Next dimension's my intention*
*In visions, invasions!*

Reli might . . . *might* . . . have been dancing behind the bar, just a little bit.

Beatrice awoke, still dreamily drunk in the champagne-filled claw-foot tub. Before opening her eyes, she wondered aloud, "When am I?"

Devin lay opposite her in the tub, head thrown back, snoring soundly. The fire was nothing but embers, and the wind was whipping in from the open window. Beatrice got up and shut it.

She stoked the fire a bit to get it going again. It was still very cold in the room, and the champagne made her feel sticky on her skin and woozy in her head. She splashed some water on her face from a nearby basin to fix this. The water was frigid.

MacCleary's nice suit was draped over a chair. Beatrice stared at the jacket for a good thirty seconds before going to it and pulling the device from the pocket.

She slid her finger over the screen and the device lit up immediately. She touched the middle pyramid in the opening picture and a menu appeared.

Under MUSIC there were thousands of tracks, regular studio recordings and live shows, everything from Mozart (recorded live in Austria) to underground Clash bootlegs, plus a few famous speeches MacCleary must have seen firsthand, nestled amidst a crowd in his space-time scenesterdom. Beatrice would have to hear all those speeches eventually.

Beatrice touched PHOTOGRAPHS. Instantly pictures montaged across the screen—shots of glaciers and volcanoes, Civil War battles and Indian chiefs, famous artists holding up paintings of politicians looking official and unofficial, even a fetching portrait of MacCleary riding a horse on a mountain trail. The MOST RECENTLY CREATED file was chock full of pictures of a tanned blonde girl and a very black girl, nude and coyly posing wearing MacCleary's cowboy hat. The date-stamp for the photo read 1869.

*He not only met them before he met you,* Beatrice realized, *he met them before you were even alive.*

But the photos got her thinking. There was an historical question she had to answer—for the sake of curiosity and her college thesis . . . and she needed to do it alone.

Would he care if she borrowed his device and indulged in a single trip by herself?

One trip would be okay, she decided. She'd be right back . . .

A mild July 11 on the New Jersey shore at dawn. Beatrice watched the boats rowing across the Hudson River from New York. The duelers had to meet in Jersey, since in New York duelers were prosecuted. Dueling in New Jersey was also illegal, but the laws were not strictly enforced.

She could see the stern-faced Alexander Hamilton even from

afar. He was as striking as all the statues and ten-dollar bills portrayed him. Yet he looked sad.

Beatrice skulked behind her stand of trees. Why was she scared? She wasn't about to fight in a fatal duel.

The better question was why she was here. How would watching the lethal spectacle improve her thesis? She couldn't source her observations with written documents. All she'd have was her word that she'd been there. Still there was no way she was missing this, fearful or otherwise. Her thesis and her research were, in her opinion, dead, irrelevant, without meaning. She believed in her soul that observing the event firsthand would jump-start her commitment, giving her writing hard-won authenticity.

She also wanted to know what *really* happened.

The fact she'd never seen anyone shot, that she'd never even held a gun anywhere, anytime, however, was starting to get to her. She wasn't sure how she'd hold up.

As the boats docked, Beatrice tried to take in the significance of Hamilton's life and what was happening.

*Founding Father. Early economist. Political philosopher, constitutional lawyer, author of the* Federalist Papers. Hamilton would never turn fifty, and he'd already had a bigger life than modern men twice his age.

*Bank founder. Continental congressman. George Washington's own aide-de-camp.*

They were climbing up the banks of Weehawken now, heading for the woods. Beatrice wondered if Hamilton was taking stock of his life in the same way she was, but if he was, she couldn't tell.

Hamilton's son had been shot in a similar duel over honor not long ago, and by all historical accounts Hamilton was inconsolable after his death. His son had fought a duel of honor with a man named Eacker who had found young Philip Hamilton's behavior in his theater box seats "hooliganish," and Philip had fought to regain his honor. And lost.

Today, it was former vice president Aaron Burr who was fighting for his perceived honor. After his decade-plus rivalry with Burr that had made its way from the Senate floor to the White House to the press, Burr had had enough of Hamilton's meddlesome critiques and issued the challenge.

Like Reli and her family before her, Hamilton had been in the whiskey business, fighting alongside George Washington and General Henry "Light Horse Harry" Lee over the whiskey tax, until its repeal the previous year, 1803. Hamilton had charged six cents a gallon to small batch-whiskey distillers and a whopping nine cents a gallon to large distillers to get a piece of the action on one of America's most popular goods—corn whiskey. Distillers had literally taken up arms against this in the Whiskey Rebellion.

The lots drawn by the opponents' seconds gave Hamilton choice of weapon and position. Save Hamilton and Burr, all backs were turned when, from a portmanteau bag, appeared a box with the Wogdon & Barton pistols. They'd had to carry them covertly so that all others present had plausible deniability—no one had technically seen any pistols in the boat when they'd left New York. Hamilton chose his gun—the same pistol that had shot his son—and took his position. Burr did the same. Their seconds, the rowers, and the doctor present all remained facing away into the woods. Beatrice cowered a little lower, her mind racing.

*Hamilton wrote in his journal last night that he's going to* delope—French for *"throw away"—his fire. Burr will later call the statement "contemptible, if true." Burr will aim for Hamilton's heart.*

The men, standing proudly in position, ceremonially raised their weapons. Hamilton's sad but steely gaze met Burr's icy sneer. The count was given, and two cracks like thunderbolts rang out. From over Burr's head, a tree branch shattered.

Hamilton had been hit over the right hip, instantly causing

him to stagger and fall. Burr moved toward him, flashing a look of what might have been regret, but then quickly steeled himself and walked away.

Everything else happened in fast-forward, it seemed. All present had turned to view the results of the spectacle. The doctor was tending to Hamilton as best he could, and then they rushed him back down to the boat. Burr, striding arrogantly back through the trees with his second and rowers, also headed for the banks of the Hudson. One of the men shielded Burr behind an umbrella, as if this event could somehow have been kept a secret.

Beatrice knew only too well what would happen from there. In the boat, the wounded Hamilton would tell his doctor to be careful, that the gun still had a shot left in it that he hadn't used. He'd die the very next day. Burr would survive relatively unscathed, eventually dodging indictments for murder in New York and New Jersey. And that was history.

She waited breathlessly until everyone had departed. The smell of gunpowder still hung in the morning air. She crept up to the site of the duel and counted the paces. They'd been about thirteen feet from each other, when Hamilton's gunshot had smashed into a branch.

Had he deloped out of honor? Had he shot wide because he'd been hit? Had he committed suicide by duel? Had he fired off the round by accident due to the pistol's unreliable hair trigger? Or had he just simply lost?

Beatrice had just watched the event unfold, and she still couldn't tell what had happened anymore than the other participants and reporters on the scene who would later agree on the facts. So what was history? A lie invented by those who were never there, spun by unreliable witnesses whose recollections contradicted those of other witnesses? History was not even the inevitable polemic of the victor. Few historians took the side of Aaron Burr, the duel's winner.

What was the meaning of history, then, if historical facts were unverifiable and truth was unattainable? That nobody knew anything . . . not even the individuals who'd been there?

Had she cracked history's conundrum?

Had she finally solved the mystery of history?

Beatrice knew this much: Instead of certitude and hard-won authenticity, her time trip to New Jersey had infused her thesis with . . . doubt.

She would not return to the History Department.

Maybe instead she should study under Reli, who had once told her, "There is more to life than the life of the mind."

All at once, Beatrice wanted to get the hell out of 1804.

The device buzzed. Its battery bar said 5% REMAINING.

But Beatrice was oblivious.

She was clicking to SETTINGS and returning to Russia three seconds after she'd left.

She grabbed the still-snoozing MacCleary's suit, then his wrist as he lay in the tub, and hit the DEFAULT icon.

Suddenly, the pair fell through the doorway of Trooley's Tourist Tavern, just as the Universal Truth Machine was packing up their instruments, and Reli was counting out the cash in the till.

All Reli could think of, seeing Beatrice and the naked, champagne-drenched friend, was how much fun she'd missed.

"I'll see you later," Beatrice said. Then she vanished.

The sound of boisterous jazz music filled the bar as amply as the cigarette smoke and bodies did. Short-haired women in short-fringed dresses and men in sharp suits danced on every available bit of floor.

Other than the fashion and lack of some wall decor and visible booze bottles, it was the exact same Trooley's Tourist Tavern that Beatrice had always walked into.

All around, people were sipping from brown-bagged bottles

and large teacups. Prohibition had done little to deter the bar's main business. It masqueraded as a high-profile jazz club, but everyone around knew the real deal.

Beatrice had seen photographs of evenings just such as this on the walls of the Trooley's she frequented. It was every bit as much fun as she'd hoped. The element of danger concerning what she knew the immediate future would hold made it even more exciting. But she had to work fast.

Behind the bar was a man Beatrice recognized as Michael Trooley, Reli's grandfather. His picture would later be hung over the pool table along with all the other Trooleys who'd run the place. He'd hired some flapper girls to actually sling the drinks, so he stood there in an impeccable pin-striped suit, watching the action. Every so often he would meander over to the door to keep an eye on who was arriving and departing, and how.

Beatrice wasted no time. She approached Trooley at the door and held out her hand.

"Mr. Trooley, pleased to meet you. My name is Beatrice Baxter."

"Good evening, Miss Baxter, pleasure to meet you."

"Thank you. Sir, I don't mean to alarm you, but I am an avid patron of your establishment and I need to tell you this: I have it on good information that in the near future you're going to be raided."

Trooley lit a cigarette and chuckled robustly. He had the exact same sonorous laugh as Reli—confident, bemused, carefree. "I think not, my dear. Every policeman in the precinct does business here."

"It's not the police . . . one of your competitors hates you for your superior whiskey and will pay the cops to take you down. The Pussycat Palace Club down the street."

Trooley shrugged. "Let me buy you a drink, Miss Baxter."

Navigating their way through Charleston-dancing couples,

Trooley and Beatrice sat at the bar. Beatrice noted in passing that it was the exact same seat she'd been reading in when her evening began.

The jazz was jumping—it'd be a nice track to play back for Reli. Beatrice touched the RECORD icon on the screen of the device in her pocket as Trooley hailed a bartender. Two teacups of red wine were placed in front of them.

"I know about bootleg whiskey, and the snake heads as the secret whiskey ingredient. You have to hide it, all of it, tonight, or you might lose everything. What you have is almost priceless to your family."

"Valuable, maybe," Trooley said, mulling over her words. "Nothing is priceless."

"This information is. And your bar could prosper for another century with a treasure trove like what you've got."

"And why are you telling me this, may I ask?"

"Let's just say I've invested quite a bit in the future of your bar." She wordlessly handed Trooley the matchbook she'd had in her pocket since the start of the evening. It commemorated the 140th anniversary of the bar, reading "1866–2006."

Trooley sipped from his teacup solemnly amidst the melee. It was almost too loud to think properly.

Definitely too loud to hear the device in Beatrice's pocket beep urgently.

Repeatedly.

And then go silent.

Devin MacCleary woke up still drunk, which was understandable considering he'd been half-submerged in a bathtub full of some of the best champagne in history, and had drunk a considerable quantity of it both awake and asleep.

History. The future. He didn't know why he bothered with any of it. He should have just taken Beatrice to Costa Rica 0007 and thrown the device into the ocean. They should go back right now. He'd left the device's charger back there, anyway.

He was very cold. He opened his eyes.

Reli had thrown Devin's suit over him and propped him upright in a booth. He was still naked.

"I can't figure if this is the best or worst night of your life, bro," she told him seriously.

"For real," the drummer of the band, Lex, added, tossing back the last of his champagne. "If people knew your bar got this kind of action, you'd be jammed all the time."

"Jam!" cried MacCleary. "Truth Machine jaaaaam! Aurelia . . . Reli . . . *really* . . . you gotta hire these guys."

The singer stared hard at Devin and Reli in turn. "So, Bar Fraulein? What do you think of it? Your man says yeah."

Reli shrugged. "Yeah, sure. Call me tomorrow and we'll book a date. You handle all your own publicity."

The band members grinned amongst themselves. "Cheers," said the singer, and with that, they left.

MacCleary looked earnestly at all four of the Relis he was drunkenly seeing. "Beatrice broke my heart again, Reli. She left me for the last time. I don't think she'll come back."

"Well, I'm sorry to hear that, Dev."

"S'okay. She'll be happier then. I'll be happy now, before my old future happens."

"Do you want some water or coffee or something, dude?"

"No! But, hey, if you want some champagne, there's a nice . . . niiiiiice. . . . bottle of Comet Vintage Veuve Clicquot in the cooler." MacCleary burped. "I told you I'd be right back. Right back from 1811!"

"Comet Vintage, huh? I probably shouldn't open that, what with it being priceless and all."

"Then save it . . . in case the band doesn't get you enough business. But I think they will. And if they don't, I'll buy the place in *gold!*" He slapped the banquette victoriously to accentuate this point.

"You really give a damn about this place, huh? That's very sweet of you." Reli used the latter sentence several times a day at patrons, but this time she actually meant it.

"This place, this time, you. It's your fault, you gave a damn about me first! Damn. *And* you're hotter than all the whores this place ever had."

"Well, that really is very sweet of you, Devin, thank you." Reli laughed and shook her head.

"Hey . . . *hey* . . . I'm naked."

"Yep."

"You should get naked, too."

Reli couldn't have put it better herself. Locking the door, she shut off all the lights save the oil lamps, then walked back down the long bar to the booth, shedding garments like a snake sheds her skin.

Trooley returned to work, unperturbed by the anachronistic matches. *Don't say I didn't warn you,* Beatrice figured. She'd at least *tried* to save the bar.

A good-looking man in a white suit, shoulder-length blond hair, and a white Panama hat sat on the other side of Beatrice. He was reading a large stack of loose notes that appeared to be hieroglyphs.

"Do you mind if I ask what you're reading?" she inquired.

"Well, the devil of it is, I'm not sure," he replied. He had a British accent and an immaculately trimmed mustache. His blue eyes shone out from his suntanned face. "I'm just back from an expedition in Cairo for the university—I'm in the Egyptology department—and I can't make heads or tails of it. It appears that the Egyptians had devised a way to combine acid with metal rods in small pots that may have served as electrical units . . . but I can't quite make out from the hieroglyphs exactly *how*. It's fascinating."

"You mean they might have had electricity in the pyramids?"

"Indeed, as preposterous as it may seem. It's a strange beast, electricity. Power, force . . ." He tilted his head toward hers. "*Magnetism*. Intriguing."

"You're the intriguing one," Beatrice decided. "Tell me more."

Trooley's Tourist Tavern was rocking. Reli could barely keep up. Patrons were lined up three deep all along the bar. From the stage, Universal Truth Machine was singing a song about whiskey that people were flipping out over, dancing and whooping along under the fierce guitars. Behind the bar, Devin helped to sling drinks to the crowd. Every time he and Reli brushed past each other, they smiled.

One addition had been made to the decor of the bar. Near where Beatrice had always sat, on the back shelf facing the drinkers, was a fishbowl containing a single bright blue and purple crown-tail fighting fish. Reli and Devin had named it Beatrice. Underneath the bowl, a small sign told all the patrons whose eyes visited it: WELCOME BACK . . . WHENEVER.

Running out of time turns out to be the best time of all for the patrons of Trooley's Tourist Tavern. History may be written by the winners, but it is just as intriguing for the bystanders. And no one may just stand idly by in . . . the Twilight Zone.

# I BELIEVE I'LL HAVE ANOTHER

Loren L. Coleman

The miracle of powered flight. What some once called the pinnacle of mankind's mastery over his world. But between takeoff and landing, mankind's world is about to change forever—leaving two hundred people hanging on the cusp of one man's cynical faith. A man with a glimpse of God's flight plan. Stow your tray tables. Seatbacks up. This plane is already descending . . . into the Twilight Zone.

When the Rapture came, it caught me on the afternoon shuttle between La Guardia and Dulles, Flight 1602, descending from thirty-five thousand feet at three hundred fifty miles per hour. I was enjoying my second Bloody Mary and a small bag of wasabi peanuts.

My first reaction was pretty routine. A startled, "Son of a bitch."

My second: He's *effing* early!

The whole thing crept up unawares on the entire plane. A small, distant, plaintive wail, barely able to be heard above the drone of the engines. Only in the last few seconds, as it suddenly rose in volume and clarity, did I recognize it as a single, pure note blown on the Golden Trumpet. It neither wavered nor worried. Gabriel hit it perfect (and with ten thousand years of practice, I would otherwise have been surprised). A solid ten. Nine-point-seven on the *New York Times* arts page.

The Trumpet. A sudden chorus of angels singing out in breath-stealing harmony. Then a clap of celestial thunder. If you'd never heard celestial thunder before that day, you probably thought that the sky had split open. Maybe you even wanted to look, but of course everyone was still blinded by the sudden flash of purest, whitest light that washed over the earth with the intensity of an Obama press conference.

Something like this happens, you expect a more physical reaction. The ground trembling. People getting knocked over by a mighty shock wave. At the very least you should worry that your drink has spilled (mine hadn't). Part of the eerie Otherness, though, was the complete lack of any physical sensation. The 737 gave only a slight bump as the Rapture lightened its load by a mere thousand pounds.

Five people.

Dammit.

Don't misunderstand me. I hadn't expected to get "called home," as they say. I still had things to do. Places to be. I wasn't insulted, and quite honestly, if I had been among the chosen, I would have had some very choice words on the subject.

But among the Raptured five were half of the plane's flight crew.

*That* I had not expected.

Besides some cursing among the first-class passengers and a scream from the flight attendant who had been inside the cockpit, the whole thing happened with little furor. There was a slight uproar from coach-class seating, though not as much as I would have expected. Yet. And one clear, distinct shout from far back near the plane's tail section.

"Elvis has left the building!"

So I knew there was at least one demon on board. Or a Graceland nut. Either way, I marked that one down as trouble.

My eyes burned with the after-glare of celestial light. Bright purple spots swam in my vision. I had at least thirty seconds before the flight attendant stumbled back from the cockpit and caused a near panic, easily a minute before the undercover air marshal would pull his gun. So I closed my eyes, popped a few peanuts into my mouth, and felt around for the plastic cup resting on my tray table. Trust me. If there is a better complement to powered flight than vodka, tomato juice, and spicy nuts, God kept that one to Himself. Wasabi scrubbed away any aftertaste. Tomato juice salved the burn of the wasabi. And the vodka was Chopin—which was reason enough.

Unfortunately, there would not be enough time to really enjoy the last of my cocktail. With regret (and one final sip), I folded the tray table off to one side and handed the half-filled cup to my seatmate on the aisle. Nice lady. Expensive shoes. A regional manager for Halliburton (I just knew) and heading into D.C. for an affair with a married three-star at the Pentagon.

A business proposition in every sense of the term.

There were now as many Christ-our-kings and God-in-Heavens being shouted as curses. People were beginning to catch a clue. More voices shouted out as people began to notice that some of their traveling companions were missing.

"My husband? Where did he go?"

And, "That little girl, she just disappeared!"

"But I'm still a virgin!"

A part of me wanted to understand the thought process behind *that* one.

Our forward-cabin flight attendant was not about to give me the time. The cockpit door slammed back hard as she put her entire weight behind it. (All right, maybe one hundred ten pounds, but those doors are *light*.) Her little cap sat on the side of her head, wrenched around and held in place by a few bobby pins. I had found it rather charming during boarding. Now it was just sad.

"The pilot," she shouted. "Both pilots! They're gone!"

Which left only the navigator to attempt any landing. Not an unreasonable situation. But her outburst wasn't exactly helpful, damaging what little calm had remained aboard the plane.

"What?" seemed to be the overall response. Followed closely by at least a half-dozen shouts of "How?"

Coming in third, but still placing, was a man at the back of first class who asked, "Was there a bomb?"

And that took care of any remaining fragmentary restraint. Especially from the air marshal who leapt out of his front-aisle seat (the one across from my contract-hustling Halliburton neighbor), digging a Glock 9mm out of his shoulder holster.

Brandishing a gun inside an airplane at over thirty thousand feet is never a good idea. Especially when your first words aren't "I'm an air marshal," or "This is all under control." Or, even better: "The safety is on and I'm not going to put my finger near the trigger while on this pressurized aircraft."

First, it encourages anyone else with a gun to reach for their weapon as well. I had high hopes and better than average odds that this was an unlikely possibility. Second was the very real chance of an accidental discharge. That direction lay madness, panic, and the very unpleasant thought that I would never get back to my Bloody Mary. Maybe it seems to you that my priorities weren't quite straight, but then, Hey! I'd just missed the Rapture train. Allow me to take what simple pleasures were left.

Besides. Chopin!

I'm certain the next few minutes looked more impressive than they actually were. I mean, it helps when you have at least a feeling for the ultimate set of actuarial tables. But just as quickly as the atmosphere on the plane seemed to be deteriorating, I was moving. Having left my drink in (hopefully) good hands, I met the flight attendant near the head of the first-class aisle, stuck out a foot, and tripped her forward into the arms of the senator who had been riding at the back of first class. This was the guy who had asked about the bomb, so I didn't feel bad when a flailing hand raked two bloody furrows down the side of his face. So long as it kept him busy for a moment.

That left the air marshal. I didn't *know* he was about to cause a rapid and violent depressurization event, but the smell of sulfur in the air suggested that it was possible. And his wild-eyed stare made it seem more so. Not less. Which was the only thing that made me reach for the gun, clamping a hand down over the back end. The air marshal spasmed, and the Glock's hammer fell down (hard!) on the fold of skin between my thumb and forefinger. Yeah, the guy had cocked it back while pulling the gun free.

The bright spot of pain and more than a little anger lent me enough strength to wrench the gun from his grasp. I stiff-armed it back into his face, and he went crashing down to the floor. Stunned, but hardly out for the count. It gave me time to eject the clip and toss it to the senator who was untangling himself from the stewardess, while I traded the pistol to the would-be Halliburton whore for my cocktail.

Standing at the front of the cabin, I felt fourteen pairs of eyes slowly focus on me. Some in surprise. At least two pairs in mild anger. And the dazed air marshal with something akin to smoldering rage. A ten-year-old girl riding next to her mother stared at me with her mouth forming a perfect little "O" of amazement. Suddenly, I had become the center of attention in the middle of a terrifyingly stressful moment. I wondered if that had been a rather stupid choice to make.

From the back of the plane, I felt a strong wave of anger surge forward. And then I was sure.

"If we can all calm down," I said, "I think I can help get us through this."

The senator, holding the flight attendant in one arm, stared down at the pistol clip in his other hand. "We're going to be all right," he said with all the conviction of a campaign pledge. And he heard the lie in his own voice, I knew.

The little girl curled over next to her mother. Peeked back. "Is that true?" she asked in a very small voice.

There wasn't much wiggle room in the question. Not really. So I swirled the last of my Bloody Mary in its cup, drained it, and allowed myself one last second of Zen-like tranquility as the smooth blend worked its own form of magic. I felt a warm flush spread out through my chest. Considered the very real problem of an aircraft caught in slow descent with no real pilots left aboard, a demon flying coach, and about two hundred people upon whom He had just turned His back.

Were we going to be all right?

"Probably not," I said. "But that shouldn't stop us from trying."

There were things that needed to be done, and (from the expectant looks of my captive audience) things that likely needed to be said as well. But since it is impossible to hold an audience captive for long with only an empty cocktail glass—especially one made from plastic, give me a heavy glass tumbler and I'll give it a shot—I decided it was the better idea to get straight to work.

"There's a demon in coach," I said, moving up the aisle. I stepped over the air marshal, who sat up behind me, and handed my empty cup to the flight attendant. "I need salt, or sugar. Lots of it."

"You're insane," the air marshal said. He held his hand to a bloody nose. "And you're under arrest."

If only. "Don't mix them," I warned her, "but get me all you have of one or the other."

Whether she was humoring the guy who had just taken—and thrown aside—a gun, or believed I was speaking in metaphor, at least she was calm enough now to not incite more panic. She smoothed down her flight dress. Tried to adjust her cap, and then pulled it free and tossed it aside.

While she hurried to the forward galley, I knelt next to the little girl who shrank away from me. Her mother covered her with a protective arm. "Can you do me a favor? I need you to be strong, and tell me if you see or hear anything strange." One green eye, peeking through a crook in her mom's elbow, blinked slowly. She nodded and I nodded back. "And I need a few strands of hair."

"Get away from her," her mother warned. She had gray at her temples and a strong brow over fierce green eyes. A natural, confident woman. The best (and the worst) kind.

Fortunately, I had somehow drafted a Washington politician to my side. The senator leaned over, pinched a few strands of stray golden hair from the little girl's head, and gave a quick yank. She yelped and the mom glared, but that was as far as it went.

The flight attendant returned with a dry coffee cup filled with an inch of white powder. Dipping a finger into the substance, I tested it on my tongue. Artificial sweetener. Well, it would have to do.

I crouched at the curtain that protected first class from coach. It had always amazed me, that power of suggestion. Twenty square feet of fabric, and so far as most people were concerned, their world ended at the first thread. Out of sight, out of mind, as the saying goes. Thou shalt not pass and get thee gone. (Under the curtain's hem, I saw a reddish-golden light glow bright and hard. There were a few shouts of despair from coach.) I hoped those rules still applied. Belief might be the last weapon we had left to us.

The senator hunkered down next to me, watching as I carefully set the young girl's hair on the floor and then crossed it with a small, continuous line of sweetener. The powder weighed down the hair, which suddenly curled and waved as if it were something alive.

"You know what you are doing?" the senator asked.

Not exactly, though I didn't see any reason to worry him with that. I had instinct and a little inside information to go on. Not much more. From both ends of the powdery line I drew a small arc back to the walls on either side of the curtained opening. One side was a wall to the forward lavatory. Solid enough. The other wasn't much more than a plastic cubicle wall. Worth a moment's delay. Maybe.

"Are you with . . . them?"

Hard to say which *them* he was referring to. Like most Americans, I'd like to believe that my elected representatives are on the side of truth, justice, and God. Experience, of course, has taught us to be wary.

Then again, I had thought well enough of him at the time to toss him the Glock's clip. So—I decided—play the odds.

"I'm in insurance."

And I gave him *the look*.

It caused him to lean back. Just a touch. "I'm covered," the senator said.

I considered that. I didn't have the man under any policy I'd written, not for one side or the other. So he obviously didn't know what to believe. Five minutes ago, I'd have given him a coin flip at best. Now?

Grimacing, I shook my head. "No. Not for this."

"It happened, then?" There was a sound from the back cabin, like the flap of enormous wings. He leaned back. Shook his head. "This is real? It seems like there are still a lot of people here."

"I'm surprised we lost as many as five. Didn't take into account the flight crew. Flying with God as their copilot, I guess."

"Then how do we land this plane?"

That was the question. Then again, with the world falling to hell below us, I was quite tempted to let the whole thing just continue on until we ran out of fuel, wasabi nuts, or Bloody Marys. Cleaner. Quicker. And with some luck we'd bypass that whole trials and tribulations thing.

"I said *you're under arrest*," the air marshal tried again. There was a quality in his voice. A new confidence I didn't like. When people took safety in something they believed in, they often got confident. And dangerous.

So when the little girl whispered, "He's coming," I naturally assumed she was talking about the smoldering marshal.

She could have been. As I stood back above my work and turned, I caught the marshal just as he moved for me down the aisle. Like some perpetual motion engine of law enforcement, he was determined to remain in motion along the path he'd chosen earlier. Maybe he was taking the bloody nose a bit too personally. Or his lack of selection for the Rapture. As snubs went, the former was more immediate and the latter far more severe. Of course, most people had trouble with the long view. Hence, only five.

My earlier neighbor, the industry pro, had risen from her seat to stand in the aisle behind the advancing air marshal. She still held the clip-less Glock in her hand, as if unsure what exactly to do with it. Under better circumstances she would certainly have handed the man back his gun. Law and order was also about belief as much as it was about the strength to enforce it. In most cases, the air marshal would have been invested in the highest authority. But anyone willing to do what she had been flying to Washington for, all in the name of personal interest, had to be considering the implications of the last ten minutes, and what that might mean to her future.

Basically, she seemed to be giving me the benefit of her doubt.

Too bad that just wasn't going to be enough.

With a snarl of rage, the air marshal leaped forward, hands outstretched. I believe he might have been thinking to strangle me. In the back of my head, I felt the probability stretch out along long lines of chance. The foundation of creation, of weight of original sin, and the power of personal choice, all coalescing into a new moment where I'd have an equal chance of surviving (or, at least, of remaining free to act) or falling. The same choice and chance that had once been faced (and lost) by the Morningstar himself.

Fortunately for me, the senator had not yet chosen to abandon my side. He stepped into the narrow aisle with me, grappling with the frenzied marshal. My tax dollars at work. Finally.

Together we threw the crazed man back. And, really, that should have been the end of it. Except that he stumbled right back into the Halliburton Blonde, who tangled up with him in a quick flurry of arms and legs. Then she sat back hard, and he spun around with his gun pointed out at arm's length in a classic shooting stance.

It caught me halfway down the aisle, thinking to secure the man before he caused more trouble. I pulled up short, staring into the dark tunnel of the Glock's barrel, never once doubting that there was a bullet in the gun. No clip, true, but I hadn't thought about the very real (and still painful) fact that his gun had been cocked before. And why cock a gun over an empty chamber? The simple answer: You didn't.

There had been one bullet already in the pipe. Of course there had.

I was reasonably sure that the marshal now meant to kill me. It wasn't anything personal. Like I said before, there were certain probabilities that would likely play out once someone drew a gun aboard an airplane.

"Mister!" The little girl, breaking away from her mother's hold as she half-stood in her chair. "Mister, he's *here!*"

He certainly was. I felt the stench of warm, sulfurous breath on the back of my neck, and the entire forward cabin filled with a reddish-golden glow. Like a small, cramped room bathed in firelight. It played in the eyes of the air marshal, dancing with terrifying fear. It reflected painfully off the diamonds worn around the throat of the military-industrial merger waiting to happen.

It touched everyone but the clear green eyes of the ten-year-old who had frozen in place. I felt her terror as it turned me around, but saw that she, at least, had been untouched by corruption. It made me wonder (albeit briefly) how such a strong, pure soul had not been called.

Because it wasn't going to matter much longer. Standing in the aisle, curtains thrust aside, bathed in an infernal aura, was the demon.

And I'd be damned (possibly very soon, in fact) if he wasn't also wearing a white Elvis jumpsuit, with dark, jet hair greased back into a proper pompadour, and a rhinestone-studded cape that spread out behind him, furling and unfurling, like jeweled wings.

Now I can't say one hundred percent that there hadn't been a demon flying coach already made up as an Elvis impersonator. As disguises go, in fact, that wouldn't be half bad. Demons want to be noticed, and yet dismissed. Never taken seriously while being afforded some measure of respect for what they are or what they are about to do. And, after all, didn't they all want to be the King? That's where the whole mess had started with them.

Though while it's true that His design allows for some of the most unheard-of coincidences, many of which have been accepted as bona fide miracles in the past, I felt the celestial actuarial tables were weighted rather against this. More likely the demon had felt my earlier aversion to Graceland fanatics, and chose that face to reveal based on the belief that I would think far less of its abilities. Maybe it was right. Remember what I said about the power of suggestion and the weapon that may be fashioned by belief? It works both ways.

Considering all of this (and taking a few extra seconds to wish for a final cocktail before reaching any ultimate destination), it took me a moment to realize that I was, in fact, still breathing, and Elvis had not taken a step forward into the first-class cabin. He was caught behind the line of my making, which glowed about his feet, soft and white and sugar-free. It gave me another moment to breathe, and think. To see a few of the coach-class passengers (newly converted to the call of a false Graceland) spreading out behind him. And to remember the guy with the gun at my back.

The air marshal's mouth moved up and down, without sound, like a fish gasping for air. Finally, he managed: "What. The. Hell."

"Yep," I said.

At some point the brain simply recognized evil no matter what kind of face it wore. The guy had to start coping with that. In the years to come (assuming we had years), this kind of thing would grow more and more common. Creation would be left on its own, running out of control, with no subtle hand or small, quiet voice guiding us forward. There would be a great deal of work to do for people like me. Policies to sign (and enforce) from the only remaining carriers who would matter. Despair and the betrayal of being left behind would test the faith of even the most righteous. Opium would be a more likely opiate of the masses. Elder religions would come back into their magicks. Public television would lose its funding.

There might be no more wasabi nuts.

No more Chopin!

The blanket of anguish and apathy that had settled over me with smothering force was suddenly ripped away, and I saw what Elvis had tried to do. Too bad for him he had pushed it a step too far.

There were things that needed to be done, and things that needed to be said. Unfortunately I once again wouldn't be given time to go about this the easy way. Not as the senator had flipped his coin again, then reached out and swiped at the temporary wall I had built.

Disappointing, sure, but haven't we all come to expect about as much from our public servants?

With a howl (and a quick hip gyration), Elvis leaped forward. And as much as He allows me an occasional peek at the gears and underpinnings, the mechanics of His design, I was fairly certain at that moment that I was a dead man. I stumbled back, right into the grasp of the air marshal, who seized me by the back of my neck and held me with great (and painful) newfound strength.

So we both stood there, watching, as it was the ten-year-old who stepped into the aisle, hands on her hips, and shouted at Elvis with that perfect, self-righteous indignation only a ten-year-old flying first class could muster, "You don't belong here!"

Elvis pulled up short, and his aura lost a few watts of brightness. He loomed above my little savior with fire and brimstone burning in his black eyes. Maybe he would have rallied quickly with his followers from coach and the senator creeping up in his shadow, but before he could, the girl's mother had joined her daughter, putting one protective hand over her shoulder.

"Leave her alone!"

Now others were moving. Taking some measure of faith in the defiance of others. Not many, but enough. The businessman in the wrinkled suit. An Asian twentysomething with enough electronics hanging on him to open his own tech-support company. They stood, stepped into the aisle, and blocked Elvis from reaching me. Even my Halliburton neighbor strode forward now, and I felt my heart leap with joy (or at least the hope of survival) when she pointed and actually shouted, "Get thee gone!"

I don't think Elvis expected that. I know I hadn't.

Salvation. Redemption. Mysterious ways. All that jazz.

Which put me in the very advantageous position of having the air marshal's ear right when the demon's power was at an ebb, confronted by the strength some of my traveling companions had managed to muster. Young indignation. Protective motherhood. First-class righteousness.

Law and order?

He had the shot, right over the small stature of the golden-haired girl. "He's trying for the cockpit," I warned the air marshal, and hoped that it would be enough.

It was. A gun, pulled on an airplane, wants to go off.

The report was deafening, much louder than it should have been, even in the tight confines of a 737. It seemed very familiar. Thunderous, even.

Elvis screamed, belting out from the diaphragm. His aura flared bright and brilliant and burning, folded back in on itself, and with a final hip-bump he disappeared in a flash of the whitest light. Purple spots swam in front of my eyes. When I blinked them clear, I saw that the demon had also taken with him his coach-class followers and the senator, too. How the mighty had fallen.

And in the distance, did I hear the dying, plaintive note of a trumpet?

Something we still had to take on faith, I suppose. Even now.

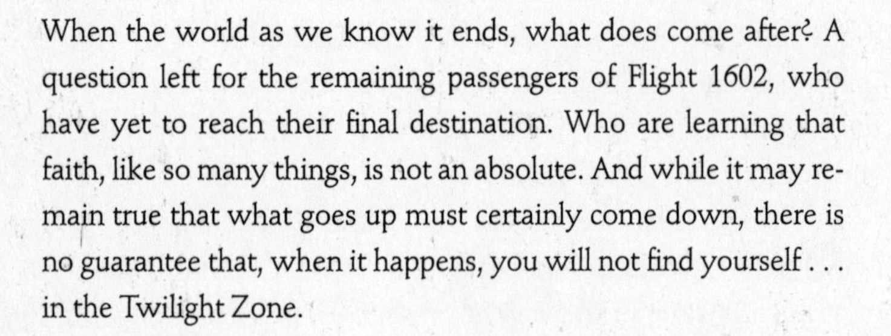

When the world as we know it ends, what does come after? A question left for the remaining passengers of Flight 1602, who have yet to reach their final destination. Who are learning that faith, like so many things, is not an absolute. And while it may remain true that what goes up must certainly come down, there is no guarantee that, when it happens, you will not find yourself . . . in the Twilight Zone.

# THE IDES OF TEXAS

Douglas Brode

Since the dawn of civilization, when the first men crawled out from their caves and attempted to make some sense of the universe around them, the human race has chosen to believe that all is not chance and chaos; that there is a meaning to the world as well as our lives in it; that each of us, however humble or great, has his destiny. But what happens when what appears precisely that is interrupted? Does this create anarchy, or is there a remote possibility that what seems some cosmic mistake may actually provide the means to fulfilling one's fate? Join us now as a living legend leaves history behind to take a sudden, if surprisingly temporary, side trip into . . . the Twilight Zone.

As the first light of dawn broke over San Antonio on that nasty morning of March 6, 1836, the foreboding sky above appeared to mirror events taking place below. The last of the Alamo's 186 defenders, struggling in the semidarkness to offer the beau geste of a final stand, died on the sharp bayonets of Santa Anna's troops.

The finishing attack, a culmination of thirteen days of brutal siege, lasted less than an hour. After the first wave of General Martin de Cos's advance force slipped close to the undermanned fortress under cover of the starless night, they breached the Alamo's north wall, the Texicans' most vulnerable spot. Once General Castrillón's volunteers reinforced Cos, whose men had suffered a terrible toll from Kentucky long rifles above, the outcome became frightfully obvious to all.

Travis, the Alamo's young commander, died early on. Bowie, the pioneer who had led so many of these rough-hewn types to the Texas plains from Creole Louisiana years earlier, was discovered weak and ill on his cot. Even so, the bear-sized co-commander, his reddish hair marbled with silver, employed his signature blade to take down three of the enemy before dying.

Now, scattered Mexican patrols sought out any member of the defending force still hiding in the shadows. Their stark and simple orders: Take no prisoners!

So much blackpowder smoke filled the old mission that the advancing lancers could not discern anything clearly. While scouting the chapel area, one group, under Lt. Jesus Ramirez, noticed a tall, rangy figure standing stock still, patiently awaiting them. Something about his stature frightened the men as they inched close. Juarez noticed his buckskin garb, as well as what everyone in the Americas knew to be his "curious" fur cap. "Cwocky, Cwocky!" they screamed. For this was the famed David Crockett: Indian fighter, bear hunter, former U.S. Congressman.

The Mexicans advanced with caution: How many would die trying to take down this tallest Texican? Before they could rush him, a cold, bitter wind swept a smoke cloud between the last defender, ready to use his spent rifle as a club, and themselves.

*So this,* Crockett thought, *is the land of the stranger, where I rise or I fall. Always did wonder when and where the final reckoning would occur. Now, I know.*

When the smoke dissipated a few seconds later, the seven lancers gasped. No one stood before them. Could they, in their trepidation, have only imagined Crockett? Was he already among the dead, what they'd perceived merely an apparition, the product of their collective fear? That, Lieutenant Ramirez guessed, was one of those things he'd never know, not for certain. Yet one fact could not be disputed—how glad each man was to remain alive at the end of the battle.

It would be a story each soldier in the unit would tell his children, a tale that they would conclude with the fearful words: *May I never again encounter that indomitable presence!*

"Welcome to the city of brotherly love."

Crockett stirred, head pounding, body aching. Never had he experienced such a profound sense of disorientation. He tried to sit up, managing to do so only with great difficulty. Dizzy, he glanced up at the fellow who'd spoken, his tone combining sincere concern with puckish humor. A little chap, he stood beside the couch where Crockett found himself lying.

*Am I dead? Them Mexicans was a-closin' in, but I don't recall feeling their lances penetrate my hide. Still, I reckon that's what happened. This fella must be the gate-keeper. Wonder if I made it On High? Or mebbe this—*

"My name is Angus McCracken," the bespectacled soul, whom Crockett guessed to be around thirty-five years old, continued with a smile. "It's an honor to meet you, Colonel." Crockett took the fellow's hand, which he'd extended for shaking.

"My pleasure, or at least I hope so. You ain't planning on escorting me Down Below, I hope 'n' pray?"

"No, no," McCracken laughed. "Nor are you dead, sir."

"Huh! Been in an' outta b'ar traps all m' life, but I sure can't figger how I twisted away from that un."

"I'll show you," McCracken replied, placing an arm around Crockett's waist for support. Once the hero known as the Lion of the West had risen, his new companion helped him cross to the small room's far side. Lining the wall was a glass booth covered with meters, bulbs, levers, every sort of technical apparatus and scientific equipment known to man. Smoke billowed out of the side outlets as well as a release gauge up on top of this mechanical contraption.

"What, in the name of all that's holy, is that?"

"My latest invention. I call it a time machine."

Several hours later, Crockett sipped a cup of black coffee as he sat across a small dining table from his host. While David, who had not enjoyed a full meal during his period of near-starvation inside the Alamo, consumed a large dinner, McCracken rambled on about what he referred to as his "experiment." An amateur scientist, he had devoted most of his life to building weird devices that might lead to progress for mankind. He'd tried to create a boat that could travel underwater, a wagon that might fly into the sky. And what he'd just recently completed: a machine able to move people forward or backward in time.

"Why me?" Crockett bellowed. "If ya wanted to make this here monstrous piece o' work, what'd ya pick on me ter do it?"

McCracken looked as if he might break into tears. "Colonel, you've always been my hero. When I was a child I read stories about your courage on the battlefield."

"Well, there's 'stories,' an' there's history. My first engagement with the Creeks? I got sick to m' stomach. When it was over, fell down on m' knees, lost m' lunch. Admitted as much in that autobiography I published."

"That may be the fact, Colonel. But time has turned you into a legend. In truth, not many people read your book anymore. But they devour the monthly *Crockett Almanac*s, all about your adventures in the Rocky Mountains—"

"Why, I never stepped foot in the Rockies!"

McCracken grinned. "See what I mean? There hasn't been a man to compare with you since the fall of the Alamo. That's why you're here. Colonel, I believe we need you. Now more than ever."

"Hold on a minute, bub. Since the fall of—?"

"Nine years ago today. Though I'm sure it only seems like a few minutes to you, I employed my device to draw you out of that battle at the last possible moment."

Frowning, Crockett leaned across the table. "Mind telling me just where I am? And when?"

"Certainly! David Crockett is alive and well and living in Philadelphia on March 6, 1845. Isn't that wonderful?"

"Ain't so sure. Don't mean to sound unappreciative, Mr. McCracken, but maybe you shoulda left well enough alone."

McCracken couldn't wait to show his guest the brave new world that had developed in Philadelphia during the past decade: advances in urban transportation, new systems for lighting the downtown area, and recent improvements in such important matters as running water and sewage removal. Also, restaurants that offered cuisine from around the world right here, so every citizen could try international delicacies to cultivate more sophisticated tastes. The inventor couldn't believe Crockett's reaction: While this throwback to the now-all-but-bygone frontier did marvel at what he observed, the colonel grew nostalgic for the old ways.

"I know, I know," Crockett said as they strolled through a magnificent three-story building in which one could purchase virtually any goods from the globe's four corners. Crockett wore a suit that McCracken had ordered for him; his buckskins were hanging in a closet of the inventor's home. "Beautiful, sure. But not fer me. I miss the old trading posts, the rustic general stores. The way we were."

"Davy," McCracken sighed, as they were now on first-name terms. "If I'd known how unhappy you'd be, I never would have—"

"Y' meant well, Angus. I do know that."

The one place Crockett deeply desired to go was Liberty Hall, to see the great bell that symbolized the land he loved and had done so much to tame and settle. McCracken noticed his new friend's eyes light up at the sight, Davy grinning from ear to ear when he considered the large crack running the entire distance from the bell's top to bottom.

"Y' know, Angus, when I first got t' Congress, I set out t' patch that up. Got me some mortar, marched right in, made m'self t' home, spent a day fillin' that space. Looked just like new. Wall. I let it sit fer two days, then struck it with a gong. Soon's I did, the mortar fell away, an' there was the crack again, big an' bold as ever."

"If David Crockett couldn't fix it," Angus admiringly observed, "I don't guess anyone could."

"I allus took it as a sign from On High. Democracy by its very nature can't be perfected. Too complex, too many edges. May not reach the ideal, but in the real world, it's the best mankind can ever know. Way I see it, that crack reappearin' was God's way of tellin' me so. 'Davy,' the Good Lord was a-sayin', 'do your best to make things better. *Go ahead!* Just understand: There will always be limitations to what you, or any man, kin accomplish.' "

Angus marveled at the profound philosophy that this uneducated soul spouted in impromptu poetry which conveyed the voice of the common man. "You really do believe that?"

"To everything there is a season. Yup. All that happens is fer a purpose. Sometimes, though, it kin be pretty tough figurin' out precisely what that is."

"Including my bringing you here?"

"I wish I could figure out what I'm supposed t' do. Ain't been able to so fer." Crockett's voice turned melancholy.

"So you still wish you could go back to where you came from? Even knowing that to do so would mean instant death?" The only time and place other than here that Crockett could be placed, according to the paradigm that McCracken had created for his time machine, was precisely where he'd been picked up: in

Davy's case, a split second before his death at the hands of the Mexican soldiers.

"In all honesty? Yes. More I think on it, the Alamo wasn't just somethin' that happened to happen. It was in my stars. Why, I'd been born fer it. I feel . . . robbed!"

"I had hoped you might do wonderful things here. I understand now this was a mistake. A man belongs to his own generation. Let's head back to my place and fix it."

Crockett looked happier than he had since the moment McCracken had brought the buckskinned buckaroo into his own time period. An hour later, the colonel appeared sadder than he had throughout the past two weeks. "What's wrong?" he demanded, growing a little surly.

"I just don't know." McCracken had helped his guest into the machine, set the controls, and pulled the lever. Nothing happened. The inventor could only guess that, when trying it out for the first time, something had gone wrong. Perhaps that explained why so much smoke poured out, which had surprised him. "It's just not working."

"So 'm stuck here?"

"I'm . . . afraid so. For the time being, at least."

"Why, if that don't beat all." Crockett began pacing around the room like an animal confined to a cage.

"I'm so deeply sorry."

"Sorry don't make it right."

"I know. Davy, let me go out and buy some equipment to try to fix it. That's all I'll work on, day and—"

"Look me in the eye," Crockett insisted. McCracken did as commanded. "You really think you can get this infernal thing-a-ma-jigger goin' again?"

"Probably not." McCracken found it impossible not only to lie but even put a positive spin on the situation when staring into Crockett's honest-as-oak face. "But I swear to you, Davy, I'll give it everything I got." This did not visibly hearten his guest, Davy's eyes growing misty.

For the next week, Angus came and went, purchasing gadgets, sending all the way to New York for others not yet available in Philadelphia. Hours passed; he labored hard. Crockett, who had grown uncomfortable with the suit, went back to wearing his buckskins. This made McCracken feel even worse. He had learned the hard way that, as an old adage put it, the road to hell may be paved with good intentions. By saving Crockett's life he'd robbed his hero of a birthright—a gallant death at what had, during the past decade, come to be considered America's greatest shrine of liberty.

"Where you goin'?" Crockett called out as McCracken headed for the door.

"Post office, see if the new materials came in. Care to come along?"

"Nah. Don't feel t' home out there."

"We've got to keep hoping. Sooner or—"

"Later, I'd imagine. Much later."

Guilt-ridden, McCracken ran off to get the goods. Left alone, Crockett continued his daily ritual of reading the papers, particularly intrigued but also disturbed by front-page news about Texas. Initially he'd been thrilled to learn that two months after the fall of the Alamo, Sam Houston and his ragged group of volunteers had defeated Santa Anna's army along the San Jacinto River. Texas had immediately declared itself a sovereign country. More recently, though, the governments of Texas and the United States agreed to abandon the former following its nearly decade-long status as a republic, entering its Lone Star into the American flag.

Two days before leaving office, President John Tyler signed the legal papers; the Mexican government announced this was tantamount to the United States declaring war on Mexico. The new president, James K. Polk, nervously sent troops, led by that old warrior Zachary Taylor, down to the Rio Grande to protect what were now U.S. citizens. Mexico's moderate leader, Jose Joaqin de Herrera, considered Polk's offer of many millions of dollars to maintain friendly relations fair. The military quickly deposed him, sending troops up to the Rio Grande, now a powder keg waiting to explode. Reading this, Crockett grimaced. Somebody ought to do something! But . . . who?

An hour later McCracken returned, ready to begin again, if fearful his latest experiment might achieve no more than everything else he'd tried. He found the house empty.

"Davy?" he called out. "Where are you?"

No answer. McCracken headed into the dining room. There he found a scrawled note waiting on the table:

*My good friend Angus—*
*When you read this, I will be long gonne. Not in yer counfounded time travel thing, but on my own too sturdy legs. 'Preciate how hard ye be tryin. Yet I cain't stay confined no longer. Mebbe you was right. Mebbe there is some work needs to be done: here, now. If so, you was correct bringin' me forwerd in time. If that indead be the case, my chore now is to discover it. First though I muste earn me some money. Go ahead!*

*Yours trooly,*
*David Crockett*

"Oh, Davy," Angus wept. "Forgive me if I have done wrong. I hope and pray you are right. And that, in time, there truly will be some meaning to all of this. Like that old song you so love: 'To everyone there is a purpose.'"

"I'm half horse, half alligator, and a little teched by a snappin' turtle. I can outride, outwrassle, outshoot, outsmart, outrun any man in Tennessee. My pappy could lick a den o' wildcats before breakfast, and I kin lick my pap—"

"Thank you. Next?"

The theatrical team had been interviewing actors for their new show all morning. Each subsequent hopeful appeared more poorly fitted for the title role than the previous. This weak attempt caused Anne Semple, the show's producer, to wonder if mounting a play to mark the tenth anniversary of the fall of the Alamo was such a good idea after all.

The piece, which she'd penned out of respect for that battle's greatest hero, bore the title *Wildfire*; the central character was Jeremiah Nimrod, a fictionalized version of David Crockett, dead nearly a decade. Every nation needs its epic hero: Crockett had become America's Heracles. The fly in the buttermilk, as a Texas native like Anne Semple would put it. The larger-than-life image of this man whose memory she hoped to enshrine made it difficult to cast. Every one of these seasoned actors auditioning for the role *played* at being Colonel Crockett. Anne and her colleagues sensed this wouldn't work. What they needed was not a traditional performance, but a presence. This caused her to consider closing down the show before any more money could be wasted. After all, who could embody such a figure?

"Let's 'go dark' for lunch," she whispered to her assistant, who had interrupted the latest actor while signaling for the next. "I can't take anymore."

Quickly, the fellow instructed the group of hopefuls to return in ninety minutes. Then he, Anne, and the four key members of their team exited the Philadelphia theatre.

"Miss Tinley's Tea House?" the assistant, George, suggested. A pleasant and refined place, this was where a respectable lady like Anne Semple ordinarily dined.

"I need a beer," she announced. "Let's try Barney's Beef and Brew down the street." Refined women did not ordinarily retire to such male-oriented establishments. Then again, they knew Semple to be a suffragist, demanding voting rights and equal opportunity for all American women.

Twenty minutes later, they sat around a large table, partaking of a hearty stew washed down by large mugs of ale, processed in the brewery located behind the restaurant. The repast helped them relax, at least a little.

"I'd hate to see this wonderful project close down simply because we have a casting problem," Michael, one of the largest investors, sighed.

"I know, I know," Anne replied. "Never did I think this would become such a serious problem."

"Let's face it," George agreed, "without a strong central figure, it doesn't matter how much time or cash we lavish on theatrical trappings. It just won't work."

Michael was about to make another suggestion when a large, lumbering man, holding a mug in one hand, obviously drunk, approached. "What's a woman doin' in here?" he demanded, eyeballing Anne with fiery orbs.

"My good sir," George said, about to rise and face the ill-mannered fellow, "would you please leave us to our—"

"Sit down," the huge oaf bellowed, pushing George back in his seat before he had a chance to try to be Anne's white knight. Everyone in the bar fell silent, nervously waiting to see what might happen next. "Too many changes goin' on these days. Now why don't you git—"

"To my way o' thinking, yer the one who ought to 'git.' And do so quicker'n a cornered jackrabbit."

All eyes were drawn to the speaker, an impossibly tall fellow who had quietly slipped out from the backroom. In simple clothes, fists clenched, he obviously served as the establishment's bouncer, on hand to stop confrontations before they erupted. Momentarily, the ill-mannered assailant stood stock-still; big as he was, this newcomer had him beat by an inch. While the bouncer spoke in a soft voice, all understood this was not a man to be trifled with. Still, the amount of brew that the oaf had consumed filled him with false courage. He lunged forward, furious.

"This is a man's world and this is a man's saloon!" he insisted, raising his right arm. Faster than anyone could imagine, the bouncer casually grabbed hold of the oncoming fist, twisting the brute's arm, then swung the fellow about so the bouncer could easily escort him to the doorway. A mild shove and the ill-mannered lout flew out onto the street, angrily shrieking as he stalked off. Arms crossed over his chest, the bouncer waited, making certain the drunk wouldn't try to return. He stopped by the table on his way through the main room, right in front of Anne Semple, nodding humbly.

"Sorry for the slight scuffle," he apologized. "He won't be botherin' you ag'in."

With an irresistible smile, the tall man, whom Anne guessed to be about fifty, bowed graciously and left. Once he'd returned to the backroom, Anne eyeballed her colleagues. Even before she could speak, the delighted look in each man's eyes made clear they knew what she was going to say.

"That's him. That's Davy Crockett!"

"Citizens of the great state of Tennessee. It has been my privilege, first as a Democrat, then a Whig, to represent your interests in the halls of Congress. Now, you have seen fit to vote me out of office. Well, lemme jes' say: You can all go to hell; I'm goin' to Texas."

The tall bouncer put down the script, considering the group of men and one woman seated before him. He stood on the stage of the theater where *Wildfire* was set to premiere in two months' time, having accompanied the producing team when, after lunch, they convinced him to join them for a few minutes. Now, he could not believe what he was hearing.

"So far as I'm concerned," Thomas, set to direct, shrugged, "he's our man."

"Precisely what I was looking for," Anne agreed.

"Now, hold on a dang-burned moment," the subject of their approval interrupted as all the others buzzed happily. He stepped down, approaching them where they'd gathered in the front row, close to the stage. "You people better think this through. I'm no actor."

Anne sweetly smiled as she explained what the group had decided that very morning. "But you see, Mr.—"

"Newman. D. C. Newman."

"You see, Mr. Newman, we don't want an actor. Rather, we've been looking for someone who has the stature to embody David Crockett for an entire generation."

"Huh! Still ain't certain I'm yer best bet."

"We are!" the group exclaimed in unison.

"Look at it this way," Anne coaxed. "Clearly, you come from Tennessee; the accent is so authentic! If not for us, or yourself, please do this for the country."

"How's performin' in some show supposed to help—"

"There's going to be a war. No sensible person in the United States or Mexico wants it, yet war is coming at us like a loose wagon rolling downhill. As a nation, we must be prepared. Not just militarily, but patriotically. That's why I decided to mount this play; I want to employ the figure of Crockett to reignite pride in being an American."

Michael agreed. "You say those lines so naturally, it's as if you were born to recite them."

"In truth," Thomas added, "it's almost as if you'd written them yourself, the conviction is so complete."

"I don't see how we can pull it off without you," Anne concluded. "And, as I said, before we happened to discover you, we were agreed that the show ought to be shut down."

"A happy coincidence," George ventured.

"That, or—" The man who'd identified himself as Newman paused, searching for precisely the right word. "Fate?"

"Fate or coincidence." Anne nodded. "I guess that all depends on how one views the world: chaotic or meaningful."

"Huh! When you put it that way, guess I can't refuse."

There was no reason to wait for the reviews to pour in; audience reaction told them all on opening night they had a hit on their hands. When Jeremiah Nimrod faced off with a bear (more correctly, a man in a fur suit) and grinned him down to the ground, or outboasted as well as outfought Mike Fink, the burliest of all river men, the full house of men, women, and children broke into spontaneous applause.

One major change had been made. In the original script, Nimrod was to whip a band of Indians. The star, for truly Newman was best considered that as he made no pretenses to being an actor, insisted such stuff be removed. "Crockett was a blood brother t' the Cherokee. He hated every minute he spent in the army," he blurted to Anne as they conferred in her office. "I don't want to play such scenes."

She stared at him. "Since when did you become such an expert about Colonel Crockett?"

That caught him off guard. She watched as he stumbled to find the words. "Uh, ever since I agreed to do this part, I been researchin' over at the library. If folks are goin' to think of me as him, I'd best be well-prepared."

"I see." Anne nodded, sounding none too convinced. "But don't you agree that most people recall Crockett as a great Indian fighter?"

"He hated that reputation." Quickly, Newman added, "At least, from what I have read, that's what I gather."

"All right, then, we'll rewrite the scene so that you will fight a group of outlaws on the trail instead."

"That'd be fine an' dandy."

So that's what took the place of an Indian battle when the play debuted in mid-May. As the crowd cheered Nimrod/Crockett/Newman after he'd saved a fair damsel in distress, the onstage embodiment of heroism caught his breath. Out of the corner of his eye, he sized up the audience. Immediately, he noticed a familiar face in row three: Angus McCracken, the lovable crackpot who'd brought him here.

For a moment, Crockett worried that the little fellow, theater lights dancing off glasses perched on his nose, might stand up, shout something, give him away. Not a chance. As they briefly made eye contact, Crockett could tell that McCracken appeared happy for him. Clearly, the scientist understood the positive impact this show could have, particularly after they concluded the Philadelphia run and took the play on the road all over America.

Davy sensed McCracken hoped he'd found the purpose to his being here. But the tall man sensed his unwitting mentor in the reserved seating knew him well enough to grasp how he felt now: This was something, at least. Something good. But would the show be enough to satisfy Davy Crockett's hope of striking the kind of blow for freedom he'd been all ready to offer just before being swept through time and space? No.

However nice this might be, whatever good they might achieve, Crockett had grown to believe if this was all there was, it wouldn't satisfy him. He'd still spend his life wishing he'd died defending the Alamo. He must find a way to do more.

The theater company received a royal welcome when they reached Washington, D.C., three months later. President Polk himself was in attendance on the first evening and clapped harder and longer than anyone else at the end. The company performed *Wildfire* for three full weeks before they headed on to the next city. Rarely was there an empty seat to be found. David Crockett—or Newman, as he billed himself when he played Nimrod—took satisfaction in their impact. As Anne had predicted, a new wave of patriotism swept the land.

But it went beyond that. In each city where the show was performed, parents brought their children to see it. And then bought them souvenir coonskin caps before heading home, as well as little flags the kids waved. This happened none too soon, for U.S. and Mexican troops eyed one another ever more warily across the Rio Grande. Their play was no longer another of many road shows crisscrossing provincial America, but the centerpiece of a "From Sea to Shining Sea" movement, as well as a virtual Davy Crockett craze.

"Mr. Newman!" Anne ecstatically told her star as they met for lunch at the elegant hotel where top members of the company stayed while in D.C. "We've received an invitation to visit the White House. The president and his wife want to meet us in person!" To Anne's surprise, the tall man seated before her did not look any too thrilled.

*Whew! That don't sound so good,* Crockett mused. *Met Polk many a time. While that was almost ten years ago, fer him if not fer me, likely he'd recognize me. Seein' me up thar' onstage was one thing, what with the lights an' commotion. But standin' face to face? Ooooh! That never occurred to me . . .*

"Sure sounds like an honor," he replied.

A family just then stopped by the table, the children anxious to meet the person they referred to not as the actor D.C. Newman or even the character Jeremiah Nimrod, but as the spirit of the man they adored. "Hi ya, Davy!" One little tyke hopped right up on his lap and hugged him, causing the big man to smile.

"You're less excited than I thought you'd be," Anne said after the fans had left, speaking of the invitation.

"No, no. That'd be swell."

Nonetheless, when the appointment came around, the star could not attend due to illness. Though two fine doctors came by and found nothing wrong, he insisted his attendance might ruin the event for the others and that he'd best stay in bed. But he asked that they please send the president his best regards.

In fact, President Polk looked downtrodden that the man he most wanted to meet did not show. Still, he and Mrs. Polk graciously showed their guests the White House. Polk was particularly proud to display the only known painting of the actual Congressman Crockett completed in his lifetime. In 1824, more than eleven years earlier, Crockett had agreed to pose, not like most politicians in a fine suit, but wearing authentic buckskins, his rifle Old Betsey cradled in one arm, happily waving his hat with the other.

"I thought you'd enjoy seeing this," Polk told Anne. "Here is the real man, the great man, himself." While President Polk waited for her reaction, Anne could only gasp. Her face turned white, then red. "Miss Semple, is anything wrong?"

"No, Mr. President," she coughed. "It is a wonderful likeness. So real I feel I could almost reach out and—"

"I know! Such a shame Mr. Newman isn't standing beside you at this moment. He's convinced the entire country that he *is*

Crockett. Wouldn't it have been fascinating to compare him with the real thing?"

"You're him. I know that's impossible, yet . . . you are. And please don't tell me I'm crazy."

"Annie Semple," the big man standing on the balcony of his suite, overlooking the lights of the capitol, said as he turned, "you're 'bout the least crazy person I ever met."

After returning from the White House, Anne had marched directly to the rooms where Newman had lived since their arrival in Washington and rapped on the door. No answer. Anne knocked more fiercely and, from the far distant side of the suite, he had called out: "Come on in, Annie," as if there was no doubt in his mind who'd arrived.

"How can this be?" Anne asked, staring up into his eyes as she traversed the room. "You clearly aren't a day over fifty. Yet you—he—would be sixty by now."

"Ain't so easy to explain."

"Try me."

For the next two hours, under the cover of darkness, the two strolled the D.C. streets together. David Crockett told Anne precisely what had occurred, starting from the moment Angus employed his time machine to pluck the last Texas fighting man left inside the Alamo out of smoke and darkness, in so doing bringing him almost a decade forward in time.

"If it was anyone but you telling me this, I'd say that you were mad. Or the greatest tall-tale teller this side of . . ." She laughed.

This side of who?"

"This side of Davy Crockett. From what I've garnered in my research, he loved to tell whoppers on the stump."

"And there are those who've always held that I'm crazy. Andy Jackson for one, when I turned down his offer to run as his vice-presidential candidate."

"Why in heaven did you do that?"

Crockett grew glum. "'Cause I woulda had t' back down on my Indians' rights crusade. I had no intention of—"

"That's what I love about you." She eyeballed Crockett. "You do realize, David, that I'm in love with you?"

"Oh, come on, now, Annie. I'm at least twenty years older than—"

"Thirty, counting the decade you slipped by. Then again, I've always been attracted to older men."

Crockett firmly but gently took Anne's hands. "You ain't in love with me. You're in love with an idea."

"You *are* an idea. The living embodiment of everything that's best about America."

"Don't go to overpraisin' me. I got m' faults, too."

"Thank goodness. Otherwise I might think you were God, returned for a Second Coming."

Crockett howled at that. "Not even close."

They paused under one of the modern lamplights. "Close enough for me. David, do you believe Mr. McCracken will ever be able to fix that machine of his?"

Crockett thought about that for a moment. "Nah. He was out there in the audience that first night. So he knows how t' locate me. I have no doubt he's been workin' away t' the best of his ability. Had he come up with something, he'd a-been in touch long ago."

"So you're stuck here."

"Seems that way."

Annie leaned up on her tiptoes, kissing him gently. "Won't you allow me to help you make the best of it?"

"I'm jest afeard t' do anything that might hurt you."

Anne laughed joyously. "Oh, David! Every woman dreams of holding her ideal man from the past in her arms. But I actually get to do that! It's . . . I don't know—"

"Perfect?"

"Yes. Precisely."

"Yeah, well . . . That's what worries me. 'Cause I'm a realist. An' as such, I don't believe that perfection can long exist in this world."

All the same, Crockett and Anne Semple became loving friends for the remainder of the tour as it continued on and on, and of course she kept his secret. New Year's Eve came and went as the troupe swept into the northwest, then on over to California where Col. John Fremont had been headquartered in case the coming war spread all the way up the western coast. Finally the company drifted down into the southwest.

All along, Anne had planned on staging *Wildfire* in San Antonio on March 6, 1846, on the tenth anniversary of the Alamo's fall. When they arrived, Crockett was fascinated to note the little village of three hundred had transformed into a city of three thousand. Its shopping and financial districts now stretched closer to the old mission on the river's far side. Though a thin stretch of open plain still remained between the center of commerce and the shrine, Crockett assumed that in the next few years, the concept of progress would see the bustling town overcome this silent temple. He hoped and prayed its sanctity would remain rock-solid.

The reaction their play elicited in the grand theater that night suggested the Alamo likely would survive. If he'd played a small hand in assuring that, then McCracken had indeed done the right thing bringing him here. However, Crockett still had some misgivings. The show's successful run was over. Did that mean his final chore was completed? If so, why didn't he feel satisfied, content, justified?

"What's wrong?" Anne wanted to know. They sat across from one another at a café one night after the show, sipping coffee.

"Ain't sure I know myself." Melancholy now, Crockett cast his gaze out the window.

"You need to go there, don't you?"

He nodded. "Seems all wrong, comin' this close to the spot where I'm supposed to have met my Maker and not pay a visit. Disrespectful, almost."

"Go ahead!" Anne responded, using his favorite phrase.

"I'd ask you to walk with me—"

"David, I know this is something you must do alone."

Crockett smiled his appreciation. "Sure 'preciate the way you understand me without m' havin' to put it in words."

"It's just," Anne gulped, "I have this strange feeling that I'll never see you again."

"Why, Annie! I'm only goin' a mile away, and I'll be there fer maybe half an hour. What could happen?"

Captain Jesus Ramirez motioned to his six volunteers, men who had been with him twelve years now. During that period, the group had become so close they barely needed to speak, able to communicate through eye contact and body language. Thank goodness for that, as they were on the most dangerous mission of their lives.

A short while ago, Santa Anna, banished after losing all of Texas to the rebels a decade earlier, had been called back to retake command of the army. The Napoleon of the West, as he called himself, had assembled his favorite officers, Ramirez—a young lieutenant when he led a lancer squadron at the Alamo—among them.

In his raspy voice, Santa Anna explained that war with the United States would begin in a month. First, though, he needed to strike hard and fast with a symbolic gesture. The anniversary of the Alamo's fall was approaching. Santa Anna asked for an officer willing to take a bold risk. He would slip into San Antonio in white peon's linens with a small group of saboteurs, then blow up the mission on that night. This would set the pace for the upcoming conflict while also uniting all of Mexico behind him.

"Please, sir! Let it be me," Ramirez had called out. This pleased

Santa Anna, who prized loyalty and courage. So he assigned the task to Ramirez, free to pick six men to travel north with him. Santa Anna could have no idea how important this was to Ramirez, or those lancers he took into his confidence. Never once, during all the time that had passed, did any of them dispel from their minds the strange event they witnessed: Crockett, apparently dissolving into the morning mist before their very eyes. The image haunted their dreams; they met regularly to speak about it, try and guess what might have happened over wine and beer. Eventually all had admitted that they hoped to return someday to the Alamo, perhaps to learn if it had been real or a living nightmare.

Now, they were there. As darkness descended, they had slipped their barrel of gunpowder inside the crumbling walls and were readying to set the fuse. However spooky the place, none had yet experienced anything out of the ordinary. Once they'd blown the Alamo sky-high, they could return to their base not only to receive their commander's grateful thanks, but would be able to put this out of their minds once and for all.

"Who'd that be?" a voice called out from over by the chapel.

The Mexicans gasped. What they saw was not some night watchman, arrived to check on things. Standing in the starlight they perceived the tall man they'd encountered once before. Though a bold man, Ramirez had to restrain himself from calling out in horror: "Cwocky! Cwocky!" This must be a ghost, for he appeared the same age as when they faced off with him ten years earlier. As they summed up their courage and stepped closer, he now clearly saw them in a stream of moonlight and at once knew precisely who they were.

"Wall, hello, boys! Looks like we got us a date with destiny."

The loud explosion caused Anne Semple, waiting for the great love of her life to return, to spill her coffee and leap up out of her seat. She darted into the street where other citizens were swiftly congregating. The town marshal, his six-gun by his side, hurried up. Some people pointed across the way to the Alamo, witnesses who'd seen the explosion explaining it happened just outside the old walls. The marshal nodded for the men to follow him.

Anne hurried along, already guessing what had more or less happened. When they arrived at the site, they found three dead Mexicans, dressed in civilian garb, blown to smithereens; alongside them was the tall fellow who had played the part of Crockett in the play everyone had so enjoyed. The marshal sent deputies running off in all directions to see if there might be any more Mexicans trying to escape. He himself set about figuring out what had happened.

The lady who had brought the show here, a proud native Texan herself, was the one who figured it out. Mr. Newman had wanted to see the Alamo firsthand. Stepping into the structure, he must have discovered a group of saboteurs about to blow up the place. Maybe he'd played David Crockett so many times onstage he had begun to believe that's who he really was, and so attacked them before any damage could be done. Unable to dislocate the fuse, he'd carried the powder-barrel out on his large shoulders, three Mexicans trying to slow him down. All were killed by the explosion.

"How strange," said the marshal, certain that Anne Semple must be right. "I mean, most actors would have changed clothing after the show. But he was still wearing his buckskin costume."

"To the saboteurs," Anne added, "he must have looked like Crockett come back from the grave to stop them."

The following morning, Angus McCracken of Philadelphia worked on his time machine, hoping to yet fix it and contact the star of that show to tell him now it could be done. As had happened many days before, he was frustrated to realize he'd made no progress. Exhausted, he fixed himself a cup of tea, then slipped on his spectacles and sat down to read the paper. Halfway through the front-page story—which told of the strange coincidence of an actor who'd just played David Crockett stopping an act of sabotage on the Alamo precisely one decade after the famed battle—Angus began to shake so furiously he had to set his cup down.

"No coincidence," he sighed. "Fate!"

*So, Davy, this was, after all, your purpose. What you were born for. I didn't rob you of your birthright. Instead I provided you with a greater destiny. Thanks to you—and, I might add, me—the shrine was preserved. We did it, Davy. Each in his own way. Together.*

With that, Angus McCracken broke into tears. Yet he was not sad. Rather, in a strange way, he felt happy. *This,* he thought to himself, *must be what people mean by "an up-cry."*

And as for the colonel? He had won his last battle, after all.

As a famous ballad once put it, "history books tell they was all cut low." Every one of the Alamo's 186 defenders, including David Crockett himself. But did the colonel's death occur, as the hard cold facts insist, on March 6, 1836? Or could there exist an alternative truth in which that event transpired a decade later? Newspapers of the time record Crockett sightings all across America for ten years following that fabled battle. Were people merely seeing what they wanted, perhaps needed, to see . . . or did their eyes witness a reality that the brain had trouble accepting? Not an easy issue to deal with, then or now. Yet a question that must be raised, if not necessarily answered, in . . . the Twilight Zone.

# THE BLOODTHIRSTINESS OF GREAT BEAUTY

M. Tara Crowl

In a far corner of the Twilight Zone, a vicious battle rages. Day after day, year after year, warriors strap on their armor, wield their swords, and march into combat. Savage as hell and dressed to kill, they tirelessly pursue the elusive, ephemeral battle prize: fame. Livia Mendelssohn joined the battle six years ago. She may look sweet and innocent, but don't be fooled; this once-delicate flower has hardened into the most ruthless of warriors. She has stars in her eyes, blood under her fingernails, and desperation so deep she'd claw, bite, or crawl over corpses to reach that glittering beacon of celebrity. Some might call that madness. Here, it's just survival. The quest for fame demands nothing less in this dark corner of the Twilight Zone called Hollywood.

Livia Mendelssohn was twenty-six, but she told people she was twenty-three. Everyone lied about their age in Tinseltown. Here, youth was king.

Not that it had done her much good—her greatest feat so far was a bit part as Girl Number 4 on that sleazy soap opera for two weeks. Then there was the humiliating role as Whiny Customer on that mattress-store TV commercial, and then the stint as Yente in the summer stock North Hollywood production of *Fiddler on the Roof.* The theater, she ruefully reminded herself every night, was a half-block from the city's biggest porn studio.

Cynical about all auditions, she was especially skeptical about this one. Staring at the audition-room door, she felt a drop of sweat course down her spine. For God's sake, couldn't they afford air-conditioning? The looks of the actresses around her made her sweat even harder. They had been classically trained, had worked in TV or films since their preteens, and were so drop-dead gorgeous they could have stripped to their lingerie and posed for an impromptu Victoria's Secret catalog photo shoot.

Hearing another girl's audition through the thin wall, Livia robotically recited the lines herself. At this point she knew them so well she could have done them standing on her head, underwater, on sodium pentothal. She'd done so many auditions she could sleepwalk through them.

Her cynicism notwithstanding, she recognized her presence here as a major coup. *Variety, People Magazine, Entertainment Weekly*, showbiz gossip columns, Internet blogs, and conversations over crab cakes and Cobb salads at the Ivy blathered about nothing else. The big-budget studio production of *Cleopatra* she was trying out for silenced all other gossip. The project had all the right elements—a giga-buck producer, a violence-crazed, prima-donna director, and a coke-snorting, tequila-chugging, woman-abusing mega-star actor. Ah, Hollywood.

The extravaganza had everything except Cleopatra—an omission the studio had described as "deliberate." They wanted to cast far and wide for the hottest, most jaw-dropping, most ravishing unknown actress on earth—"a vixen with enough *vavavoom* to launch a thousand ships." Someone at the studio had neglected to tell the hopeless hack who'd hammered out that shamelessly pilfered Marlowe quote that it referred to Helen of Troy, not the Queen of the Nile.

Livia had no doubt that after scamming—and no doubt bedding—half the starlets in Hollywood, the principal players would hand Cleo's diadem to Angelina Jolie, saying no one could top her for intellect, talent, integrity, acting skill, commitment, social conscience, political passion, work ethic, dedication, and love of indigent African children, to say nothing of lewd, lascivious lust. Who could top that?

The door opened, and Livia was hit with a blast of air-conditioning cold enough to freeze meat—hell, live steers. She was almost hit as well by the stunningly voluptuous, auburn-haired actress who spilled out of the room in a painted-on red dress. All the actresses had worn the same basic ensemble at the insistence of the audition manager, but this girl's outfit was so sensationally skintight, with a sky-high hem and a plunging neckline, that it made Livia's look like a cherry-red paper sack. Livia couldn't picture the Queen of the Nile in such a getup, but what did she know? Pausing only to toss her long Titian-hued hair extensions back over her shoulders and out of her eyes, the girl shot Livia a pitying smile, as if apologizing that she had to pass through that door. Livia grimaced and stared at the floor as the girl hightailed it away.

"They're ready for you," a high-pitched voice shouted to her from within.

The voice's owner, a petite, immaculately groomed boy in a perfectly tailored suit, let her in. He looked her up and down with a staunchly disapproving glance. Typical pompous Hollywood assistant.

The assistant shut the door, then led her into a meeting room. The terrifying triumvirate sat at a mahogany conference table that was surrounded by matching leather-padded armchairs. The table was littered with bottles of Jack Daniels, Chivas Regal, and Dom Perignon icing in a bucket, three black thermal coffee carafes, and an assortment of glasses, more ice buckets, bottled waters, and sodas. Jars of pâté, beluga caviar, and a wheel of brie along with various crackers and breads were also spread out.

There were other dishes as well. One of the sugar bowls was either filled with powdered confectioner's sugar or Bolivian marching powder. Another held a stack of brown folding papers, and a third was filled with Purple Haze.

Livia averted her eyes in horror. She felt like Goldilocks facing the Three Wicked Werewolves the day they forgot to bring their bear suits.

Rounding the conference table, she stood before them as if facing a firing squad. On the far left was the Papa Werewolf-Bear, producer Alan Hakim. Sixtyish, with thick, black-dyed, blow-dried hair and a fashionable deep-sea tan burned permanently into his skin by an overpriced Rodeo Drive tanning salon, turning it parchment-dry and brown as an old hide. He sported a custom-tailored jet-black Brioni power suit—the exact model James Bond wore in *Casino Royale*. The tabloids often photographed him roaring around town in his vintage James Bond Bentley convertible, his bevy of D-cup Bond-style bombshells in hot librarian eyeglasses, brandishing pens and notepads at port arms, their low-cut dresses showing off their spillage to maximum advantage.

His past life was a matter of some dispute. Left-wing blogs claimed his first name was Ali and that he was a Saudi prince in exile—hinting at more than one or two al Qaeda connections—and that he'd made his fortune as a black-market arms dealer. Thirty years after receiving his first Best Picture Oscar, Hakim remained a Hollywood institution. He was the kind of person who brought his stars fame and notoriety, but whose wake was strewn with the wrecked hopes and trashed lives of almost everyone else.

In the triad's center, the thirty-eight-year-old director—famous for transmuting misogyny and mayhem into preposterously profitable blockbusters—leaned back in his reclining leather office armchair. Staring vacantly into space, Malachi Chung had hard, sharply chiseled features, eyes black as anthracite and a thick ebony ponytail that fell past his narrow, scrunched shoulders.

After breaking into Hollywood with the critically acclaimed

Korean film *Engorged,* he had dominated the box office with his last five movies. According to *Entertainment Tonight*, he planned to infuse Shakespeare's *Antony and Cleopatra* with the shocking tableaux of his signature sado-eroticism.

Though now purportedly clean, Malachi had in the past suffered a notorious affinity for heroin, which had landed him in rehab no fewer than five times. His eyes were so stupefyingly empty, Livia wondered if he was high now.

He was the trio's Middle Werewolf-Bear.

Finally, on the right was Lucas Bright, the group's dazzlingly handsome but painfully stupid Werewolf-Bear Cub. One would be hard-pressed to find an American teenage girl (or gender-bending boy) who hadn't fantasized about him. With his photogenically muscular physique, he was dashing enough to look at home in a tuxedo but a good ole Southern boy at heart, with a hint of Dixie skulking somewhere in his voice. The hottest young star in Hollywood, he would play Julius Caesar.

Stunned by their presence, Livia stood frozen as a popsicle in front of the three moguls. At first, they didn't seem to notice. Lucas squinted moronically into his BlackBerry. Alan stared so intently into the notebook computer perched on his lap that Livia assumed he must be watching Internet porn. Finally, Malachi woke from his stupor and broke the silence.

"What are *you* doing here!" he thundered, jumping to his feet.

His outburst brought everyone else to attention.

"She's come to clean the office," Alan said without looking up, his eyes glued to his computer.

"Then where's her broom?" Malachi asked, still confused.

"She flew in on it," Lucas said, putting down his BlackBerry.

"Look at that nose," Malachi said, pointing and cackling.

"Looks like a badly busted knuckle," said Alan.

"She's got the eyes of a sheep-killing dog," Lucas said.

"A wolverine," Alan said.

They hooted with derision.

"Definitely the mouth of a wolverine," Lucas said.

"Look at those teeth," Malachi said, staring at her mouth intently.

"She could gnaw the chrome off a trailer hitch," Lucas said.

More lurid laughter.

"Who sent us this wolverine anyway?" Lucas said

"The L.A. Zoo," Malachi said.

"Put the animal back in its cage," Alan said, returning to his computer porn.

More hysterical hilarity.

"Come on, guys," the undersized, suit-clad gofer said timidly. "She came all this way to read for the part. Even if she's not right for Cleopatra, she might be right for another role."

"Not unless we're shooting *Return of Bigfoot,*" Alan cracked.

"Bigfoot on a bad hair day," Lucas said.

"*Revenge of the Abominable Snowman,*" Malachi said.

"Come on, her agent sent her," the gofer said.

"Oh, an *agent* sent you!" Alan shouted at Livia, feigning wonder. "Excusez moi!"

He filled his glass with Chivas and passed the bottle to Malachi. "And pray tell, who the hell is this zookeeper and where does he keep his beasts?"

Livia took a deep breath. "Scott Temple at Timeline Artists."

Alan threw up his hands. "Temple? Temple is where my lawyer does Rosh Hashanah. Temple is not a man who wastes my time with a wolverine in my audition room."

The assistant looked sheepish. "Look, Alan . . . I owed the guy a favor." He darted over and whispered to Alan, who looked like he might explode. He drained his scotch and poured another tumbler-full.

"Sorry, man. The guy said she was hot," the assistant said.

With an unexpected surge of defiance, Livia decided they wouldn't dismiss her—not so insultingly, and not without a fight.

"I prepared!" she insisted. She fought to control her cracking voice. She wouldn't, *couldn't* let them see her cry. "Give me five minutes. Just a few lines."

The Three Werewolf-Bears stared at her.

"Fine," Alan finally barked. *"Blow me away."*

And there it was: her main chance, her opportunity to shine. Livia closed her eyes and felt the old energy surge—that performance-induced adrenaline rush. In spite of the hellish beginning, she could still wow them. Miracles did happen.

"My desolation does begin to make a better life," she began. Pausing, she steadied her voice.

> "*'Tis paltry to be Caesar;*
> *Not being Fortune, he's but Fortune's knave.*
> *A minister of her will; and it is great*
> *To do that thing that ends all other deeds,*
> *Which shackles accidents, and bolts up change,*
> *Which sleeps, and never palates more the dung—*"

"Unbelievable!" Alan yelled. He turned to his cruel cohorts. "Bigfoot thinks she can act. Will wonders never cease?"

"Let me tell you something that most girls like you never get to hear," Malachi said, his eyes cold and steely. "You have *no talent.*"

She fought tears, holding them back as long as she could.

"Now hear me out," Malachi said. "You deserve to hear this. Every minute you spend in pursuit of this career is a tragic waste of everyone's time. *You will never be a star.*"

"Don't take it so hard," Lucas said. "I hear they're hiring at the Light o' Love Pleasure Palace."

"Can wolverines dance?" Alan asked.

"Good question," Malachi said.

Livia's chest heaved, and an agonizing sob tore out of her.

"I didn't know wolverines cried," Lucas said with mock incredulity.

And Goldilocks fled the room as fast as her legs could carry her.

At times like these Livia couldn't imagine life without Jenny.

Loyal, trustworthy Jenny was the best, most sensible friend a girl could hope for. With sensible hair, sensible eyeglasses, a plain sensible nose, a sensible brown blouse and plaid skirt, Jenny was unfailingly sensible where Livia was foolish, solid where the actress was flighty. She was Livia's loving, sensible alter ego.

"Screw 'em all," Jenny said, toasting Livia with a glass of Chardonnay.

Not for the first time, Livia was grateful for the dim lights in The Low Down, their favorite dive; her eyes were still red and puffy from the afternoon's crying jag.

"'Screw 'em'? If I could screw 'em, I would. That's the only way to make it in this town. You've got to sleep your way to the top."

"The feminist in me is having an aneurysm right now," Jenny said.

"I'm serious! Look at Marilyn Monroe. She seduced her way from obscurity to stardom."

"She had three failed marriages and died young, alone, and depressed!"

"But she died *famous*. Marilyn was a great actress and an icon." Livia pointed to a framed photo print on the wall. The screen queen's dazzling smile outshone all the surrounding celebrity pictures.

"Granted, Marilyn was the real thing," Jenny conceded.

"She's one of history's great beauties! Up there with Helen of Troy."

Jenny snorted. "Let me guess—you want to be 'the face that launched a thousand ships.'"

"Some illiterate publicist thought that was Cleopatra." Livia laughed.

"Cheers to Helen of Troy!" Jenny hooted, raising her glass. "Loving her was more like a thousand deaths—she caused the Trojan War—but it was fun while it lasted, right?"

"How about Cleopatra?" Livia asked. "She brought all of Rome's and ancient Egypt's emperors weeping to their knees. Now actresses like me are begging for the chance to haltingly, ineptly portray her. 'Had Cleopatra's nose been shorter, the whole world's face would have been changed.'"

"That's a good one!" Jenny worked in a small bookstore specializing in rare texts, so she spotted the quotation. "Pascal. But the world would have been better off if Cleo had been a little homelier! Her ambition nearly destroyed Egypt. She drove Mark Antony, her one true love, to suicide. Believe it or not, beauty doesn't solve everything—and sometimes it generates new woes."

"I don't care. I'd die young if it meant I could have a legacy like that. I would do *anything* for great beauty."

Livia shoved her empty glass across the bar. The dumpy, grizzled old bartender in thinning gray hair, a white shirt, and apron lumbered over and rolled his eyes as he refilled it.

"'Anything for great beauty'?" Big Sam said. "C'mon, Olive—you don't mean that."

"Yes I do, Sam," she insisted. "And don't call me Olive."

Jenny leaned forward and set her wineglass on the bar. "'Great beauty is invariably bloodthirsty,'" she told Livia gravely.

"And I thought I was dramatic. Where the hell did you get that one?"

"Gary Jennings in *The Journeyer*. The account of Marco Polo's travels in the Far East."

Livia stared at her blankly. "I give up. What does that have to do with anything?"

"It has *everything* to do with your situation. Look. Marilyn Monroe's death was ruled a suicide, but that's a load of crap—she was murdered!"

"You believe that? That's a total conspiracy theory."

The bartender, leaning over to wipe down the place next to Livia, interrupted their debate.

"One hundred percent true, m'lady," Sam rattled in a gravelly voice. "She was whacked."

"Thank you!" Jenny held up her drink to him. "Sam Giancana's son exposed it all in *Double Cross*: Hit men killed Marilyn in an attempt to expose Bobby Kennedy as her lover, drive him out of the Attorney General's office, and end his crusade against the mob. The author claimed his father—a notorious mob godfather—had a part in it."

"Same thing today," Livia said. "Hollywood is a battlefield! Men like Alan Hakim, Malachi Chung, and Lucas Bright are capable of anything, and we women have to be armed to the teeth. Irresistible beauty is the best weapon of all."

"So Jennings had it right," Jen said. "Great beauty *is* bloodthirsty."

"It's the greatest weapon in a woman's arsenal: brutal, bloodthirsty beauty."

"Forget about those movie assholes," Sam recommended. "Who wants to work with psychopaths anyway? Remember what happened to Marilyn."

"But they control everything in Hollywood!" Livia said.

"Tell you the truth, I'd love to meet Lucas," Jenny confided, "if he weren't such a jackass. I swooned all over him when we saw *Time Bomb*."

Despite being endlessly sensible, Jenny was a sucker for man-candy, and Lucas Bright was gourmet, Godiva-caliber man-candy.

"He's sexy," Livia said, "but his ego isn't."

"Why do you want a film career so much?" Sam asked. "Hollywood isn't the center of the world."

But Livia ached for it. "A life of anonymity won't satisfy me," she said sadly. "And this is the one place where there's fame for the taking. To me, Hollywood's not just the world's center. It *is* the world."

Naturally the elevator in her building was broken again, and Livia's legs grew heavier with each of the six flights of creaky stairs. Yellowed paint peeled from the wall in a patch just before the third-floor landing, and the scent of mold hung in the air. Still, the occasional paychecks from acting gigs and meager supplements from her parents barely covered the rent.

Finally she stumbled into her sad excuse for a one-bedroom apartment and gave it a distressing once-over, taking in the Castro convertible couch with mismatched pillows and her collection of stuffed teddy bears for a back, the busted door she and an old boyfriend had sanded, varnished, and converted into a living room table, the two frayed studio chairs flanking it, the eighteen-inch, twenty-year-old portable TV up against the wall on a former nightstand. She continued into her 5' × 6' bedroom and fixed briefly on her grandmother's cherrywood antique vanity, the only piece of furniture she cared about. She smiled at its exquisite beauty and the fond memories of her grandmother it summoned.

She tossed her purse onto the bed, then caught sight of herself in the mirror. The smile dropped from her face like a rock. Normally she looked like your typical dark-haired, fun-loving, healthy-living "girl-next-door"... when her spirits were up, her hair done, her makeup on, her clothes matched and pressed.

Now, however, that girl-next-door look wasn't cutting it. She needed to look *hot*. Pouting, she struck a sexy pose. She and the mirror would prove those bastards wrong. Doing a model turnaround, she opened her eyes and stared salaciously into the antique looking glass.

But drained and drunk, her cheeks drawn, eyes hollow and haggard, she looked like . . . well, like Bigfoot on a bad hair day!

Still, she was determined not to cave in. She was, after all, a professional thespian. Instead she pulled herself together, hit the invisible marks, and dutifully recited her lines, even though her only audience was the monstrous reflection mocking her so remorselessly.

> *"'Tis paltry to be Caesar;*
> *Not being Fortune, he's but Fortune's knave.*
> *A minister of her will; and it is great*
> *To do that thing that ends all other deeds."*

But the monster in the mirror would not lie. Livia looked and sounded pathetic. Savage and sadistic as the three psychos were, they were *right.* Furious, she ripped the red stiletto heel from her right foot. Throwing herself down on her bed, she flung the shoe blindly across the room, inadvertently shattering the upright mirror atop her grandmother's vanity. Crashing and clattering, the glass shards scratched, gouged, and scarred the cherished cherrywood antique.

Overcome with grief, convulsing with sobs, Livia buried her face in the overstuffed purple teddy bear her beloved grandmother had given her as a child.

"Buck up, Livia," a soft female voice intoned. "We can repair your stupid vanity."

Who was in her apartment? Livia looked up, searching frantically for the disembodied voice.

"Don't be afraid," the voice said with a foreign accent Livia couldn't identify.

Suddenly Livia saw the woman standing in front of the disfigured vanity. Hips canted, arms akimbo, her honey-hued skin, high flaring cheekbones, and wide voluptuous mouth framed fierce feline eyes, their pupils pale-gray and vertically distended.

*Cat's eyes,* Livia thought, staring at them fixedly.

Shaking her head, the woman casually flung her waist-length mane of raven hair over the front of her body. Tall, angularly slim, the sublimely gorgeous creature wore a gossamer-thin, floor-sweeping gown of sheer silk, as luminously black as burnished obsidian.

She wore no jewelry save for the four delicate gold rings that adorned her wrists and ankles.

"Who the hell are *you*?" Livia asked, not in the mood for any more abuse.

"I am Isis, daughter, She of the Throne. Egyptian goddess of wisdom and simplicity, patron of nature and magic. I've heeded your conjurations."

"My what?"

"Your divine desideratum."

"Decide what?" Livia said drunkenly.

"I've come to grant your more fervent desires."

"This is a joke, right?"

"Caesar, Antony, and Octavian didn't think so."

"You're Cleopatra."

"I'm incarnating her earthly presence as it was two thousand years ago."

"Then you're . . . ?"

"You've prayed to me often enough. I'm Isis, the patron goddess of great beauty."

"What's that got to do with a plain-looking, no-talent loser like me?"

Isis raked her up and down with a hard stare. "I don't know about talent. That's some other deity's department. You'll have to ask my boss, Osiris. But the plain-looking loser stuff I can fix."

"Yeah, you and about ten million dollars' worth of plastic surgery."

"I can do it for far less than that."

"Less than what? I couldn't afford a canceled stamp or an expired supermarket coupon."

Isis's eyes glowed and the corners of her sensuous mouth crept upward. "Then you have the wherewithal."

"The where with what?" Livia slurred.

"You can afford my services."

"What's the catch?"

"You'll have to live with the consequences."

"What consequences?"

"The bloodthirstiness of great beauty."

"Oh, I get it. Is there some kind of weird sacrifice to the gods involved? I have to cut off a toe or something?"

"A simple touch from my palm to your head will do it."

"Will do what?"

"Make you blindingly, achingly, dangerously, inescapably desirable. Every man you come into contact with will be instantly smitten."

"You're going to turn shit into gold?"

Isis winked, and Livia's heart fluttered. "Just watch me," the goddess whispered.

She leaned forward to touch Livia's head with the palm of her right hand, but pulled back suddenly. "There's just one more thing. In the morning you'll find a tool to aid in correcting today's wrongs. I won't see a daughter of Isis ridiculed."

Despite all she'd heard, Livia was dubious. "You mean the audition? I can't correct that. They kicked me out of the room. They called me a monster."

Isis was undeterred. "Sands shift for the gods and goddesses."

"Well, that's great in ancient Egypt, but we're not there anymore."

Isis shushed her, holding a slender finger to her lips. "You won't be disappointed." She placed her cool palm on Livia's forehead and Livia felt a thunderbolt blast flash through her skull, face, and throat. Then she felt Isis's palm press firmly against her chest. A second thunderbolt detonated in her chest, knocking her backward onto her flimsy secondhand mattress.

The pounding on the door woke the groggy girl up.

"You made too much noise last night. You're two months behind in your rent. I'm sick and tired of your antics. This has happened for the last time. Open up!"

Livia groaned and pulled the comforter over her tender head. She had a killer hangover.

"Hold *on,* Sayid!" she shouted, hating herself for living in this ratty apartment building with its chronically broken elevator and the crankiest landlord in Los Angeles.

Still wearing her dirty, hideously wrinkled, red cocktail dress, she flung open the door to find the middle-aged, half-bald, eternally angry landlord, Sayid. As usual, he wore a dirty wife-beater tank top, his meaty fist poised for the next door-hammer.

"Maybe I wouldn't have made so much noise if the damned elevator had worked for once!"

Waiting for him to fire back, Livia watched Sayid's expression shift from rage to alarm to shock. His mouth gaped, and his eyes grew wide as saucers.

"Hey, forget about it. I'm sorry I bothered you. Really."

"And the rent, I—"

"I said forget about it. I know times are tough. Really." Turning, he limped away. Glancing over his shoulder, he smiled at her sheepishly. "By the way, you're looking marvelous," he said with a wink.

She gasped. She'd never seen Sayid smile.

Livia closed the door. Judging by the severity of her headache, she'd had far too many cocktails with Jenny. Had she done anything stupid?

God, she looked a mess. That must be why Sayid was so nice. He felt sorry for her. She walked up to the mirror. She was still wearing last night's rumpled dress. Her hair was messy, her lips chapped, her eyeliner smudged. But wasn't her mousy disheveled chestnut hair somehow thicker, shinier, more lustrous? Wasn't her skin brighter?

She backed up to examine her entire body. It was impossible, and yet . . . she could swear her figure had changed overnight. Her breasts had swelled, her waist had shrunken; she was altogether more shapely.

With a start, she remembered the proposition extended to her by a self-proclaimed goddess. In her own bedroom! She laughed at the audacity of her alcohol-induced dream. Yet she was sure that she had broken the mirror above her vanity, and here it was, intact and spotless. And here she was, and she'd be damned if she hadn't come down with a serious case of sex appeal overnight!

Remembering the goddess's words about leaving a gift, she flung open her bathroom door. No golden elixir or beauty potion. Nothing in the kitchen, either. She opened the drawers of her dresser, looking for anything out of place. What kind of gift would a goddess give, anyway? As a last resort, she pulled open the door to her closet. And there it was.

A regal, shimmering, Grecian-style white dress with gold trim.

It lay on top of all the other clothing, suggesting that it outshone all the dresses in her closet—perhaps all dresses everywhere.

And it did.

Hot blood coursed through her veins as she waited outside the door to the audition room. No pacing this time, no nerves, no line muttering—just anticipation.

The door opened and a statuesque Middle Eastern girl emerged in the same red dress and heels all the other actresses had been ordered to wear. The girl had the same shell-shocked look that all the others had had upon leaving that den of vipers, but Livia detected in this girl fear as well—fear that grew as she looked over Livia and took in the white Grecian dress Isis had given her.

No one had looked at her that way before, but she'd been its bearer so many times she knew exactly what it meant. Livia's beauty intimidated her.

She smoothed her gorgeous new dress, lifted her chin high, and strode in.

"What the hell is this?" Alan Hakim shouted as she entered. "Did somebody tell you to come back here?"

She walked straight up to the long table and stroked his leathery face. "Mr. Hakim," she cooed, "you're gonna wish I'd never leave."

She didn't even wait for his reaction but hopped onto the table. Slinking down the tabletop, she began speaking the lines she would now never forget. Only this time, she was not Livia Mendelssohn; she *was* the legendary Nile Queen.

> *"Give me my robe, put on my crown; I have*
> *Immortal longings in me: now no more*
> *The juice of Egypt's grape shall moist this lip:*
> *Yare, yare, good Iras; quick."*

Catlike, she hopped off the table again and whipped her head to the right.

> *"Methinks I hear*
> *Antony call; I see him rouse himself*
> *To praise my noble act; I hear him mock*
> *The luck of Caesar, which the gods give men*
> *To excuse their after wrath: husband, I come:*

*Now to that name my courage prove my title!*
*I am fire and air; my other elements*
*I give to baser life. So; have you done?*
*Come then, and take the last warmth of my lips."*

She leaned down and gave Lucas a sensuous, lingering kiss. He shuddered at the touch of her fingernails running down the side of his neck.

*"Farewell, kind Charmian; Iras, long farewell."*

She tossed her hair and walked briskly out.

Not five seconds passed before the producer's voice rang out behind her:

"Where do you think you're going?" Marching after her, Alan grabbed her wrist and pulled her back in the room.

The Three Werewolf-Bears were all staring at her, gape-jawed.

"Were you on the schedule today?" Lucas asked, finally finding his voice.

"No, you miserable moron," Malachi said. "This is the same girl from yesterday."

"Which girl?" Lucas asked.

"The wolverine," Malachi said, staring at Livia, stunned.

"You mean Bigfoot?" Lucas queried.

"Look at her, you coke-crazed cretin," Alan said. "She's not a Bigfoot any longer. What was your name again?"

"I think her name just became Cleopatra," Malachi said.

"It's Liv . . . Liv Lux." Marilyn changed her name—why shouldn't she? "Let's just say I was having an off day." She stepped forward and looked each of them in the eye.

"Let's break for the day," Alan said, treating Livia to his biggest, widest werewolf smile. "My assistant will bump the rest of the appointments. They can be rescheduled—or canceled. Either way. I don't care."

Livia smiled back at him seductively. She liked the sound of his words.

Alan met her by the door. Putting a hand on her back, he felt the silky patch of skin, the Grecian dress's plunging neck- and back-lines leaving the upper portion of her torso exposed. When Alan placed his hand on her back, her silk skin felt electric.

"You're coming with me," he said.

When the headwaiter seated them at the big circular booth of the Polo Lounge, arguably the most famous restaurant in Beverly Hills, she'd found Dom Perignon already chilling in the ice bucket. She also noted that the staff treated Alan with a deference that could only be inspired by total terror.

"Dry gin martini with a twist," he snapped at the drink waiter impatiently. "And, boy, I want you to shake that martini sixty times, not one less, then shake your ass back here. That should take you sixty seconds, starting three . . . two . . . one, NOW!"

The petrified waiter skittered away.

When the food waiter appeared, Alan ordered a porterhouse steak smothered in onions, French fries au gratin, and for Livia a house salad with oil and vinegar . . . without consulting her.

"I've been around long enough to know what you little ladies like," he said, winking.

"And Mr. Hakim, I bet I know *exactly* what you want," she purred, totally into her Cleopatra-seductress role—so into it the part now seemed second nature to her.

"Your voice—it's pure ambrosia," he whispered.

"I hope I get the chance to impress you with my other talents, Mr. Hakim," she said throatily.

Riveted, Alan leaned across the table toward her. "I'm cow-simple over you. You've turned me into a raving fool."

The waiter returned with his martini. Without taking his eyes off Livia, he downed it and slammed the empty glass on the table. "Perfect. Another, and shake this one seventy times." The amazed waiter whisked the empty glass away and disappeared.

"Tell me what you want. Anything—jewelry, cars, a trip to paradise—you name it."

It was good to be a goddess.

"I want nothing, Mr. Hakim—"

"Alan, please."

"—Alan." Fluttering bedroom eyes, she ran a finger across his bottom lip, somehow aware that the candlelight heightened her captivating radiance. "Nothing, Alan, except the chance to entertain the world. I was born to act."

"Yes, of course you were." He was so absorbed in her presence he barely heard his or her words.

"I will work very hard for you. I will do a very good, very *thorough* job. I will do *anything* you say."

"And I will work you *very hard*."

"And I will work like a *slave*."

She gave his leg a painfully hard squeeze under the table.

Alan Harding's next martini appeared, shaken a full seventy times.

By the time dessert arrived, he had jacked the shake-count up to a hundred-plus.

"I'm not sure you should have made psycho-producer your first conquest, but it's a start."

Perched on the bungalow's baby grand in a white silk nightie, Isis cupped her glorious face in her hand and gave Livia a coy, eye-batting smile.

Livia woke with a start and rubbed her eyes. Sunshine filtered through the window's wooden blinds onto the white marble floor. The Jacuzzi in the room's opposite corner was still gurgling, reminding Livia of their hours of steamy pleasure in it the night before. An empty bottle of Dom Perignon sat on its ledge, and two plush white bathrobes, each embroidered with the logo of the Beverly Hills Hotel, lay crumpled a few feet away. The bungalow where she'd spent the night was a long way from her dingy Hollywood apartment.

Livia glanced at the mass of grotesquely tanned flesh splayed across the ivory comforter, which had forced her onto the thin edge of the huge bed and finally onto the floor. Gray hair tufts seemed to sprout randomly across his back.

"I got the part!" she whispered to her guardian goddess.

"Isn't that splendid!" Isis glowed like a proud mother. "Now let's see if you can really fill Cleopatra's sandals and match her legacy."

"I'll surpass it!" Livia said, leaping out of bed. "Look how they fall at my feet. I plan to make myself the most irresistible woman in history."

"If you say so," she said. "Just remember my warning."

"That 'bloodthirsty' stuff again? Don't you see he'd die before seeing me harmed? He's head over heels!"

"I suppose you know better than I." Isis glowed a little brighter as Alan stirred. "But now Prince Charming wakes. Ciao!" She vanished with a flash of light.

Alan groaned as he awakened. "Good God, Toni, how'd you let me *drink*—" His eyes opened and saw Livia. Confusion, realization, and finally rapture crossed his expression. "Ah yes, my queen. My divine Cleopatra. What a night we had!" He reached out and grabbed her around the waist, trying to pull her back into bed.

"Now, Alan," she said, teasingly pulling away. "You'd better pull yourself together and get home! Won't your wife be worried?"

He squinted and let out a cough that attested to an unhealthy smoking habit. "My wife? That ancient hag? How could I go back to her now?"

Ten years earlier, posters of Alan's supermodel wife, Toni Harding, covered the bedroom walls of her conceited high-school quarterback-boyfriend who'd dumped Livia for a brainless cheerleader with a bodacious body and hellaciously hot panties. Deep down inside, she'd always blamed their break-up not on the IQ-challenged cheerleader but on Alan's super-sexy spouse. She'd been the boy's malevolent muse. Revenge on Alan's trophy wife was sweet.

Alan straightened the gold chain around his neck and grabbed his diamond-encrusted white-gold Rolex Oyster off the floor where he had flung it during the evening's festivities.

"Darling, there's no question—I'm leaving her. I won't live another day without you."

"I want you to stay with her, darling. I don't want anyone getting hurt."

Like hell she didn't. However, she would not attain the stature of a global sex-goddess by seducing one megalomaniacal producer.

Alan's BlackBerry buzzed and he grabbed it off the nightstand. "Jesus Christ," he muttered, "if that hermaphrodite assistant of mine schedules one more morning meeting for me, I'm gonna rip out every tooth in his queer head." He slipped into his new James Bond Brioni power suit—this one an $11,000 Pure Escorial Jet Black—and kissed her roughly. "Relax! Order breakfast, lay by the pool!" he ordered, rushing out the door.

Just as Livia lay back in bed, basking in luxury, her purple cell phone rang. Snapping it open, she knew who it was.

"Jenny! I have so much to tell you!"

"Liv?" The voice was deep and growling. "This is Malachi Chung."

"Malachi!" she whispered breathily, rolling onto her stomach. "Where have you been all my life?"

"Pining away for you. Alan says you're Cleopatra, and I need to discuss our vision of her with you. I'm only shooting inserts. Meet me on the lot in an hour."

"I can't wait, darling."

She clicked the purple phone shut.

"Make her bleed!"

Hearing Malachi's voice, she lingered in the shadows by the doorway of the set where no one could see her. A buxom Latina actress lay naked in a bathtub on a small bathroom stage. She talked and laughed to someone offstage.

"Ready, Rosita?" Malachi called. The girl nodded and let her head fall to one side. "Roll sound . . . roll camera . . . action!"

Suddenly, a burly redheaded man burst on the stage with a baseball bat. He ran to the bathtub and beat the woman with it over and over. She bellowed lusty, B-movie ululations worthy of Beverly Garland, the legendary horror-flick scream queen. As her arms and legs spasmed, the screams pumped out of her repeatedly. Hidden in the shadows, Livia reminded herself to breathe.

"You like that, bitch?" the man thundered.

"Cut!" Malachi yelled. He stepped onstage. "Yes, yes, yes! Insanely hot." He wiped sweat off his forehead and peered in Livia's direction. She took a tentative step out from the shadows. "That's a wrap!" he yelled, eyes on her.

As the cast and crew chatted and milled about, he strode toward her. "Did you see that? How sexy was that?"

"*So* hot," she answered, even as she wondered if anyone really bought into his savage-sexy bullshit.

"That scene is brilliant. Seminal. Merging brutality and beauty—*that's* true art. But you—well, you're a sensation all on your own." His gaze was so carnivorous she felt violated—not that she minded. "Where did you come from?"

"Your imagination, of course. I was made to fulfill your secret desires and your most prurient passions."

"And to service my masterpiece! The ultimate cocktail of gore, insanity, psychopathy, sado-erotica and *Shakespeare!* Do you have any idea how delicious this film will be?" His eyes lost focus for a moment, and she shuddered, thinking what sordid stuff he was determined to put her through in her film debut. "Come with me. There's an empty stage where I can take a few shots of you."

"I didn't know I would be on camera today . . ." She gestured to her simple blue cotton dress.

"Never fear, my Devil with a Blue Dress On. Everything becomes you, and the camera will love you."

And it did. To her amazement, the lens lusted after her almost as hungrily as Malachi.

"Incredible," he marveled later, staring at the digital-assist footage when he wasn't darting around adjusting lights and camera settings. "It's impossible to make you look anything less than desirable and divine."

Livia arched her back and tousled her hair. "I exist solely for your work and your happiness."

Malachi peered through a camera. "Because of you," he said, "this film will be the most stunning artwork I shall ever conceive, write, and direct."

"I would be nothing without your genius," she pandered, as if Shakespeare would have nothing to do with the production.

"You were designed for *me,* my Cleopatra. You tantalize my eyes and inflame my desire. But that is not enough. I want more."

"Take it all."

She gasped as he swooped her into a low dip, kissed her voluptuously, vehemently, then yanked her back up. His cheek to hers, he whispered:

"Lascivious Liv, you intoxicate me." Holding her hand, he spun her away, then whipped her back in to him. "I'm a man who knows what he wants. My scripts, my sets, my actors, my cameras, my lights—I control them all. And what I want is *you,* Liv Lux." He grabbed the back of her neck firmly, fingers massaging her skull. *"I want to rip you apart."* His hot breath tickled her face.

"Is that who I think it is?" Overhead lights illuminated the stage, exposing their lovers' embrace. Alan Hakim approached them in a red shirt, a tan vest and matching jodhpurs, black riding boots polished to a mirror-gloss and heeled with gleaming steel rowels. He strode toward them with short, determined steps, a black riding crop under his armpit. He stopped five feet from them, legs apart, cracking the crop on his right boot-top.

"My director with my newest star? What are you doing, Malachi? Purloining my property?"

"Malachi was just screen-testing me," Livia said, pulling from the director's grip. She faced Alan, hands clasped behind her back.

"She's stunning on camera," Malachi told him.

"Of course she is," Alan said, eyeing them suspiciously. He took Livia's hand and kissed it. "But preproduction doesn't start for three weeks. Don't put her to work before then." He put his arm around her. "Princess, let's go for lunch."

Malachi grabbed her hand and pulled her from Alan. "Actually," he said, "*I* need to have lunch with her. We need to discuss her character."

Alan bristled and stepped closer so that Livia was sandwiched between them.

"I'm sorry, boys," Livia said, "but you're both out of luck. I've promised the rest of the day to my best girlfriend—we have an awful lot to catch up on."

The two men stared at her downcast, but each seemed satisfied that she wouldn't be with the other.

"Go play with your girlfriend then, doll," Alan said, squeezing her arms and kissing her on the cheek.

Malachi pulled her into a long, tight embrace. "Can I see you tonight?" he whispered.

Alan cleared his throat pointedly.

"Booked through the night." She pulled away and put a hand on each of their shoulders. "You boys play nice while I'm gone." She looked back just once as she left. The bigwigs slavered in her wake like lovesick, dreamy-eyed puppies.

Two men subjugated in less than two days.

Not bad, for an aspiring goddess.

Jenny's bookstore was a rare haven for intellects nestled between the trashy apparel shops and flavor-of-the-week nightclubs on Hollywood Boulevard. Jenny told Livia that it had been there since the 1950s, before the neighborhood's glamour decayed into seediness.

Outside the glass storefront window, Livia kicked a few French fries off Tippi Hedren's star in the sidewalk. Even when Hollywood gave her the cold shoulder, she faithfully defended its glitz and tinsel.

She sauntered into the store, pulling off her sunglasses and planting them on top of her head.

"Jenny!" she yelled.

The shop was usually empty but always charming. Amber light shone from antique green lamps onto cherrywood bookshelves and plush chocolate-colored chairs adorned with thick ribs of corduroy. Livia fell into one sideways, her high-heeled tawny boots dangling over the side. "Jenny!!"

"You're impertinent, you know that?" Jenny called from the stockroom.

"But you love me!"

Jenny emerged and sat in a chair facing her. "How're you holding up? Feeling any better since the other night?"

Livia grinned like a six-year-old showing off a new front tooth. "You wouldn't believe how much better!"

She recounted her sudden power in new sex appeal, her triumphant intrusion into the audition room, and her seductions of both Alan Hakim and Malachi Chung. Nothing was omitted except the deal she had made with Isis.

"And the best part is, I'm only just getting started," she said.

Jenny pursed her lips in disapproval. Getting up, she strode to a bookshelf.

"I *know* what your books say," Livia whined. "'No good will come of any of this.' But those books were written by bitter people who never really lived. They're *stories*."

Jenny triumphantly pulled out a volume of Shakespeare's *Antony and Cleopatra*.

"Remember what happened to Cleopatra?" She tossed the thick book to Livia. "And your other idol, Marilyn Monroe?" She walked to another shelf, pulled out *Double Cross*, and tossed that to her, too. "Whacked by the mob. Remember how they treated you the other day? Alan Hakim is a bigoted, *married* mogul who's famous for his temper! And Malachi Chung is a heroin addict—"

"*Former* heroin addict!"

"—who's built a career wreaking violence on women!" She kneeled in front of Livia. "Olive, I'm serious. I'm happy for you—believe me, I am. But you've got to be careful."

A chill flashed through Livia like a cold black wind—but it passed.

"Don't be so uptight," Livia said. "Look, I appreciate your concern. I really, really do. But this is my chance—this is what I've been dreaming about my whole life! Besides"—she grabbed Jenny's hands—"don't forget who my co-star is."

Livia had her. Jenny couldn't suppress a sly smile. She knew Jenny's fantasy lover. Livia had seen his poster in her bedroom, his shining countenance facing the head of her bed. Lucas Bright was Jenny's objet d'amour.

"I'm bound to get to know him at some point—we'll be on set together for six months," Livia said. "And once I do, I just might have to introduce him to a very special someone."

Jenny groaned. "But wait—doesn't he have a girlfriend? The singer from the Wind-up Dolls, right?"

"That was ages ago. Supposedly he's dating the girl from that new lawyer show."

"The female partner?"

"No, her daughter. But that's probably just for publicity."

Livia felt something in her purse: the little purple phone buzzing with an unknown caller once again. Livia raised a knowing eyebrow at Jenny.

"Hello?"

*"This is Lucas,"* the caller said. *"How's it going?"*

Livia pressed the button to put it on speaker phone. "I'm all right. How about yourself, big boy?"

*"Cool, cool. So I was thinking, since we're gonna be working together, we should have a drink. Get to know each other."*

"Sounds good. But I already had plans to hang out with my friend Jenny."

*"So bring her! I'm down with threesomes."*

Livia nodded knowingly at Jenny, who blushed. "We'll meet you at the bar at Chateau Marmont at eight?"

*"Nice. See you girls there."*

"Ciao!"

She snapped the phone closed. "I prefer the term 'Fairy Godmother,'" she instructed.

Jenny jumped up and danced around the store, giggling, more animated than Livia had seen her in years.

"Can I borrow your lucky bracelet?"

Every person in the posh bar, male or female, gaped at Lucas Bright.

But he only had eyes only for Livia.

Jenny had regarded the night as a test and prepared accordingly: She had rehearsed in her mind all the bon mots and scintillating conversation she would bestow on that handsome hunk of Hollywood manhood.

Oblivious, Lucas ignored her chatter—and ogled Livia.

"What was it like, growing up in Louisville?" Jenny asked, scooting closer to him in the booth.

"We didn't have Liv."

"Why did you take up acting?"

"To meet beautiful women like Liv."

"Who's your favorite co-star?"

"Liv."

"Who did you vote for in the last election?"

"If Liv was on the ballot . . ."

Livia's phone rang, but quickly she silenced it. Malachi, the caller ID said. She sighed and returned it to her purse.

"But don't you miss the south, Kentucky bluegrass, sweet tea, and all that?"

"Not when I'm with Liv."

Lucas brushed his chin-length dark blond hair back behind his ears and took a long swig of Blue Moon.

A rough hand grazed Livia's bare knee—definitely not Jenny's.

"What was it like working with Marla Marsden on your last film? Isn't she brilliant?" Jenny wouldn't let up.

"I don't know," Lucas said with shrug. "She wasn't Liv."

He gestured the waitress over and ordered two shots of whiskey.

"But she's one of the most talented female directors of our time!"

"No hard feelings, but I changed my mind about a threesome," he said, unable to take his eyes off the actress. "I just want Liv."

His hand traveled slightly up the inside of Livia's thigh.

Disgusted by his obvious under-the-table grope and Livia's patent refusal to stop it, Jenny was dispirited and distressed. Not with Lucas so much. He was what he was: a scumbag in a drool-worthy package. Her best friend, however, disappointed her. She wasn't the old Livia—loyal, principled, true to the core. This Livia had the face of an angel, the heart of a whore, and the soul of a chiming cash register. Finishing the last of her blackberry martini, Jenny excused herself to go to the restroom.

Lucas rose to let her slide out, but instead of returning to his seat, he joined Livia on the opposite side.

"Move," he ordered.

"Manners, little boy," she chided—but she shifted to give him room.

He grabbed her face roughly. "I don't know what you're doing," he said, "but you're driving me crazy."

"Must be the old Caesar and Cleopatra thing," she said lightly.

She tried to ignore his smoldering eyes, wide jaw, and strong arms. He was a million times more attractive up close.

"I want you, Liv. I've wanted you since you kissed me in that audition."

She tried to breathe evenly. "Look, Jenny will be back soon—get back over there and behave."

"Who?"

The waitress brought the shots of whiskey. He downed one and handed Livia the other. "I'm having more fun without her." His sex appeal was overpowering. Finally she understood how she made men feel. She took the shot obediently. "Good girl," he said, caressing her shoulder.

Her cell phone rang again. She cursed it as she hunted for it in her purse. Alan, the caller ID read. She silenced it and put it away.

"Alan Hakim?" Lucas said, staring over her shoulder. "Why is he calling you at nine thirty at night?"

"How would I know?"

"Are you lying to me?"

"Did I answer it? I'm here with you, Lucas." She ran a finger lightly down the inside of his forearm. "Here is where I want to be."

"Good." He pulled her face close to his. "You're my Cleopatra, no one else's." He kissed her, setting her body on fire. A few moments passed before she opened her eyes—and saw Jenny standing at the table's edge, arms crossed.

"Fairy godmother, my ass," Jenny snapped. She threw the borrowed bracelet on the table and stormed away.

"Jenny, wait!" She tried to climb out of the booth, but Lucas blocked her. "Let me out!" she insisted. "She's my friend!"

"Your friend?" he scoffed. "I've never seen a *friend* act so jealous. She wasn't having any fun. Let her go—you'll make up tomorrow."

Watching Jenny push through the bustling restaurant made Livia uneasy. Neither had ever abandoned the other in a time of stress. But a group of three supermodel types making eyes at Lucas quickly distracted her. She'd be crazy to pass up a date with the hottest actor in the world. Jenny had been her friend forever—she'd come to her senses and forgive her in the morning. And after all, this was for her career. She'd never be famous if she didn't think of herself first.

They left the bar two hours later, both of them blitzed. The ravenous paparazzi waiting outside caught them sneaking out holding hands. To their delight, Lucas brazenly kissed her for them.

"Cleopatra," he whispered, kissing her hard in the backseat of the Lincoln that picked them up, "don't leave me tonight."

"Your place?"

Tugging her hair, he shook his head with a grin. "Your place is closer. And anyway, I want to see where a princess lives."

She felt like Goldilocks again—Baby Werewolf-Bear was just right.

The elevator worked for once, and their ardor gained steam through their ascent to the third floor. But when the elevator doors opened, the enchanted spell was abruptly broken. Like a tiger awaiting its prey, Malachi stood by the front door with a bouquet of bloodred roses.

"What the hell are *you* doing here?" Lucas demanded.

"Meeting my girlfriend, you piece of shit!" Malachi slammed the bouquet down, sending roses tumbling down the flight of stairs.

Livia shushed them both. "We had a late meeting to discuss our characters!" she insisted to Malachi. And to Lucas: "I don't know why he's here!" Fearing another reprimand from the landlord, she shepherded both men into her apartment.

"You *bitch!*" Malachi spat. "I'll make you pay for this. I'll make both of you pay." He sucker-punched Lucas, knocking him to the floor—not a difficult feat, considering Lucas's intoxicated state.

Malachi pinned Livia's wrists together behind her back and yanked her so close she could smell his drunken, drug-fouled breath. "I thought you were something special. Now I know you need to be punished like the rest of them." She screamed as he whipped piano wire out of a pocket and wrapped it around her wrists. He silenced her screams with long, malicious, malodorous kisses.

Lucas, however—who was wobbling to his feet—tackled him. Malachi was fast, wiry, and fought dirty, but Lucas had the strength of his chiseled muscles. Wrestling on the floor, Lucas threw drunken punches, while Malachi scratched and kicked. Since her wrists were wired behind her back, Livia could only watch. She didn't even notice the unlocked door swing open.

"Children, get up." Alan Hakim stood in the doorway. He wore a Hawaiian-print shirt—all multicolored coconut trees, pineapples, surfboarders, and bare-naked women—1960s tie-dyed Levis, and red flip-flops. A yellow straw boater was cocked jauntily on his head.

His pistol was also pointing . . . straight at them.

*Oh no*, Livia thought, *it's a goddamn, no-shit .45-caliber Magnum Desert Eagle—the most powerful automatic pistol made.* Her crazy, gun-fetishing ex—the creep who had played Perchik in *Fiddler on the Roof*—had one just like it.

The room froze.

"Malachi. I expected to see you here. I saw you pawing on my golden girl today." His voice was as level as the Desert Eagle, but his ruddy face was crimson with rage. "Even went to the trouble of wiring up her hands so you could force yourself on her against her will. I'll deal with you in a moment.

"But Lucas—this is a surprise. Thought you'd try your hand at taming the vixen, did you? You're out of your league, son." His voice wavered now. Keeping the gun aimed at Lucas, he took a sideways step toward Livia. "This minx heeds only real men, namely *moi*—a man with five decades of proven experience around the feminine gender, a man who can—"

"What are you going to do, you leather-skinned, arms-peddling, al-Qaeda-sucking perverted old pimp?" Lucas snarled from the floor. "Spank her with your truss? She's been with me all night."

"Is that right?" Alan moved closer to her, pistol still extended. "Was my golden girl a bit of a tart?" Whipping around, he aimed the quivering gun in her direction, and she whimpered in fear. His voice softened: "Did they seduce you with visions of fame and glory, promising to make you a star? You told me you want to entertain the world." His voice took on a harder edge. "Let me tell you a secret. No one in this town makes it big . . . *unless Alan Hakim says so!*"

Trembling, Livia nodded her head in frantic agreement, her eyes all the while locked on the pistol. Its muzzle's maw gaped big and black as a dug-up grave—a midnight grave. "It wasn't like that. It was—"

"Shut up!" Alan bellowed. His body heaved with deep breaths, and Livia braced herself for the explosion that was sure to come. But there was nothing—instead, an interminable silence.

She opened her eyes, and then the strangest thing happened—the invincible producer, the man who controlled everything and everyone in his power, lost it. A goofy grin and a faraway look replaced the rage in his expression.

"You know, none of you would be here if it wasn't for me. Especially you, Malachi, you deceiving, ungrateful, sadistic, heroin-shooting bastard. That sickening schlock you call art has made me a pretty penny—but I've peered into your pit viper's soul. I guess that's why I'm so delighted to—"

*BANG!* Alan fired an ear-cracking Magnum slug into the twisted heart of Malachi Chung.

The bullet hole was big enough to drive a Hummer through.

Livia dropped to her knees, shaking. With all her strength she tried to break out of the wire binding her wrists.

"And you, you shit-for-brains piece of redneck white trash," he growled at Lucas. "When I found you, you were a nineteen-year-old hick straight from the trailer. If I hadn't given you a chance, you'd still be in the fields of Kentucky picking cotton. I *made* you! And I can take it all away!"

"That's what you think—"

*BANG!* A super-powerful .45-caliber Magnum bullet blew away the gorgeous face of this year's *People* magazine's "50 Most Beautiful People" cover boy.

"I see you're a trifle saddened," Alan said, turning to Livia. "Probably think you should call 911." Silent laughter shook his shoulders. "Doesn't really matter now. No use checking their pulses either—or poking mirrors in their mouths, giving them mouth-to-mouth, shocking them with fibrillator paddles. These boys are deader than beached carp, deader than Nebuchadrezzar's nuts, deader than the dark between the stars. Irrevocably, irretrievably, terminally, totally *DEAD!*"

A moan arose from Malachi's crumpled body. His extremities jerked as life oozed out of the bullet wound in his chest. Spooked, Alan silenced him with another Magnum round to the neck. He shuddered, then kicked the lifeless figure. When Malachi failed to react, he returned his attention to Livia.

"Now then! Where were we?" he continued, glancing around the apartment as if surveying it for the first time. "A Hefty bag—do you have one?" Livia nodded, unable to form words, her hands still wired up behind her back.

He darted into the kitchen, haphazardly slamming drawers and cabinets until he discovered the box of garbage can bags under the sink. Fingers shaking, he wiped down the gun with Mr. Clean and the tail of his Hawaiian-print shirt, then dropped it into the bag.

"Yes, that's it," he muttered as he sealed the plastic. "We'll find a nice river for you."

"What are you doing?" Livia asked.

"Escaping—my jet can be ready in fifteen minutes. A deserted desert island. St. John. No, Fiji! No need to risk getting wrapped up in this hassle." As he related the plans for his getaway, his speech became increasingly incoherent but his plan still had a maniacal logic to it. Even in extremity, Alan Hakim had a knack for taking care of business—a desirable trait for both a producer and a murderer.

Then he remembered her role in the evening's misadventure. "And you—you have to come with me!" The brilliance of this solution made him giddy with satisfaction. "Yes—that's right! We'll run away together!"

Her breath froze in her chest. "No," she said, shaking wildly. "No, no, no. I don't want to go. I'm staying here. I want to act."

"Acting is clearly no longer an option. Anyway, on our desert island I'll have no other means of entertainment. You can act for me—only for me."

"But I don't want to go to Fiji."

"Take comfort in the fact that you have no choice. I can't let you stay here and bungle my escape." He pondered the situation. "In truth, you're as implicated as I am. We are in your apartment, and I'm assuming witnesses saw you with that foolish child tonight." He held up a finger, remembering something relevant. "As a side note, don't even think about calling anyone or trying to escape. Not that you have the ability with your wrists wired up like that—quite a beneficial twist, I must say. I have several more bullets in this gun and no reservations using them on you should you misbehave."

He nodded toward her bedroom room. "Now sit in there while I make the arrangements. You have five minutes to decide what you want to take, then I'll pack for you."

He whipped out his BlackBerry and started dialing.

Dazed, she sat down on the bed in front of the damaged vanity.

"Lucas," she muttered under her breath. His star power was no good to her now. "Malachi?" she groaned softly. She would never be his leading lady. "Jenny!!" she wailed mutely. But for once, Jenny couldn't help her. Then, more urgently: "Isis!!"

The goddess appeared, her cheeks flushed with excitement. "This is getting really good," she said, smiling with mean merriment.

"This is *terrible!*" Livia moaned. "Do you derive some sick pleasure from watching this?"

"Me and the others—you know, in the heavens," she explained, "we're all loving it. *So* dramatic."

Livia fumed, imagining gods and goddesses enjoying her life's tragedies like they were a soap opera. But there was no time for carping complaint.

"What do I do next?" Livia asked.

"Well, it seems to me you have three choices," Isis said. She flashed a toothy grin. "I love it when things come in threes."

"Yeah, well, what are they?"

"Simmer down, Liv. First, naturally, you could take him up on the offer. Be whisked away in his private jet, settle down for a discreet life in Fiji and whatnot."

"But I don't want to live on an island! I want to make the movie! I want to make a hundred movies!"

Isis whistled low. "Well, I can tell you this: With the director and Julius Caesar dead and the producer on the lam, you're gonna have to put that dream on hold. So on to option number two."

Livia closed her eyes, still trying to assess the situation.

"Hey!" Isis snapped delicate, manicured fingers dangerously close to her eyes. "Keep it together! Option two. You refuse. You could escape—maybe out this window. But he said he'll kill you, and after what you just saw, I wouldn't take that threat lightly. Anyway, you're on the third floor. I doubt you'd make it in one piece or even alive. And even if you do—well, I have a feeling he'd hunt you down. He's obsessed with you now, and of course, you might always rat him out. Especially seeing as how you'll be all over the tabloids after the paparazzi photographed your lovefest tonight. The cops will be on you like a bad smell."

Livia groaned. "Can't you make this go away?" she implored. "You didn't tell me it was going to be like this. You didn't say things would go all wrong!"

Now Isis's eyes burned bright with anger. "I didn't tell you *what?* I gave you ultimate beauty, ultimate magnetism. *I gave you exactly what you wanted.* You're gorgeous. You're seductive. Men give you anything you want. Isn't that precisely what I promised you? Didn't I also tell you the inviolable truth of invincible pulchritude? It is invariably, inevitably, unavoidably, irreparably, inextricably, incomprehensibly . . ."

*"Bloodthirsty,"* Livia whispered.

". . . bloodthirsty," Isis repeated.

"Yes, but—"

"But *what?*" The goddess's eyes were now as hard as green glittering diamonds. Looking into them was painful. "You mortals can't figure out what you want, not one of you. No wonder my old friend Circe turned you into pigs."

Light-headed, Livia tried to organize her thoughts. "The third choice! You said I have three choices—what's the third?"

Isis regained her serenity. "Ah yes, the third choice. Sometimes in circumstances such as these a terminal option is called for."

She shook one hand briskly and stroked the palm with the fingers of the other. A thin snake appeared—brown and white with vertically pointed pupils bisecting the eyes on the sides of its head. She gazed fondly upon it before holding it to her face for a gentle kiss.

"Cleopatra used to amuse herself by testing poisons on prisoners and animals. She deemed the bite of the asp the least terrible way to die. Its venom brings heaviness to your body, without spasms of pain." She moved her eyes from the snake and leveled them with Livia's. "That's why she chose it for her own death."

Livia blanched at the suggestion. "You want me to *kill* myself?"

"Hey! You're the one who's in peril here. I don't much care what you do. You've amused me, but I'm rapidly losing interest."

"But I haven't even acted in my first movie!!" Livia cried.

"I gave you a fair warning. My hands are clean," Isis said crisply.

Alan's voice thundered from behind the door. "What's going on in there?"

"Don't forget—" Isis raised a suggestive eyebrow. "Yours is not the only mortal blood the asp craves."

Alan slammed the door open. He'd left the ammonia-scrubbed gun in the living room, but the determination in his eyes was no less menacing. The man was living a scene he'd produced a hundred times in movies, and he operated under a sense of control.

"Enough funny stuff," he said. "You're trying my patience, precious. We're going now. What do you need packed?"

Isis had vanished. In her place, the asp sat quite still on the floor. Its wide-set eyes trained upon Livia, it anticipated her decision.

The asp somehow gave her heart.

She would not go down without a fight.

"No," she said to Alan.

"What was that?" Alan said. He tore the thin comforter off the bed. Picked up a framed picture of Livia and Jenny and hurled it. She ducked and it slammed against the wall, then clattered to the floor.

Lying on the floor next to her was the same shoe that had shattered her mirror two nights earlier. She imagined launching it at Alan, watching it sail in a perfect arc before hitting his head. The sharp heel would slice a gash in his forehead, the blood oozing down his tanned cheek in a ghastly tableau worthy of Malachi's movies.

Yet she was crippled by the piano wire still binding her tender wrists. Inexplicably the strange words came unbidden from her mouth:

> *"With thy sharp teeth this knot intrinsicate*
> *Of life at once untie: poor venomous fool*
> *Be angry, and dispatch."*

The asp responded, leaping forward and sinking its venomous fangs into Alan's ankle. Panic set in as Alan collapsed. In only minutes, the poison would work its way through his veins and the job would be done. The almighty producer had no control over this scene's outcome.

Three dead bodies and a disoriented, intoxicated young woman: That's what the police officers who answered the disturbance call on the 6100 block of Hollywood Boulevard found upon storming the run-down apartment. Details were released to the media the next day.

The public became instantly fixated on Livia, and overnight the Bloodthirsty Beauty was a global sensation. She had it all: looks, charm, and an unforgettable personal story. She was history's loveliest murderess. The press were eating her alive already. They couldn't get enough of her.

A seven-figure movie contract quickly followed.

The night of the signing, she and Raoul Diabolo, the devilish studio head who had signed her, partied until dawn. Afterward he passed out in the stretch limo from too many Xanaxes and martinis, and she returned to her Beverly Hills Hotel bungalow alone. On her arrival she found something better than a drugged-out besotted executive: a huge expensive gift basket overflowing with red roses, jars of caviar, tins of pate, bottles of Remy and vintage wines.

On top of the goodies was a large, oblong, diamond-studded sterling-silver Cartier case with a note on top of it signed:

*"From Your Mysterious Admirer . . ."*

It was from Raoul, who else? She knew it in her bones.

Oh, what could it be? Diamonds, gold, pearls?

She fondled and kissed it. She wanted the contents to surprise her. Averting her closed eyes, she held it to her bosom. She popped open the lid, lowered her head, and looked.

But when she lowered her gaze, all she saw was an empty silver gift box and the tail of the asp sticking out of her plunging black neckline.

Like the press and public, the asp was sucking the life from her. It just couldn't get enough.

Alan's widow, Toni Harding, slipped out of the bathroom where she had hidden and watched. She bent over Livia until their eyes locked. Her Chanel Number Five smelled like it had been applied with a paint-sprayer. Livia wanted to say so, but the asp's venom had already paralyzed her mouth and vocal cords.

"I hope you like your present," Toni Harding Hakim purred. "It's a gift from me to you for stealing my husband." She was really aging well. She looked even better than she had in the posters that had plastered Livia's high-school boyfriend's walls ten years ago. *Has she gotten a face-lift?* Livia wondered as the lethal poison coursed through her veins. Toni touched her French-manicured fingers to preposterously plumped lips gleaming with gloss, then pressed them on Livia's rapidly paling cheek. She strode purposefully toward the door.

What was that outfit she had on? Even as Livia's vision faded, the ensemble looked familiar. A long white Grecian dress with gold embroidery, her only jewelry four wrist and ankle rings of simple elegant gold . . . just like the dress and rings Isis had given her.

Reaching the door, Toni Harding Hakim turned and said,

smiling toothily over her shoulder: "By the way, doll, welcome to Hollywood."

Livia wanted to howl with rage, but a firestorm of toxicity was coursing through her throat, lungs, heart, and brain. Still, in her dying mind she mustered a last, mute roar of protest. As her mental screech reached a furious, pain-racked crescendo, Isis and her fellow deities watched the climax of the show in ecstatic suspense. The heavens echoed with cackles as Livia's spark of life dimmed, faded, and was gone.

Livia Mendelssohn: another warrior slain in the carnage of the savage, endless battle. Such is the price that fame exacts in that dark corner of the Twilight Zone called Hollywood.

# EYE FOR AN EYE

Susan Slater

It is often said that "nothing ventured is nothing gained." Edie Holcomb, divorced and overworked, longs for a weekend away. But her venture takes her far beyond her expectations . . . perhaps, beyond her imagination . . . on a journey to the Twilight Zone.

Sliding behind the steering wheel, Edie started the rental and quickly turned the heater to three before pulling a New Mexico map from the glove box. At least she couldn't get lost. Ha! Her friends would laugh at that. She had been known to screw up going from point A to B in a straight line. But not this time. She shook out the map and traced the route with her index finger: Highway 64 from Taos, west across the Gorge, cross 285 at Tres Piedras, continue on 64, and follow the signs to Durango. Piece of cake. Yeah, right. What the map didn't say was beware of wildlife. Was she taking a chance starting out well after dark? Probably. But as usual she was running late. Just another stressor. One she'd promised her shrink to work on.

Still, a chance to get in a day's skiing, eat a few good meals, poke around antique shops . . . *and* some alone time—hadn't she packed a couple paperbacks? It sounded blissful. Besides, when would she get this chance again? Monday morning and it would be back to the grind—all work and no play. No wonder thirty-five was beginning to feel like eighty. So, the weekend was hers to do whatever she liked. She just needed to make the most of it.

She smiled—she was beginning to feel good already. She folded the map, switched on the high beams, and accelerated.

She owed this trip to her shrink—she would have never gotten away if Caryn hadn't insisted. The ol' doctor-knows-best ploy. But it worked and Edie promised to review the list of stressors that they'd worked on together: thou shall not be late, thou shall not spend recklessly, thou shall not overeat—well, maybe that one could wait. She was counting on enjoying the Snickers bar she'd stashed in the console. She'd cut out of the meeting before dinner, so the Snickers should be guilt-free.

She sighed. What wasn't guilt-free was the way she'd snapped at Caryn on the phone. She'd only called Edie to say thanks . . . again. She credited Edie with saving her thousands in construction costs on her dream house. All because Edie had looked at a photo of the lot and saw mounds in the shape of graves. Caryn had had the ground consecrated, the freak accidents had stopped, and building was progressing without a hitch. Blind luck. Happenstance. Anyone could have guessed there were graves. But Caryn insisted that no one could see them, only Edie.

What hocus-pocus BS. Contrary to what Caryn thought, she didn't have special powers. No gifts from the beyond or visions like her Great Aunt Edith, the one she was named after. Everyone knew her visions came out of a bottle.

The ring-tone suddenly sounded shrill and insistent . . . well, enough of that. What a great way to start the weekend—she'd turn off her BlackBerry. No texting, no pesky e-mails, the world could wait. She dug one-handed in her purse while keeping an eye on the road, only to have the BlackBerry squirt from her grasp and clatter to the floorboards. Damn. She was always dropping the thing—one more time and it probably wouldn't work. But she didn't want to answer it anyway. She'd hunt for it later; it wasn't going anywhere.

She was making pretty good time, but it was interesting how

perfectly black a moonless night could be—on a two-lane road without neon signage and homes tucked behind rolling hills. No sightseeing at this hour. But she was warm and had found one static-free radio station. Life could be worse. Or maybe not.

Coming to a stop at the intersection of 285 and 64, she watched a highway patrolman drag an electric signboard to the center of the two lanes in front of her. "Weather warning: Closed to through traffic until further notice."

Ridiculous. She pressed the down button on the window and took a peek at the sky—not a cloud in sight. She crossed the intersection and pulled behind the patrol car, then braving the cold, hopped out. A blast of wind plastered her dress to her body. She turned her back into the gale, and felt the material cup her backside like a second skin. She sensed rather than saw eyes take in the spectacle and for the first time that day was pleased she was wearing the knit. Cold be damned.

"Hey, you're gonna freeze. No use talking out here when my heater's running." He motioned toward the patrol car, walked to the passenger side, and opened the door. He was right, the car was toasty. She sank into the seat and didn't try to pull her dress below her knees. He was cute—not just a little cute, bona fide darling. And definitely her age.

He slid his seat back so that he could comfortably turn toward her. She tried not to stare at his ring finger as he slipped off his gloves. But no ring—not even an indentation.

"Kenny Walsh." He held out his hand.

"Edie Holcomb." His hand was warm and engulfed hers. She was reluctant to break the connection.

"Now, how can I help?"

"I need to get to Durango. I'm surprised by the weather sign." Hadn't the TV weatherman given the storm off of California a 70 percent chance of going bust? This was the week before Thanksgiving and snow could be expected, but the year had been dry. Ski resorts were panicking. Even man-made snow wasn't doing the trick.

"Don't expect much precip before midnight but that's a nine-thousand-foot pass. If there's moisture in the area, it'll be snow before you know it. And trust me, you don't want to get caught in a storm out there. Zero visibility, roads slicker 'n snot . . ."

"But won't I be in Durango before there's any danger of that?"

"Well, yeah, guess you're right. I'd say you don't have to worry for a while—should have plenty of time. You're lucky, you know. I've been working this stretch of highway for ten years and this year's the latest we've ever closed. Things are usually shut down by mid-October. This is one mean mountain for weather." He smiled, softening the weathered skin around his eyes. He could be a bit older than she'd first thought, late thirties, maybe. But hazel eyes, blondish-brown lashes, curly thick hair that he self-consciously finger-combed off his forehead . . . she found her breath coming just a bit quicker.

"Guess I am lucky. I can't imagine backtracking to Espanola and then up 84. If I read the map right, that's the only alternative."

"Not a lot of roads out here. But you should be okay if you get going." He turned on the car's headlights, then flipped them to bright to take in the roadblock. "Stay to the left; you'll get around the sign just fine." She hated getting back out in the cold but took a deep breath and hurried to her car. A quick wave and she was off, around the sign, and headed west.

The snow totally ignored its schedule. In a scant hour, big, fluffy flakes slipped down the windshield and puddled under the wipers. Double damn. She slowed to sixty, then fifty, and finally forty-five. Kenny hadn't been kidding, the road was treacherous. She lost traction on every curve. She knew she was climbing but her headlights were useless—like throwing the light from tiny, twin flashlights into a wall of cotton. She switched to low beams. No better. Absolutely no visibility. Her speed was now fifteen miles per hour and decreasing.

The elk came from the left up and over the edge of the drop. She probably would have been blindsided in broad daylight, never expecting an animal from that direction. But would she ever be able to forget that eight-point rack, the majestically crowned head that turned for one brief second to look directly at her? Because then she did everything wrong—hit the brakes, held them, didn't turn into the spin. She didn't see, only felt, the car violently fish-tail, leaving the highway to spin a hundred and eighty degrees, bumping rear-end first up, then down a slight embankment, coming to rest with both front wheels off the ground, headlights aimed toward the treetops.

She tried to quiet her breathing by relaxing, leaning forward to rest her head against the steering wheel and taking inventory. Nothing broken, nothing bleeding, nothing really hurting . . . she ventured a couple deep breaths. No searing pain. Ribs intact. She seemed to be all right. Now if she could just stop shaking.

She turned the lights off and then the ignition. Quickly the windshield clouded with snow, and she realized just how dark and how quiet the world could be when wrapped in a cocoon. And how cold. Warmer clothes were in her luggage—in the trunk. Think. She'd been a Girl Scout. Surely she'd learned survival skills. But badges in folk dancing, culinary arts, and animal husbandry weren't going to help her now. Wait. The BlackBerry. Surely, there was a wrecker service out this way—even if it had to come from Taos. She stretched sideways across the passenger's seat and felt along the floor. There. She snatched it up and dialed 411, only to watch the smartphone futilely search for a network. She dropped it back in her purse. Useless. Now what?

She was pretty certain the high-centered car wasn't going anywhere. It would take a truck and a winch to get it back on the road. Nothing less. So, what did that leave? Walking out? Stay on the road, continue west—but then what? No one would be coming along; the road was closed—she assumed from both directions. She was still three hours—driving sixty-five—from civilization. Unless someone lived out this far. But that was doubtful if the only road was closed much of the year. Weighing the options, instinct told her to stay put. Run the heater intermittently with a window cracked but first get all her clothes out of the trunk. Wrapping up in layers, extra socks, ski pants, mask and hood should keep her from frostbite. And she'd reassess in the morning. She popped the lever that opened the trunk.

Trying to hold the car door open while she crawled out was the first challenge. It was a full three feet to the ground, the car was tilted and stiletto heels made any leaping an act of faith. She pushed against the door with both hands, turned sideways, dangled her feet above the ground, then slipped off the seat to stand upright while still leaning against the door before wiggling to her left and letting it thud shut. Hauling two overstuffed bags out of the trunk and up the slight incline, then hoisting them onto the backseat would be her next challenge. Two inches of snow made guesswork out of maintaining footing. She took a step and slipped on loose gravel.

At first, lights above her and to her right didn't register. Then, oh my God, someone was coming. A car. Hurriedly, she jerked open the rental's driver-side door, leveraged the heavy door with her shoulder, leaned in, fumbled for the lights, turned them on, and watched as a pickup slowed, then stopped.

"Here! I'm down here!" Could she be heard? Ignoring the near impossibility of four-inch heels navigating a snowy incline, she scrambled upward. Above her, a hand suddenly thrust through the swirling snow.

"Grab on here. Let's git you on the road."

". . . trying to make it to Durango . . . dodged an elk." She was out of breath and bent double, gasping for air when she reached the road. Altitude. She wasn't used to this. But she was on solid ground.

"Probably not gonna git there tonight." He laughed at what he seemed to think was uproariously funny. Then he sobered. "Least I can do is git you to someplace warm. Anybody else in this wreck?"

She shook her head.

He led her by the arm to the pickup, opened the door, and waited until she could pull herself onto the seat. "I assume you got some luggage down there?"

She nodded, and found her voice. "Trunk's open. Purse is on the front seat." Deep breaths, gulps really, but starting to slow. He closed the door and was gone. The truck's interior smelled musky. Funky. Not really unpleasant, but sort of an animal smell. Like chickens had been roosting in it. And it was old—a real museum piece. She found herself hoping she wouldn't be riding in it for long . . . and its owner, a scarecrow of a man, tall, lanky, grease-stained sweatshirt over too-loose jeans. Difficult to guess his age, maybe fifties. But it was the eye-patch—a black square with rounded corners hugging his left eye, secured by black ties knotted in back of his head and buried in a wad of dirty blond hair—that gave him a menacing demeanor.

Then she admonished herself. Looking the gift horse in the mouth wasn't too wise. Didn't he save her from a cold night? If not something worse? And it was obvious that he'd survived something horrendous himself—disease, an accident, maybe. She was startled by a thud directly behind her. Her luggage, of course. He must have put it in the truck's bed.

The driver-side door opened, "Here's yer keys and purse. I closed the trunk and locked the car. Don't want nobody taking what ain't their's."

She idly wondered who would be out in this weather looking

for something to steal. Didn't seem likely but, again, she was thankful for the help.

"Thanks. I didn't catch your name."

"Larry, and yer?"

"Edie. I really appreciate this." She smiled.

"Don't mention it." He turned toward her and smiled back. Missing teeth caused his lip to curve inward, making the effort more of a sneer. He slipped the truck into gear, and carefully made a U-turn. "Gonna take you back up the road to an inn. You'll be warm tonight and in the morning Bob can call you a tow."

"A bed-and-breakfast?"

"Yep, guess you could call it that."

"That's great." Suddenly she didn't care about the cab's smell. A B&B! What good luck. Nothing sounded better than a hot bath, warm sheets . . . maybe get started on one of the novels.

"You were real close. It's just up here at the end of this road." The pickup bounced to the right and down a slight incline. How could he even know where the road was? Snow obscured everything. Wipers were almost useless, but as they pulled up in front of a rambling farm house with dormers, she noticed they were the only vehicle. Looked like she might be the only customer.

"You go on up and check in. I'll bring yer bags."

A bell on a desk in the hall summoned the proprietor, who turned out to be "Bob." A nice man, as clean and squat and chubby as her driver was mussed and lean. But then she sucked in her breath. Bob also wore a black eye-patch.

"Mill accident."

"Pardon?"

"I saw you noticed . . ." He gestured toward his left eye. "Happened years ago, nasty accident. You passed the saw mill on your left . . . corner of 64 and 285? Closed now. Regular death trap. No OSHA in my day."

"And Larry?"

"That ol' conveyor belt made us twins. Only good thing is we're both right-handed."

"I'm not sure I'm following."

"If you're right-handed, you don't want to lose your right eye—you compensate better if it's opposite your dominant side." This time Bob winked with his good eye. "Nope, under the circumstances, we were both lucky. Now, enough about me. Let's get you checked in and tucked in."

She put her credit card on the desk and moved to sign the register.

"Sorry, I shoulda said we're not set up to take those. More out of laziness, just never got the paperwork done. Cash is always good, or a check."

"How much is a single room?"

"Fifty-five."

Wow. That was a bargain. How long had it been since she'd paid fifty-five dollars for a room—and breakfast? "Plus tax?"

"Nah, I don't bother. More of that paperwork." He grinned, scrunching up his good eye and making the eye-patch bounce against a fat cheek. "Listen, why don't we settle up in the morning—give me time to print out a receipt."

The accountant in her was screaming "audit," but there she went again, looking at that gift horse. She should be so thankful to be out of the weather.

"That'll be fine."

"You like a sandwich? Kitchen's closed, but I could rustle up something. There's coffee and hot chocolate in the room."

"Hot chocolate sounds perfect. I'm past being hungry—a warm bed trumps any thought of food at this point."

"I understand. Guess you'll be needing me to call the wrecker in the morning?"

"Yes, thanks." Information traveled quickly around here, she noted.

"Away we go, then. I'll get the boy to bring that luggage up in a few minutes."

She wasn't sure who the boy was—to date, she'd only seen two people, Larry and Bob. But as long as she didn't have to drag her own luggage up a flight of stairs . . . She always overpacked. Another stressor. She made a mental note to add it to the list.

The room was toward the back of a long hallway on the second floor. An *unlighted* long hallway. There were bulbs in the ceiling fixtures—maybe they were trying to save money. Bob opened the door with an old-fashioned metal key—one of a circle of many. "I want to apologize about putting you in a converted storeroom. We're expecting a big party tonight—snow's slowed 'em down. 'Fraid this is all I have left."

"If it has a bed, I'll be fine."

But after he left, she looked around. The bed was a thin, ticked mattress of cotton batting thrown onto a rough wooden frame. There were no sheets, just two khaki green blankets—both wool, both scratchy. And she wasn't really sure they were clean. There were no women's touches—no starched linens, fluffy towels, aromatic soap—in fact, there was no bathroom. Must be down the hall. Funny, Bob hadn't pointed it out. There was a Coleman camp stove on a card table in the corner with a blue-speckled, enamel-over-tin coffeepot—a package of cocoa next to it. That was positive. But she wasn't going to feel safe lighting a propane camp stove indoors.

A soft knock interrupted her inventory and she opened the door to a young man in Goth black, including spiked locks with neon pink tips that fell forward over his forehead. Large black-rimmed sunglasses completed the look. She congratulated herself once again for not having children.

"You want these in there?" Chains hanging off his belt clunked against the door as he leaned in to point.

For just a moment she was tempted with a smart retort, *No, just leave them out in the hall.* But she stepped back so he could enter.

"Yes, please. You can put the smaller one down there." She pointed to the foot of the bed. "I'd like that one on the bed. Easier to unpack." She watched as he moved forward, wrestling with one bag at a time as he carried them through the doorway. She wondered why he hadn't popped up the pull-handles. It was like he'd never seen luggage before.

She watched as he struggled to lift the large case onto the bed. He seemed frail—thin, undernourished, and decidedly weak.

"Here, let me help you with that." She stepped forward, grabbed one end of the bag and lifted, knocking him off-balance. He caught himself before he fell, but his glasses slipped to the floor.

It was all she could do not to scream. He grabbed up the glasses and slammed them back on—but not before she'd seen the pink, pulpy indentation where his left eye had been. This was no mill accident—this was recent and still not healed.

She forced a smile. "Thanks. You've been really helpful." She reached for her purse and held out a five-dollar bill.

"That's okay." He waved aside the money, turned, stumbling over his own thick, black motorcycle boots, and bolted out, leaving the door open.

In all her life she had never seen so many empty eye sockets. And that included a couple bad pirate movies. Three in thirty minutes—all left eyes. What kind of coincidence was that? She walked to the door to close it and heard angry voices coming from somewhere downstairs. Tiptoeing into the hall, she stood and listened. Sounded like Bob and Larry were upset about something. She couldn't make out the words, but the anger was real. She inched along until she could hear clearly—thankful now for the darkness.

"You're flirtin' with the devil. We've been lucky so far—you know that for a fact, Bob Hutchins. There's no good reason to tempt fate."

"Only money. She's young—healthy. That means functioning kidneys, liver, lungs—maybe there's someone out there needing a heart. That'd put some green in your pocket."

"Let her go. I don't want to get my three squares behind bars . . . or worse."

"Losing your nerve? Never thought I'd see the day."

She didn't wait to hear more. Organs. They were talking about selling organs and they were talking about her. Or parts of her. Get out. She had to get out. She willed rubbery knees to carry her back to the room. Yes, her imagination was working overtime, but her sixth sense was screaming, *Hurry.* She didn't know where she would go, but she wasn't staying there.

She rummaged through her bags, kicked off the mud-stained Manolo Blahniks without a second's regret at having ruined an eight-hundred-dollar pair of heels, pulled on a pair of raglan socks, silk long johns, sweatpants, two silk undershirts, and a sweatshirt, then thrust her feet into a high-topped pair of UGGs. All before allowing herself a really deep breath. A scarf and stocking cap, and she was ready to go.

Wait. Money and identification. Grabbing her purse, she dumped it on the bed, picked out penlight, BlackBerry, billfold, car keys, and stuffed all in the pockets of a quilted, wool buffalo plaid jacket. Then frantically she made one more comb-through of her luggage to find something even vaguely resembling a weapon, but airlines made pretty certain there'd be nothing—no nail file or cuticle scissors.

She shivered. It was now or never. She slipped into the hallway, closed the door, and turned away from the voices—still debating her demise? She didn't want to find out. She couldn't dwell on what might be—she had to concentrate on getting away. Time was on her side, if she made use of her advantage. They wouldn't be expecting her to leave. Moving quickly and quietly, she discovered another staircase just two doors down from her room—

another set of stairs that descended into darkness. She wasn't good at taking chances, but what choice was there?

The voices had faded by the time she'd reached the first floor and the door in front of her seemed to lead to a side yard. Her luck was holding; it was unlocked. She slipped out, closing the door behind her and hesitated, listening for someone coming her way. Nothing. The night was clear, but bitter. The snow had stopped and a bright, almost full, moon hovered above. She didn't have a plan, but instinct said get back to the road. Getting lost in the woods at nine thousand feet in winter might not have pretty consequences.

But she'd keep to the tree line and out of sight of the house—that made good sense. The snow wasn't deep, maybe three inches, just slippery. It took her thirty minutes to reach the road by walking along the edge of a stand of aspen. Their black and silver gnarled trunks stood out in crisp relief against the white. She'd never looked over her shoulder so many times in her entire life, but there was no one following her. No cars or trucks, no flashlights, or shouts in the darkness. The night was eerily quiet, moonlight on snow dazzling in its pristine freshness.

Was she safe? Would they even check her room before morning? Depended on who won the argument, probably. But maybe, just maybe, she had escaped. She would be all right but she needed a vantage point—someplace high above the road that would give her a clear view in both directions. And offer some protection from the elements. It was probably around thirty degrees—below freezing with a slight wind chill. She was dressed for an overnight in the wilds, but not a comfortable one.

A mountain juniper about forty feet above her would work. Its low-lying branches offered the perfect cover. Not warm exactly, but out of the wind. Adrenaline would keep her from frostbite. Keep her awake and focused. She needed a plan and she had no earthly idea what it was going to be. At least from that vantage point, she could keep an eye on the rental car. She thought they would expect her to run—not expect her to stay close. But was her logic their logic?

She heard the car coming around the curve before she saw it. She froze. Friend? Someone who could help? Or someone called by Bob? Then in a wave of relief that left her faint, she realized it was a patrol car. Kenny? It didn't matter. Anyone in uniform was a welcome sight. She slipped and slid to the edge of the road and, jumping up and down, waved her arms as the car neared.

In a cloud of powdery snow, the car skidded sideways, ABS whining before shuddering to a stop.

Kenny opened his door and got out.

"Hey, are you all right? That looks like your car."

"It is. Played tag with an elk."

"This is the night for accidents. First snow, I guess. Got a call on one this side of Tierra Amarilla. Roll over. Pure luck that I was out this way." He'd moved around the patrol car to get a better look. "I don't think your car's going anywhere. Guess it'd be best to get you back to Taos and get a wrecker out here in the morning."

"Sounds wonderful."

He started down the incline. "Then let's get your luggage and get going."

"My luggage isn't there."

He'd slid to a stop by the front of the car. "That's not your stuff?" He was pointing to the backseat.

"What stuff?" She clicked the remote on the key ring and climbed down to stand beside him as he opened the door.

She felt faint and knew she was trembling. But there was the knit dress thrown to one side beside two open suitcases, the water-stained heels on the floor; the contents of her purse spilled out across the front seat.

"Hey, hang in there . . ." He caught her as she slumped against the car. "Let's get you back up to some warmth." He half-carried her to his car, helped her inside, bumped the heater up a notch, then retrieved her luggage.

"Are you sure you're all right?" He slid behind the steering wheel, handed her purse over, but didn't seem to be in a hurry to leave.

"No, I'm not." She slid the zipper back on the envelope-shaped black leather clutch. Everything seemed to be there and she didn't need to pat her pockets to know they'd be empty.

"Were you injured?"

"No, nothing like that—"

Then she told him everything. Larry, Bob, the Goth kid, all without left eyes, the room with a camp stove, the conversation that seemed to point at killing her. "Wait, tracks. I wasn't thinking. There would be tracks from the pickup."

He watched her closely. Sympathetic? Disbelieving? She knew she sounded hysterical.

"Snow would've taken care of tracks. But let me show you something." He slipped the car into gear.

She knew where he was taking her and wasn't surprised when he turned down the road to the inn. He pulled into the same circular parking area where Larry had dropped her earlier . . . only now when Kenny stopped and trained the car's external spotlight straight ahead before sweeping it from side to side, she could only stare.

The two-story structure was cavernous—burned, gutted, all but the stone façade that supported a part of the roof and two dormers with broken glass. The wide front porch listing away from the structure was missing steps and a railing.

"When . . . ?" She could hear the disbelief mixed with fear in her voice.

"About ten years ago. I was a rookie just joined the force. Whole place blew up during a raid—meth lab explosion."

"Let's just go. I don't want to see anymore."

Without comment, Kenny wheeled the Crown Vic around the semicircle and gunned it down the driveway to pop up onto 64, heading east toward Taos.

They rode in silence; Edie lost in thought. This was not a trick of her mind. Not some paranormal happening that Caryn could use, say "I told you so." She pressed her cheek to the cool window and took a deep breath. She wasn't crazy. She didn't just go off imagining things. Her life was real. There was a perfectly logical explanation for this.

Kenny broke the silence. "Bob was Robert—"

"Hutchins, I know."

Kenny paused, searching her face before continuing. "He inherited the property from his uncle. Larry was a local mechanic who, along with his son, hooked up with Bob somewhere along the way. But the combination was deadly—cop's nightmare. Can't tell you how many times we were out here. If it wasn't drugs, it was stories about luring unsuspecting victims to their deaths. Offering housing to those stranded on the road—there were even rumors about organ sales. Some people said they'd given up their own eyes to make money."

"Not rumors, truth."

"Before anyone could prove anything, they'd blown themselves up." He paused again. "It's a well-known story in these parts. Popular. Somebody comes up with a new rendition for the paper every Halloween."

"That's it." She hadn't meant to shout, but bounced forward on the seat. "I knew it. A simple explanation." She marveled at the relief she felt, that she heard in her voice. "Was there a feature this year?"

"Yeah. Even ran a picture of Bob . . . complete with eye-patch."

"You know, I'm not saying I saw it; I don't remember seeing it, but I could have. Hotel lobby, newspaper just lying on a table . . . and then when I went off the road, I hit my head . . . I imagined the story was real. Out there where it happened, my *imagination* filled in the details." She looked at Kenny hopefully, but he was busy maneuvering the car past Blueberry Hill at the outskirts of Taos. She took off her gloves and held her hands out to the heater and felt the chill disappear. Hadn't her suitcases been on the backseat? Exactly where she had left them after changing clothes? She had simply internalized the details of a story of local lore and with the help of a head injury . . . God knows she had always had an overactive imagination—

"Where should I drop you?"

"Sage Brush Inn. I'm sure they have vacancies—maybe I'll get my old room back." She smiled. Relief. It was like awakening from a nightmare. Maybe she'd sleep in tomorrow morning, have the desk call a wrecker, pick up another car . . . she'd blow off Durango; that was a given. She could never drive that road again. Not for a long time, anyway. She needed some distance on this one.

"Here we are." Kenny pulled the patrol car close to the door, retrieved her bags, and set them on the sidewalk just as his two-way squawked. "Gotta go. You take care."

"Thanks. I appreciate all you've done."

He shrugged. "Glad I could help." That shy smile and then he was gone, back in the car and turning onto the main drag.

Tough to be a cop. Up all night. All kinds of weather. Always rushing to one catastrophe or another . . . She picked up her overnight, pulled up the handle on the rollaway, and pushed open the heavy, hand-carved wooden doors.

The desk clerk jerked upright and quickly stood. Must have been sleeping. It was pretty late. Or early. She glanced at her watch. Nine twenty? That would have been about the time of the accident—she must have hit her wrist on something.

"Room for one?"

She nodded. What a strange little old man. The thick lenses in his glasses made him look like a frog.

"Downstairs or up?"

"Either."

"And how many nights will that be?"

"Just the one." She couldn't wait to get back to civilization—her home, work . . .

"I can give you a break, seeing how it's pretty late—tonight *and* tomorrow night for the price of one."

"No. Thank you, anyway." She was freezing. Had they turned the heat off in the lobby? Maybe if she put her gloves on. She thrust her hands into her jacket pockets—no gloves. Of course. She'd left them in Kenny's patrol car. She wasn't eager to write off a new pair of cashmere-lined lambskin gloves. She put her purse on the counter and dug out the BlackBerry. She'd call the station and leave a message, then pick them up in the morning.

The clerk seemed fixated with the BlackBerry, peering at it with those watery amphibious eyes. No, she was being unkind. It was late. She was tired.

"Is there something I can help you with?"

"Well, yes, there is. Do you have the number for the New Mexico Highway Patrol?" She saw his hesitation and hurried on, "I need to leave a message for Officer Kenny Walsh. I was in a one-car accident earlier and he gave me a ride back to Taos. I left my gloves in his patrol car."

"Officer's name?"

"Walsh. Kenny Walsh." Hadn't she just given his name?

Edie took a step back. Only then did her peripheral vision take in the small, open cardboard box next to the register. The label on the end facing her read, OCULAR PROSTHESIS—GLASS/BLUE-GRAY. She willed herself to look at the clerk. Slowly he slipped off his glasses and wiped a glob of yellow mucus from the corner of his left eye with a brown-stained handkerchief. Not an empty socket this time, but a perfectly stationary, large, glassy orb stared back—with a blue-gray iris.

He was saying something, but she felt the room start to spin and wasn't certain of what she was hearing. Something about Officer Walsh being dead, blown to bits some ten years back while serving a warrant on a suspected meth lab out on 64—

The BlackBerry clattered to the floor as her knees buckled.

What lies beyond imagination man often refuses to accept. But it is there that the eye can see the truth in the shadows, along the edges . . . of the Twilight Zone.

# THE COUCH

Peter Farris

Time, they say, is of the essence. To turn back the clock is a luxury none of us possess. Yet Herbert Menkel, like many middle-aged men, simply must accept the dour and mundane existence he's created. A life of routine and quiet despair, confined to a marriage that's lost any sentiment of love or companionship. But the memory of a strange encounter in his past returns, a moment that could be the key to happiness and freedom. Herbert's story begins with a simple relic stored in the attic of his seaside Connecticut home . . . and ends . . . in the Twilight Zone.

Herbert Menkel hated two things in life more than his clownish, shoe-salesman name. He hated his wife and her dog.

In that order.

Herbert was downstairs in the basement, feet propped on his old desk, flipping through back copies of *Sailing World* and *Ocean Navigator*. He'd been gazing at pictures of a Catalina Mark II Sloop, a forty-footer, when he heard the garage door, then the back door, followed by the woofs of their goddamn golden retriever, Daisy.

Iris, his wife, and her declarative stomps through the kitchen and living room were not far behind.

Herb tried to return to the dreamy attention he was paying to the gorgeous sloop, with its large central cockpit and state-of-the-art sail controls. He turned the magazine vertically, like a creep admiring the latest *Penthouse*, imagining not a pair of luscious breasts but a custom helm seat where he could watch the sun set, adrift in the Caribbean.

Neither dog nor wife in sight.

But his fantasy was lost, evaporating, as it did every evening. Herbert followed the noisy routine upstairs, his eyes going from the magazine to the ceiling where every creak and footstep resounded like a death knell. Another day gone. Never to be relived.

Iris opened the door to the basement, Daisy barking as if an earthquake was imminent. Herb closed his eyes mournfully and sighed. He felt his head retreating between his shoulders.

"Herbert! HERBERT! Daisy needs to be walked and fed! I've worked like a slave and there's still dinner to make. HERBERT! ARE YOU LISTENING?"

"Yes, dear. I'm coming. I'll walk the dog. Why don't we order take-out?" Herbert said, his tone soft and gutless.

"And just throw two hundred dollars' worth of Whole Foods groceries away? Why don't we just put the free-range chicken and fresh sage out in the front yard and burn it! And speaking of fire, you better not be smoking those stinky cigars down there, Herbert Menkel! I can smell them from here! You're going to get CANCER!" Iris hollered, punctuating the end of their conversation with the door slamming and more barks from the nasty beast of a retriever.

Herbert sighed again. He realized that after many years with Iris he was very good at sighing. A professional sigher. He tossed the copy of *Ocean Navigator* onto his desk. Looked at the cigar smoldering in an ashtray. A couple more puffs, he thought. He should hear the rush of water through the old pipes any second. Iris loading the washer. Then the television. She insisted on listening to the local news from the kitchen. Which meant turning the volume up so high it rivaled any quality public address system.

Five minutes and she'll be back, he figured. Per routine. For Herbert and Iris their first conversation of the day usually took place under such dysfunction. Iris at the entrance to the basement, yelling down. Herb muttering his replies from behind stacks of sailing magazines.

*And she'll use my full name,* he predicted. With total accuracy.

Just as he brought the wet tip of the cigar to his lips, Herbert heard footsteps. Then the door and its terrible rusty moan.

"Herbert Menkel, will you puh-lease walk Daisy? I just cannot do it all by myself! HERBERT MENKEL, ARE YOU LISTENING?" Iris said, her voice a histrionic caterwaul Herbert likened to that of a rabid monkey, or a cat being dipped in turpentine.

"Yes, dear," Herb replied with a squeak. He stubbed the cigar out in the ashtray and shuffled up the stairs.

Herbert managed to avoid Iris for a few more minutes. He knew what was coming. Dinner. He'd sit across from her as always and she'd talk and talk and talk. Work. Gossip. Politics. Business. Her opinions on everything were spoken as if the future of the country depended on their very utterance.

Daisy stood by the front door waiting for Herbert. He held the leash in his hand. She never wagged her tail. Never looked happy to see him.

Herbert noticed the neat stack of bills on a table in the hallway. He tried not to think about when the ominous-looking envelopes would be opened. And how the bills enclosed would be paid.

The words *"Please write your account number on your check or money order"* drifted through his mind when Daisy bit him.

The retriever never bit him hard, not hard enough to draw blood anyway. But it wasn't a playful bite, either. It was an act of meanness from a mean animal. Always happened when Herbert put Daisy's collar on. She led him out the door. He had to jog to keep from being yanked off his feet.

Outside in the yard Herbert stepped in shit. Daisy woofed at him. Herb didn't speak dog, but he knew those woofs were laughter.

"Why don't ye just divahce her, Herbaht?" Monte Doogan said to Herbert over coffee in the breakroom.

"Divorce?" Herbert replied, as if he'd never heard the word before. Monte shook his head.

"Maybe she's cheatin' on ye, Herbaht. Evah considered that possibility? If I caught Lorraine messing 'round on me, I'd find the cahksuckah and throw 'em both into the Pawcatuck Rivah!"

Herbert sipped his coffee. He smiled at his best and only friend. Monte was a hillbilly from Eastern Connecticut. A lost breed of New England ape. Known for his talent with a chain saw, sculpting tree trunks into bears and hawks and other woodland creatures. He delivered office equipment from a distribution center that Herbert managed in quiet, effective bursts of competence.

"Think 'bout it, Herbaht. Iris drives ye fackin' nutty, that I knows. If I was yous, I'd cat and fackin' run to tha hills," Monte said, departing with a wink and a tip of his filthy hat. The Red Sox cap Monte never took off looked to have been buried in motor oil and fertilizer for several decades.

"Sound advice coming from a guy with four ex-wives," Herbert whispered in response. He took another sip from his coffee.

It was almost quitting time.

Herbert knew something odd was up when he pulled into the driveway. Iris was home early from her job at the insurance company. He hesitated, his hand wavering near the doorknob. Herb looked around, expecting to see a camera crew. Practical jokesters lurking in the bushes. Nothing but the hum of the ocean. The shore. A breeze.

Herbert nearly fainted at the sight of his wife, singing a tune, hustling food from a pan to a dish to an oven. A pleasant aroma in her kitchen. A full pot of coffee. Iris hated the smell of coffee. She never drank it. She forbade Herb from brewing it in the house.

Herbert didn't trust anyone who didn't drink coffee.

Iris turned and lavished a gaze so false and rehearsed he thought for sure this was hell and his car had been struck by a train or crashed into the Pawcatuck River. Before he could find a knife and prick himself to see if it was only a dream, Iris brought him a steaming cup of black coffee, wrinkled her nose at him, and returned to her chore of preparing what looked to be an exquisite feast.

Herbert steadied himself. Seated at the kitchen table, he noticed a three-pack of his favorite brand of cigar. Even Daisy the retriever sauntered up and nuzzled him with a wet nose and a flash of pearly whites.

*This surely must be what hell is like,* Herbert thought.

But he'd seen this act before.

"I thought we'd eat in the dining room for a change, Herb," Iris said. She carried a baking dish to the table. A hot, aromatic casserole. Brown rice. Steamed cauliflower. Veal cutlets.

Herbert decided just to eat quietly. He sensed what was coming. It was all too good to be true.

"So I spoke with Jim Mitchell over at the bank today," Iris said, nervously picking at her food.

"Oh?"

"I've been working on a business plan. Put a lot of work and effort into it. You know it's a dream of mine, Herb!"

*Oh, boy. Here it comes.*

Herbert was very familiar with his wife's entrepreneurial fetish. Something she'd failed to mention during their unremarkable courtship, but had become an obsession once Herbert muttered the two saddest words in the English language: *I do.*

First it was the antique store, then the nightclub, the trendy boutique, the art gallery, the gym for toddlers, the movie theater for the blind. Iris Menkel had quite a reputation among shop owners up and down Main Street of Craftbury, Connecticut. And she damn near bankrupted the two of them every time. Herbert had squandered a rather healthy inheritence, amassed large deficits on his six credit cards, but most of all, he'd sold his sailboat. The only thing that had given him true happiness. Six years ago. He hadn't been on the ocean since.

Herbert nodded. His eyes betrayed him. Iris was gauging him as she would a derelict on her doorstep holding an axe.

"So, Herb, I met with Jim Mitchell and we discussed a potential business loan. He heard me out and just loves my proposal," she said, the wine turning to snake oil in front of her.

*I'm sure he loved your proposal,* Herbert wanted to say.

"Are you ready, Herb?"

Iris clasped her hands, the prestige moments away. Herbert nodded. Someone very dumb and sad had taken over his mind for the past thirty years and was at the controls now.

"I plan to open a restaurant right off Main. Now, Craftbury doesn't have a lot of independent eateries. Sure, there's the fast-food junk and take-out. But here's the genius of my restaurant. We'll only serve leftovers! That's right! Leftovers! I plan to call my diner 'Yesterday's Lunch.' Everything on the menu will be at least a day old. Jim Mitchell thinks it's a really niche idea! Can't you just see the neon sign out front, Herb? Herb?"

Herbert was nodding uncontrollably. He wasn't so much following Iris's big pitch as he was seizing up like an epileptic caught in a strobe light. He regained enough composure to reach for his cup of now-cold coffee.

"Sounds like a winner, dear," Herbert finally said.

Some other vestige of Herbert Menkel, deep down in his brain, perked up and shouted, *Did you really just say that?*

"And I've raised the capital to get started on Yesterday's Lunch," Iris said, beaming.

"You have?"

"It's a win-win. I worked out the details with Jim Mitchell. Just a matter of refinancing this and that, freeing up some equity, taking out that second mortgage you and I have talked about—"

Coffee didn't spew from Herbert's mouth, but it did trickle over his lip and drip onto the china-white tablecloth.

"Second mortgage?" he sputtered.

"Everybody's doing it, Herb. After six months, we'll be the talk of Eastern Connecticut. It's a slam dunk! Herb? Herb? HERBERT MENKEL!"

Iris's voice climbed to registers shrill enough to direct a flight of bats into a brick wall. Herbert found himself in the kitchen. His legs moved involuntarily, as if a switch in his brain had malfunctioned. Herbert freshened his coffee, grabbed the cigars. Daisy growled. He tiptoed down into his basement refuge.

For the next few hours Herbert studied the floorboards overhead through a haze of cigar smoke. Iris was hard at work slamming kitchen cupboard doors, clanking dishes, stomping this way and that, and watching *Entertainment Tonight* with the volume on AIR RAID. Herbert winced. He sighed. He eventually fell asleep in his chair, a copy of *Sailing World* on his chest, rising and falling with his snores.

That night he dreamt of his old sloop.

The Caribbean. A stranger on the beach.

And the weirdest single event of Herbert's life.

A solo voyage to St. Lucia. Drunk on the beach, a much younger Herbert relaxed under a full moon. Dark waters lapped against the shore. A ragged-looking man approached. A dreadlocked local, walking stick in hand. The smell of strong ganja. His name, he said, was Dahntay.

"White mon, sitting all alone here on the beach. How a boy like you get all the way down here?"

"My sloop. I sailed," Herbert said, pointing to the slips a quarter of a mile away.

"I see. A mon of the water. Then you must know my God, *Agwe*?"

"God?"

"*Agwe,* mon. God of the ocean, protector of all that is salty," Dahntay said incredulously.

"Sounds like a good guy."

"Oh, he is, mon. *Agwe* is good *and* evil *and* righteous."

Dahntay produced a spliff the size of a zucchini. He lit the end and passed it to young Herb, who had been feeling particularly adventurous since arriving in the Lesser Antilles. He liked smoking ganja and listening to Dahntay, who could have been anywhere from twenty to a hundred years old. It didn't take long for Herb to get very stoned.

"Oh, mon. Young sailor like you should see *Agwe* firsthand. You see them starfish over there? Dead as can be, am I right?"

Herb looked at the sea stars a few feet away, probably a dozen in all. Dumped from a fishing net, most likely, and most certainly dead. His eyes drifted back to Dahntay, who had hustled from one of his many pockets a leather pouch. Herb watched in dreamy amazement as his new friend rose, approached the pile of starfish, and with a pinch of whatever was in that little leather pouch, sprinkled it around.

A minute passed. Herbert took his dreadlocked friend for a crackpot. But then there was movement on the sand. Undeniable. The sea stars began to twitch. Arms flexing. Herb couldn't believe his eyes. Dahntay sang a little tune.

Then the little creatures, once dried-up and dead, began to dance by the light of the moon.

Herbert woke up to a quiet house. He felt weak, worn out, as if the dream of that magical night on the beach had sapped him of his strength. The first thing Herbert did was call in sick at work. Then he went to the attic.

*I've still got that stuff. I know it.*

He rummaged through boxes and foot lockers. Pictures of him and Iris on the sloop, sailing Long Island Sound, the Atlantic, the Caribbean. Happier times. But as if his eyes were suddenly seeing clearly, Iris acquired the appearance of a crazy person. It had taken thirty years and a really outrageous dream for Herbert to finally apprehend the downright wackiness in Iris's gaze.

*She's nuts. She's fucking nuts. And I sold my boat for her?*

Herbert found the leather pouch buried under old nautical maps and motor boat manuals. The leather was soft and worn. Oil-stained, the stitching barely held the contents inside. Who knew how old Dahntay's gift really was? Herb had forgotten nearly everything about that night, including Dahntay's pouch. It was oddly heavy, though it supposedly contained nothing but an ashy powder. Herbert studied the round sack in his hand. *Must weigh close to three pounds,* he thought.

*Agwe.*

Herbert showered and dressed. On his way to the garage Daisy the retriever appeared with a leer and a well-timed growl. She'd shat on the kitchen floor, knocked around her food and water dishes, spilling their contents. The dog wore its contempt for Herbert as easily as its golden coat of hair.

"Get leukemia and die!" Herbert shouted in a voice he'd never heard before.

Daisy flinched and crawled under the table. This was not the Herbert she'd known all her life. The pushover, the introvert, the sad sack. Daisy watched him enter the garage from behind a fortress of chair legs, a soft whimper her only retort.

Herbert drove along Craftbury's shoreline, eyeing the ocean with a nostalgic sadness. Fishing boats dropping their lobster pots. Cruisers and day sailers dotted the blue water. He passed Craftbury's famous marina, with its million-dollar yachts and catamarans. Herbert imagined that his cherished old sloop was out there somewhere.

With someone else enjoying it.

Midmorning and the parking lot at Stop & Shop was half-full. Mainly housewives and old ladies. Herbert parked near the front entrance of the grocery store. Inside his jacket pocket he massaged the leather pouch with one hand, walking in a kind of daze through the automatic door to be greeted by bright lights and fresh produce. Herbert never thought for an instant that his behavior was strange. He was enjoying whatever trance or spell *Agwe* had over him. And Dahntay's odd prediction so long ago on that dark beach came back to him like a lost radio transmission.

*Take it, sailor mon. One day you might wake up and have a need for* Agwe. *The ocean always giveth. And the ocean always taketh away. That, sailor mon, is the essence of* Agwe.

Taketh away? Herbert liked the sound of that.

He headed for the seafood department.

A young kid asked Herbert if he needed any help.

"Just browsing," Herb said.

The kid shrugged his shoulders and returned his attention to a clipboard. Seemed he had a floor to hose down next. Most of the store's seafood selection was displayed behind glass, but there was plenty of dead shellfish iced down in barrels and trays. Herb studied a bushel of crawfish, some snow crab clusters, whole steelhead trout in a bed of ice.

Glancing around, Herbert removed Dahntay's pouch, untied it. Just a pinch of dust. No one was watching, except for the security cameras, but the guard usually watching the monitors was busier checking out the new teenage girl at the register in lane five.

Herbert sprinkled *Agwe* over the crawfish and snow crab, got a second pinchful, and powdered the steelhead trout. Then he waited. And waited. The kid turned around and eyed Herb curiously. He pretended to be really interested in a tray of Maine mussels.

Then the snow crab began to twitch.

Herbert heard a soft *plop* and realized the clerk's chewing gum had fallen out of his mouth, landed on the display window. The other *plop* was one of the whole trout flopping off the ice tray and landing on the floor. Its reanimated brethren followed. Soon five whole fish were flopping away from the seafood department. Not the panicked death-rattle spasms of a fish out of water. The trout advanced earnestly, an eerie intelligence to their bouncing, hopping movements. After all, they didn't *need* water anymore.

A woman screamed. Then he heard the kid speak.

"Mistah, them crab legs are moovin'."

Herbert tucked the leather pouch back in his pocket and backed away, right into a display full of tortilla chips and salsa. He turned, an icy panic gripping him, and double-timed it down the nearest aisle. By then the chorus of screams had gained in volume. Old ladies shrieked, a man jumped over the pharmacy counter to safety. Children cried. Customers in the checkout lanes curiously craned their necks, mesmerized by the sound of breaking glass and manic shouting.

Herbert passed an end-cap full of batteries. The front door was in sight. The security guard almost knocked him down on his way up aisle seven, his gun drawn, his face twisted with fear.

An awful alien *hiss* filled the grocery store. Herb broke into a run at the sight of five dozen crawfish scurrying down the aisle in pursuit. Like demonic field mice, they overtook the security guard. An old woman with a purse full of coupons was next. A stock boy swatted at the crawfish with a broom. They made a terrible shriek.

On his way out Herbert heard gunshots.

Craftbury was so close to the state line Herbert could throw a rock from his beachfront yard and hit Rhode Island. And that's where Herb found himself, cruising along the coast road toward Madangasset and its world-famous fish market. It was midday. The events inside Stop & Shop, unnerving and fantastic as they were, simply drove Herb farther down the rabbit hole. He was on a mission.

And he needed supplies.

The twenty thousand square foot fish market was located on Madangasset Beach, a tony resort popular with the uppity hedge-funders of Litchfield and Greenwich Counties, along with the usual millionaire mummies who trickled down from Boston every summer to bake their flesh and drink martinis. Herbert found a parking spot between two Range Rovers. He had to call the credit card company to find out his available balance. There once was a time when he didn't even look at price tags.

The market was cool and smelly. Herbert pushed a cart past beds of ice. Aproned fishmongers worked the chains and slabs behind the glass displays of seafood. Herbert methodically explored every department, assessing the merchandise like a builder shopping for plywood and nails and paint.

Blue crab, alaskan King crab legs, jumbo prawns, crawfish, sea scallops, rainbow trout, mackerel, red snapper, haddock, whole squid, lobster, razor clams, shrimp cocktails. Herbert selected all his purchases with an eye for design and functionality.

Each seafood piece had to serve a purpose.

Iris arrived home from work as expected, doing her usual entrance accented by slamming doors and cupboards, Daisy the dog woofing its way around the kitchen until Herbert appeared. But Herbert knew tonight would be different.

He couldn't wait for Daisy to go into the living room.

Where he'd done some rearranging.

Herbert quietly opened the door that led up from the basement to the kitchen. Iris didn't hear him. Sacks of groceries were scattered along the counters. His wife had a pot boiling already. Herb turned to his right and saw Daisy frozen at the threshold as she studied what he'd done in the living room.

"HERBERT! Come help me with dinner! I am TOO TIRED TONIGHT! Did you hear the news today? People went crazy at the Craftbury Stop and Shop! I had to drive all the way to Stonington. HERBERT!" Iris yelled over her shoulder.

"I'm right here," Herbert whispered.

"Oh," Iris said, turning around. "What's the matter with you?"

"I was ill today. I called in sick at work. But I'm all better now."

"You're *sure* of that? Well, what did you do today? Sit around smoking cigars and reading old magazines? That's some life, Herbert. And what's that awful smell?"

Iris looked to Daisy, the dog mysteriously rigid in the doorway. "Sweetie? Whatcha lookin' at?"

The retriever took several cautious steps into the living room. By then whatever was in there began to make that terrible alien *hiss* that had frightened Herb so much in the grocery store. A pleasant chill pebbled his flesh.

"I did some shopping, dear," Herb said. "I bought a new couch."

Iris suddenly jumped at the sound of Daisy growling ominously. The hiss in the living room had grown to a crescendo. Iris ran. Herbert didn't try to stop her.

When she saw the couch, Iris shrieked. She turned to run but Herbert blocked the doorway. In his hand was a leather pouch, empty of all its magical contents. Iris reached out, her face taut with fear, just as Daisy the retriever leapt toward the now-moving couch.

But what ate the dog was no piece of furniture. What had been a wicker loveseat was now an undulating mass of scallops and salmon, with lobster claw armrests and a headrest made from crab legs, with beady black crawfish eyes peering out from the unmistakable impression of a face Herb was proud to have made. Mackerel cushions and an oyster-covered back wiggled and wormed as prawns and shrimp plopped and hopped toward the slobbering retriever.

Daisy foolishly launched herself against the beast, Iris screaming in protest. The squid tentacles Herbert used as trim along the lower frame of the couch snatched the dog. By then the crawfish and razor clams had worked their way through the dog's coat. The squid tentacles pulled Daisy's body toward the couch in a slurping, schlupping din of pure hunger.

The crab legs danced back and forth, black eyes glittering in ecstasy. Their little claws snipped and snapped in unison. As if to signal that the couch was happy with its meal.

And it wanted more.

Daisy was disappearing, a matted gooey mess of fur as the lobsters and prawns and fish heads sucked and slurped at the retriever. Iris vomited in a wastebasket. She felt Herbert's hands close on her arms.

"Herbert! No! NO! NO!"

"Come, dear. Let's sit for a spell."

With a powerful shove from Herb, Iris tripped and fell into the waiting claws of the couch. The squid tentacles roped around her neck and pulled her toward a welcoming committee of blue crabs and dozens of pinchers. Catfish faces under the armrests smiled and licked their whiskers in anticipation. The prawns and shrimp scurried around her like cockroaches. Oysters clapped a percussive voodoo beat as Iris was consumed in seven wet and awkward gulps.

Herbert had to open the door to let the couch out.

Thank God it was dark. Couldn't imagine a neighbor seeing his inspired creation. He followed the undulating mass of reanimated seafood as it squished its way down the beach. He waved good-bye as the couch disappeared hissing and belching into the waves.

"An offering for you, *Agwe*," Herbert said.

He admired the full moon. The tide. He smiled at the slimy trail the couch had left through the sand.

"The dog was extra."

*And the ocean giveth. And the ocean taketh away.*

Dahntay's words from so many years ago crept once more into Herbert's dreams. He dreamed he was on his sloop, the sun at his back, sailing through calm waters. A course set for the Antilles. On the foredeck Herbert gazed at the horizon. He'd never been happier.

And while Herbert slept peacefully, some crab legs worked together to form a bridge up the staircase of his house. Crawfish pushed as two giant Maine lobsters mounted the carpeted steps. On the first floor red snapper and bay scallops had formed ranks like an infantry awaiting marching orders. And in ways only sea creatures could understand, instructions were passed along.

A whisper in the darkness. A hiss. A slurp.

"It's the second bedroom on the right."

Desperation is a powerful emotion . . . one that can often lead to madness. Yet for one crucial interval as he stared at the moonlit waters of Block Island Sound, Herbert Menkel relished the mysterious beauty of the ocean. For some men find great comfort on the open sea. But in those dark depths was a magical force Herbert could never understand. The ocean giveth, and the ocean taketh away . . . only in the Twilight Zone.

# WHERE NO MAN PURSUETH

Norman Spinrad

Joe is, well, a middle-class racketeer running a middle-rank Mafia franchise operation. He wouldn't even call himself a good man, but he's not the worst of men either, now is he? Okay, so he's a gangster, but he's never killed anyone in the course of doing business, and he's never put out a contract.

But then, he's never had to.

Not yet.

Would he if he had to?

Joe doesn't know and he doesn't want to find out.

But he will.

Or has he already?

Perchance in dreams?

Because when the wicked flee where no man pursueth, they're likely to find themselves somewhere and somewhen where the past can become the future and the future can become the past—a somewhere and somewhen known as the Twilight Zone. . . .

And you say that you've never—"

"Look, Doc, I'm a Catholic, maybe not such a good one, but if I had, wouldn't I be telling this at confession to a priest, not to a shrink?"

"We're bound by an oath to maintain doctor-patient confidentiality, too." He gives me this oily grin. "I'm from Vienna, you can trust me," he says like I'm supposed to laugh.

"Huh?"

"Just a little inside joke."

I made this guy for a sleazy scam artist as soon as I walked into his office. The building's a dump, there's no couch like there's supposed to be, just a leather-upholstered easy chair seen better days, a desk looked like secondhand from my high-school principal's office with which I had been all too familiar, and this guy in maybe his late fifties behind it in a cheap gray suit with an open-necked white shirt needed a trip to the dry cleaner's, hippie-style wire-rim glasses, graying ponytail to match behind a high bald forehead reaching about halfway back.

Maggie had found this shrink's ad in one of her magazines, said something about how he had trained with L. Ron Hubbard or Dr. Phil or another of those heavyweight psychiatry stars could get themselves on *Oprah,* but offered bargain-basement rates. And the whole thing was Maggie's idea, not mine anyway, I never believed in this stuff, I went along mostly to get her off my back.

"If *Tony Soprano* can take his problems to a shrink, then why the hell can't you?"

"*Hello?* Jesus Christ, Maggie, there ain't no Tony Soprano, he's just a character in a TV series, remember?"

"*So?* So *you're* just a character in your dreams. Unless . . ."

*"Unless?* Unless *what?* How many times do I have to tell you *I've never killed anybody!"*

"You sure, Joe?"

"Am I sure? You think it would just slip my mind?"

"Maybe. Like I read in *Psychology Today,* a guilty conscience could push it out of your waking memory and into your dreams. I mean, in your line of work. . . ."

Well, Maggie has a lot of time on her hands to watch daytime television with the kids gone off to college and all, and she likes the phony judge crap and the talk-show bullshit better than the soaps, and she reads these chick lit romances, and those damn self-help magazines full of starvation diets, fortune-telling astrology, New Wage fruitcakery, an' all, and while it's all a load if you ask me, which she doesn't, at least I gotta admit she might know a little more about this dream interpretation stuff than I do.

I mean about all I know about it is the dream books some of the marks read to pick numbers, and once in a while one of them dreams something that *does* give them a winning number, or so they claim.

And the dreams . . .

By this time they're really getting to me.

"Always different, always the same, sort of, Doc, know what I mean?"

"Sort of," says the shrink. "Why don't you give me three examples? One's just a dream, two could be a coincidence, three establishes a pattern, game theory, know what I mean?"

*"Sort of,"* I grunt, but I kind of do. Like when some bar owner's late with the protection money, well, sometimes shit happens, a second time the month after just might be coincidence, but the third time, gotta give him a Dutch uncle session or it's gonna degenerate into a serious enforcement issue.

He gives me a go-ahead nod and a rolling hand signal, and I'm paying by the hour, now ain't I, so . . .

"I've always dreamed I'm a kid again a lot—"

"You're back in the fifth grade in your eleven-year-old body, but you're really an adult, the teacher's giving you a hard time, or you're out there in the schoolyard with the older kid that's always bullied you but you know karate—"

"Wow! Amazing! Howdya know that, Doc?"

"Quite common in the literature, a lot of people have dreams like that. Sometimes they're wish fulfillment dreams, sometimes they're—"

"Bummers. Yeah, well, they used to be mostly fun stuff, like you say, kickin' the crap out of fuckin' Tommy Murphy, gettin' my grown-up hands into Mary Coangelo's thirteen-year-old pants, winnin' the ballgame with a grand slam in the bottom of the ninth, like that. But three, four months ago maybe, they started to go bad . . . come to think of it, I think that's how this whole damned thing started . . ."

"You began killing people as a kid in your dreams?"

"I told you I've never killed anyone, damn it!" I shout like an asshole. Like I've been taking to shouting it at Maggie in a way that's starting to make her think I'm keeping some hit from my youth from her all these years. Like if I was to lose it that way being questioned by the cops all I'd succeed in doing was convincing them I was hiding half a dozen stiffs in the basement.

"Not even in your dreams?"

"Not even in my dreams, Doc," I tell him, getting ahold of myself. "Well, not exactly, but . . ."

*"But?"*

"But, well, I've *already* done it when the dream starts. It's never my fault, you understand, Doc, I had to do it to protect myself, or the son of a bitch was just asking for it, or . . ."

I gotta stop and take a long deep breath, three or four actually, because talking about it is like puttin' me right back in there bodywise, I'm startin' to feel that nervous lump in my gut, that hollow behind my eyes, that cold sweat comin' out on my nuts, that twitchy-itchy feeling that I've forgotten something, that they're closing in on me, that they're gonna find out . . .

"Go on . . ." the shrink says in this nothing nerdish way.

This guy don't give away much with his mouth, but there's something about the way he's hunching forward a little, something about the way his eyes are getting glossy behind those hippie glasses like he's stoned on reefer and getting off on this somehow, a pervo thing, or like some down-on-his-luck grifter hoping that this is gonna somehow turn into the main chance.

Or maybe that's part of the job, like you gotta not exactly be sympatico if you expect to make it as an enforcer, what do I know about this shit, and I'm paying for this, ain't I, so . . .

"Okay, Doc, so I admit it, I've *already* killed someone when it starts, even in the kid dreams, I've disposed of the body in a professional manner, I've gotten rid of whatever leads to me, I've done such a good job that *I've forgotten I've done it myself, until—*"

*"You've killed someone and you don't remember?"*

He gives me a halfway freaked-out look and you don't need to be a shrink or a mind-reader to know what he's thinking, like if this guy can forget he offed someone in a dream, how can he be so sure he's not forgetting he's done it for real? Maybe more than once? How do I know I'm not sitting across my desk from a homicidal maniac so far gone he doesn't even know it?

Is that a question so good he don't even have to ask it? For sure, this is the first time I've found myself asking it. Is that what you pay shrinks for? Is it such a good idea?

I sit there looking at him for a long time saying nothing and neither does he as I run back through my memory looking for any holes. There aren't any. Or any that I can . . . remember. But would I know if there was . . . ?

"Until what . . . ?" he finally says.

"Until it begins to fall apart, and the dreams sorta run backwards," I tell him, and it's like magic or something, I'm right back there in one of these kid dreams, it's really happening, well, sort of, except that I'm awake, and I know it, and I'm babbling it across the desk as it's happening, or maybe it's the babbling of it that's making it happen, or maybe it's somehow both . . .

I'm thirteen years old, I'm upstate, in the country, where we used to spend the summers when I was a kid, or anyway me and Mom and my sisters did in the cabin we rented in this bungalow colony, with Pop staying in the city to work on the docks and come up only on the weekends.

I love it up here, there's a bunch of kids more or less running wild, ball fields, handball courts, woods, a lake, wild blackberry brambles everywhere, orchards not that big a hike away to steal apples from, and best of all two whole months with no school, no homework, only two days a week of Pop givin' me crap about studying hard so I can go to college so I don't end up like him or worse even though I'm not even in high school yet.

Not that I intend to do either. In fact I *know* I'm not going to because I haven't, I'm *me* inside the little punk's head, the grown-up me that's talking to you now, remembering everything that's going to happen, what's gonna be the future for this kid.

Right now, sunset is coming on, and I'm sitting at one of the picnic tables outside the kind of candy store-bar-pinball parlor, where there's enough light from the windows so we can keep playing poker, me, my main man Richie, Dominick, and Ted, and Richie and me are giving the usual secret hand signals that let us know who's holding the best hand so we can control the bidding between us and split our winnings. Not like this is *cheating,* Doc, it's *teamwork,* and ain't that what made America great?

Yeah, okay, so I'm a little wiseguy already, we all are, poker games, craps, running this and that on kids younger than you are, same kind of stuff the bigger boys running on you, beatings sometimes when you don't cough up your allowance money or your gambling winnings when you got 'em, the law of every jungle, asphalt or otherwise.

Worst of us is Big Al, almost sixteen, and that's what all the guys call the big fat prick if they know what's good for them and even if they don't, because, yeah, he may be overweight, but most of it's muscles, he's built like a gorilla with a brain to match, and if you don't watch your ass when you're around him, and even if you do, every once in a while he's gonna kick the crap out of you when it's your turn, just to remind everyone who's the top all-beef hotdog around here.

But Big Al, he ain't too bright, else why would he be hanging around with kids mostly a couple years younger than him, and it's usually Big Al who Richie and me take the lion's share of our winnings off in these poker games, not *cleaning him out* all the time—*that* he'd not be stupid enough not to notice, and *we're* not stupid enough to try.

But Al's not here now for some reason I can almost remember, has something to do with Richie's black eye, I think, which makes for a crummy game of seven-card stud, not just because me and Richie are missing our main mark, but also because a four-handed game don't work as well as a five somehow, if you know anything about poker.

And oh shit, here comes Big Al's mother with the local deputy sheriff, which gives me a kind of hollow feeling in my gut and sucks my balls up tight into my scrotum, but doesn't surprise me at all, why the hell is that?

"You bums seen my Al?"

Dominic and Ted shrug.

Richie and me exchange looks and try not to look nervous.

Why is that?

Oh yeah, we haven't seen Big Al for a couple of days now, strange, come to think of it.

So why ain't it surprising?

"Come on, where is he?" Big Al's mom screeches. "You think I don't know he plays cards with you here every afternoon before dinner?"

"Yeah, kind of weird, come to think of it, ain't seen him at all for a couple of days," Richie tells her, but it don't sound very convincing, Richie's not a very good liar. And besides—

"Yeah yourself, Richie," she snaps back at him, "then how did you get that fresh shiner?"

Of course the bitch *knows* her son's the main bully around here, she's *proud* of it, after all there's nothing else about him she can be proud of, and it's better than even money that when a kid shows up with a black eye that he got it from Big Al.

"Uh . . . playing softball . . . got hit by a line drive. . . ."

Big Al's mom don't know squat about softball, so she doesn't know Richie is a hotshot shortstop not likely to take a liner in the face. The deputy probably knows from softball but not that Richie's an ace shortstop, so maybe Richie gets away with a lame one like that if it doesn't take him what seems like a year to think it up and slowly spit out. Like I said, Richie is a lousy liar.

He's gonna get us caught.

'Cause Richie's not the bravest guy around either. Even these country cops can get it out of him, probably won't even have to bring on the rubber hoses.

Caught doing what . . . ?

I'm almost remembering . . .

"Ah hate t' haveta say this, Miz Fiorellio," Deputy Dawg drawls, "but looks like we'd better dredge the bat cave."

Oh no! It's probably gonna be full of gut gas now and floating!

They're gonna find Big Al.

I don't just *remember,* Doc, I go back in time, I'm back there yesterday.

I'm walking with Richie along the abandoned narrow-gauge rusted-out railway line that leads back through the woods to the bungalow colony from the bat cave. The bat cave isn't really a cave, though the bats that pour out of it at sunset are real enough, it's a sunken mine—coal, iron, copper, nobody knows—that went down too far, hit an underground river, flooded, and had to be abandoned.

Big Al is why Richie's walking back from the bat cave with a shiner and I'm trying to come up with a story explaining it that will hold water when the grown-ups start looking for the son of a bitch and don't find him, and someone remembers seeing the three of us going up there and two of us coming back and the local yokel cops dredge the sunken mine shaft where, according to what passes for tough country boys up here claim, they've fished up the rotting corpses of those what had it coming to them many times before.

The grown-up me inside the thirteen-year-old kid knew that you're supposed to tie weights to a corpse when you ditch it in a drink, and preferably with chains instead of ropes that might rot away too fast, or it's liable to fill up with dead man's fart gas and float to the surface, as well as the moves that allowed me to do what was necessary when Big Al demanded we both take turns sucking his dick and socked Richie in the eye.

But I didn't have either ropes or chains with me, so we had to just drop his fat ass down the well and hope for the best.

Oh shit!

I *know* they're gonna nail me!

"*And?*" the shrink demands eagerly, like what I've been telling him's left him with a boner and it's up to me to come to a punch line that gets him off.

"And *nothing,* Doc, that's the end of the dream. They all always end like that."

"Nothing like that in the literature . . ." he mutters. "Suppressed memories *inside* dream timelines, time sequences running backwards . . . very strange . . ."

"No shit, Sherlock. Why do you think I'm here in the first place?"

"Uh . . . well, they could be wish-fulfillment dreams."

"Are *you* nuts, Doc? Who would wish he was gonna take a fall for a homicide?"

"You'd be surprised . . ." the shrink sort of mutters under his breath with a weird dreamy look on his face. "Guilt can do funny things to the mind."

"Guilt for what?" I shout at him. "I *told* you I never offed anybody, what's the matter, don't you believe me?" I say it in a movie-gangster voice, half rising from my chair to leer at him cockeyed like Tough Tony wiseguy.

He turns pale. "What kind of work you say you do . . . ?" he stammers.

"I didn't. You sure you want to know?"

He cringes a little.

Why I want to do this, I'm not sure. Probably just because I'm getting pissed off. Who wouldn't be?

"Maybe I don't," he mutters, then tries to get more professional. "Uh, *was* there a bully called Big Al in the country place where you spent your summers? It'd be natural if you had fantasies of, uh, getting him off your—"

"Are you kidding, Doc? There wasn't even a country place, my pop couldn't afford stuff like that! And the only Big Al I've ever known is still alive and he's—"

I stop myself, because I was about to say he's just *muscle,* not a real enforcer, he don't even have the smarts for that, you gotta be able to talk the talk a little, and Big Al's just a particularly big and particularly ugly plug-ugly your real enforcer might have use for when dealing with particularly hard-core ass-pains. Or to take a murder rap himself if necessary.

"He's what?"

"Just a business associate," I tell him.

"Interesting . . ." the shrink mutters like Mr. Spock. "Very interesting." He picks a pencil off the desk and starts nibbling on the eraser, an ex-smoker, and probably recently. He sort of waves it back and forth in front of his face like a guy conducting a phantom opera got only one note, like what do they call it, a metropole, a . . . *metronome.*

"Why . . . don't . . . you . . . tell . . . me . . . another . . ."

"Like . . . what . . . do . . . you . . . mean. . . . ?" I mimic back at him.

"Like . . . one . . . where . . . you're . . . an . . . adult . . ."

I find myself unable to stop watching his damn nervous tic with the pencil, like my old Uncle Marty always bobbing his head like one of those trick plastic birds do it forever in a glass of water without a motor.

"Like . . . a . . . wet . . . dream . . . ?"

Like Maggie wagging her finger under my nose when she's really pissed off at me and reading me out.

"No . . . like . . . just . . . business . . ."

Like . . . funny . . . he . . . should . . . say . . . that . . . dumb . . . line from a dumb movie about the business he don't even know I'm in, maybe he's starting to guess, anyway he must know *his* business better than I been thinking he does, because this time it's not like I'm telling him the dream like it's a story, it's like a movie and I'm back there in it. I know I can't change anything, but I don't quite remember how it goes even though I know I've seen this one before, even though I know I've *been* this one before. . . .

I'm lucky, maybe not Luciano lucky, but say Tony Soprano lucky. I've got bigger turf, I've got a bigger crew, I've got one of those so-called consiglieres. It's not just the numbers and the local bookie operation and a couple of whorehouses one step up from street walkers and the neighborhood protection collections, I'm into the coke trade, a string of upscale whorehouses, a couple of clubs I own outright, pieces of a dozen or so bars.

If this ain't exactly the big time, it's not the small time no more neither. We got a house out on the Island with enough grounds you might call it an estate and a wall around it makes it a *compound*, Maggie's got her own BMW, I've got a big black Mercedes limo with a driver and a bulletproof window between me and him no less, and he's wearing a *uniform*.

Like this is my sweet future, only it ain't so sweet now, because that's where I am now, in the backseat sucking nervously on a ten-dollar cigar the size of a donkey dick as my convoy zips back out of the city and away from the screwup on the docks, a pearl-gray SUV riding point in front, a blue one behind the limo, desperately hoping I'm gonna get back to the compound in one piece, where I'll have some firepower protection.

If this was one of those old gangster movies, no problem, they gotta find the stiffs, get to a phone, call up a crew, and beat me to my rabbit hole and nothing to worry about except the cops who don't give high priority to this kind of thing, especially since this was ordered from higher up the food chain where they probably got 'em on the pad.

But this is not a movie, this is not the 1930s, everybody and his kid cousin, everybody and his kid cousin's *dog* fer chrissakes, got a cell phone, and the survivors must've had cell phones.

So I'm smoking like a chimney, I'm pouring myself a second scotch from the limo bar, whacking it down, I'm stroking the piece in the shoulder holster I never worn before tonight every five minutes to assure myself it's still there, as if it's gonna do me any good, and freaking out every time something in the next lane paces my limo for a few car lengths.

I never expected this when I got into the life—does anyone? I don't know, but *I* didn't. I never was muscle, I never even thought about doing a hit, never even carried a gun—well, hardly ever. For sure never thought I'd ever get involved in fulfilling a contract.

Yeah, sure. Never thought a phone call like that would be part of the deal. Never believed that these are the dues you're gonna have to pay sooner or later.

"Think of it as a Roach Motel, Joe, you and that cockroach Nickie the Dickie go in, and he don't come out," says that voice like Arnold Schwarzenegger doing Don Rickles. "A personal favor to your favorite uncle. I *am* your favorite uncle, now ain't I, Joe?"

"Yeah, sure."

Yeah, sure, like there are *personal favors* in this business, like you can tell your favorite uncle, sorry but I'd rather not, nothing *personal* you understand, Unc.

*Making your bones,* what they call it in the movies, like it's some kind of, what, coming of age ceremony, a bar mitzvah, getting your foreskin chopped by the jungle-bunny chief, yeah, sure, what a load. Like Don Whoever's gonna waste your cherry on a pointless hit just to let you in on the secret handshake.

This is supposed to be a meet to make a deal between me and Nickie been ordered from higher up, that's the story I've been told to have my consigliere tell Nickie's. Nickie's got a private garbage hauling company called Earth Angels, I've got a bunch of my bars, and clubs, and cathouses what need their crap hauled away, and my operation being in Tony the Tuna's garbage franchise's territory, I've been using Keep on Truckin like I'm supposed to. But now I've been told that for reasons that are none of my business I'm supposed to cut a deal to give my business to Nickie.

Now I ain't chickenshit, or a pussy, or nothing like that, I may not have ever had a hard-on to make my bones and become a made man—more Hollywood bullshit, anyone who's running a franchise operation of my size is as *made* as he needs to get, namely passing at least high six figures a year up the food chain—but I've never killed anybody, never ordered a hit, never put out a contract.

Not that I wouldn't if I had to, just business like they say. But I never had to—who needs it? It's dangerous stuff. If your protection goes wrong, or the cops get pissed off, or there's some other kind of screwup and you get nailed, it's at best a long, long stretch, and at worst sweating out the legal eagles' endgame on death row.

We get to the docks first, that's the game, tell Nickie eleven thirty, he'll arrive at eleven on the bean, we get there at ten forty-five and set it up. The two SUVs full of my guys, that's standard, he'll have two of his own plus his limo. My driver parks the Mercedes halfway out on the dock we agreed on, that's all arranged too, and Nickie's limo will meet me out there. My backup cars park on the shore end of the dock on the left, Nickie's gonna be on the right, that's by agreement too.

But what Nickie the Dickie hasn't exactly agreed to is that two of my guys are out of the SUVs and hiding *under* the dock where Nickie's backups are gonna park. With a couple bundles of stick dynamite with three-minute timers each so they can get out of range after they roll them under the vehicles.

Nickie himself is gonna be my job, should be no sweat because he's about a hundred years old never known to be packing, or at least not for the last fifty years or so, and me being the triggerman is a sucker punch, because everyone knows I've never used a gun.

First time for everything.

Sure enough, Nickie's convoy arrives right at eleven, half an hour early, as anticipated, so my guys are already in position, hanging on to the crossbeams under the dock with their bombs as his backup vehicles park and his long black stretch limo drives out onto it, to where I'm waiting.

Nickie gets out, an old guy wearing a black suit and white shirt, a matching homburg, even got a trimmed mustache dyed black, like he's auditioning to play himself in some gangster movie, but the black cane with the ivory eagle head is a necessity at his age as he limps halfway to my limo and stops.

I get out of the car and walk towards him. This is supposed to be the signal for the guys under the docks to set their timers and roll the bombs under Nickie's backups. My signal is supposed to be the explosions.

There is something of a cock-up.

The first two explosions go off too quick, when I'm still maybe ten feet away from Nickie, big balls of flame and black smoke like in the movies, not as loud as on a movie sound track, but enough to have Nickie yelling, "What the fuck!" and drawing his attention away from me.

But it's not gonna be for very long, I gotta whip out my piece, a .44 Magnum revolver I'm told don't exactly require first-class marksmanship.

I aim the gun in the general direction of Nickie's gut and pull the trigger.

Seems like two explosions at once, the third bomb going off up the dock, the bang from my gun with a recoil that just about knocks me on my ass, as my shot tears through Nickie's throat, just about blows his head off.

I stagger forward, put another slug into his chest just to make sure, as if I had to, and I'm hearing shots from up the dock but no fourth explosion as I run back to the limo. I glance back there as I climb back in and see that one of Nickie's backup vehicles has been blown to hell and gone according to plan along with his muscle, but the other one is laying on its side with two of Nickie's guys crouched behind it trading fire with my men.

My driver starts the engine, I drop down on the floor as we tear-ass up the dock and through the line of fire. I stop hearing shots a couple minutes later, as my backup teams break off the gunfight, and their SUVs catch up to my Mercedes to form up the convey. At least that much has gone according to plan.

Who knew it would end up like this? I guess you could say I'm a real gangster like in the movies, but this ain't the movies. I never bargained for this, this is the real world, and in the real world more guys like me than not never get called on to do a hit until they're high enough up to do the calling themselves instead of the dirty work.

Matter of luck is all, and tonight mine run out.

Or not.

Because, hey, here comes the off-ramp finally, and my lead SUV is turning right onto it, and the limo is following, and—

—*wham, bang, smash,* as the trailing SUV slows down and starts making the turn, a garbage truck comes up alongside it on the left and smashes it into the guardrail, and I recognize the snot-green and piss-yellow colors of Earth Angels, Nickie the Dickie's carting company. It's his guys, or what's left of them—

—and a red Cadillac Esplanade van is now on my limo's back bumper—

—and there's another Earth Angels garbage truck at the bottom of the off-ramp—

—and an RPG launcher sticking out of its death seat window—

—and its grenade is launched—

—and my lead SUV explodes, showering my Mercedes with metal and flaming gas and blood and guts, and guys are piling out of the Esplanade with Glocks and M-16s and—

*"And?"*

"Where the hell am I?"

I wake up someplace else, sitting in a chair sweating in front of some plainclothes cop's desk, and he's giving me this fish-eyed stare and—

No, wait a minute, he's a shrink, not a cop, and there's no murder rap to pin me on, I never killed anyone, just like I keep telling him, just like I keep telling Maggie, I've . . . I've just been sitting here *dreaming* that damn dream again while I was *awake* and spilling my guts to this guy . . .

"Wha . . . wha . . . what happen?"

Me and the shrink both say the same dumb thing at the same time.

He's still waving his pencil back and forth, only in his own face double or triple time like some old lady trying to brush off mosquitoes with a fan, and staring at me like he's trying to avoid crapping in his pants and afraid he's not gonna make it.

I'm staring at him staring at me and waving the thing like he was and getting pissed off.

Real pissed off.

"You hypnotized me!" I yell at him.

He cringes back like I just gave him a big breath of wino halitosis. "It's a standard recall technique . . ." he stammers.

"You're at least supposed to ask my permission, ain't you!"

"It worked, now didn't it?"

"Worked *how,* you son of a bitch?"

"What we call *catharsis.* I hypnotize you so you're telling me everything while you're reliving the memory in a dream state, and telling it unblocks the guilty memory that's been giving you these nightmares into your waking consciousness, and that should—"

"*What are you talking about?* I don't have no Mercedes limo! I don't have a string of upscale whorehouses! I don't have a fancy compound out on the Island! I never even heard of no Nickie the Dickie! And how many times I gotta tell all of you I haven't killed anyone yet!"

*Yet?*

"Yet?"

He says it anyway, but he don't have to, I heard myself say it. But what the hell did I mean?

The shrink gives me the strangest look, like I'm some fascinating bug under a microscope, but a germ that can give him the Turd Flu or AIDS or some other fatal disease. "But . . . but you really are . . . you're really a gangster, *aren't* you?"

Well, what can I say to that? The son of a bitch hypnotized me into more or less admitting it. And just maybe he can help me figure all this out, so . . .

"What if I am?" I grunt belligerently. Makes me want to stroke the piece in my shoulder holster like in the dream, but of course in the real world I'm never packing.

"The wicked flee where no man pursueth . . ."

"What's that supposed to mean?"

"Let's say for the sake of argument that you *are* a gangster . . ."

"Let's say for the same sake of argument that the business that I'm in ain't like in the movies, let's say it's like I got a McDonald's franchise. I don't kill the cows or chop up the meat, I just sell . . . stuff and services . . . to my customers and pay their cut to the franchisers upstairs . . . and mind my own business . . ."

"Okay, so you run whatever . . . whatever . . ."

"*Rackets* is okay. For the sake of argument."

"So you run your . . . rackets, just doing your business, and you don't—"

"Even order anything much worse than a little roughing up when necessary. Not even a knee-capping. Well, hardly ever. Let alone *kill anyone!*"

"So you're *afraid* to kill anyone?"

"You sayin' I ain't got the balls to do it if I have to?" I yell at him.

He cringes back from me.

"I mean you don't *want* to kill anyone—"

"Of course I don't! Who wants to get involved in a hit? The homicide squad's usually not on the take, a murder-one conviction's not a hot career move, and it's a capital offense now, ain't it, not three-to-five with time off for greasing the parole board."

"So you're not *afraid* to do it if you have to, but you don't *want* to—"

"Just good business."

"But you'll do it if you *have* to?"

I gotta think about it. But considering what the consequences would be if I turned down the contract, not for very long.

Not for very long? I *already* been thinking about it.

In these damn dreams.

I'm not having *guilty* dreams for what I never done yet, they're like *rehearsals* for what I'm maybe gonna have to get done right if and when that's the way the dice come up. I'm always about to get nailed or worse because of some detail or something gets screwed up, now ain't I?

"So I gotta get it right for once to make them stop!" I find myself proclaiming, like there's a lightbulb over my head and I just found the Lost Chord.

"The dreams?"

"Yeah, of course, Doc, what else? I *told* you I never killed anybody yet, I'm not *guilty* of anything . . . well, anyway not no capital felony. They ain't your blocked memories or cathartic enema, they're not about my *past,* they're dreams of my *future*—"

"Your possible *futures! Prescient* dreams of a kind—there's plenty of that in the literature, but not like this . . . they're . . . they're a set of alternate future scenarios!" He looks like he's practically creaming in his pants for some reason.

"Yeah, yeah, like my *maybe* futures, if I can't avoid it. At least I gotta know I'll get it right if it's ever got to happen—"

"And if you get it right in a dream—"

"The dreams go away."

I'm practically creaming in my pants myself. "I got it, Doc. Hypnotize me again. But this time you give me one of those . . . what do you call it, hypnotic suggestions. To know I'm dreaming and not wake up until I know I'm home free, I can't get nailed."

"Do I have your permission to—"

"I just told you—"

"—to try to *communicate* with you, can I try to make it interactive, can I write it up for publication? If this works, it could make me the next Oliver Sacks."

"*What* kinda sex? Whatever! Just do it!"

I'm a *cop.*

The worst kind of cop, a vice squad creep accustomed to screwin' freebies from the same junkie skanks I run through the revolving door when their pimps forget to grease my paw with the weekly payoff, the vice equivalent of old-time beat cops grabbing apples off fruit stands.

But I been going a mile too far, lots of miles in fact, taking whatever smack the hookers I been screwing are caught holding, selling it to those I encounter *not* holding and feeling the pain. Stealing the goods from the hookers the street dealers sold it to, and then using the very same heroin to steal their customers in the bargain.

And lately I been shaking down pimps and street dealers directly, taking both goods and proceeds, whichever I find them holding, and even forcing them to buy back their own inventory from me at inflated wholesale prices.

What are they gonna do, call the cops?

The cops is us.

I'm standing in an alley full of garbage cans and bum piss puddles over the corpse of a skuzzy pimp and sometime small-time smack dealer with a rap sheet long as an elephant's trunk, got what was coming to him, lying here in his own blood with his pockets turned inside out and his throat cut in an unprofessional manner and the broken bottle lying there right upside his head.

Standing beside me in a trench coat and a fedora with its brim pulled down over his face like Bogart as he eyeballs the scene with me is a homicide lieutenant.

"You know this guy?" he asks me.

Well, what can I say? Everybody on the vice squad knows who everyone else is running so I'm not gonna get away with denying that one.

"Yeah. One of my snitches."

"Any idea who did it?"

"Are you kidding? A penny-ante pimp well-known for dealing smack to his own five-dollar junkie whores doesn't exactly lack for people like to see him dead or ready to cut his throat for the next fix if necessary, so we don't lack for the usual suspects."

"But things aren't always what we think they seem, now are they?" says the homicide dick, looking up at me.

Damn strange thing for him to say. Strange-looking homicide lieutenant. Wire-rim hippie glasses, graying ponytail down behind his head. Don't go at all with the Dick Tracy outfit.

And I know this guy from somewhere else . . . don't I? And *he's* looking at *me* as if he knows things about me better than I know them myself.

And somehow I know that I'm not going to get away with lying to this guy.

But I know I gotta try anyway.

Because *I* killed the scumbag.

What was I supposed to do?

My own goddamn snitch turns out to be an Internal Affairs undercover running a number on me! It's enough to have Mahatma Gandhi reaching for his revolver! Okay, everyone knows there ain't no honor among thieves, but looks like there ain't even honor left among crooked cops. I mean, this son of a bitch's cover's long since made him one of the bad boys, Internal Affairs or not.

He arranges a meet in this crummy alley we used, or one like it, to make sure we keep things private, tells me he's got a tip for a juicy bust. He's there when I arrive, dancing back and forth nervously like he always does, but he's wearing wire-rim glasses, which he never has before, and the eyes behind them aren't the usual weaselly jump and glitter, but cold and hard like greased steel ball bearings.

And since I last seen him, which can't be more than a couple weeks ago, he's gone bald on top of his head to halfway back, and somehow managed to grow a long gray ponytail.

*"So?"*

"So I got a hot tip for you," he says, giving me a look like a hungry cat about to sink his fangs into a canary. "A significant bust."

"Yeah? Who?"

"*You,*" he says, whipping a little .38 snubnose out of his flasher raincoat pocket and pointing it one-handed at my gut in an unprofessional manner so's he can whip out a badge and shove it into my face at the same time.

"What the—"

"You are under arrest. You have the right to remain silent . . ."

The rat's reading me my Miranda, and I don't have to look at his badge to know it's Internal Affairs.

"You think *you're* gonna get away with popping *me?*" I snarl at him. "I got as much on you as you got on me, they put me on the stand and I'll sing your song, and it's gonna be 'Melancholy Baby,' you rat-fink bastard!"

He gives me this smug little smile, the kind you want to punch out right away, and I know I gotta make some kinda move to take him out before he even says it.

"Go ahead, asshole, rat out my cover. You really think what I've been doing on the side hasn't been authorized by my captain?"

Well, of course I'm not that stupid. I am screwed. I am looking at fifteen years' minimum on the Rockefeller Law alone, and that's the least of it. And vice cops in the joint have worse things to worry about than serving out a long stretch, like living long enough to do it.

He shoves the badge back in his coat pocket, fishes out the plastic cuffs, motions with his pistol for me to hold out my hands. I hesitate.

"Do it!" And he signals with his gun again.

I give him a sad ya-got-me shrug, move in closer, slowly stretching out my arms to let him cuff me—

—as I kick him with all my might square in the balls.

He folds, hunching over, and reaching down two-handed without thinking like any guy would to cradle his yowling nuts—

Dropping the gun in the process.

I scoop it up, grab him by the ponytail, and yank him as upright as a slimeball like him can get, shove the pistol right in his face.

"Now what, wiseguy?" I snarl.

"Now what yourself, asshole?" he comes back at me. "You gonna shoot an Internal Affairs cover? Murder one, Joe. Murder one plus for killing a cop."

He's right, of course. I gotta think fast.

Well, maybe not that fast, I've got the gun on him, and he ain't going nowhere in the next thirty seconds, now is he?

Cold and clear. Got time to get it right this time.

I gotta off this rodent. I can't let him out of this alley.

But I gotta cover myself. I gotta be able to have it pinned on someone else.

Hey, no problem! I realize.

I can just pin it on more suspects than homicide can know what to do with and they'll give up trying to sort 'em all out, not worth the effort, Captain; lots of scurve coulda offed this creep, junkies without the money for a fix, one of his hookers high as a kite. Right, it's a wonder he lasted this long, we really give a crap . . . ?

But it's gotta look like it happened on the spur of a red-hot moment.

I glance around sidewise. Nothing but garbage cans. Still holding the pistol on him, I slide over to the nearest one, flip off the cover, rummage around blind—

"Hey, what are you—"

My hand closes around the neck of some kind of bottle, I pull it out, smash the bottom of it against the wall as I roundhouse the rat with my gun hand across the temple. Using the pistol like brass knucks, he goes down like the sack of shit he is.

I don't bother checking to see if he's out cold or not, who cares, I saw open his throat with the broken end of the bottle until the blood's spurting out his jugular, not as easy to do as the movies make you think. Then I wipe the bottle off with a dirty pizza joint napkin from the garbage so the crud'll mask any of my prints I mighta missed, and drop it by his head to make the murder weapon nice and obvious for Homicide, and empty his pockets of cash and smack to supply the motive.

Slick as that, I got it right, and I'm home-free.

*"The guilty flee where dead men pursueth."*

I'm staring back at the homicide detective lieutenant.

Suddenly I'm freaking, suddenly I'm shaking. The same trench coat and fedora. The same glasses. The same damn ponytail. Why didn't I see it before?

I see it now.

The homicide detective and the dead snitch have the same face.

Worse, maybe it's just the same *mask.* Because I somehow know there's someone else behind it.

"What's that supposed to mean? I'm not guilty of anything!"

It's like I'm talking to that someone else somewhere else where he's not a homicide cop and I'm not exactly lying.

"But you haven't gotten it all right yet, now have you? And you won't be home-free until you do."

This dead man's spook, this homicide creep, this nightmare witch doctor, *knows.*

And he's right.

Whichever he is, he's got the goods on me to nail me to the gurney with the needle. Like we're playing out the script of some TV show, like in a dream, where you know what's gonna happen but you know you can't do anything about it, that it's gonna rerun forever until you finally get it right.

That he knows.

But he doesn't know that I know what I gotta do now.

Or for some reason he doesn't care. Like it *is* just a TV show he's watching. Like it's all a dream.

Maybe it is. But it doesn't matter, does it? Because one more little detail to take care of and I can't get nailed, and I'm home-free. I know it. And he seems to know it.

And it's not like he hasn't been asking for it, now is it?

I reach under my jacket for the shoulder holster I know is there, pull out my .44 Magnum, and blow him away—

—and I wake up standing over the cheap desk with the shrink facedown on it with half his head blown off and the famous smoking gun somehow still in my hand. Hands are pounding on the door; sirens are howling outside for my ass like a wolf pack.

What the hell happened?

To make a long story short of insanity pleas, guilty verdict, appeals, more insanity pleas, that are still going on, I still don't know, even after telling the whole truth to the jury and appeals court judges more times than I can remember . . . I mean, that should be enough to prove I was crazy sooner or later, shouldn't it? It sure convinces *me.*

Welcome to the Twilight Zone, Joe.

But, hey, spend this much time in a solitary cell on death row, and you look to find a bright side.

You could say I finally got it right after all.

At least in the last dream.

Yeah, that's right, after I did, those nightmares never came back.

When I made my bones good and proper, I blew them all away.

Picture of a man who's found his answer.

Picture of a man who's rid himself of his nightmares.

Picture of a man likely to spend the rest of his life paying the price.

Picture of a man who's escaped from his bad dreams only to awake into a worse nightmare in what we call reality.

Picture of a man who has learned that one way or the other, he'll never escape from his jail cell solitarily confined in the Twilight Zone.

# THE LAST CHRISTMAS LETTER

Kristine Kathryn Rusch

A perfect Christmas for Joanne Carlton is giving her family, her grandchildren, and the grandchildren of her extended family a Christmas they will always remember in her home. The smell of cookies fills the air, decorations cover the walls, the tree perfectly in place, wrapped presents already under the heavy branches. And every Christmas card hung except for one. A very special card. An impossible Christmas card that could not exist, yet does, and made this a Christmas Joanne Carlton would always remember as well, for this was the year she received a Christmas card sent directly from the Twilight Zone.

I can't believe you did this, Joanne," her sister said on the phone. "Just because I can't come to Wisconsin for Christmas doesn't give you the right. It's mean."

Joanne Carlton leaned against the oven. It was warm with the afternoon's baking. The entire kitchen smelled of vanilla, cinnamon, and cookies.

"I didn't do anything, Annie," Joanne said tiredly.

"Nice try," her sister snapped and hung up.

Joanne rested the phone against her forehead and closed her eyes. For nearly fifty years, she had put up with her sister's histrionics, usually laughing them off. Annie was volatile. Annie was temperamental. Annie was the emotional one, while Ginny was the pretty one and Joanne was the smart one.

Joanne was also the oldest and had been, from the beginning, the one everyone expected to be responsible.

But she wasn't responsible for this.

She set the phone back in its cradle, then wiped her hands on the towel she had looped through her belt.

The grandchildren were coming for the annual cookie decorating party, something everyone in her extended family—the family *she* raised, not the one she was raised in—looked forward to. Cookie decorating and then, in four days, Christmas.

Her entire house was spotless. She had decorated every room, and had trees on every floor. In the basement she had set up the white flocked tree she had bought one year when the children were young, upstairs she had the artificial tree that her late husband had once sprayed with pine scent because he couldn't stand the smell of plastic, and on this floor she had a real tree that her son Ryan had begrudgingly helped her put up in early December.

Her house looked like Christmas, felt like Christmas, and smelled like Christmas, and that was what she wanted—a sense of the holiday so strong that years from now, when her grandchildren thought of Christmas, her house would rise in their memories as the perfect place for the perfect holiday.

The children would have their perfect holiday, but for her, some years were harder than others. This was one of the hard years.

She walked into the entry. Christmas cards hung from the garland that looped the mahogany banister leading upstairs. She picked up the pile of cards that had arrived this week, the ones she hadn't had time to hang.

Strike that. The ones she'd been avoiding hanging.

She plucked out a card that had ostensibly come from her father. It looked like a card Daddy would pick out: garish red and green, with Santa and Rudolph on the front. Santa was shaking his finger at Rudolph, whose nose was glowing red.

*We can't call your room the Red Light District,* Santa was saying, *and no, I won't explain why.*

Inside, the card read HAPPY HOLIDAYS, with the "I" dotted by the image of Rudolph's red nose. Underneath was tight precise writing that said simply, *I love you, Button. Merry Christmas. Daddy.*

The disturbing part of the card wasn't the slightly risqué slogan or her father's unblemished handwriting (despite his shaking fingers). It was the Christmas letter tucked inside.

She had opened it the day the card arrived and started to read, then stopped with tears in her eyes. Obviously, Annie had gotten one of these letters too and it had upset her as much as it had upset Joanne. Soon, Joanne would probably be getting a call from Ginny, and while she wouldn't be angry—not like Annie was—she would profess a mild shock and dismay over the way that Joanne "of all people" had handled the holiday.

Even though Joanne had had nothing to do with the letter.

She unfolded the piece of paper and leaned against the banister, the garland tickling her neck. The letter looked like every other Christmas letter Daddy had written in his long life.

Joanne would have sworn that it had been typed on the Royal that his mother had given him (at great expense) when he went off to college in 1932. He had used that Royal throughout his life, having the keys repaired when they needed it, and stockpiling ribbons in the 1980s when the demise of the typewriter became apparent.

The arch of the lower case "a" was broken, and the enclosed part of the lower case "e" was filled in because no matter how often he cleaned the keys, he could never get that "e" to work right again.

He—or whoever had done this—hadn't photocopied the letter, like Daddy did in his last two decades. Instead, the letter had obviously been mimeographed.

The ink was slightly blue and blurry. But even if that hadn't tipped her off, the faint smell still embedded in the paper would have. That sharp powerful odor, only approximated these days in

Magic Marker pens, always brought her back to her father's office where she ran the mimeograph machine for him.

He would set up the machine, carefully aligning the typed original with its gluey purple back on the drum. Then she would operate the crank handle, watching as each page appeared, glistening and wet from its contact with the mimeo ink.

She was there every week, copying his pop quizzes and helping with the year-end exams. But she loved mimeographing the Christmas letter because she got to read it first.

Joanne could still remember some of his openings, having studied them as they came through the mimeograph machine, one blurry page after the other:

*Yes, it is the bleak midwinter and you will probably get this letter after the festivities have ended. Still, the information contained herein doesn't lose its freshness with the passing of the holiday.*

Or . . .

*Every year, I look at the snow glistening on our yard, the pine trees providing a nest for the winter birds that gather despite the weather, and I feel the urge to share the triumphs and tribulations of my family with the people whom we love but see only too rarely.*

When she went away to college, she missed that voice, and greedily snapped up a copy of the Christmas letter as soon as she got home for the holidays.

Annie had inherited her job. Annie had lasted only one year ("Jeez," she said to Joanne, "you didn't tell me that turning that dang crank hurts your arm.") before giving the job to Ginny.

Ginny secretly told Joanne that she hated the smell: "It makes me dizzy."

Joanne loved it. She missed it when her father became practical and retired the mimeo machine for a half hour at a copy shop. Some pimply kid ran the copier behind the desk while Daddy read his newspaper, and Joanne always felt the process had gone slightly wrong. No pimply outsider should take over the family copying task, no matter how slight it was.

Joanne once told her father she had learned to write by reading his letters, and he was surprised by it. But she felt it was true. Even though he had written essays—what now would be called "creative nonfiction"—those influenced her less than his newsletters.

Although she never did tell interviewers that. When they asked where she got her inspiration for her novels, she cited her favorite authors—Fitzgerald, King, Le Guin—and never once mentioned her father.

Lately, she had been regretting that oversight. She might not have a chance to rectify it. The doctors said he would probably never regain consciousness.

At the thought, Joanne's hand started shaking. The newsletter crinkled in her fingers. So she carried it to the kitchen and set it flat on the table she had covered with a vinyl cloth in anticipation of the grandchildren.

*December 15*

Right there, the date was unbelievable. Daddy had slipped into the coma on December 2. The nursing home had moved him to hospice on the 10th. Hospice was offering only palliative care.

The fact that he was still alive only a few days from Christmas showed the inherent strength of that ninety-five-year-old body. It was efficient from the marathons he had run until his knees gave out at seventy-two, and the lap swimming he had substituted until he got pneumonia in October.

He had been so angry then, knowing he was going to miss the Regional Masters Competition that was going to be held in Minneapolis at the end of November.

*I would've won my category, Button,* he said to Joanne—actually more like wheezed at her, his breath whistling as if he had swallowed a bit of tubing.

*You're the only one in it,* she said.

*No, Button, that's where you're wrong. There were fifteen people at State, and I beat all of them, including some whippersnapper who hadn't even turned seventy-five yet.*

She remembered when he turned seventy-five and was trying to find something to substitute for the running. That was the year he had discovered the Masters age group swim program and he was determined to race.

*This'll keep me going, Button. You'll see.*

She blinked hard and made herself focus on the warm house, the table before her, the vinyl cloth ready for the grandchildren's mess. She held the newsletter flat and tried to read it again. This time, she got past that date and into the body itself.

*December 15*

*The magic of the season arrived with suddenness and gusto the day after Thanksgiving. For the first time since retailers moved the Christmas season from Advent to November, the Christmas music on the radio seemed appropriate and I began thinking about my holiday newsletter.*

*Of course, I think about my newsletter all year. How does a man describe his adventures in a world he doesn't really understand in a short pithy way that makes him seem less like a fool and more like the hero?*

*I hark back to my own great-grandfather on that summer day in 1934 when he first took me across that mysterious divide between our world and Luminaria. My mother had called me home from college, convinced he was about to die. And apparently he thought so, too, or he wouldn't have taken me with him . . .*

Joanne stopped reading. She knew the story, since her father had repeated it most of her life. Only there was no mention of Luminaria. Instead, her father told the tale to illustrate how hardy his side of the family was.

His great-grandfather had fallen off a ladder at the age of ninety-five. Daddy had been called home from college and spent the day at his great-grandfather's bedside. In the morning, Daddy had awakened to the whir of blades against grass. He peeked out the window to see his great-grandfather mowing the lawn—not with any power mower (they didn't exist in 1934), but with one of those push mowers that Joanne had tried once and given up on at half the length of the lawn.

*He couldn't stand how overgrown the lawn looked through the window,* Daddy would say, *so he hopped from his bed and had the entire thing mowed by ten A.M.*

And lived for another five years, mowing lawns, shoveling snow, and bowling until a few days before the end.

Luminaria. She shook her head just as the buzzer went off. She got up and walked into the kitchen. Whoever had written this newsletter had known her father. That much was clear from the lawn-mowing story—and from the mention of Luminaria.

Luminaria had been Daddy's world. It lived in the bedroom she shared with Annie before Ginny arrived and they moved to a bigger house. In that house, Luminaria moved to Ginny's room, because she was the baby and she had a special bed she needed tucking into.

Daddy always told stories of Luminaria. It was his fantasy world, filled with knights and pretty princesses named Joanne and Annie and Ginny, and a benevolent queen who sounded a lot like Mom, and dragons and sea monsters and talking cats with names that matched those of the family cats.

The stories never ended, just like they never began, but they continued from night to night, unless Daddy had to work late. Then Mom read a story from a book—*Where the Wild Things Are* or *Horton Hears a Who*—which was nice, but just wasn't the same.

At some point, Joanne stopped showing up for the stories. She listened to music, read her own books, or talked to boys on the telephone.

She couldn't even remember where the Luminaria stories left off for her, only that look in Daddy's eyes when she told him she didn't want to hear any more. *Stories,* she said, *are for babies and little girls.*

These past two decades, he had never said what he thought of her making her living from stories, stories of the fantastic kind. Stories she had once dismissed.

She wiped at her eyes and opened the oven. Warm steamed air swept over her. The last batch of sugar cookies were a perfect golden brown.

At moments like this, she got flashes of her mother—who taught her how to bake, how to make a home pretty, how to make people feel comfortable even when they didn't belong. Most of the traditions she brought to her grandchildren came from her mother and her mother's family—the recipes, the cookie frosting party, the way the meals were served.

She put the cookies on the cooling rack. Soon she would have to start mixing the frosting for the kids. They would arrive in about two hours, energetic, giggling, and ready to make a mess.

By then she would have the frosting done, the sprinkles and red hots set out, the Christmas carols on her stereo, and the tree lights flickering merrily.

She had to put this thing with her father aside.

But she couldn't yet. She went back into the dining room and grabbed the letter. It seemed longer than it had before. She had thought he (or whomever) had sent a single page. Now she held two.

She sat down slowly. She wasn't thinking clearly, that was all. She was doing too many things—cooking, cleaning, decorating, and now the letter. She was also running to hospice, making sure she spent an hour at least with her father every day.

And her sisters were too far away. "We have a choice," Ginny had said on her last phone call. "We can come see him when he's in a coma or we can come for the funeral. I'd like to be there for both, but I can't, and I know Annie can't either."

Annie, who had screamed at Joanne on the phone not so long ago about this letter.

Joanne found the paragraph where she had left off.

*The light* is *different in Luminaria. That's the first thing you notice. I was nearly blinded by it seventy years ago, and my great-grandfather laughed.* You never get used to it, lad, *he said,* but you do come to crave it.

*And he was right. At times like this, when winter falls without warning—the sky dark, the world gray except for the white snow—you crave the light. I've only seen light like it one other place, and that was the Mediterranean on that cruise the girls put me on nearly a decade ago, trapped with a bunch of old people, going from port to port, pretending to see the sights.*

*My great-grandfather took me through my mother's garden, past a pile of rocks he called Stonehenge. To call those rocks Stonehenge was to call a Matchbox truck a Big Rig. Still, the magic shimmered in the air, and I knew as I stepped through that shimmer my life would never ever be the same.*

*That was his gift to me, this place, and when he was dying five years later—really dying, a fragile wisp of a man buried under my mother's homemade quilts—he sent everyone from the room but me.*

*Then he grabbed my hand. His grip was so tight, I think I*

*still have bruises from it. I didn't know a dying man could cling to something that tightly.*

*"Have you gone back?" he whispered.*

*It took me a moment to understand him. "No," I said.*

*"You have to now," he said, "if only to visit me."*

*Then he chuckled, but he didn't let me go.*

*"Remember," he said. "You have two lives. Never confuse them. The real world is here. That world—ah, it's marvelous, but you can't live there."*

*"You just told me to visit you there," I said.*

*He smiled. "I said you can't* live *there, my boy. But there's nothing wrong with dying there."*

*Then he patted my cheek with his other hand, and closed his eyes. Even though he lived for three more days, he never opened his eyes again . . .*

Joanne set the letter down again. She rubbed her thumb and forefinger over her nose. Whoever had written this had managed her father's voice beautifully.

But she understood Annie's anger. Who would play this trick, especially now?

She was standing before she realized it, heading to the phone. Halfway there, she realized she had been about to cancel the frosting party.

But she couldn't do that to the kids. She had too many generations to consider, too many things to worry about.

She went back to the table and picked up the letter. This afternoon was about the children. She would worry about her father later.

She folded the letter back up, wondering how he (or whomever) had gotten it into the card. Three pages seemed like a lot to cram into a regular-sized envelope, with only one stamp in the corner.

She buried the envelope under the pile of cards, hoping to

forget it, and knowing she wouldn't be able to. Then she went into the kitchen and prepared the frosting.

Halfway through, she turned on the Christmas music loud enough to drown out her thoughts.

But no matter how many times she sang along with winter wonderlands and jingling sleigh bells, it wasn't visions of sugar plums that danced in her head.

It was mimeographed sheets of paper, telling, in her father's inimitable prose, the story of her life.

By the time the children arrived, her mood was lighter. It was hard to be sad when little hands, newly freed from snow-covered mittens, grabbed hers, when cold cheeks pressed against hers, and when slightly sticky lips brushed against her skin.

Six grandchildren, ages four to ten, and three of their parents—all her children because they loved the tradition.

Her dining-room table was covered with plates of unfrosted sugar cookies, bowls of frosting—red, green, yellow, blue, pink, and white—and more edible decorations than they could use in an entire year.

Sing-alongs with Frosty and Rudolph and lots of chatter. Little fingers in bowls (parents grabbed filthy hands—*you can't do that, hon*) and voices clamoring—*What do you think of that nose, Grammy? Gots more frosting? I like frosting. Izzat how you spell Mommy?*

Too many cookies got eaten, too much frosting ended up on faces, and (predictably) one of the four-year-olds giggled herself sick in her sugar high and then passed out as it wore off.

No one would eat a good dinner that night, but they would all remember the occasion—and not just because of the red hots stuck in their hair.

Joanne was packing up cookies in the special tins she bought just for the occasion so that everyone could take some home, when Ryan joined her in the kitchen.

"You've got shadows under your eyes, Mom," he said.

"It's a busy time of year," she said.

"Bull." He took one of the tins from her and wrapped up the cellophane like she had taught him years ago. "You usually get jacked by this time of year. It's Granddad, isn't it?"

To her surprise, her eyes filled with tears. "This is the first time ever he missed cookies."

She hadn't realized it until she said it aloud. He only decorated a few every year. He sat at the head of the table, did his "example cookies"—usually piled with frosting and sprinkles—and then got out of the way. He had always been the only person who wasn't wearing frosting or flour by the end of the day.

But he had also been the one to carry in the extra cookies, and help Joanne pack up the tins. And he had watched avidly as generation after generation of children learned how much fun it was to make the ugliest cookies on the planet.

She smiled up at her own son. Ryan had come in here, not just to talk with her, but because he remembered that his grandfather had done the same job.

"Have you visited him?" she asked, not sure she wanted to hear the answer. Her own sisters had disappointed her, and one of her daughters hadn't visited her grandfather since he left the hospital for the nursing home.

"Leonardo has been insisting," Ryan said.

Leonardo was Joanne's oldest grandson. The rest of the family called him Leo, but Ryan loved the boy's full name. Joanne's father had shaken his head when he heard it.

*Leo the Lionheart,* his father had taken to calling the boy, and the nickname was proving true.

Who would think that a ten-year-old would be the one to insist on seeing his unconscious great-grandfather?

"You've been taking him to hospice?" Joanne asked.

"Every day we can manage it." Ryan sounded as baffled as she felt. "He's the one who keeps reminding me when it's time to go."

She heard the reluctance in his voice. It was the same reluctance she felt whenever she thought of going to the hospice care facility.

"Leonardo wanted to take some cookies over today," Ryan said. "I'm supposed to pack up the best for him."

Joanne hadn't thought of that, probably because she knew her father would never eat them. Ah, well. They'd last. Eventually the nursing staff would enjoy them.

Still, she picked out the best "example cookies," the ugliest ones, dripping with the most frosting and decorations. She had an old tin, an extra one she'd kept for years for reasons she no longer remembered, and she carefully packed the cookies in that.

Her grandson came into the room just as she was finishing. Leo looked like a little lion. He had a round face and a flat catlike nose. His eyes were a light brown that matched his brownish-blond curls.

A streak of green frosting ran from his right ear to his nose, and his eyebrows were dusted with red sprinkles. She had a hunch he did that last on purpose.

"You wanna come and see Grandpop?" he asked Joanne. Grandpop was what all the kids called her father. Her own husband had been their grandfather, but his death was long enough ago that Leo was the only one who remembered him, and then only dimly.

"I'll see him a little later," Joanne said. "You tell him all about the cookies."

Leo took the tin. "He's sorry he missed out, but he said you'd understand."

Her breath caught, but Leo didn't seem to notice. He took the tin out of the kitchen as if he were holding gold.

Ryan watched him go. Joanne's hands were shaking as she packed the last tin.

"He's been doing that," Ryan said. "It's like he realizes Grandpa can't talk, so he's talking for him. I'm not sure if it's sweet or creepy."

"Or both," Joanne said.

Ryan nodded. "We'll stop at hospice. You sure you don't want me to stay and help you clean up?"

She shook her head. "I've done it for years. It's my chance to eat the leftover frosting."

He chuckled. She grinned, then picked up the remaining tins and carried them into the dining room. The littlest two grandchildren—four-year-old cousins born days apart—had fallen asleep with their faces mashed against the table. The five- and six-year-olds—both boys—were stirring all the different frostings together to see what color they would get.

The eight-year-old had her arms crossed in disapproval. She was the only grandchild who hadn't gotten covered in food.

Their mothers looked exhausted. Joanne helped wake up the little ones. Then she took the frosting from the boys and carried it into the kitchen. She dipped a clean spoon into it—it was now a muddy brown—and took a taste, closing her eyes. She loved butter frosting. It was the best thing of all.

Her youngest daughter, Nikki, leaned her head into the kitchen.

"Mom?" she said. "I was going to ask you. Did you get a letter from Grandpop?"

"A Christmas newsletter?" Joanne asked.

"Yeah."

"I got a Christmas newsletter purporting to be from your grandfather," she said carefully.

"So you didn't send it," Nikki said.

"No," Joanne said. "If I had, I would have made him photocopy it instead of mimeo it."

Nikki frowned at her. "Mine was photocopied," she said. "On that green and red construction paper he loved. Remember?"

Joanne did remember. Throughout the late eighties and early nineties, all of her dad's Christmas letters were on thick red and green paper. The family joke was that they could cut up the letters and make them into daisy chains for the tree.

"It's weird," Nikki said. "I thought you mailed it for him."

Joanne shook her head. "Ask Ryan. He's been seeing your Grandpop more than the rest of us."

Nikki's face colored. She nodded and backed out of the kitchen. Joanne swirled the spoon in the frosting, regretting the tone she had taken with her daughter. It was the holiday, no matter what was going on, and there was no cause to speak to Nikki that way. No matter how hard Nikki tried, she would never be as considerate as her brother. Yet Joanne always expected her to be a lot more sensitive.

Joanne was the one who wasn't being sensitive. That letter was disturbing. She wondered who else had gotten a copy, and how she would ever find out.

It never took as long as she expected to clean up. Within an hour, her house was back to normal, as if the kid tornado hadn't hit at all. When everything was done, she grabbed her coat and purse, and headed into the snow.

All she planned to do was say a quick hello to her father, then buy herself a nice dinner. But she drove the car past hospice, and down a road she had traveled most of her life.

The family house looked naked this winter. Usually she came over on the first weekend in December and decorated. The last few years, Ryan and Leo had helped, hanging icicle lights from the eaves and wrapping multicolored lights on the two evergreens up front.

But they hadn't done that this year.

The sidewalk needed shoveling—she would have to remind the neighbor boy (had she paid him lately?)—and ice had formed on the porch steps. She unlocked the front door and let herself inside.

The place was starting to smell musty and unused. She had cleaned up her father's mess shortly after he went into the hospital, expecting him to return at any point.

But he hadn't returned. And the Thanksgiving decorations she had put up—her mother's decorations—came down without being replaced by the Christmas decorations. His Christmas cards had all gone to hospice in case he did regain consciousness, as did his little six-inch television, the one he usually kept near his chair in the kitchen.

She ran a finger across the fireplace mantel, noting the dust. She would have to clean this place, but she didn't see the point. He wasn't coming back, and the family would have to decide what to do with the house itself—something she didn't relish.

She grabbed a flashlight out of the front hall closet, then stopped. The familiarity of it all. She had made these same movements ever since she was a little girl. She knew where everything was and where everything belonged.

Losing the house would be like losing both parents all over again. Even if the house stayed in the family, this configuration—the flashlights and extra blankets in the front hall closet, the ice skates (unused in more than two decades) hanging from their peg behind the door—would be gone. The house would be different, its soul altered because the beings that inhabited it would be different.

She shook off the thought and climbed the stairs, listening to the familiar creaks and groans under her feet. She let herself into her father's bedroom, and opened the closet door.

The closet was a walk-in, and in the very back were the stairs leading up to the attic. She climbed them, ducking more than she had as a child.

She flicked on the dim overhead light. Dust motes rose around her. The attic was cold. She had forgotten to turn on the small heater that Daddy always used to keep back the gloom.

There were more boxes up here than she remembered, and a stack in the corner of all of her mother's personal things, labeled in Joanne's neat handwriting—from another moment in her life that she would love to forget.

Joanne turned her back on that stack of boxes and headed to an older stack, pushed behind an ancient wardrobe.

She flicked on the flashlight, and ran the oval of light over the boxes, reading the labels—JOANNE (SCHOOL), PHOTOGRAPHS 1941–1955, GINNY (BEAUTY PAGEANTS), and on and on. Finally Joanne saw the box she was looking for. It wasn't in the back after all. Someone (her father? He knew he wasn't supposed to come up here alone.) had slid it nearer to the stairs.

The box was twice the size of the other boxes, and it was labeled XMAS LETTERS. She opened it and found her father's original drafts in perfect order, starting with last year's.

*December 19*
*I'm getting a late start this year because Mother Nature has decided that winter will start on time for once. Too often she's been late with the snow and cold, and I'm never in the seasonal mood until the air is properly crisp. Of late, however, she's been early, and that's equally frustrating, for when Christmas comes, it feels as if someone had postponed it to the end of January instead of the end of December . . .*

Joanne sank to the floor, reading each letter, going slowly back in time.

*December 1*
*I have dreaded this letter ever since August. So many of you don't know, because we only communicate at this time of year,*

*that my beloved Lucille left us that month. I stood over her open grave, tossing in a perfect white rose like the one I had given her on our wedding night, and thought of this moment.*

No more letters, *I decided.* There is no point.

*But there is a point, dear friends, and the point is you. This afternoon, my daughters and I, along with my grandchildren and their children (three now!) stood at that same gravesite, covered in brown grass and frost, and watched as the stonemason put the beautifully carved headstone in place.*

*Annie thinks it a bit plain. Ginny likes its simplicity. But as usual, it is Joanne who understands.*

*"Art Deco," she said, placing her hands together like she has since she was a little girl. "Mama would be so pleased. . . ."*

Joanne placed the pages upside down so that they stayed in order, some of the words so familiar she could recite them from memory. The oldest letters dated from early in her parents' marriage, long before she was ever born.

Her father had married late, and relished the idea of a family, saying he hadn't been ready before, and hinted at things he had done, things his readers (but not the daughter he hadn't yet had) would clearly understand by implication. She had read these older letters dozens of times, and each time, they had raised questions.

She had forgotten to ask her father about those questions.

Now she never could.

She set the letters down. When he was gone, she would copy them for the whole family—a bit of history for everyone—and make a little booklet out of them. Maybe she would go to one of those self-publishing places and create something lovely, something worthy of him.

But this year's reaction to the surprise letter ruled out one thing: She couldn't send that booklet at Christmastime, not without letting everyone know it was coming.

She gathered up the letters and held them for a moment. That surprise letter had driven her here, to see if what she remembered was what her father had done.

She had remembered a lot, but she had forgotten so much more—the occasional elegiac note, the puckish sense of humor that would appear, the way he could turn a mundane moment into the most important in the world.

She was glad she had come, on this night of doing the cookies. It was a way of keeping him in the celebration, even though he physically couldn't be present.

She neatly stacked the letters together. She was about to put them back in the box, when the flashlight beam caught something at the bottom.

A mahogany box, long and thick and ornately carved. She had seen four others like it. One belonged to her mother. Her father had given it to her as an engagement present so she had a place to keep all of the love letters he had sent to her. Mother had done that, too, and Joanne knew where that box was.

Her father had made Joanne promise she wouldn't read anything in it when he was alive—*I didn't write those letters for you, Button*—and she had kept that promise only because, as a child, she had been unable to break the tiny lock her mother had attached to the beautiful silver clasp.

The other three boxes came to each daughter on the occasion of her high school graduation, a place for her future love letters. *I trust,* Daddy had said to all three of them at the moment he gave them their box, *you never got letters in high school. You're barely old enough now to get them.*

Joanne reached into the cardboard box, her hand shaking, and pulled out the mahogany box. This box matched the others. It had the silver clasp—tarnished now—and the same odd carvings along the edge. There was no lock, like there was on her mother's love letters, yet Joanne still felt like she was about to touch something forbidden, something that didn't belong to her, and never would.

She almost let it wait until her father was really and truly gone. But the flashlight beam flared—something she had never seen one do before—and for a moment, she thought she saw her name carved into the wood.

She squinted. What she had thought was her name was one of those scroll-like carvings that existed on the other boxes. If the carvings said something, they did so in a language she had never seen before.

She set the box on her lap and ran her fingers across it, feeling the warm wood beneath her fingertips, the gentle edges of the etchings, and the roughness of the silver clasp. Then, before she could change her mind, she threw back the clasp and opened the box.

The scent of sandalwood rose from the interior, which surprised her and made her sneeze. Inside were more letters, looking just like the ones Joanne had thumbed through.

*December 19*
*It's always summer here in December, something I will never get used to. Yes, it's summer in Australia in December as well, but I've never been Down Under, and I come here all the time. Summer is the busy season—more bugs than any other place on Earth (if, indeed, this is Earth), flowers bigger than my head, and animals on the move, trying to find the proper home for their growing families.*

*I can empathize, even though my family is long since grown . . .*

She frowned, thinking that the date was familiar, and so she looked at the pile of letters still resting beside her leg. Each letter that he had mailed had a corollary in the box. Last year's letter, dated December 19, had a matching made-up December 19 letter, as if she had had two fathers, one who lived in this little house that he had raised a family in and paid off twenty-eight years ago, and the other who disappeared into a sunlit world of December summer.

She read random snippets of the other letters from the box:

*The water here is brighter blue than the water at home. It tastes fresh, like snow melt with a tang.*

and . . .

*He passed me this morning, my great-grandfather, looking trim as ever. His hair was black, not the thick pile of silver I remember from my childhood. He wore an Edwardian suit, complete with pocket watch and long golden chain, and made me think of those illustrations of the rabbit from* Alice in Wonderland.

*He didn't say hello and neither did I. We both knew it wasn't the time. We would speak on some future date, when it was more appropriate, when we actually had something to say . . .*

and . . .

*Saw my first dragon in June. They're bigger than I expected and more fearsome. If you jump when you see a lizard, imagine how you would feel at one blown up to the size of a horse, with round reptilian eyes and a slitted tongue. Each tooth is larger and thicker than my finger, and the fangs that curve beside the black lips are the size of horns of plenty.*

*I was terrified. Deep down mortally terrified, knee-knocking, all-but-peeing-myself terrified. I hid behind some tree with big flat leaves and hoped I was downwind.*

*Apparently I was because it lumbered in the other direction, and then when I was really and truly sure it was gone, I leaned my head against the tree's sharp bark and felt both humiliation and embarrassment.*

*In my imagination, I am the archetypical hero, the man who would rush a dinosaur wearing nothing but a loincloth and carrying a dull knife. But in real life (although I hasten to call this place real life), I am a middle-aged guy in blue jeans and an Abbey Road T-shirt who hides behind giant leaves and tries not to wet his pants . . .*

She laughed in spite of herself. Not because the letters were particularly funny, but because they were wry and honest. She remembered that quality from her teen years when she did sneak into Ginny's room to listen to the later Luminaria tales.

The hero in Daddy's stories was never particularly heroic. The monsters were hapless—had they been intelligent and strong, the hero would have died. Instead he survived through instinct and sheer luck, somehow always making it back home in time to have supper and tuck his precious daughters into bed.

Joanne riffled the letters, but didn't read any more. Although she did note that the typeface of these letters always matched the typeface of the Christmas letter from the same year.

She closed the box and cradled it to her chest. Part of her wanted to take the box with her, bring it to the safety of her own home, and hide it in her attic so no one else knew it existed.

But she was Joanne The Responsible One, and she would forever feel like she had a secret—a noxious secret—from the others.

She leaned her cheek on the box's edge, feeling the soft warm wood against her skin like a caress. Then she replaced the box in the bottom of the cardboard box and put all the other letters on top of it.

She stood carefully, so that she didn't hit her head on the

slanted ceiling, and brushed off her pants. More dust motes rose. She shut off the flashlight and headed back to the stairs, turning off the overhead light before heading down.

For the first time ever, she was cautious—if she fell and hurt herself, no one would find her here. No one had known she was coming.

She reached the bottom, the closet that smelled faintly of the pipe Daddy had given up thirty years before, and the leather from his (rarely worn) dress shoes, and she let herself out of the closet and into the bedroom.

There, in the light, she saw herself in the mirror above the vanity and got another surprise. What a comical figure she made—a middle-aged woman dressed in a Santa sweater and black pants, dust stains on her face, and frosting with sprinkles along her hip.

Certainly not the beautiful princess of the Luminaria letter or the lovely daughter who needed her father's protection from the once-imaginary suitors.

She wasn't quite sure how she ended up here, looking for bits of the fantastic in the dark. That she had found it surprised her.

That some of it sounded familiar surprised her even more.

She had to go home before heading to hospice. She took a shower and found a different set of holiday clothes to wear, this one—a black and red glitter sweater over black pants—a little more tasteful.

As she left the house a second time, she grabbed her cell phone and speed-dialed her youngest sister.

"I was just going to call you," Ginny said, sounding breathless. She didn't say hello or anything—she hadn't since she bought her first cell phone years ago. "I finished up earlier than I expected. I'm flying in tomorrow and I'm staying until the inevitable. Have you already done cookies?"

"This afternoon," Joanne said as she slid into the car. She felt an odd sense of relief that her baby sister was coming—not to help her with their father. Lord knows, no one could help anymore—but to simply be there, beside her, so that Joanne would no longer be alone.

"Damn," Ginny said. "I love doing cookies."

"I could whip up another batch," Joanne said.

"Naw, I'm sure there are other traditions I'd forgotten that I'll love just as much."

"Will you stay with me?" Joanne asked.

"Hotel, babe," Ginny said. "Pampering and fifty-seven channels."

"Doesn't sound like any hotel around here." Joanne almost mentioned that Ginny could stay in their childhood home, but she didn't. Her sister, who had started her fashion company for women over forty when she hit that magic age and no one would hire her, had more than enough money to do whatever she wanted.

Ginny laughed. "I've booked the ticket and rented a car. I'll be there for dinner tomorrow. We can talk then."

She was clearly going to end the call, but Joanne caught her first.

"Ginny," Joanne said, "did you get a Christmas card this year from Daddy?"

Joanne half-expected her sister to say she hadn't. Instead, Ginny said, "Oh, yeah. It was cute. That red-light-district thing? So Daddy."

"It didn't bother you?"

"What? The card?" Ginny let out a gusty sigh. "Don't tell me. It got Annie's knickers in a twist. She should be old enough by now to understand that Daddy has a bawdy sense of humor."

Joanne smiled in spite of herself. In years past, the red-light-district aspect to the card would have bothered Annie. She probably hadn't even noticed this year.

"The newsletter," Joanne said.

"I *loved* it," Ginny said. "It read like a great story from Luminaria. Made me feel like a little girl again."

Her response made Joanne lean back against the seat in surprise. The car was getting cold. She turned the ignition, and started the heat, making certain she pressed the garage door opener.

"You there?" Ginny asked.

"Yeah," Joanne said. "It's not the newsletter's content—"

Although it was. The newsletter's content bothered Joanne so much she couldn't read it—

"It's the *fact* of the newsletter."

"The fact of it?" Ginny repeated, obviously not understanding.

"That it exists at all," Joanne said. "Daddy went into a coma weeks before it got mailed."

"Oh." Ginny said it as if she hadn't put that together.

"Annie blames me. She thinks I wrote it and sent it."

"Daddy clearly wrote it," Ginny said. "The dates didn't bother me either. I figured he'd written it a long time ago, like a good-bye newsletter, and made sure someone would mail it for him if he couldn't mail it for himself. It's just the kind of thing he would do."

It *was* the kind of thing he would do. "I didn't mail it for him," Joanne said.

"I didn't say you did." Ginny sounded a little annoyed now. "Daddy has friends, you know."

He did. A large group of them with whom he spent countless evenings, going out to dinner, bowling, or drinking and playing darts at a local bar. They had been visiting him faithfully.

"Maybe that's what happened," Joanne said. "The letter just seems so . . . this year, you know?"

"No, I don't," Ginny said. "Did you *read* it? He didn't mention a single thing that happened this past year. That's why I figured he'd had the thing in storage, waiting for this moment."

Joanne didn't confess that she couldn't read it. Maybe she had just taken that opening and grafted the events of the year onto it.

"Was yours mimeographed?" Joanne asked.

"Yeah," Ginny said. "That's why I figured he planned this years ago. Do you know how hard it is to find a mimeograph machine? Especially one that works? Not to mention the paper."

Joanne hadn't thought of that. She hadn't thought of any of it.

"I guess that's it," she said softly.

Ginny sighed into the phone. "Annie really got to you, didn't she? What did you think Daddy did? Crawl out of bed, type and mimeo a letter, and then sink back into his coma?"

Joanne winced. Annie had always been blunt. Ginny had learned how to be even more blunt.

"No," Joanne said.

"The letter's sweet," Ginny said. "Read it. And get Annie out of your head. She's always veered to the negative, and it's gotten worse as she gets older."

Which was true, no matter how much Joanne didn't want to admit it.

"So buck up, enjoy your holiday, and I'll be there to help with Daddy and festivities and everything. I'll even buy you dinner at the nicest place in town."

"There's no need," Joanne said, but realized she was talking to a broken connection.

Ginny, as usual, had hung up without saying good-bye.

Joanne stared at her phone for a moment, then smiled ruefully. Her baby sister always made her feel better.

Joanne folded her phone and tucked it into her purse. Then she backed the car out of the driveway, and headed to hospice.

She probably should have gone to dinner first. She was hungry, despite all the cookies. But it was getting late, so she went to see her dad.

Already the hospice house had dimmed the lights in the entry. She used the admissions code they had given her and let herself inside. Someone had left fudge on the reception desk with a sign that said, PLEASE! TAKE SOME!

Joanne smiled as she signed in, but didn't take anything. Lights illuminated the single nurses' station in the back. The remaining rooms were private, designed to look like bedrooms so that the dying would feel comfortable—if they were aware at all.

She walked down the hall to her father's room. The night nurse peeked out of one of the other rooms, saw Joanne, and gave a little nod.

Joanne nodded back. She slipped into her father's room. A holiday nightlight in the shape of a tree made the room a festive green and red. A small light glowed from the nightstand behind the bed.

Next to it stood the pile of cookies that Leo had taken with him with a note—*Merry Christmas! Love, Leo*—in her grandson's careful handwriting.

She smiled as she sat down next to her father. He looked even less substantial today than he had the day before. This light, however, gave his now grayish skin some color. His head was propped up by pillows, tubes taped into him everywhere. His blue eyes were closed and were slowly sinking into his skull.

She took his hand and was startled at how cold his skin was. Instinctively she looked at the monitor, saw the green line that tracked his heartbeat, and then covered his hand with her other one.

"We did cookies today," she said, "although I suspect Leo has already told you about that."

She talked to her father, telling him about the day, the baking, the fact that Ginny was coming—everything except the letters.

He didn't look at Joanne. He didn't even move while she was there. Eventually, she ran out of things to say.

She leaned over him, bussed his cheek, and headed out into the night.

It seemed colder than it had before, the air clearer. She drove to a diner not far from her house and ate meatloaf with homemade gravy—comfort food.

Then she went home to a decorated house that still smelled of cinnamon, vanilla, and Christmas love.

The rest of the days before the holiday blurred. She had dinner with Ginny, listened as Ginny told Annie to lighten up and get her butt home to see Daddy one last time, bought turkey and all the fixings for Christmas dinner, wrapped the remaining presents, and somehow got to midnight service on time despite all her errands.

She had no time to look at Daddy's letter. She barely had time to think about it. She visited him, of course, but each day it seemed like he became more and more insubstantial.

Part of her prayed he would go soon, while the other part hoped he would wait until the holiday was over; she didn't want to forever associate Christmas with her father's death.

He hung on, through Christmas Eve and into Christmas Day. She wouldn't be able to see him until late, so Ginny did the family duty, spending the morning with him.

By the time she got back, Joanne had a feast for the table. Her downstairs Christmas tree, the one that stood in her living room, was buried with presents. She had something for each grandchild as well as her children and their spouses. The few gifts she had received in the mail were there as well, along with the pile that Ginny had brought with her.

The guests arrived, more presents went under the tree, the children begged—as they did every year—to open the gifts before dinner, which didn't happen, and one of their parents reminded them (in a voice that made Joanne think of her own) that they had already opened some gifts at home and they could learn to be patient.

Ginny helped serve the turkey and stuffing and the dozen

different kinds of breads and all the salads, pouring coffees and sodas and waters, acting as if this were an upscale Manhattan dinner party instead of a family Christmas.

And as the adults savored their after-dinner coffee and the kids tried to amuse themselves without shaking the presents to death, Joanne heard Leo's voice.

"It was weird," he was saying. "Like I've never seen so much light and there were bugs and everything. We walked over the snow and into that spot and then it was too hot and I was going to take off my coat, but Grandpop wouldn't let me. He said we were only staying a minute."

Joanne looked at Ryan, who was frowning. They both got up. The other adults didn't seem to notice. Joanne and Ryan wound their way through the kitchen into the living room.

Leo had the kids sitting in a circle, even the littlest ones, and they were watching him as if he were a magician. He was pacing, his hands gesturing.

"We snuck up on this place Grandpop said was a grove, then he did this"—and Leo put a finger over his lips, lowering his voice to almost a whisper—"and then he pointed."

Joanne could imagine her grandson and his great-grandfather in their winter clothes, crouching behind some plants in a grove, staring ahead. The image was as vivid as the images she saw when she wrote . . .

Or the images she had seen as a little girl when her father told her tales of Luminaria.

She shook off the thought.

"And over there," Leo whispered, "was this tiny lady, like Tinkerbell, only prettier, with wings. And she hovered, y'know, like hummingbirds do. Then she saw us and flew away . . ."

The kids groaned as if they were disappointed that the little woman had vanished. Then, from the dining room, one of the adults said, "I think it's time for presents, don't you?"

And the spell was broken. The kids stood and everyone headed to the tree.

Everyone except Joanne and Ryan. They went back into the kitchen as if the movement were prearranged.

"Did you tell him about Luminaria?" she asked her son.

He shook his head. "But he spent a lot of time with Grandpop. I'm sure Grandpop did."

But Joanne's father always told stories of thinly disguised heroes and princesses (or princes with the grandsons). He never talked about himself in the first person or anyone else.

Except in those newsletters she had found earlier in the week.

"Grandma, you coming?" Leo shouted from the living room.

"Yes," she said, and grabbed a glass of water, heading into the living room with Ryan right behind her. They took the last chairs as the present free-for-all began.

Three days after Christmas, Daddy died. He had always called the days between Christmas and New Year's the Last Nothing Days of the Year, because the real holiday was over and everyone was simply waiting for the next year to begin.

The arrangements were all made; Annie was the only person who had to fly in, and she had no trouble booking a quick flight. The funeral was scheduled for the thirtieth, and the burial, of course, would wait until spring.

The planning was less work than Joanne thought it would be. Ginny handled most of it, claiming she wanted to be useful.

Joanne cleaned her father's house and her own, took care of the visiting relatives by finding them places to stay and people to eat dinner with. It took no time at all.

She found herself looking for things to do.

Which was how she ended up in the entry of her house, holding a pile of late-arriving Christmas cards, feeling the annual dilemma. Hang them on the banister for a few days or simply acknowledge them and toss them?

She decided to hang them when her father's card slipped from the middle of the pile and landed on the carpet. For a moment, she stared at that familiar handwriting, her name in his flowing script, and then she sighed.

She set the other cards on the table, picked up her father's, and carried it into the living room. She sat in her favorite chair, and opened the newsletter.

She read it slowly. The line that caught her, made her breath actually leave her body, was this:

*I have made an appointment with my great-grandfather in that flashy stone building where he keeps his office. It'll be the first time we've talked since he came here permanently in 1939. It never felt right to talk to him before. Indeed, the few times we've passed each other on the street, he's averted his gaze, as if he wasn't allowed to look at me yet.*

*My appointment is three days after the holiday. But Christmas, not to be missed, has to come first. Then I'll give myself the gift of a visit I have looked forward to for my entire life . . .*

Three days after the holiday. Ginny had been wrong. There were dates and mentions of the current year.

Three days after the holiday was December 28, the day Daddy died.

Joanne wasn't sure she would point this out to anyone. She wasn't sure the line had been in the letter before Christmas. She could have sworn she only received a one-page letter in the mail, but it had since grown to four pages.

And Ginny was right. Except for the first-person passages, it read like a Luminaria story. Although this one had an ending.

*This is going to be my last letter. You can only straddle worlds for so long. I've stood in our world for a very long time. The new world beckons.*

*I've always imagined myself a hero, even though I am not. Still, I am off to battle dragons. Any man who has already stared down his own death knows he has seen the worst. Dragons are large, yes, and fearsome, yes, and smelly, yes. But they are also vulnerable.*

*Death is not. It comes no matter what you do. At least in our world.*

*In this new one, who knows? Certainly not me. Maybe I am foolish for choosing a life of adventure, but I have never been foolish before. I look forward to it and I step into it with only one regret.*

*I cannot come back. The time for straddling is done. I must move on.*

*Some of you, I will see again. And the rest—I will think of you daily, and miss you hourly.*

*I love you all, more than you will ever know.*

*Forever and ever,*

And then he signed hers in his familiar precise handwriting:

*Daddy.*

Joanne cradled the letter against her heart, her eyes closed, her questions answered.

Daddy had sent this letter. Not through a proxy. Not planning months ahead. But from an odd place, the one where he straddled both worlds.

He combined his holiday letters, looking forward as he never had before. But thinking of what he had left behind.

*Some of you I will see again.* She knew he hadn't meant her. He meant Leo, and maybe some of the other great-grandchildren.

She should have minded. She, after all, was the responsible one, the one her father had always relied upon. The one with the imagination, who created books from nothing.

But she didn't mind. She didn't want to leave the here and now for a place of winter bugs and bright sunlight and giant dragons.

She liked her holiday decorations and the cookie tradition and the giggle of grandchildren. She liked holding hearth and home together.

Adventurers needed a place to come back to, to rest their weary feet, and know that they were safe—even for an evening.

She provided that place. She created it, hoping to leave a bit of it in the minds of her own grandchildren, so that when they grew old enough, they would create a marvelous place to come back to as well.

*Some of you, I will see again. And the rest—I will think of you daily, and miss you hourly.*

*I love you all, more than you will ever know.*

"I love you, too, Daddy," Joanne whispered.

Then she folded the letter, and put it away.

A world: Christmas trees, a decorated home, the smell of fresh-baked cookies and the family who love her and whom she loves. Joanne Carlton's world is grounded solidly in the real world we all live in. But for an instant in time, Joanne Carlton finally understood that her world is sometimes not the world of others, that there are adventures to have and dragons to slay. With one Christmas letter, Joanne Carlton got a glimpse of the other side—the side sometimes called . . . the Twilight Zone.

# AN ODYSSEY, OR WHATEVER YOU CALL IT, CONCERNING BASEBALL

Rod Serling

Once again, I am pleased to be able to provide another previously unpublished story from Rod Serling himself. As with many of his stories, this one deals squarely with a theme that he examined so often in his television scripts—the power of imagination, this one set squarely against the backdrop of America's national pastime. But what happens when a man's dreams are faced with the reality of his life? There's only one way to find out . . .

There is a gigantic silver-buck moon hovering high in a September night over Shea Stadium, touching the darkness and softly dispelling it. And down below, leaving the New York Mets dugout, is Albert Patrick Hogan. Feast your eyes—the word must be "feast"—feast your eyes on Hogan: He glides, not walks. The grace of the man must be seen, must be experienced—muscles and ligaments in a ballet; shoulders and arms and legs in a rhythmic dance that glorifies the symmetry of the human body. Watch him as he saunters past the on-deck circle, picking up a bat in a single graceful notion. Just the one bat. Other men—lesser men—pick up the lead-weighted stick and swing it, or they fiddle with trouser belts, or kick mud off cleats, or furiously rub rosin bags to dry out the moist residue of fears that collect in palms—the ritual, the liturgy of baseball that marks any plover's obeisance to the nerves and tensions of the sport. But not Hogan. Oh, no. Hogan carries the one bat over to the Plate. It is the heaviest bat in the National League. And when he gets to

Home Plate, the universe narrows down to a ninety-foot rectangular corridor between the high mound of the pitcher and the small square arena of the man with the bat. Then the two opponents face one another in a special moment of truth.

Hogan plants his two thick legs into the dust like mighty oaks ready to be driven deep into the earth. Then he gazes out like a calm eagle toward the pitcher's mound. See the smile flicker on his lips. A part of the man. A clue. A hint. A suggestion of his preeminence. He's the best. Nobody touches him. Nobody comes close. The probing gray eyes scan the outfield, then the three runners on base. Those eyes. They, too, bespeak the quality. He has the best eyesight in the National League. But the smile never touches them. The smile is simply the unspoken awareness that Hogan has no peers. He must play in this league because there's none better. In Heaven, maybe.

Against Cobb and Ruth and Gherig—the Ghost Greats who have preceded him. Maybe up there with the Big Umpire looking on, he might ultimately play a game with equals. But for the moment he must content himself with being the giant among the pygmies. He must play the Wagnerian symphony in a concert hall full of harmonicas and combs with toilet paper. The smile carries with it a small pity. The young left-hander facing him keeps wetting his lips with his tongue. The infield moves way back onto the grass. Nine enemies with nine constricted throats and eighteen perspiring palms—because that's Hogan at bat.

Hogan's mind is an express train on tracks, zooming past the landscape and taking note of everything. Hear his thoughts. Listen to the smooth meshing gears of a mind singular in what it can encompass and assimilate in flashing fragments of moments. Listen to Hogan think:

*Pity them—the Dodgers. Pity them. Without Koufax they are a rabble. They are three hundred Spartans at Thermopylae without Leonidas; they are the Continentals at Valley Forge without Washing-*

*ton; they are the Union at Vicksburg without Grant. Pity them, I must. They are shattered and demoralized and bankrupt before I lift my bat. Look at Parker at First. Much too close to the bag. I can pull to the right and leave him naked. And there is Willie Davis in center—way out on the track. He knows I have power. A decent lad, full of humility, with a modicum of talent. But he's an opponent nevertheless—frail, as they all are—but still the opposition. So I can bloop it over Second and let it drop a hundred feet in front of him. It's no trick, really. Not when I know how I'll be pitched to. The left-hander is the new kid out of Spokane. He knows of my awesome control of the bat and he can do nothing but fastball me. So I already know how I'm to be pitched to. There is Hunt playing too far back. I can drag it along Third and leave him with a ham omelet all over his face while I squeeze the run in. There are so many possibilities. And all of them relatively simple. I feel a sadness sweeping over me. God, I wish there were opponents left. Men of mettle, worthy of combat—deserving of competition.*

The smile flickers and fades. The bat hovers higher over his shoulder. All that can be heard in the vast stadium is the wheezing, fluctuating breath of the nervous left-hander on the mound as he quickly checks the three runners on the base paths and prepares to face his Armageddon. It's hopeless and he knows it's hopeless. That is Hogan there. Invincibility stares at him from Home Plate. A wave of panic washes over him, carrying away what little vestige remains of strength and talent. That's Hogan at the Plate. Hogan who bats .480. Hogan who steals bases with frightening ease. Hogan who pulls a ball left or right with precision that is almost mystical. Hogan whose power is so legendary that whole teams seem to collapse when he picks up a bat. Hogan. It is an unspoken battle cry that sweeps silently across Shea Stadium where fifty thousand human beings know with certainty that more history is being made in front of their eyes. Hogan will bring back the pennant to New York for the first time in over a decade. He can outthink and outplay any man in the sport.

Hogan, Hogan, Hogan. God loves the boroughs, else why was Hogan born?

The platinum orb of moon stares down, from its sky perch on Shea Stadium, and the figure of Albert Patrick Hogan standing at Home Plate. The stillness is unearthly. The vast multitiered place of battle is also a place of sound—but where is the roar of the crowd? Where is the screaming, raw excitement of fifty thousand faithful? Suddenly there is a whisper of noise. But only an errant wind. Another sound—this the distant throaty roar of Pratt-Whitney engines from an aircraft heading toward Kennedy Airport miles away, and the occasional rise and fall of traffic hum on the parkway that runs past Shea Stadium. The New York Mets are playing at St. Louis that night, the Los Angeles Dodgers have an off day and they're out on the West Coast. There is no one in Shea Stadium *except* Albert Patrick Hogan. Other men—those lesser men—are at home and hearth. But Hogan, Hogan is no dreamless suburbanite. Hogan is no plodding, dull, faceless component of the times. Hogan has verve and imagination. Hogan has dreams. He rises to his full five feet six inches, hitches up his little potbelly, swings at an invisible ball thrown by an invisible left-hander, then watches with his piggish, myopic little oyster eyes a nonexistent trajectory of an imaginary white pellet disappearing over the center field fence. Now Albert Patrick Hogan starts to run around the base paths, ears cocked to the phantom screams of the phantom crowd calling his name. He rounds Third, breathing heavily—ancient Schlitz beer sloshing around inside the flab-covered recesses of his fifty-eight-year-old insides, then continues to chug toward Home Plate. He tips his cap to these invisible wraiths who scream his name, thanking him in roaring tribute for having belted one for God and Country, the City of New York and the Beloved Mets. He is not Albert Patrick Hogan, a fifty-eight-year-old schlep who sells hot dogs at Shea Stadium. He is Hogan. The mighty Hogan. The incomparable Hogan.

"Hogan, Hogan, Hogan." The soundless voices scream out from evanescent throats—and Hogan wears a humble and gentle smile.

"Hogan—schmuck! You're some kind of a friggin' nut—you know that? A nut! How many times I gotta tell you that you ain't allowed in here when the team's not playin'? How many times, schmuck, huh?" The voice is that of Bull Walsh, one of the stadium guards who wears a badge and has no imagination and is one of the lesser men. He shines his flashlight through the wire mesh of the screen behind Home Plate and has just finished watching Hogan point toward the center field fence—the spot where he would park the pitch. He has then watched him run around the base paths like some ungainly farm animal with a hernia.

"Schmuck," Walsh calls out again. "Off the field. You hear me? I mean, off the field—like now!"

The grandeur dissolves. The crowd noises fade off into the night. The cheering multitude disappears and becomes fifty thousand empty seats. The billion-candle-powered incandescent lights over the field go black. There is only the moon and Albert Patrick Hogan—sparse, bony shoulders slumped as he turns disconsolately to the dream-killer with the badge. The ecstasy departs with the batting average, the eagle eyes and the humble smile of the Adonis forced by circumstance to leave Mount Olympus and pit his mammoth strengths against tiny mortal man.

The real Hogan now stands up. This is "Fats" Hogan—the nickname he has collected with the rest of the flotsam of his life. He is a heavy-breathing, spindle-shanked, florid-faced little man who sells hot dogs up and down the aisles of the Third Base bleacher side of Shea Stadium. He has been doing this since they built the place, and before that at the Polo Grounds—thirty years in all. Thirty years of pushing knobby knees and dead-flat feet up and down the concrete steps, the big metal box riding hard on his protruding gut, the leather strap rubbing angry indentations into the back of his lobster-red sunburned neck: a Humpty Dumpty gnome, visible but never seen. He's omniscient. He blends with the green infield, the white shirts, whatever the color of the sky. He's an accoutrement. Like a men's room sign or a seat number.

"Get your Honey-Gee red hots on a Spaulding roll," he calls out, while his perpetually bent back protests in concert with the rest of his tired limbs. Thirty years for Hogan. A million tons of ground meat shoved into gelatin coverings; thousands of gallons of mustard, tons of onions; a small fortune in change passed down to the beckoning, hungry faithful—always at the far end of the row, while the equally faithful, but less hungry citizenry pass down the Honey-Gee red hot on the Spaulding roll with grudging, but silent, impatience, anxious for Hogan to leave, anxious to get back to the ball game—unwilling participants of the ritual; the dollar bill passed right to left, the hot dog passed left to right, the change passed left to right—down the steps goes "Fats" Hogan, the steam curling up around his red face, watering his little eyes, sticking small shafts of queasiness into body and mind that thirty years ago began retching at the smell, the sight, the flavor of Honey-Gee red hots on Spaulding rolls.

Off-night at Shea for the Metz. Off-life for Albert Patrick Hogan, who is the sole manufacturer, distributor, and also consumer of illusions. He walks with them up and down the concrete steps. He carries them into the grimy little bar on Ninety-eighth Street where he goes after each game. He fondles them on the lumpy mattress in his little room a block from the bar.

He's a sloppily formed, overaged Walter Mitty, dreaming the dreams of the desperate, because man does not live on rancid beer and frankfurter steam alone.

He suffers Bill Walsh's touch and allows himself to be escorted back up the concrete steps to the first tier and then down the long cavernous corridor toward an exit. When they get to the parking lot, Walsh studies him for a moment.

"Lemme ask you somethin', Fats. You sick? Is that it? Is that why you alla time play games like this? I mean, all that crap you were doin', pointin' to center field and swingin' away like you had a bat—and then runnin' around the base paths like that. You sick?"

Albert Patrick Hogan wears a distant smile. He shakes his head. Explain his dream to Bull Walsh? In Lithuanian, he could try. In Mandarin. In geometric symbols. It would all be the same. Walsh could never understand.

"Ain't you ever had any hopes?" Hogan asks him in a sad voice. "Ain't you ever aspired? Why do you suppose people read books?"

Walsh stares at him, uncomprehending. Walsh does not read books.

"When I go down on that field," Hogan says patiently, "it's like a mental constitutional."

Bull Walsh stares at him. He has the rational, ordered, file-cabinet mind of a simple citizen with one job, one point of view and one set of criteria that differentiates between sane men and nuts. "Constitutional" is the name of some big mother of a ship that used to be at the Brooklyn Navy Yard. Beyond that, there is no "constitutional" in his language. He raises one bushy, County Mayo eyebrow and sticks out a bulbous middle finger to top the small area above Hogan's spread-out stomach.

"Lemme give you a piece of advice, Fats," Walsh says, tapping with the finger like a ruler on a blackboard, accentuating each word. "One of these nights there's gonna be, like, an ambulance around here. And a coupla guys with white coats. They're gonna take a look at you playin' the part of the number-one nutsy out there and are gonna stick you in a rubber room at the Bin—and Mayor Lindsay won't be able to get you out with a court order."

The wan smile on the face of Hogan—a little touch of the

dream returns. He looks superior. "Walsh," he says. "You give me advice—I give you advice. Go take a flying fig at the September moon!"

He swipes away Walsh's finger, turns and walks across the vast, empty parking lot toward a 1950 Dodge sedan that he owns and curses and cajoles and sometimes makes run. He climbs in behind the wheel, ripping his sleeve on the broken window handle, and starts the engine. The dream hovers over him. He smiles at the thousands who surround the car. It's a Rolls-Royce given him a month before at a gigantic ceremony at New York City Hall. Senator Javits presented him with the keys.

As if in a fog, he drives to his tiny, cramped room. And then, on that hot night, lying in his ovenlike room, he applies baby oil on the painful knobs on the back of his neck and looks across the yellow, cracked dresser mirror and studies himself. And after a bit, he does not see the piggish little face or the oyster eyes or the rising hump of his back or the distorted stomach or the yellowed teeth. Then he is not Hogan. He is something else again . . . He is . . .

He is . . . the best. He is the "Babe"—moon-faced with the giant shoulders on toothpick legs. . . .

# ABOUT THE AUTHORS

**David Black** is an award-winning journalist, novelist, screenwriter, and producer. His novel *Like Father* was named a notable book of the year by *The New York Times* and listed as one of the seven best novels of the year by *The Washington Post*. *The King of Fifth Avenue* was named a notable book of the year by *The New York Times*, *New York* magazine, and the Associated Press. He divides his time between upstate New York and Manhattan.

**Douglas Brode** is a novelist, screenwriter, playwright, film historian, and multiaward-winning working-journalist. He teaches courses in popular culture and modern media at the Newhouse School of Public Communications, Syracuse University. The most recent of his more than thirty books on film and television is *Rod Serling and The Twilight Zone: The Official 50th Anniversary Tribute*, coauthored with Carol Serling.

**Loren L. Coleman** is the author of twenty-six novels, with short fiction work appearing in many Tekno Books anthologies. He began watching *The Twilight Zone* (in syndication) as young as five years old, which may explain a lot about his life. Today, when not locking himself away in a small room to invent worlds and create people from the mysterious ether of his imagination, he coaches youth sports, manages Catalyst Game Labs (a pen-and-paper game company), and occasionally sets out in search of the perfect martini. His personal Web site can be found at www.lorenlcoleman.com.

**M. Tara Crowl** grew up in Murfreesboro, Tennessee, and recently graduated from film school at the University of Southern California. She currently lives and works in Los Angeles.

**Peter Crowther** is the recipient of numerous awards for his writing, his editing, and, as publisher, for the hugely successful PS imprint. As well as being widely translated, his short stories have been adapted for TV on both sides of the Atlantic and collected in *The Longest Single Note, Lonesome Roads, Songs of Leaving, Cold Comforts, The Spaces Between the Lines, The Land at the End of the Working Day,* and the upcoming *Things I Didn't Know My Father Knew.* He is the coauthor (with James Lovegrove) of *Escardy Gap* and author of the "Forever Twilight" SF/horror cycle (*Darkness, Darkness* and *Windows to the Soul* already available, and *Darkness Rising* due in summer 2010). He lives and works with his wife and business partner, Nicky, on the Yorkshire coast.

**Loren D. Estleman** has published more than sixty novels and two hundred short stories in the areas of suspense, historical western, and mainstream. He has won seventeen national writing awards, including five Spurs, four Shamuses, and the Elmer Kelton Award, bestowed by the German Association for the Study of the Western. In addition, he has been nominated for the Edgar and the American Book Award. In 2002, his alma mater, Eastern Michigan University, presented him with an honorary doctorate in Humane Letters. He lives in Michigan with his wife, author Deborah Morgan.

**John Farris** has been called "the best writer of horror at work today" and was awarded a Lifetime Achievement Award by the Horror Writers Association in 2001. His thirty-nine titles have sold twenty-two million copies worldwide in twenty-five languages. His most recent novels are *You Don't Scare Me* and *High Bloods*. He wrote and directed the cult-classic film *Dear, Dead Delilah,* and has written many other screenplays. He had a short-lived career as a playwright in his twenties. His only produced play, *The Death of the Well-Loved Boy,* Farris fondly recalls as having received "the worst reviews since Attila the Hun." He lives near Atlanta, Georgia. Please send favorable reviews and notes of appreciation to kingwindom@gmail.com.

A graduate of Yale University, **Peter Farris** has collaborated on numerous screenplays with his father, John Farris. Their script *You Don't Scare Me* was optioned by New Films International and is currently in preproduction. Peter's first novel, a racing satire called *The Eggshell,* was described by legendary motorsports journalist Monte Dutton as a work that would make him "the Salman Rushdie of NASCAR nation." While waiting for an editor brave enough to buy *The Eggshell,* Farris has written a second novel and is hard at work on a third. He lives in Cobb County, Georgia, with his girlfriend, Heather, and a black cat named Grimm.

**David Gerrold** is the author (and father of) *The Martian Child,* the basis for the 2007 movie starring John Cusack, Amanda Peet, and Bobby Coleman. He's also known as the creator of *Star Trek*'s Tribbles, *Land of the Lost*'s Sleestak, and his own much more terrifying Chtorrans in *The War Against the Chtorr.* He's published more than fifty books, including *When HARLIE Was One, The Man Who Folded Himself,* and *Jumping Off the Planet.* In his spare time, he redesigns his Web site, www.gerrold.com.

**Nancy Holder** is the *New York Times* bestselling coauthor of the dark fantasy series *Wicked,* which has been picked up by Dream-Works. She also writes the young adult horror *Possessions* series. She has received four Bram Stoker Awards for her supernatural fiction and has written many books set in the *Smallville, Saving Grace,* and *Buffy the Vampire Slayer* universes. A true Disney geek, she can frequently be seen in the Twilight Zone Tower of Terror gift shop, purchasing more bath towels for her Disney-themed house. She lives in San Diego with her daughter, Belle, the cats, David and Kittnen Snow Vampire, Panda, a psychic Cardigan Welsh Corgi, and by the time this book comes out, they will have another dog, the Pembroke Corgi Tater Tot, la Comtesse de Pommepomme-Yip.

**Lee Lawless** is the author of several award-winning plays, two screenplays, and a vast compendium of postmodern rock and roll music. In addition to her avant-garde short films and visual artwork, Lawless was a contributing editor of *The Weekly World Wiretap* e-zine and *Harlem Today* magazine. She plays guitar, cowrites and sings for the apocalypse-rock outfit Universal Truth Machine, and lives in a possibly haunted historical building in Harlem, New York City.

One of **Jane Lindskold**'s earliest story sales was "Good Boy" in the anthology *Journeys to the Twilight Zone*. Since then, she has published more than sixty short stories and twenty-some novels. Her novels include the six volumes of the "Wolf Series" and the three books in the "Breaking the Wall" series. She lives in New Mexico with her husband, archaeologist Jim Moore, and assorted small animals.

**Jean Rabe** is a book hoarder, a museum patron, a student of Egyptian symbolism, and a goldfish fancier. She is also the author of twenty-seven novels and more than five dozen short stories. When she's not writing or editing, she delights in tossing tennis balls and tugging on old socks with her three dogs. Visit her at www.jeanrabe.com.

**Kristine Kathryn Rusch** is a bestselling, award-winning author who has written under a variety of names in fantasy, science fiction, mystery, and romance. Her latest novel, *Diving into the Wreck* from Pyr, is based on the award-winning novellas first published in *Asimov's Science Fiction* magazine.

**Robert J. (Bob) Serling** is Rod Serling's older brother and a prolific author himself, with twenty-five published nonfiction and fiction works, mostly dealing with the airline and aerospace industries. Among his seven novels is the bestselling *The President's Plane Is Missing*. Before becoming a full-time freelance author, he was aviation editor of United Press International and at age ninety-two is regarded by his peers as the dean of aviation writers. He served as technical advisor on Rod's acclaimed *TZ* episode "Odyssey of Flight 33."

**Rod Serling** (1924–1975) worked in the television area for twenty-five years, developing, in addition to the landmark *Twilight Zone* series, *Night Gallery* and *The Loner,* and countless drama anthologies, including *Requiem for a Heavyweight* and *Patterns*. During his career he won more Emmy Awards for dramatic writing than anyone in history. He also wrote the screenplay for the very first *Planet of the Apes* film, which embodied everything Serling was interested in as a writer. He continued to write for television while teaching in Ithaca, New York, until his death in 1975, leaving an indelible imprint on television that would inspire countless future writers and artists.

**Susan Slater** is the author of six published mysteries—four in the Ben Pecos Indian series, *The Pumpkin Seed Massacre, Yellow Lies, Thunderbird*, and a novella, *A Way to the Manger,* and two standalones, *Flash Flood* and *Five O'Clock Shadow*. Her novel *0 to 60* is women's fiction and has been optioned for a feature film. Susan lives thirty miles west of Taos and writes full-time.

**Dean Wesley Smith** is the bestselling author of over ninety novels and hundreds of short stories. Some of his first sales were to the *Twilight Zone* magazine and its sister publication, *Night Cry,* in the 1980s. He is best known for his work on *Star Trek, Men in Black,* and *Spider-Man* novels, and is currently writing thrillers under another name.

**Norman Spinrad** is the author of some twenty or so novels, five or six dozen short stories, a classic *Star Trek* episode, a couple of flop movies, an album's worth of songs, political columns, film criticism, literary criticism, mini-cookbooks, autobiography, and a bunch of assorted other stuff. The latest to be written is a new and literarily revolutionary novel called *Welcome to Your Dreamtime,* in which you, the reader, are the viewpoint character, and sections of which have been published in a weird assortment of magazines as freestanding short stories. The latest to be published is *He Walked Among Us,* a novel so far ahead of itself that it had to wait until it had become something of the fave rave of a radical viral Internet distribution experiment before any traditional publisher would bring it out in paper.

# ABOUT THE EDITOR

**Carol Serling** has been involved with the writing career of her husband from its very inception, and all through the *Twilight Zone* years she was his first reader and toughest critic. Since her husband's death in 1975, Carol has maintained a self-contained industry working with the literary and cinematic legacy that Rod left behind . . . the latest work being this anthology written in the spirit of the Zone.